LORDLY INSOLENCE

"What would Reverend Headley think, to find you so scantily clad?" Lord Roxham mused, as his eyes raked Jessica with studied insolence.

Jessica felt panic bubbling up from deep within her. It constricted her throat so she could make no reply.

"Come, come, Miss Winslow," Roxham chided. "You are not generally at a loss for words. Tell me, at least, what I should do with you now I've found you in my library in dishabille." As he spoke he reached out to lift her thick braid, and in the process he deliberately allowed his knuckles to graze her breast.

"Please!" Jessica pulled back.

"You are afraid," Roxham dryly observed.

"No!" Jessica hotly denied . . . refusing to admit how afraid she was . . . not only of him but of herself . . . .

EMMA LANGE is a graduate of the University of California at Berkeley, where she studied European history. She and her husband live in the Midwest and pursue, as they are able, interests in traveling and in sailing.

The
Unwavering
Miss Winslow

Emma Lange

A SIGNET BOOK

NEW AMERICAN LIBRARY

A DIVISION OF PENGUIN BOOKS USA INC.

NAL BOOKS ARE AVAILABLE AT QUANTITY DISCOUNTS WHEN USED TO
PROMOTE PRODUCTS OR SERVICES. FOR INFORMATION PLEASE WRITE
TO PREMIUM MARKETING DIVISION, NEW AMERICAN LIBRARY, 1633
BROADWAY, NEW YORK, NEW YORK 10019.

SIGNET TRADEMARK REG. U.S. PAT OFF. AND FOREIGN
COUNTRIES REGISTERED TRADEMARK—MARCA REGISTRADA
HECHE EN CHICAGO, U.S.A.

SIGNET, SIGNET CLASSIC, MENTOR, ONYX, PLUME,
MERIDIAN and NAL BOOKS are published by New American
Library, a division of Penguin Books USA Inc., 1633 Broadway,
New York, New York 10019

First Printing, September, 1989

1 2 3 4 5 6 7 8 9

PRINTED IN THE UNITED STATES OF AMERICA

1

As she made her way down the long gallery of Bleithe-wood Manor, Jessica Winslow glanced out the windows, and, seeing the bare trees of the park bend dangerously before the icy gusts of a March storm that had swept in the night before, she smiled to herself.

She had quite forgotten the storm until now, for, though the principle seat of the Earls of Roxham had first been built in the twelfth century, the present title holder's father, the eighth earl, had extensively modernized his ancient, mellowed-brick home and rendered it impervious to drafts.

That she was lucky, indeed, to be so warm and secure and housed in such magnificent surroundings made the smile lighting Jessica's blue eyes particularly vivid. There had been a time when she had despaired of finding any shelter at all.

Jessica turned from the window and continued on her way. A slender, graceful figure with long legs and a feminine sway to her hips, she preferred to think of the present, not the past.

If, in the past, she had been obliged to endure a great many more trials than most young ladies of her age, she had survived, and now lived in a beautiful, comfortable home. Best of all, she worked for a darling old dear she had come to like enormously.

Jessica's mouth curved again, unbidden, as she thought of Lady Beatrice Carstairs, the woman she served as a paid companion. Despite their age difference, for Lady Bea, as she was often called, had lived seventy years to Jessica's twenty, the two had taken to one another from the first.

"You're a deuced improvement over all those puling old maids that blasted agency in town was used to send up!" the older woman had pronounced in her descriptive way only the second day after Jessica had arrived at the Manor. "If she outlives me, I'll thank Helen in my will."

Lady Beatrice referred to Mrs. Helen Ashcroft of Broadcourt in Dorset, Jessica's previous employer, the woman who had recommended her to Lady Beatrice when she had grown too ill for Jessica's limited nursing abilities.

Jessica was as grateful as Lady Beatrice for Mrs. Ashcroft's thought. She enjoyed Lady Beatrice's shrewd, agile mind, and, though their association had been a brief one, she felt toward the crusty, forthright old woman more as she would toward a relative than an employer.

In the next moment, as she made her way down the corridor leading to the apartments of Lady Mary Fitzgerald, a frown etched Jessica's brow. Lady Mary was Lady Bea's niece, and had never made much push to be friendly until today, when she'd sent Jessica an invitation to take tea with her.

Shrugging off a subtle sense of foreboding, Jessica knocked upon the door. She had nothing to fear she told herself stoutly. Lady Mary only wanted to obtain the herbal remedy for headache that Jessica had made for Lady Bea and, perhaps, to acquaint herself better with the young woman serving her aunt.

It was certainly not remarkable that they had not developed a closer relationship. Lady Mary was some twenty years Jessica's senior and a far more fluttery, vaporish sort of woman than was Lady Beatrice.

Jessica's musings were interrupted by a rather high but not unpleasant voice calling, "Come in, Miss Winslow." Lady Mary lifted her rounded figure briefly from the cushions upon which she reposed and fluttered a small square of linen edged with Brussels lace in Jessica's direction. "I am so very glad to see you, my dear. I do hope you've not forgotten your concoction for the headache. I've a great need for your herbs today, dear girl, for my nerves are vastly overset!"

Jessica suppressed a smile. Lady Mary's nerves were famous for being delicate. A more remarkable report would have been that they were steady that day.

"I am sorry to hear it, ma'am," Jessica said not without sympathy in the low, almost husky voice that Lady Beatrice had been known to commend for its soothing qualities. "I did bring the herbs, as you asked. Shall I administer a dose and be on my way? I shouldn't care to impose when you feel unwell."

Perhaps Jessica's voice did have restorative qualities, for Lady Mary at once removed her plump hand from her brow and waved her little square of linen vigorously. "But you can't impose, dear child! A coze is precisely what I need to life my spirits. Will you be so good as to pour the tea, my dear? You've such a graceful way about you that it will soothe my nerves simply to watch you."

Jessica's finely drawn mouth twitched as she sat down before the tea tray. Of her niece Lady Bea had also said, "Mary has a keen eye for putting others to use! Watch her, Jess or she'll have you drawing up the week's menus."

"But make no mistake!" Lady Mary exclaimed as she roused herself to accept the cup of tea Jessica proffered. "I did not invite you to my rooms merely to make use of you, Miss Winslow." Lady Mary looked up from choosing just the right macaroon with a sweet smile, and Jessica admitted to a small twinge of guilt for her uncharitable thoughts. "I want to thank you for all the work you have done with my twins. They adore you, I know, and Nanny Budgett advises me they've come round to minding their manners to please you."

Lady Mary's brow puckered as she stirred her tea. "They can be the worst rascals, I admit, forever getting into one scrape after another. I suppose there are those would lay their behavior at my door. A mother is ever responsible, is she not?" She cast Jessica a wounded look. "But no one ever seems to stop and think of the difficulties. When my Ronald was taken from me, not only was I left all alone in the wilds of Ireland with little or nothing of an estate left after the creditors had their way, but I had four children as well!"

Jessica, who knew very well how difficult life could be for a widow with children, thought that on the whole Lady Mary had come out rather well. The rooms in which she was ensconced were warm and cheerful, her favorite chocolates were never in short supply, and at the call of a bell there was an army of servants to see to the three of her children still at home: the twins, Julia and Giles, were seven, and Olivia was seventeen.

Lady Mary sighed dramatically. "Thank heaven for Justin! I cannot imagine what I'd have done without him. His invitation to come to Bleithewood was a godsend. I know that as my cousin and the head of the family he was obliged to offer assistance, but to bring me to his home! My dear, it was more than I ever expected."

"The earl must be a very fine man," Jessica agreed, meaning what she said. The Earl of Roxham, the Justin to whom Lady Mary referred, had not only undertaken to share his home with Lady Mary and her brood, but also with his elderly Aunt Beatrice when she, too, was widowed.

"He is!" Lady Mary smiled fondly in between nibbles on her macaroons. "And with such presence! My dear, he is a figure of the first stare in town. Handsome and elegant, he's a Corinthian and nothing less! I do wish he would take . . ."

Lady Mary looked up with a start. "Oh, but I do prose on so," she cried, making an attempt at a smile, though Jessica was interested to see the expression fade as quickly as it came. "Tell me of yourself, Miss Winslow. I know so little about you. I believe Bea said you lost your father when you were young just as my poor lambs did?"

Jessica still experienced a sense of loss when she was reminded of the death of her father, though it had occurred eight years before, but she showed little of her feelings to Lady Mary. "Yes," she said in her low voice. "Father died at the battle of Corunna on the Peninsula in '08."

Lady Mary believed it very likely that Captain Winslow had bequeathed little to his family, and sighed to herself. She felt rather sorry for the girl before her. It would not be easy to be both beautiful and penniless. Few men would care to marry a girl who came with no portion at all, while few wives would care to hire a girl who possessed such beauty.

At the thought that she, too, had reason to be disquieted by Miss Winslow's looks, Lady Mary nibbled nervously at one of her macaroons. She must come to the point of her interview eventually, but she found the task more difficult than she'd imagined it would be. Miss Winslow was proud without being arrogant, and Lady Mary's sympathy reluctantly went out to her.

Rather at random she said, "I have been quite remiss, you know, in not expressing to you how grateful we all are at Bleithewood for the change you've wrought in Aunt Bea!"

When Jessica attempted to deflect the praise by saying Lady Beatrice's improvement was due entirely to that lady's determination, Lady Mary shook her head in earnest. "You are too modest by half, my dear. Only three months ago Bea rarely left her bed much less her rooms, and now she joins us at dinner regularly. And I—who better?—know Bea can be quite difficult. Finding a companion to stay with her above a month has been the most difficult of my responsibilities, I assure you! Happily, you are too sensible to allow her occasionally sharp words to upset you."

Jessica smiled a little. The truth was she was too desperate for a position to allow anyone's manner to offend her, not that Lady Bea had offended her. Thus far, at least, her elderly employer's undeniably sharp temper had been directed entirely at the disease that riddled her joints.

"In truth, I have enjoyed Lady Beatrice very much," she assured her hostess.

Lady Mary's blue eyes widened briefly, for she, herself, had never found her aunt's sharp wit enjoyable, but she was not inclined to argue the point. The soft twinkle she could detect in Jessica Winslow's eye gave her to believe the young woman was more amused than discomfitted by Bea's wicked tongue.

"As"—Jessica continued to address her hostess—"I should like to say, I have enjoyed the company of the twins and Olivia. You've delightful children, my lady, however much their youth may lead them into a foolish start or two."

Lady Mary responded with a pleased smile. "Livy sings your praises as well, Miss Winslow!" she assured Jessica. "For which, I must add, I am truly grateful." Lady Mary's linen handkerchief fluttered into the air. "Livy's in dire need of direction from someone with your good sense. She's at such a flighty age, but she will not come to me, of course—I am only her mother!"

When Jessica chuckled sympathetically, for Olivia was at that age when one's mother seems hopelessly outdated, Lady Mary smiled, but only briefly. Almost at once her eyes slid away from Jessica's. "You know I've an elder son, do you not, Miss Winslow?" she inquired carefully after a moment.

When she'd answered in the affirmative, Jessica added, as Lady Mary only stared pensively into her tea cup, "I believe Sir Andrew is at Cambridge just now, is he not?"

Lady Mary's face fell dramatically. "No! No! That is just the problem!" she wailed. "Andrew has been sent down. I received word only yesterday that he will arrive at Bleithewood in a day or so."

Lady Mary dabbed at her eyes with her square of linen. "He is not bad! Really he is not! Andy is merely a high-spirited boy like his father! I had hoped school would settle him, but it seems I was wrong. He's always had some nonsensical notion that he wishes to go in the army. But that desire only shows how lacking in maturity he is. The army is quite dangerous!"

Jessica overcame a desire to roll her eyes by reminding herself that Mary had lost her husband. Though there was peace at long last, she could be forgiven wanting to keep her eldest son safely by her side.

"The boy must marry." Lady Mary turned an almost pleading look upon Jessica. "Marriage will settle him. We've little income from Ronald's estates, you know. If I bought Andy his colors, there would be only a pittance left to augment his soldier's pay. I cannot think he would care to live so poorly, though he maintains he would do well enough. No, no! He is too young to understand how unpleasant straitened circumstances would be!"

Jessica said nothing. She occupied herself with pouring a fresh cup of tea for her hostess, instead. That her family had succeeded quite well living on a soldier's pay she saw no reason to point out. Her standard of what was needed to be comfortable was ludicrously different from Lady Mary's, and though they'd made out well enough while her father lived, she had to admit there had been precious little left after his death.

"Thank you, my dear," Lady Mary sniffed gratefully as she took the cup Jessica offered. "You see now why I am in need of your herbs. I have been thinking of this latest start of Andy's, and what he must do, until my head positively aches.

"Fortunately," she continued, her expression clearing amazingly, "I've dear friends who have proposed a quite happy solution. Squire Multaney and his wife, Emily, believe Andrew and their daughter, Marianne, would make a happy couple. The advantage to them, of course, is the connection they would have to Bleithewood, while Andy would ally himself to a dear, sweet child who is heir to the squire's considerable fortune."

Lady Mary's frankness might have startled Jessica except that the older woman seemed to have forgotten her presence altogether as she recited aloud all the merits of the union for which she hoped. As she considered her son's reaction to her plans, her brow wrinkled. "I am afraid that Andrew will not view the Multaneys' offer with enthusiasm," she confided. "But I shall press him," she added, an unusually militant gleam lighting her eyes. "He will find it impossible to make a better match with his limited prospects. If he had not developed such a reputation for wild starts, I might send him to town, but there seems little use now. Besides, I believe the squire might succeed in curbing Andrew's impulses as I have not. He is a forceful man."

Perhaps recalling that she spoke before neither a member of the family nor a close friend, Lady Mary fell silent then. Taking a sip of her tea, she glanced at Jessica over the rim of her cup, but the expression on the girl's refined, nay ethereal, features revealed little.

"Miss Winslow, I am at a loss!" The words burst from Lady Mary with such force her cup rattled in its saucer. "Yes." She nodded unhappily when Jessica's brow lifted

11

in surprise. "Marianne is quite plain, you see, and Andy has a decided fondness for beauty. It is what got him into this latest scrape! I do not know the particulars, but there was some to-do over a schoolmaster's daughter he'd been forbidden to see. But that is neither here nor there. It is what he'll do when he sees you that has me so undone. I very much fear he will be head over heels. Oh, Miss Winslow, I do hate to say so, but I am certain you will understand I could never countenance such an infatuation. Indeed, were Andy to become set upon you, I very much fear I should have to ask Aunt Bea to forgo the pleasure of your company."

Jessica sat very still. By no sign did she betray the extent of her reaction to Lady Mary's almost apologetically worded threat. If there was a vivid flash deep in her blue eyes—and there was—her eyes were veiled by her thick lashes, and Lady Mary, though she was regarding Jessica with palpable apprehension, did not see it.

Leaning forward gracefully, Jessica placed her teacup upon the table, and, having successfully subdued the stab of resentment she felt at being told so bluntly she was an ineligible parti, she lifted her eyes to Lady Mary.

"You shall have no reason to worry on my account, Lady Mary," Jessica said quietly. She waited for a moment to be certain her firm statement had registered, and when she thought it had, she rose. "I must go now that we understand each other, my lady. I promised to read to Lady Beatrice before her nap. Thank you very much for the tea."

With a dignified curtsy she was gone, leaving Lady Mary little option but to look after her with an unhappy sigh.

The interview had been trying in the extreme, at least at the end, but had it been successful? There was no question in her mind that Miss Winslow could hold off Andy. They were of an age, both twenty, but the girl seemed the older by a decade. She'd more resolution than Andrew had ever dreamed of, Lady Mary admitted frankly.

But would she hold him off? Lady Mary, despite Jessica's straightforward assurance, could not be certain. She found it difficult to believe any girl would be content to remain a mere companion when she might be a viscount's wife, no matter if he were nearly penniless.

Certainly the girl would turn Andrew's head. Her delicately boned face was lovely to look upon, and her clear, wide, indigo-blue eyes were exceptionally vivid.

Andrew would not look away from them without a second glance. Particularly—Lady Mary nearly sighed aloud at the thought—when Miss Winslow smiled. Then they sparkled with such life even Lady Mary was persuaded to smile with her. Once, however, Lady Mary had detected a quite different light sparking in those blue depths: when a maid had not been as polite to Bea as her young companion thought she ought to be, Miss Winslow had sent the girl flying with a mere look.

With a faint shiver Lady Mary allowed her mind to turn from the spirit she did not doubt the girl possessed to what she considered the girl's crowning glory—and she did not apologize for the triteness of the appellation.

Others might have used the phrase, she thought, but rarely so aptly. Miss Winslow's hair was quite sumptuously glorious. Even the demure style the girl had adopted—a thick knot pinned at the nape of her neck—could not hide its vibrant red-gold color or its lush thickness.

With sudden decision, she rang for her maid. She would appeal to Justin. She must, though it was the start of the Season and she was not certain he would come—no matter how dire she made her need sound.

But if he did come, Justin would put the matter right, she knew. Miss Winslow's unflinching gaze would be nothing to him, and Andy's cocky grin even less. What he would do, exactly, she was not certain, but, she would trust him to act as decisively as always.

As she retraced her steps down the long gallery, Jessica was no happier than Lady Mary with the outcome of their meeting. She hoped her answer would be sufficient assurance for her hostess, but she feared it would not.

Oh Papa, she called out silently. Why did you leave us? There was no answer to her anguished cry, of course,

13

for Captain Winslow had not wished to die in battle and leave his family so little with which to manage.

Still, he had, and Jane Winslow, Jessica's mother, had found it nearly impossible to provide adequately for her children.

Jessica was eleven and her two brothers seven and four respectively when Jane married her only suitor, Charles Godfrey, a thickset, middleaged man of undistinguished birth but considerable fortune. Rumor had it he'd gotten his wealth in unsavory ways, and though Jane Winslow was much admired, the respectable folk of the town in Kent where they lived, cut her husband at every opportunity.

An unreasonable man, Mr. Godfrey blamed Jane, not himself, for the repeated rejections he suffered, and he relieved his frustrations by lashing out at her when he returned home after an evening spent drinking himself into an ugly mood.

More than once Jessica had flown to her mother's side to protect her from her drunken husband. Little more than a child, she often succeeded only in deflecting his anger to herself but there were times when her spirit daunted Mr. Godfrey enough that he would tire of the battle and lurch unsteadily off to his bed.

One night, however, Mr. Godfrey's attitude toward her changed entirely. Jessica, once more traversing the long gallery at Bleithewood, shivered, seeing not the Axminster rug beneath her feet nor the Sevres vase upon a nearby table, but her stepfather's eyes.

When she had heard her mother cry out that night, she'd had time only to throw a thin wrapper over her nightdress, and when Mr. Godfrey had turned to backhand her as he had her mother, he was transfixed by the curves that had transformed Jessica's body from a child's to a young woman's seemingly overnight.

She had not understood exactly why Mr. Godfrey's hand wavered or why the light in his bloodshot eyes gleamed suddenly with such intensity, but Jessica had lashed out with unusual vigor when he caught her by the shoulder and tried to pull her to him.

Simultaneously raking his face with her nails and kick-

14

ing his shins with her feet, she won the day, but his eyes, hot and rapacious, followed her wherever she went after that. Worse, if he came upon her when she was alone, he would touch her, though she threw off his greedy hands and ran from him.

There was no question she must escape Mr. Godfrey. Both she and Jane agreed, and Jessica willingly adopted her mother's plan that she seek refuge in marriage. At seventeen she was young, but when a cousin, Lady Sarah Renwick, who resided in London, replied to an appeal from Jane by saying she would sponsor Jessica, there had been no hesitation.

A bleak expression on her face, Jessica recalled her ill-fated stay in town. She had found no husband there . . . only disgrace.

And humiliation, she added, recalling suddenly a pair of amber eyes that had looked down upon her with galling scorn.

She would not think of it . . . of him! It would only lead to self-pity to recall the events that had forced her to give up her dreams of having a home of her own.

She must concentrate instead upon keeping the position that maintained a roof over her head. The necessity was great, for she'd no income of her own, and she could never return to Mr. Godfrey's house. Nor could she rely upon finding a new position. She remembered too well how difficult it had been to find employment in the first place. Position after position had been denied her on one excuse after another.

A lock of her hair came loose from its pins, brushing her cheek, and Jessica glared angrily at the flame-colored thing. After one look at her hair, people seemed inevitably to draw the wrong conclusions about her.

Loose and immoral, they thought her, though they did not even know her. Only Mrs. Ashcroft, old and infirm, had been willing to believe in her. And now Lady Beatrice, Jessica reminded herself.

She must hope Lady Bea would prove an ally if there were difficulty with Lady Mary's son. The old lady could carry the day against Lady Mary as long as the earl did not return home to take his cousin's part. And surely that

15

was a remote possibility for some months, at least, since Lady Bea had said her nephew never missed the Season.

2

"Do go, my dear." Lady Beatrice Carstairs looked to where Jessica stood arranging a handful of flowers and shook her gray head impatiently. "No, I shall be firmer. Go!" She pointed a finger, curved by disease, at the door, but the twinkle in her brown eyes made the command something more like a wish.

"It's Andy who's keeping you indoors, I don't doubt," she continued as Jessica crossed to smile down at her. "You are likely right to imagine the boy will pop out of the shrubbery the moment you enter the gardens. He's been a veritable shadow, I know. Has he been too awfully bothersome?"

"Not too awfully." Jessica laughed, obviously surprised by the sentiment she would voice. "In fact, I admit I cannot help but like him."

Lady Bea nodded abruptly. "I've always found him to be a good-enough lad. Doesn't ape all those absurdly languid airs the dandies in town adore. But liquor affects him like it did his father before him. Too much to drink, and he's a handful.

"Still, he's not likely to have imbibed excessively this early in the day, nor will Mary be watching out the windows to spy upon you if that's your worry." Lady Beatrice rolled her eyes. "Egad! I've never seen her rouse herself as she has over this notion that Andy must wed the Multaney chit. This tea she's arranged for today has her atwitter. What a scene it will be! All of us, even the twins, gathered about to greet a mother and daughter who live no more than five miles away."

Jessica did not, as might have been expected of a companion, sympathize with the older woman's scowl of discontent. Far from it, she laughed. "You may look put

16

out, my lady, but I've a strong suspicion you would not care to miss observing this to-do.''

"Go! That is what comes of staying cooped up indoors. You've become entirely too forward.''

But Lady Beatrice was unable to maintain her fierce frown, and as Jessica curtsied dutifully, she smiled satisfied. "Good! I shall see you at tea, my dear. And afterward,'' she added outrageously, "we shall decide between us whether Marianne more closely resembles her father's bay or Andy's new hunter.''

Jessica was still smiling to herself at Lady Bea's play when, as she sat before a bed of daffodils just coming into bloom, Lady Mary's eldest son, Andrew Fitzgerald, Viscount Avensley, appeared flourishing a bouquet he'd picked only moments before. That he'd done almost precisely what his aunt had predicted he would left Jessica torn between amusement and exasperation.

"A spring tribute for a beauty as lovely as spring.'' Smiling engagingly, Andrew extended the daffodils he'd picked for her.

Jessica did not return him as bright a smile, but she did give him a polite one. "Thank you, Lord Avensley. You are very kind.''

But when she rose to go, the young man cried out in an aggrieved tone that reminded Jessica of her eleven-year-old brother, "Surely you are not going in already.''

"You know very well, sir,'' she said, giving him a direct look he could not evade, "that it would do me no good to be found alone in your company.''

Abashed, Andy shrugged, but he fell into step beside her, uninvited. "Well, I shall walk with you, then, and no, you may not protest. If Mother makes the startling discovery that we have traversed the gardens together—and I know it is she who has made such a to-do that you are reluctant to have any conversation with me at all—I shall tell her it would not be polite to deny you escort, or so my father taught me.''

Jessica arched a delicately drawn eyebrow at him, for she did not imagine Andrew's glib explanation would appease Lady Mary, but he smiled winsomely before she could tell him as much.

17

As Lady Bea had said, he was not a bad sort at all.

Even if he had not yet matured entirely, he was good-natured and not the least vain. More important, though the young man did not disguise his interest in her, he'd nothing of the predator about him, and never so over-stepped the bounds as to make her truly uncomfortable.

"Really, Jessica," he pleaded. "There's no harm. Mother cannot be angry with you, only me. And any-way," he added with a comical grimace, "I think it is deuced bad of the fates to put an Incomparable before me and then decree that I may not even have a moment's conversation with her."

This was said so ingenuously that Jessica laughed, and instantly regretted her response, for Andrew almost stopped walking altogether and stood gazing at her with an absurdly bemused—his mother would doubtless say idiotic—expression.

Jessica glanced toward the manor and saw with a sigh that they'd a long way to go yet, so she increased her pace. "Tell me, Lord Avensley, what sort of plans have you now?" she asked to distract him from staring.

"Now that I'm not to be a scholar?" The young man laughed amiably. "Perhaps I shall simply stay here at the manor and live off Justin's largesse. The prospect has brightened considerably of late," he added with a mean-ingful look at Jessica.

She did not attempt to conceal her exasperation. "Lord Avensley!"

"No! Don't scold!" He grinned charmingly, but when Jessica would not be coaxed, he sobered a trifle and shrugged. "In truth I've no plans. I suppose I could learn how to manage my estates from Justin." Andrew gave a careless wave with his hand. "He knows an amazing amount about cow and crops, which is why his estates are so profitable. But what would my knowledge avail me? The lands my father left me are scarcely enough to sustain the few tenants unlucky enough to live there, much less the family my mother wishes me to start."

Andrew's remark about his cousin did not surprise Jes-sica, for she knew from Lady Beatrice that the earl made certain to spend several months of the year at Bleithewood, although he had other estates and a house in town. Unlike many men his class, it seemed Roxham was a scrupulous landowner.

"And even if I were interested in following Justin's lead," Andrew continued as he idly kicked a loose pebble with his boot, "he's enjoying the Season in London, where I devoutly hope he stays. If he comes home, he'll only ring a frightful peal over me. This was not my first scrape."

Jessica swallowed a chuckle at her companion's gloomy tone. "There must be some worthy occupation you would enjoy," she said, frowning faintly as she searched for some suggestion.

Andrew glanced at her, his eyes twinkling playfully. "Lacking which I will only get into the suds again?"

His good-humored insight deserved a friendly smile, which Jessica gave him despite the responding gleam in his hazel eyes. "Something like that," she conceded as she quickened her pace yet again.

"There is one occupation I should not object to," Andrew confided rather thoughtfully after a moment. When Jessica looked curiously toward him, he said, "I know it will sound ridiculous coming from me, but I should like a life in the army. I always have, but Mother will not be persuaded to buy my colors. She says she doesn't want me getting killed in some far-off land, but in truth I believe she thinks I'll be dissatisfied with only my army pay to support me. Instead she'd rather I marry a chit with only wealth to recommend her. Dear God! You'd think Mother would realize I will be bored to tears married to the squire's gold and will likely get myself killed right here in my own county in some silly prank."

"Jess! Andy!"

Jessica looked around to find Olivia Fitzgerald waving as she hurried to catch up to them. Andrew muttered something under his breath about sisters, but Jessica smiled. Though she found herself in some sympathy with Andrew, she thought it much better for her if they continued their conversation in a group of three.

"Andy, I watched from my room as you crept up to bedevil Jess, and I hurried out at once." Olivia greeted

19

her brother after she'd embraced Jessica. Unlike her mother, Olivia was possessed of a decisive and energetic nature, and when she took a friend, she gave that fortunate person unstinting loyalty. In return for the sympathetic ear Jessica was accustomed to lending her, Olivia was quite prepared to protect her from her thoughtless, scapegrace brother.

The short curls Jessica had persuaded Olivia to adopt set off her pretty, rounded face in a very pleasing way, but Andrew did not pause to remark the change wrought in his sister's appearance. Suffering a scold from Livy put him off his normally amiable stride.

"And I suppose your behavior is so exemplary that you think to set yourself up as my mentor, Livy?" he retorted, scowling. "If so, you've forgotten that Jenkins caught you kissing Martin—our youngest groom—and that Martin was only kept from being sacked, because Jess, here, had the presence of mind to remind Aunt Bea that he is the sole support of a mother and eight siblings."

Olivia reddened at the reminder of her foolish escapade—she'd only kissed Martin because her friend, Kate Verney, had dared her—but she did not admit defeat. "You should not refer to Jessica so informally, Andrew," she flared back. "To you she must be Miss Winslow."

Andrew did not give his sister's scold the benefit of a reply. "That stunt of yours will likely be enough to bring Justin down upon us, Season or no Season," he predicted gloomily.

Olivia tossed her chestnut curls, undaunted. "I am not afraid of Justin," she proclaimed proudly.

"You've never seen him angry, that's why," Andrew returned, sure of himself. "When all's right as rain, he's the greatest gun. There's no doubt of it. But you may rest assured that when Justin gives you a dressing down, there is nothing quite so awful. He can look like the very devil."

Andrew's bleak expression deflated his sister. "I imagine you are right," she conceded. "I did see him once administer a thunderous scold to a groom who'd not cared for his cattle adequately, and I don't doubt he reserves something rather more severe for those of us from whom he expects even more." Olivia chewed on her lip in silence a moment before the optimism that was natural to her reasserted itself. "But, truly, he has always treated me wonderfully," she observed, half to herself. "And Mother may well not write him about Martin. It's the Season, after all. He seldom comes home before summer, and then he'll likely bring a party of the most splendid people with him." She turned eagerly to Jessica, "Only those in the most exalted circles come. Aunt Bea says an invitation to Bleithewood is worth its weight in gold."

"And what did you expect?" her brother demanded in a superior tone that drew a glare from his sister. "Justin's an immensely wealthy earl."

"An immensely wealthy, handsome earl," Olivia bettered his description just to show she knew very well what life in town was about.

Her indignation had the happy effect of causing her brother's mood to veer. "And don't let us forget his superior accomplishments," Andy reproved with an owlish look that prompted Olivia to giggle and Jessica to smile. "Justin's a noted whipster, almost never loses at cards, has a punishing left hook, and, so Jenkins himself says, can ride any horse born no matter how ill-trained."

"Don't forget women," Olivia piped up daringly. "Tom Cathcart said he can have any woman he wants, whenever he wants."

"Livy!" Andrew cried, so taken aback that Jessica could scarcely keep from laughing.

"How old is this paragon?" she asked quickly when she saw Olivia open her mouth to defend herself.

Andrew replied, "Thirty—the perfect age for matrimony, or so all the matchmaking mamas hope, according to Mother."

Olivia, not to be left out, added importantly, "Any number have hoped to snare him over the years, but Justin has always successfully avoided their schemes. Just now most of the talk revolves around Lady Aurelia Stanhope, a widow, who is his latest flirt, and very beautiful they say."

Andrew looked over to question his sister on her source of information, but his younger brother and sister, known collectively to all as the twins, prevented him.

"It's time for tea," the two children cried simultaneously as they leapt out from behind a bush where they had hidden in the hopes of startling their brother and sister.

"Egad!" Andrew jumped. "You two will be the death of me!"

When Andrew hit playfully at them, they shrieked with delight, and Jessica, stepping back, marveled at how very closely Lady Mary's offspring resembled each other. Despite the differences in their ages, it was obvious the children had been cast from the same mold, fashioned after their father.

With their chestnut hair, hazel eyes, and energetic natures they'd little or nothing of their mother in them, and Jessica felt a twinge of sympathy for Lady Beatrice's niece. It did seem unfair that fate had not sent her even one quiet, biddable child.

"Marianne and her mother are here," Giles exclaimed, ducking out of the way of his brother's fist.

"And Mother wants you and Livy to go in at once," Julia finished for her brother while she leapt at Andrew's arm when he came close to Giles.

At once Andrew sobered. "I've half a mind not to go at all," he muttered.

Concerned that the young man might actually be weighing the idea of escaping the elaborate tea his mother had roused herself to plan, Jessica thought it time to speak up. "It is half of your mind I hope you will ignore," she said quietly. "Taking tea with Miss Multaney may be uncomfortable for you, but imagine how dreadful it would be for her if you could not be found. She would be mortified at the direct snub, and she did nothing to arrange this affair."

"Jess is right," Olivia agreed, turning to look at her brother with more sympathy than Jessica had expected she would. "Your argument is with Mother, not Marianne."

"I suppose," Andrew conceded, though when he ambled off to the house, Olivia at his side, he wore the sort of grim expression Jessica thought the Early Christian martyrs must have worn as they marched out to meet the lions.

"How do I look, Jess?" little Julia cried in her high voice, for her brother's woes were the very least of her interests that spring afternoon. When she executed a twirl to show off the pretty pink muslin dress she had donned for the tea, Giles grimaced.

"You'll fall if you don't take care," he warned. "And Nanny said if Jess was to take us to tea, we must look our best."

Jessica laughed aloud at Giles' attitude, for his lack of interest in his appearance was one of old Nanny Budgett's greatest woes. It seemed an invitation to tea with the adults was a lofty honor indeed.

"I think you both look quite splendid," Jessica assured each child in turn with a particularly fond smile. "I shall be most honored to escort you to tea. Shall we?"

She put out both her elbows, and the children, laughing, linked arms with her. "I am so glad you have come to live with us, Jess," Julia cried happily.

"We know that you are the one who persuaded Mother we've the manners to take tea with everyone," Giles added. "Nanny told us."

Jessica smiled. "It will be my pleasure to see you acting as well as I know you are able," she said, and was glad to see both children nod brightly.

One twin on either arm, Jessica came to the drawing-room door, and while a young footman jumped eagerly to open it, she straightened Giles' hair and rearranged Julia's bow.

To her relief, when Lady Mary summoned her children, they behaved impeccably, bowing and curtsying before the guests with such grace that their mother cast Jessica a grateful look.

After the twins were sent to their seats, Lady Mary accorded Jessica the honor of being presented to the Multaneys. It was Jessica's first glimpse of Marianne, and as she greeted the girl and her mother in her low-pitched voice, she fought to keep from smiling.

Lady Bea had not been uncharitable. The poor girl, with her long face and squarish teeth, did resemble nothing so much as a horse.

Lady Beatrice was watching her with shrewd, twinkling eyes when Jessica went to her, and they exchanged a significant look, but nothing more. Not even a smile betrayed Jessica, for she was aware Andrew watched her from where he stood beside the fire.

"I had your sewing brought," Lady Beatrice said as Jessica took a seat behind her. "I know how much you like having your hands busy while the rest of us are being idle," she added with a droll look.

There could be no harm smiling then, and Jessica did. "You are very thoughtful, ma'am," she said, meaning it, for she did like to keep her hands busy.

Seeing the twins were well occupied eating the macaroons and seed cakes from the tea tray, Jessica took up her needlework. She'd only just finished the first row of neat, intricate stitches when the door opened and Moreton, Bleithewood's ancient butler, entered.

"My lady," the staid old retainer announced with what amounted to vast excitement, "his lordship is returned. He will be with you shortly."

"Justin!" several voices cried at once.

In that single word, Jessica could detect an astonishing variety of tones, which distracted her, as she sat in her corner alone, from worrying what the earl's arrival might portend for her.

Closest to her, Lady Beatrice and the twins conveyed both surprise and delight, while Lady Mary, though she shared their pleasure, expressed satisfaction rather than astonishment.

Andrew, throwing an angry look at his mother, exclaimed his cousin's name with a mixture of dismay and defiance, but Olivia went rather pale and cried his name only faintly.

"Lord Roxham's visit comes as a surprise." It was Mrs. Multaney who uttered the first coherent phrase. "I know how like him it is to come unannounced, but I do wonder that he would leave town at the start of the Season."

24

"Well, I did write and ask him to come," Lady Mary admitted bravely, though she earned another scowl from her oldest son.

3

"Justin!" The twins tossed decorum aside and raced to the door before it was fully open.

The earl, when he entered, glanced over their heads to flash a strong smile at the group in general, but his young cousins, leaping to embrace him, claimed him for themselves first.

"Whoa, there!" He smiled, bearing their attack with lazy ease.

Tall, with broad shoulders and a narrow waist and hips, he possessed a taut, well-developed body that his valet had been known to say showed to advantage regardless of what he wore. Which was just as well, that same man, Hanks, had gone on to say, for the earl, though he invariably dressed with impeccable elegance, had a decidedly careless attitude toward his appearance.

Even then, his coat of blue superfine, its fit so exquisite it could only have come from Weston, was being put to a stringent test as Giles hung on one arm of it, and when Julia clambered upon his black Hessians, her cousin displayed not the least concern for their glossy shine. Far from it, to her delight, he played at walking with her while she stood upon them.

More remarkable, perhaps, it seemed that nothing the children did could detract from the earl's appearance. His cravat remained as white and as intricately knotted as ever. His buckskins continued to cling as tightly to his well-muscled thighs, and when a lock of his sun-streaked hair fell forward onto his brow, he was able to restore it to its place with a negligent stroke of his hand.

It was not difficult to see why the twins were so beside themselves, why Lady Beatrice leaned eagerly forward in her chair, why Lady Mary beamed with obvious pleasure, nor why the eyes of the Multaney ladies, mother and daughter, had taken on a rather hectic sparkle. Even Olivia, making an impatient movement in her chair, waved happily at her cousin.

The Earl of Roxham was as handsome as Livy had promised, and he possessed all the presence of which Lady Mary had been so proud.

Those encountering him for the first time invariably noticed, aside from his imposing height and virile body, his unusual eyes: brown with golden lights. Their contrast to the light coloring of his hair surprised. Subsequently the viewer remarked, if the earl chose to smile, how the golden lights sparkled and turned his eyes a lighter, warmer color.

Surrounding those changeable amber eyes were absurdly thick lashes of a somewhat darker color than his hair and matching his faintly arched brows. He had a proud, straight nose and a wide but firm mouth that more than one woman had been heard to say had a most tempting, sensuous cast.

Just then it was curved amusedly at both corners, for Giles, the budding horseman of the twins, was eagerly inquiring, "Did you bring Mars with you, Justin? Can I ride him one day?"

And Julia was asking simultaneously, "Do you like my hair, Justin? It's not short like Livy's, I'm letting it grow long like—"

"And I am very glad to see you both as well." The earl laughed with an easy affection to which both children responded with beaming looks. "Yes, Giles, I rode Mars a good deal of the way from London, and, Livy, I find your lengthening hair, if not the style, nonetheless, most becoming." He addressed each child in turn, but when he saw Giles' open his mouth in preparation for further excited speech, Roxham cuffed him lightly on the head. "Patience, halfling, I shall answer your every question later. For now, I've others to greet."

"Yes, Giles, Julia. Let Justin be, or I shall regret inviting you to tea," Lady Mary chided her offspring before extending her hand to her cousin. "We are glad to see you, Justin," she said with more energy than was her wont. "And isn't it quite wonderful that Emily and her dear Marianne should be here to greet you?" she asked, gesturing toward the couch.

"It is always a pleasure to see my nearest neighbors," Justin Stafford agreed affably. "Mrs. Multaney . . ."

Mrs. Multaney, country-born -and bred despite her connection with the powerful Leamingtons, flushed with nervous pleasure when Roxham bowed gallantly over her hand. "I trust the squire is well?" he asked, and when he received a slightly breathless answer in the affirmative, the earl turned to Miss Multaney.

His flashing smile reduced her to a twittering mass, but Roxham, who was accustomed to his effect upon young, inexperienced women, had several stock phrases to say, and by the time he turned to greet Livy, Marianne's cheeks had lost at least some of their painful heat.

Olivia, her hazel eyes sparkling, was bouncing upon her seat. In the excitement of seeing her thrilling cousin again, she'd managed to put aside any worry over what his visit might portend for her. "You look so handsome, Justin," she blurted out after she'd made her greeting, and immediately turned as red as Marianne had.

But the earl laughed in such an unaffected way, he saved her further embarrassment, and when he told her after a brief, twinkling look that she had become quite a young lady in the past year—her hair, he said, was particularly becoming in its new style—Olivia flushed pink with pleasure.

Only Andrew, older, and with more experience of his cousin, held himself aloof. When Roxham greeted him, he said, only, "Sir." and bowed stiffly.

The earl, if he intended to discipline Andrew, did not seem interested in doing so before a room full of people, however, and soon put his young relative at ease by remarking with unfeigned interest that he had seen a superb hunter in the stables.

At once Andrew's eyes lit with unaffected pleasure, for he'd only bought the horse a month earlier. "By jove, Justin!" he exclaimed proudly. "You must see him take a fence! He fairly floats over!"

After the earl had agreed to ride out the next day, he turned, at last, to greet his aunt. Jessica flinched, inadvertently sticking herself with her needle.

It was her first movement since Justin Stafford had entered his drawing room. Until then she had sat immobilized by disbelief and horror.

As she watched the tall man with tawny hair and warm, laughing eyes greet his family and friends, she saw him whirl to confront her in another time and place.

His eyes that dreadful night had been as cold as chips of obsidian, his mouth a straight, grim line, when it was not turned down in a sneer, and he had been dressed, she remembered well, in black evening clothes finer than any she'd ever beheld.

There was no question he was the same man. Though she had met Justin Stafford only once and then only briefly in the private room of an undistinguished inn with nothing but the fire and two spluttering candles for light, there was no mistaking him.

Jessica had not learned his given name that night. He'd not given it, nor his title. He'd only thought it important to inform her he was Edward Stafford's brother. Had Edward told her his brother was an earl? She did not know. He might well have. She'd had so little interest in the young man, she'd not listened to him.

And Sally? Had Sally whispered of Edward's connection? Likely she had. She'd have been impressed by it, but Jessica had almost from the first dismissed anything Sally had to say.

How very foolish she'd been! She ought to have listened better; ought, at the very least, to have questioned her assumption that the Staffords of Herefordshire had no relation to the Staffords she'd met so disastrously in London.

But she had been too relieved to find a position after Mrs. Ashcroft's health had declined so much. Now as a result, the man who had threatened her with ruin should she ever darken his presence again, held her future in his hands. All unwitting she'd walked into the lion's den.

"How is my favorite aunt?"

Her head lowered as she sought to cover the drop of

blood staining her piece of linen, Jessica hid her gasp. She could see the gold tassels swaying on the earl's Hessians only a few feet from her.

He buzzed his aunt's cheek. "You are as beautiful as ever, Aunt Bea," he said, smiling.

"Darling boy! You flatter me as always." Lady Bea laughed as she lifted her other cheek for a salute. "Feasting my eyes on you is almost the tonic for my spirits that your flattery is. I vow you grow more handsome every time I see you."

"I'm happy we agree that we're both in looks," the earl returned with a lazy laugh. "Perhaps I ought to make it a habit to stay away so long. I find I like the warmth of the reception."

"Oh, go on, you charming rascal." She swatted at him with her fan. "We always greet you this besottedly. I only hope you intend to stay long enough to allow us to become accustomed to you, though I've little hope you'll be so generous. I imagine we've only borrowed you from the Season and its, ah, distractions for a little time."

The remark, though put in the form of a statement, was obviously and unashamedly a question. The earl's response was to laugh with such amusement that even Jessica, though her heart hammered painfully in her chest, darted a quick look at him.

"It's good to see you in such spirits, Aunt," her nephew said with evident sincerity. "But I fear I cannot reward your unabashed curiosity with the plain speaking it deserves. The length of my stay must depend upon the duties I've neglected so shamefully."

"An oversight I don't doubt Mary pointed out to you," Lady Bea retorted with a shrewd twinkle in her eye. "But whatever the excuse, I am pleased to see you. I've the dearest person to present to you."

The staccato rhythm of Jessica's heart left her breathless. Once, when she'd been thrown from a horse and was reluctant to remount, her father had said to her, "Every man feels fear, Jess, but only a few have the will to turn a brave face to the world."

She clung to his words now. She would not faint,

though her breath came with difficulty, and she felt as if all the blood had drained from her face.

She could not smile, the effort was beyond her. But she could wrap her composure around her like a cloak and lift a brave face to look directly at the earl.

Now that he faced her and away from the others, his eyes were as cold as the scornful, golden-brown eyes that still haunted her dreams. "Miss Winslow," he inclined his sun-streaked head when Lady Bea presented her.

Praying that her legs would not buckle, Jessica made her curtsy and heard him add, "My cousin made mention of you and your services to my aunt in a letter to me."

For a long, perilous moment, Jessica battled a bubble of hysterical laughter. What he must have thought when he learned she was working in his very house! Given what he thought of her, he'd likely never have entertained the notion that her coming to Bleithewood was the sheer, unlucky coincidence it was.

Jessica raised her chin, giving the powerful man look for look. He would believe what he liked, that was certain, but whatever he believed, whatever he called her, he would not label her a coward. She was Captain Arthur Winslow's child, after all.

But Jessica had braced herself for naught. The twins, quiet until then, could no longer contain themselves now that Justin was meeting "their Jess."

Sliding her hand into Justin's, Julia claimed his attention before he could denounce Jessica before the others, if that had indeed been his intent. "Jess taught us how to tend a wounded bird Giles and I found, Justin. She showed us just how to bind its wing and feed it. We let it go yesterday, because it needed its freedom, but I wish you could have seen it."

"We didn't know Justin was coming, silly," Giles reproved his sister as he maneuvered into position between Jessica and his tall cousin. "Jess is teaching us to make maps with flour. Nanny thinks the maps a great mess, but now I know where Waterloo is, and Austerlitz, and Corunna, and even Vienna."

"I see that you have learned a great deal from Miss

30

Winslow." The earl flicked his considering gaze back to Jessica.

The beauty that had been only promised three years ago had been realized. She'd been pretty enough then, of course, but the intervening years had honed her features, giving them a definition they had not possessed.

Her hair was the same, however. She had worn it down that night. Not loose and tumbling, he recalled, but held back by a ribbon, and even in the gloom of that dingy inn, he'd been momentarily startled by its bright beauty. Today, bound neatly in a heavy knot, a little of its glory was diminished, but none of its allure.

And her astonishingly blue eyes were exactly as he remembered—even to the fierce pride that flung him an unspoken challenge.

"I should like to see you later, Miss Winslow," he said coolly. "Say six o'clock, in my study. Mary keeps town hours, I believe, and we should have sufficient time to conduct our business before supper."

Jessica inclined her head a fraction, feeling grateful—though she would not let him know it—that he made no mention before the others of their previous meeting. "As you wish, my lord," she replied, proud that her voice remained level.

Roxham did not allow his amber gaze to linger upon her. He turned to his aunt, and his mouth curved at once in an affectionate smile. "Let me help you to a chair closer to the tea tray, Aunt Bea," he whispered *sotto voce*. "You are my one hope for wit in this group, and I can't have you sitting away off here."

Clearly pleased by her nephew's attentions, Lady Beatrice allowed herself to be removed to a seat closer to Lady Mary and her guests, and the twins followed along, crowding next to their returned cousin.

Normally Jessica would have made nothing of being left apart. It was a companion's lot, as she had learned over the last few years.

On this day, however, she felt her status keenly. Lady Beatrice was accustomed to treating her as a member of the family, and Jessica had come close to forgetting what her real place was.

The bitter thought occurred to her that it was entirely fitting that the Earl of Roxham would be the one to remind her where she belonged. His brother Edward had been the one to compromise her and it was Roxham who had told her her ruin was no more than she deserved; he had not lifted a finger to help her.

Because of him, as much as his brother, she would live forever on the fringes of society, a paid companion, sitting, as she sat now, at the edge of the circle of the family.

The brooding thought was insupportable. Jessica would not let him place her in such an ignominious position if she could avoid it.

Gathering her needlework together, she rose and crossed to Lady Beatrice. Bending, she whispered an excuse to leave. She could not later remember what she said, though she thought she made mention of hot-water bottles.

The older lady gave her young companion's drawn face a sharp look, but Justin laughed just then, and, distracted, Lady Bea patted her hand. Taking the gesture as permission to leave, Jessica walked calmly from the room, purposefully keeping her graceful gait unhurried. Only when the door of the drawing room closed behind her did she give way. Then, no longer able to contain her anxiety, she lifted her skirts and dashed headlong up the stairs to the sanctuary of her room, where she leaned heavily against her door as if she might, with her slender body, have the power to ward off the earl in his own home.

4

"I have spent the most agreeable time telling Justin how very lucky I am to have you," Lady Bea proclaimed with great relish when she was returned to her rooms by a young footman after tea. "And I will not tolerate head-shaking," she continued sharply before Jessica could summon any response at all. "Your only fault, miss, is your absurd modesty. You deserve my praises, for you've been the greatest comfort to me. And I remind you, I've had enough prune-faced old women come to attend me to know precisely the extent of my good fortune."

Despite her worries, Jessica smiled. Lady Beatrice's antipathy for her previous companions was an oft-sounded theme. "I believe you took a dislike to my predecessors because not one of them was as poor at piquet as I," she teased lightly in return.

But Lady Beatrice, now settled in her bed, her pillows fluffed comfortably behind her, would not be turned up sweet so easily. "Nor did they read to me in a soothing voice," she scoffed indignantly. "Every last one of them sounded like crows. And who is it, young lady, who thought to warm my bed with bottles filled with hot water? One of those ancient crones who reminded me of the death that will come too soon, or you, a chit too young to be so well acquainted with the inside of a sickroom?"

Shooting Jessica a belligerent look that dared her to argue, Lady Beatrice continued repressively, "You may rest assured that I spared Justin none of it. I even added, though it will displease you to hear it, I'm certain, all the good you've done for Mary's scamps and the willing ear you've lent that silly Livy." Though her eyes drifted shut, Lady Beatrice managed to add in a determined tone, "And I have told him you deserve higher wages! You do double the duties I first told you would be yours. . . ."

Seeing that Lady Beatrice had fallen into a sound sleep in midsentence, Jessica lingered only to give her a grateful smile. She was doing her utmost to prejudice the earl in Jessica's favor, and it was not her fault that her efforts were doomed from the start.

Though Lady Bea could not know it, Jessica was painfully aware the real question was whether the earl would consent to keep her on at all. And if he did not, as was likely, would he suffer her presence long enough to allow her to find a position before she left Bleithewood? She

33

hoped to convince him it would be cruel to do otherwise at their interview.

Knowing his prejudice against her caused Jessica's shoulders to sag. She sent the better part of her wage home to her mother every month so she'd not saved much to live upon while she sought out another employer.

As she passed through the door separating her small room from Lady Beatrice's, another possibility struck her with the force of a blow.

Too agitated to sit, she paced to the window to gaze out unseeing. Might Roxham be so vindictive as to send her away without references?

Such fear seized her at the thought, for she would not find a respectable position without a word from her most recent employer, she did not hear the knock at the door and was not aware her summons had come until the maid, Annie, a favorite of Jessica's, peeked inside.

" 'Is lordship's wishes to see you, Miss Jess. Wouldn't do to keep 'im waitin'. 'E's most particular in some ways.''

"Thank you, Annie." Jessica essayed a smile, but it wavered so she gave up the effort.

"There now," Annie cried, her sympathies enlisted at once, for Jessica always had a smile ready for her, unlike Lady Bea's previous companions. " 'Is lordship's a fair gentleman for all that 'e's a stickler,'' she assured Jessica. "And you may be sure Mr. Moreton's told 'im what you've done for 'er ladyship. Likes you ever so well, does Mr. Moreton.''

To Jessica's considerable dismay tears sprang to her eyes. She'd not realized the dignified old man had taken much note of her, much less that he approved of her.

Mindful of Annie's anxious expression, Jessica blinked back her tears. "I am grateful to you for telling me, Annie.'' Her smile firmed. "And now, as you say, I had best go.''

The distance from Jessica's room to the earl's study was considerable, and as she made her descent, she found it difficult to control her thoughts. When she ought to have been quieting her mind so that she might do battle with the man waiting to confront her, she was, instead, recalling her ill-fated trip to London three long years before.

When she had arrived at Lady Sarah Renwick's home, she'd been shown to a sitting room decorated in imitation of some Oriental pavilion, with a pillowy canopy covering the ceiling and palm trees painted on the wall.

"My dear, you are not precisely what I'd expected," Sally had drawled, not bothering to rise from the backless couch upon which she reclined. "You do not take after Jane."

Jessica had not known what to reply to such a greeting. She did not, she knew, look like her mother. She had her father's hair, and it was from his family that she'd gotten her slender body and long legs. Her mother's only gift was the deep blue of her eyes.

Sally, looking at those eyes, knew what Jessica could not: that Jane's eyes had never looked out upon the world with the spark her daughter's did.

Sally frowned even as she bid Jessica to be seated. On a whim she'd agreed to discharge a dusty obligation to Jane. Her cousin had long years ago saved her from the consequences of a youthful indiscretion, and she had thought it would be amusing to return the favor by introducing Jane's girl to town and along the way to mold the child in her own image.

But Sally acknowledged she'd not counted upon a girl whose carriage proclaimed she'd a mind of her own, and whose beauty, when properly presented, would rival her own.

There was little to be done, however, as she could not send Jessica back to Kent. The admission implicit in such an action would be too humiliating. Only, she decided, Jane need not know if she never presented Jessica formally in society. Sally would only acquaint the girl with a few of the young men who came to her house on occasion—when her husband was out of town, as the earl often was.

Jessica, new to town and to society, had not known what to make of Sally's lack of friends. The only people who seemed to visit the house were young dandies with bored airs and bold eyes.

If only, it occurred to Jessica and not for the first time, one of those young men had been a nice, kindly gentleman who offered marriage, she would have wed him in an instant. But Sally's male acquaintances never made mention of marriage, nor did they proffer invitations to respectable parties.

Indeed, though they had more refined manners, they reminded her of Charles Godfrey, and the hot relish in their eyes when they looked at her left her cold as ice.

Her rebuffs did not put them off, however. They were amused, particularly as they sensed the fire that lurked beneath her cool surface, and they placed bets among themselves as to who would be the first man to bed her.

Of them all, one young man in particular pursued her. To Jessica it seemed that every effort she made to repulse Edward Stafford only piqued his interest the more.

Sally, eager to get the girl with her vivid hair and deep-blue eyes off her hands, arranged for Edward to take them both out driving. Though Jessica said she did not care for him, Sally firmly believed she could be made to accept the boy, if the young pup's interest could be fixed.

And to further matters, when she espied her current favorite among the young bucks paying her their addresses, she promptly abandoned Jessica. "Don't look so put out, dear." She had smiled back at her young cousin as she gaily descended from Edward's carriage. "There is nothing exceptional in riding around the park with a man of Mr. Stafford's character."

"This will never do," Jessica cried in real distress. "You must take me home at once."

But Edward Stafford, seeing his chance, had only laughed and rapped with the cane he affected upon the roof of the carriage. "Let you out, my beauty?" he'd cried. "What a cruel thing to ask of one who has worked so diligently to get you all alone."

Jessica could not think Sally had actually plotted with Edward, but she had made the matter easy for him, rushing off in her heedless way. At the time Jessica was angry, but it was nothing compared to what she felt when she realized Edward would not be content with a mere drive around the park.

When they had returned to the entrance and she was just thinking matters had not gone so badly, Edward, who had been looking intently out the window, suddenly seized her roughly to him. Frightened, Jessica pushed against him, but to little avail. Edward was the stronger, and there in broad daylight, in full view of a knot of his cheering friends, he kissed her full and hard upon the lips.

Eventually Jessica succeeded in landing a blow to Edward's jaw sufficient to cause him to retreat and mutter angrily about the games some vixens liked to play. Unfortunately, by that time his carriage was well beyond the park and none of the young men who had watched their embrace with great interest saw her repulse him. The damage to her reputation was done.

She demanded the carriage be turned about, but with a petulant look Edward sulkily informed her he had other plans. What these were, he could not be made to say. But when, toward evening, they stopped at a small, inconspicuous inn some distance from London, Jessica feared for more than her reputation.

It was obvious the innkeeper knew Edward, for he bowed him in obsequiously, murmuring "My lord" all the while. Reassured by this deference to his status, Edward grandly ordered a room and sent Jessica ahead to, as he put it, "prepare yourself."

Evidently believing that her resistance to him in the carriage was merely token, though why he should think so was beyond her—she'd not spoken to him for the two hours it had taken to reach their destination—Edward failed to take into account the lock that must inevitably be upon the door.

As soon as she was alone, she shot the bolt and for good measure pushed the bed, a small table, and an overstuffed chair against the door as well. Edward banged and shouted, but despite his every effort, he quite failed to penetrate her defenses.

Eventually, tired and furious, he conceded Jessica the victory and left her to keep guard sitting upright in the chair.

She must have fallen into a light doze, for at some time

after nightfall a sharp rapping at her door awakened her. Startled, she cried out, and an authoritative voice, distinctly more mature-sounding than Edward's, informed her curtly, "I am Edward's elder brother, Miss Winslow, and I shall see you in the parlor below in five minutes' time."

Giving her no opportunity to protest his imperious command or to accede to it, for that matter, he strode away, and as she listened to him descend the stairs at a determined pace, she sat irresolute. It might only be a trick of Edward's designed to lure her from her refuge, but if the man were, indeed, an elder brother, he might represent some way out of the predicament into which Edward had plunged her.

A new scratching at the door came then and tipped the balance in the man's favor. When Jessica answered, she was met with the sound of a woman's voice, identifying itself as belonging to the innkeeper's wife and begging her to go down to the parlor. "Please, miss," the voice quavered. "He means to tear the door from its hinges. There are the other guests to be thought of."

Hoping to set matters right, Jessica pushed her barricade aside and followed the anxious little woman down the stairs. Now she almost laughed aloud. Nothing had been set right by her interview with the man, except that Edward had been removed from her vicinity.

From the moment she had entered and the tall, broad-shouldered stranger attired all in black satin evening clothes had whirled around from the fire, his very size intimidating her, he had taken the offensive against her. "Do not imagine that your ridiculous pretense at innocence will succeed with me, Miss Winslow," he'd informed her coldly, his words so astounding her that she'd merely stood gaping at him as if he were mad. "Oh, you're clever, there's no doubt of that," he had continued, his golden-brown eyes—even in her agitated state she had noted the contrast they made with his tawny coloring—narrowed upon her. "The bar on your door was an excellent touch, but believe me, I am aware of the rig you and Sally Renwick think to run at my brother's expense. She's already tipped your hand, you see, by com-

38

ing 'round to my house demanding to know your whereabouts and informing me that Edward must marry you. As if a woman who plots her own downfall can be compromised."

"But I—"

Before Jessica could say a word in her own defense, he cut her off curtly. "You came away alone with Edward of your own free will, did you not?"

"Yes, but—"

"And you suffered his kiss in broad daylight in the heart of London, did you not?" the stranger had continued relentlessly. "You may as well admit the point," he snapped after a moment, when Jessica began to shake her head. "I was approached this evening by at least five bucks who were eager to tell me of Edward's latest conquest. The Icy Vixen, they termed you."

When Jessica's face flamed, the elegantly clad man had laughed sardonically. "I see you were not aware of their pet name. I must say my brother's taste has improved," he added as his eyes traveled over her person with cool consideration. "You are a trifle young, but there would be enjoyment teaching you what pleases in bed."

"Stop," Jessica cried, so infuriated by the look with which he had as good as undressed her and by the crudity of his words that she lifted her hand to slap his face.

Her hand was stayed in midair, however, though the man never moved an inch. "I would counsel against such a move," he had said, the light that flamed of a sudden in his eyes speaking louder than his soft words.

Jessica took a prudent step back from the fury she'd stirred.

"A wise move," he'd commended with a thin smile. "I only wish you could display such wisdom in this matter. But you are determined to play the innocent miss to the end. A stupid game." His shrug was contemptuous. "Particularly considering your connection with Sally. Her reputation is too well-known to lend your efforts the least bit of credence."

"But Sally is my cousin." It was all Jessica could think to say. She had not chosen Sally, surely he could see that.

He did, but it did not matter. "I am told certain traits

39

run in families. You prove the point, it seems." Then, weary of bantering words with her, the daunting man reached inside his coat and withdrew a pouch.

"This is the last you will see of Edward. I scarcely think it necessary to say, I am removing him from your grasp. In parting I shall leave you an inducement to keep your distance, if the warning that I will ruin you utterly should you show your face in society again does not do the trick. I would have no other young man caught in your toils in Edward's stead."

"But you are mistaken in me," Jessica managed to get out at last as he hefted the heavy pouch in his hand. "Ask Edward. He will tell you this entire affair is of his contrivance."

It never occurred to Jessica that Edward would fear his brother's wrath more than he would fear behaving dishonorably, but she was soon to learn that Edward Stafford had no intention of suffering reproach for the likes of her.

"Do you think I have not spoken to my brother?" Edward's brother demanded scornfully, dashing all her hopes with the one question. "He has told me how Sally made to leave you unaccompanied, and how you enticed him with sweet kisses to go farther afield than the park. He says you only put him off when he would not stop to buy you a ring. At least the boy was not so overcome by your charms that he gave into that bit of blackmail. Not that a ring would have succeeded in bringing Edward and his wealth to the altar," he informed her, his eyes as cold as ice. "I would never allow him to wed such as you, but I am pleased he showed some spirit."

The elder Stafford shrugged as the pouch he dropped upon the table made a dull, thudding sound. "Good night to you, Miss Winslow, and may we never have the dubious pleasure of meeting again."

So saying, he stalked from the room, leaving Jessica to stare numbly after him. A few moments later she heard shouts from the courtyard and then the sound of a carriage racing away at a dangerous pace in the dark of night.

The next day Jessica learned she'd actually heard two carriages leave. The Stafford brothers had departed each in his own carriage and left her to find her own way back to town.

Squeezed in with a half-dozen others upon the stage coach that came through each morning from Reading, Jessica arrived at Sally's house disheveled but certain of her next course of action.

It was what she should have done when she entertained the first doubts as to Sally's suitability as a chaperon. The hope of a marriage to shelter her, her brothers and her mother as well, had been a sentimental fantasy in which she ought not to have indulged.

Sally was not in, or so her butler said. Only later did Jessica hear from her mother that their cousin had written to say how sorry she was for Jessica's "mishap," but that she understood from Edward that Jessica had been compensated.

As if she could ever be compensated, Jessica had thought, as she sat in a small room in the boardinghouse she'd learned of through a maid at Sally's. Mrs. Twig's house was respectable, but it was a far cry from a home of her own.

She applied for a position, any position through an agency. The vicar in Donbridge, Mr. Ashcroft, had written her a reference, and in the end it was he, not the agency, who had connected her with Helen Ashcroft. She was his sister-in-law, and when he learned she needed a companion, he had recommended Jessica. . . .

"Come in!"

A light kindled in Jessica's indigo-blue eyes. He sounded precisely as imperious as he had three years ago. Then she'd been a child, a witless fool. Cowed and incoherent before him, she'd conceded him the day.

Well, she was three years older now and had survived with honor despite him, though her circumstances had been far from easy. Mrs. Ashcroft had had a son who, with his wife and two daughters, lived with her. It had not been an amiable situation, but Jessica had managed.

She would do so again. No matter what the earl's decision, she would not crawl or cower. She would meet him as the equal she was.

5

As Jessica had known full well, it was no simple matter to remain brave when she came face to face with the earl. With deliberate insult, he made her no greeting whatsoever. While he lounged against his desk, his long legs stretched out before him and his arms crossed over his chest, he left her to stand uncertainly before him and stared at her through cold, heavy-lidded eyes as if he could not decide whether she was worthy of the exertion of simple speech.

Despite her determination to remain composed, Jessica felt her cheeks heat at his contemptuous treatment, and nettled as much by her own loss of composure as by his rudeness, which, after all, she had expected, she forced her chin up.

"You sent for me, my lord?" she demanded, her blue eyes challenging his impassive gaze.

A single tawny eyebrow flicked up at her temerity. "Which is why you are here, Miss Winslow," he returned coolly. "Sit down." Roxham motioned with his chin to a stiff, high-backed chair before him and waited for Jessica to seat herself.

She took her time, being careful to keep her spine very straight and to fold her hands composedly upon her lap before she looked up again.

Roxham was not blind to her ploy: she thought to gain the offensive by making him wait on her. A grim light flickered briefly in his eyes. She was a more challenging opponent than she'd been three years before. She had matured in the interim in more than looks. But it mattered not. The outcome between them would be the same.

"I am curious, Miss Winslow, to hear the tale you've concocted to explain your presence in my home. You will understand my curiosity, of course, for I am certain we both recall that at our last meeting I warned you against

42

as little as setting even one of your dainty feet down in my general vicinity.''

The earl's voice, silky with danger, raised the hairs on the back of Jessica's neck, and it did nothing to bolster her courage to know that even a man disposed to believe in her would find her answer difficult to credit.

''In truth I never connected you or Ned with the Earl of Roxham, though, of course, I realized the family names were the same. I suppose I never imagined there could be so unfavorable a coincidence.''

Jessica bit her lip, when Roxham arched his eyebrow in mocking response. ''You would have me believe Sally never once made mention Ned was brother to an earl and had grown up in one of the largest homes in the country?'' he scoffed, addressing what he considered the least likely of her several absurd contentions.

''I grant that my ignorance of Edward's connection to you must surprise,'' Jessica allowed with a brave tilt to her chin. ''Nonetheless, the truth is that I knew nothing of his connection to Bleithewood nor that his elder brother was my new employer. I'd never have come here, had I known. I am not so stupid.''

The earl leaned forward slightly to emphasize his words. ''You are certainly stupid if you expect me to believe that balderdash, Miss Winslow.''

A mere point of light flashed at the very back of Jessica's blue eyes. So fleeting was that explosion of feeling, it is possible that another would not have noticed it. Justin Stafford, however, as more than one of his friends had been known to remark, had a ''deuced keen eye.''

Given the color of her hair, he'd always suspected the girl was passionate, and he was gratified to see his suspicions proved right. She was not the calm, demure wren she tried to appear with her plain clothing, her neatly coiffed hair, and her contained expression.

''As you've only a passing acquaintance with veracity''—Roxham smiled thinly as a brighter light flamed in Jessica's eyes, betraying, before she could control it, that he had struck home—''I shall tell you why I think you've come to Bleithewood.''

He raked her blue bombazine dress with a derisive look

43

before lifting his eyes to fix her with a steely stare. "Your fortunes do not appear to have improved since last we met, Miss Winslow. Indeed, I should say they've deteriorated to the level you deserve, but I suppose that is why you've come: to exact some measure of revenge and even our accounts.

"I salute you, ma'am," he went on mockingly, and Jessica, frustrated, could do no more than open and shut her mouth with a snap, "for having the forethought to arrange to arrive at Bleithewood just as the Season started. Normally I'd not have returned home until the summer, perhaps later, and you'd have had time to wreak your havoc. Did you hope to find Ned here? After three years did you hope to find him still susceptible to your charms?"

Jessica was prepared for the question. It was what she'd thought Roxham would ask, but she found she could not answer him with the degree of coolness she'd rehearsed. "I never tried to charm your brother," she replied sharply. "I did not care for him."

"And that, Miss Winslow, I believe as much as I believe in pixies," the earl returned contemptuously. "Not only is Ned a handsome boy, he has the wealth you've never been in a position to overlook. But perhaps," he continued, his eyes narrowing accusingly, "you knew full well Ned was not in residence and thought, instead, you would persuade Andrew to elope with you."

"I hoped to do no such thing," Jessica denied the accusation vehemently. "I've no ambition to tie myself to a boy just sent down from school."

Roxham never thought to dispute her use of the term "boy," though, had he stopped to think on it, he'd have known she was of an age with Andrew. With her blue eyes flashing and her determined chin thrust up, she was indisputably the lad's senior.

"And in the unlikely event you failed to secure the lad's cooperation," he continued, his golden-brown eyes never leaving her, "you must have thought back to that pouch of coins you gained so easily before. I've regretted the impulse that bade me give you it ere now, but never more so."

44

"Now it is my turn to say I do not believe you one whit." The words burst from Jessica before she could control them, but she did not regret them. She was too angry now to attempt to hide it. There was a faint color in her cheeks, her eyes sparkled, and her voice was low with the force of her emotion. "Those coins were never meant as charity, and you well know it, my lord." Her mind returned momentarily to the dim room in which she'd stood, a bewildered young girl desperately in need of assistance. "You intended to humiliate me with that gesture." Her eyes blazed with her indignation and, too, her hurt. "And you succeeded!"

"Humiliate you?" Roxham demanded contemptuously, his own eyes sparking hotly in response to hers. "It is only possible to humiliate a lady, and you, my dear, are no lady. You would ensnare a boy in a marriage for nothing but your own gain. You lie without compunction, whenever it behooves you to do so. And, now, to revenge yourself upon me, you would use both Andrew and Livy to their disadvantage."

"Livy?" Jessica demanded, startled.

He ignored her widened eyes. Ned was proof the chit could rival the best of actresses. "Livy," he returned angrily. "How else do you explain your arguments on behalf of the groom who assaulted her but that you wish to put her in harm's way again?"

"That is preposterous," Jessica half-shouted, rising an inch from her chair at the affront. "You've only to speak to Livy to know she'll do nothing so foolish again—as well as to know who, precisely, was at fault in that affair. But then, perhaps, you've no interest in the truth, for you might be forced to admit that you, the mighty Earl of Roxham, have erred."

"He ought to have been horsewhipped," Roxham thundered, uncoiling to his full height. It did not soothe him in the least to see Jessica start back in sudden fear as he loomed over her. He was tempted to give her a real taste of fear and put his powerful hands round her delicate neck for what she'd done to Ned and thought to do to Andy and, perhaps, to Livy.

Swearing savagely beneath his breath, he abruptly

stalked away. He could not be responsible for himself if he continued to look down into her beautiful, treacherous face. Besides, he was just in control of himself enough to admit it possible she was not guilty of anything in the matter of Livy. He could not know for certain until he'd spoken to the younger girl.

Jessica followed Roxham's restless progress to the window behind his desk with wary eyes. She'd seen the flat, deadly look in his eyes and was certain he'd have throttled her had not some remnant of civilized feeling prevented him.

She bit her lip as she beheld him. He was a large man, with well-developed muscles his smooth-fitting clothing did more to display than to hide. At tea, when he'd effortlessly lifted Giles though the child was solidly built, Jessica had been momentarily distracted by the easily detected play of the muscles in his back. He could hurt her, if he chose.

Just now, with the late-afternoon sun upon him, he looked too noble to consider such a thing. His tawny hair, a blend of several shades ranging from a silvery wheat color to a sandy brown, gleamed softly while his strong, handsome profile was etched clearly like some king's upon a coin.

"You do not ask after Ned, Miss Winslow."

It took the space of a heartbeat for Jessica to realize Roxham had addressed her. He had not turned, and she'd been lost in something close to admiration of him, she realized, both bewildered and angered. Her anger now, however, was directed entirely at herself. He would feed her to the wolves, if he could, and she must not lose sight of that fact, however virile and striking were his looks.

"No," she cried hastily when he whirled about to arch an impatient brow at her. Then, regrouping her forces, she added in a low voice tight with challenge, "I have not asked after your brother as politeness demands, it is true. But perhaps, my lord, you forget it is my contention that your brother abducted me against my will, forced his caresses upon me, and deliberately ruined my reputation, all—so Sally later informed my mother—to win a wager he'd made with his friends."

The moment she'd said it, Jessica could have bitten her tongue. She'd allowed him to goad her into an ill-considered remark, she knew.

"A wager, Miss Winslow?"

She colored on the instant, recalling the letter her mother had forwarded to her. Edward and his friends had made bets as to who might have the Icy Vixen first, Sally had said.

To Roxham her blush came as a surprise. It gave her the look of a true innocent. Not that she looked a jaded schemer without it, he granted. Dressed in her service-able dark bombazine of no style at all, with its long sleeves and high, tight-fitting neck, she appeared to be exactly what she proclaimed she was: a young girl of limited means serving as a companion to an older lady.

A beautiful girl, he corrected himself grimly. The color her blush gave her only served to heighten her looks, if it were possible. She'd been decidedly pale when she entered, but now, with the faint pink in her cheeks, the earl was put in mind of a soft rose.

"I said, a wager, Miss Winslow?" he repeated sharply, irritated at the direction of his thoughts as much as at her continued silence.

With interest he watched her hands clench tightly. She was finding it particularly difficult, it seemed, to summon the collected air in which she generally managed to cloak herself.

After only a moment more, however, Jessica did manage to face him directly, an achievement that Roxham admired, though he'd no intention of saying so aloud.

"They wagered on who would be the first to win my favors, my lord." Her throaty voice may have wavered slightly, but to Jessica's credit her direct gaze did not.

As a result, she saw the flash of triumph in Roxham's heavy-lidded eyes. Though she felt stripped to the skin by that look, she could not tear her gaze away from his as he remarked with knowing softness, "How very interesting, Miss Winslow. I believe you've let something slip you'd rather have hidden. And I cannot blame you. Young girls of good repute, that group you would have the world count you among, are not, as we both know,

47

often the subject of wagers involving who will bed them first.''

Where before her cheeks had turned a delicate pink, now Jessica flushed to the roots of her hair. Roxham, almost, regretted his deliberately offensive words. He'd not expected her to be so undone.

But then he recalled how Ned had looked when he'd last seen him, and he hardened his heart against Miss Winslow. Likely the girl was such an accomplished actress that she could summon a blush upon command, he told himself.

"You may not have asked after Ned, Miss Winslow," he addressed her in a cold voice from where he stood leaning against the wall by the window. Any comfort Jessica may have derived from the distance he stood away from her was canceled by the coldness in his eyes as he fixed her with a hard stare. "Yet I think it only right you should know he never recovered his spirits after his encounter with you. For two years he drank himself into a stupor as often as he could and languished almost exclusively in unfit company. In the end, I sent him off to Italy in the double hope that its sunnier climate might restore him and that that country's distance from England might help him put you forever from his mind."

Jessica had no opportunity to voice her opinion: that Ned's behavior resulted from remorse either at having lied so baldly to his brother; or at having forced his attentions upon an unwilling young woman; or, perhaps, both.

"I shall never forgive you for your effect upon my brother, Miss Winslow, and I am determined you shall not have the same effect upon Andrew."

"I am not—"

"Spare me your protestations, Miss Winslow," Roxham barked impatiently. "I am not interested in them. Your ability to act the innocent is only equaled by your looks. . . ."

"Oh!" Jessica had had quite enough of the earl's insults. He was only toying with her, avenging Ned for her supposed crimes against him. She did not even note his compliment in her anger. All she could think was that

48

she must deny him the pleasure of turning her off by saying first that she would leave Bleithewood forthwith.

She opened her mouth to say as much when to her astonishment, she heard him say, ". . . and, I concede, by your ability to restore my aunt's spirits. She is very dear to me, and I do not take lightly the change wrought in her since your arrival. She's not been so on her mettle in a number of years.

"For her sake I have decided to allow you to stay on as her companion. But, be warned!" Roxham addressed the spark of relief not unmixed with triumph that flared suddenly in Jessica's blue eyes. "My attitude toward you, personally, has not changed. Until I am persuaded that you are no threat to me and mine, I shall remain here to watch you carefully. If I find you guilty of any misconduct—no matter how slight—I shall dismiss you on the instant."

Too uncertain whether to be relieved that she'd have a roof over her head or dismayed that she'd have Roxham's suspicious eye upon her, Jessica did not trust her voice and only nodded.

But the earl was not content with her silent response. "No matter how many may sing your praises, I know you as they do not," he warned. "You are to keep those flashing blue eyes off Andrew, do you understand?"

Recalling how assiduously she had striven to keep Andrew at a distance, Jessica stiffened. But she knew she could not afford to inform him with her eyes that she'd do as she wished and flounce from the room. "Yes, I understand, my lord," she made herself say instead.

"Then you may your return to your duties, Miss Winslow."

It was no simple matter to exit the study at anything like her normal, graceful pace. That Jessica succeeded admirably was a measure of her strength of will. Keenly aware of the earl's invasive gaze boring into her back, she longed mightily to dash out the door to safety, or, contrarily, to execute a triumphant jig at having managed to keep a roof over her head.

6

"What a pretty sight this is." Lady Beatrice scowled at Jessica in her pier glass. "My old bones are arrayed in reams of useless finery, while you, who might show this blue silk to advantage, insist upon wrapping yourself in that."

"That" was a brown crepe evening gown. Of the two Jessica owned, it was the plainer, though only because its sleeves and high waistline were trimmed with black piping and not lace, as was her green crepe.

"I vow it is the perfect dress for a dowd from . . . Leeds!"

Jessica laughed. "Please, my lady! You disparage a friend of long standing. Now, hold still if you please, or I shan't get this coiffure right, and you'll frighten your nephew half to death."

The mention of Roxham did not distract Lady Beatrice. " 'Friend of long standing,' " she muttered, her lips pursed. "By Jove, it is the truth. And a sight too long, I'd say. I've half a mind to speak to Justin. You might be impervious to my wishes, miss, but he'd have you accepting all the clothes I wish to make you a present of, and there's no mistake!"

Jessica's heart sank at the threat. She was uncertain enough about Roxham's reaction to her appearance at his dinner table, even plainly dressed. At Mrs. Ashcroft's she'd seldom eaten with the family, but from the first Lady Beatrice had insisted upon having Jessica with her when she felt well enough to go down.

"I thought we had laid this subject to rest, Lady Bea." Jessica looked an appeal at the older lady's reflection in the glass. "My clothes befit my role. If they are not the latest fashion, at least they are not frayed or worn. And they are mine."

"Oh, child, don't look that wistful way. I cannot bear

50

it so. Get on with my gray mop, then, and enough of clothes. They are yours, and you've not much to call your own, I understand.''

"You are a very fine lady, Lady Bea.''

"Hmph! Cross-grained, most say.'' Lady Beatrice essayed a fierce expression, but the affection in her bright eyes gave her away. After a moment, she left off looking at Jessica and turned her attention to herself. When Jessica had smoothed the last curl into place, Lady Bea archly turned her head this way and that. "Whatever I may be, I am in looks tonight!''

Jessica's laughter floated over her shoulder as she went across to the stand where Lady Beatrice's Norwich shawl and her own much less fine affair of wool hung. The only item of quality that Jessica wore that night was a cream-colored lace fichu her mother had given her. Though the square neckline of her dress was high, she thought it wise, nonetheless, to cover herself as much as possible. She wanted to give Roxham nothing to quibble over.

Lady Mary, Livy, and the earl were all gathered before a roaring fire in the rose salon when Lady Beatrice and Jessica arrived.

"My dear, you are resplendent in blue.'' Roxham smiled as he strolled to take his aunt's arm. She chided him for practicing his polished tongue, and he inclined his head slightly in Jessica's direction. "Good evening, Miss Winslow.''

With a swift, comprehensive glance, he took in her attire, and Jessica could have sworn she saw an ironic gleam flare in his eye. She'd no time to puzzle over it, however, for, as the earl led Lady Bea toward the fire, Andrew entered the room and made at once for her side.

"Miss Winslow!'' He bowed with a flourish. "How lucky I am to arrive in time to offer you my arm. If this is my reward for being late, I shall make a point of tardiness in the future.''

He grinned cheerfully, but he could not draw Jessica into his mood. If Andrew's interest in her had been a matter of concern for her before, it was, with Roxham's cold eye upon them, one of deadly seriousness now.

"I've no need for escort, my lord. You'd be better advised to go and greet your mother."

Andrew was visibly taken aback by the rebuff, but he could be a stubborn boy. "Fustian," he declared roundly. "I can do both. I shall escort you to the others and then greet Mother."

Annoyance had raised Andrew's voice, and rather than risk a scene, Jessica consented to lightly place her fingers on his arm.

"Lord, Jess! You'd think I was poison," he grumbled, unhappy with her grudging touch.

Jessica could not be pleased. They were close enough that Roxham might hear Andrew's familiar use of her name.

Andrew, seeing the dangerous sparkle in her eyes, cried out at once, "Dash it!" He fixed her with a petulant glare, seemingly oblivious to their audience. "I never meant to overstep. It's only that everyone else—Bea, Livy, the twins, even Nanny Budgett—calls you by your name, and, besides, it's a plaguey nuisance to be so formal. But I shall make amends. I shall fetch you some ratafia."

Jessica looked closely at Andrew. Perhaps he was only attempting to play the gallant, but he had never before been quite so insensitive to the delicacy of her situation. From the corner of her eye, she saw that Lady Mary was looking their way.

"No, thank you, really. I do not care for a refreshment."

"But you always take some," Andrew protested.

"I have a glass for Jess." Olivia appeared, holding up the two glasses she carried, and careful to keep her back to the others, she proceeded to read her brother a scold. "You are plaguing Jess unmercifully, as you would know, Andy, if you had not dashed down an entire bottle of claret since Marianne's departure. Now go! Mother is looking most cross."

Andrew, his cheeks flushed with indignation, bowed elaborately before stalking off. Watching him carefully, Jessica thought Livy's guess had not been wide of the mark. Andrew did list slightly as he proceeded to greet his mother and aunt.

To Jessica's dismay, the moment he accepted a glass of claret from Moreton, he abruptly swung about to face her, a reckless grin lighting his face. "Here's to beauty," he called out, lifting his glass and looking directly at her before he drank deeply. "Beauty does our eyes a world of good, eh, Justin?"

Jessica stared blankly at the boy at a complete loss as to what to do. He seemed intent on destroying them both.

"You embarrass Miss Winslow, I believe, Andy," Roxham drawled lazily, his eye upon the spots of color turning Jessica's pale cheeks pink. "I suggest we discuss your hunter, instead. I fancy his heart is as noble as his lineaments."

"Oh, don't let's discuss horseflesh," Olivia cried. "Tell us instead all about the latest fashions in town, Justin, do!"

"I think you'd find them beautiful enough." Her cousin smiled, surrendering easily to Olivia's pretty appeal.

As Roxham knowledgeably described the fashions of the day, including enough of the gentleman's styles to keep Andrew interested, Jessica let go a pent-up breath.

Andy seemed effectively subdued at last, thanks entirely to the earl. Where both she and Olivia had failed, he had effortlessly reined the young man in and none too soon. Lady Mary's brow had begun to pucker most fretfully.

But how sly Roxham had been as well! Jessica could almost admire how smoothly he'd managed to get a dig in at her. It had been so subtly done that only she was aware she'd been unfavorably compared to a horse. To her attuned ear, his slight emphasis had been unmistakable. Marcus, Andrew's hunter, had a noble heart, while she had only her lineaments to recommend her.

Perhaps Roxham's intent was not merely to watch her, but to run her off. If so, she vowed, he'd not find his objective an easy one to achieve. She had no choice but to stay, and on the thought she lifted her chin to a determined angle.

Roxham did not appear to note her gesture. His eyes

twinkling, he was regaling the others with a description of an outlandish hat he'd seen.

"But, surely, the crown was not a foot high," Lady Mary exclaimed when he had done.

"Tut, Mary, the boy's bamming us unmercifully," Lady Bea proclaimed before her nephew could reply. "No one would care to have swans, albeit even small ones"—she gave Roxham a dry look—"on a bonnet."

"But I assure you small, stuffed white swans did float happily around the brim of Lady Michaelson's bonnet, Aunt," Roxham protested mildly.

"But I cannot see how she managed to walk with such a large thing upon her head."

Roxham turned to Livy with a chuckle. "Very carefully, I assure you," he teased.

Sipping her ratafia as she watched the earl and his family, Jessica could not avoid remarking the elegant figure he presented. While Andy, beside him, wore a blue satin coat and knee pants and a white waistcoat upon which gleamed a half-dozen chains and fobs, the earl was clad, as he had been at their first meeting, in restrained black with only a single diamond pin tucked into the folds of his cravat.

The contrast of his black coat and waistcoat with his white cravat invited comparison with the more striking contrast of his tawny hair and golden brown eyes. And then it was impossible not to notice that his eyes, catching the light of the fire, shone as brilliantly as the diamond.

"I don't believe there are many gentlemen in London who could compare with Justin. Do you, Jess?"

Jessica started. "Ah, no. No, I think your cousin very handsome indeed," she said, looking down to smooth a wrinkle from the skirt of her dress. She was not piqued to admit what was the truth. She'd been to town and knew full well there were not many men there with such presence as the earl. She bit her lip because, until Olivia had recalled her to her senses, she realized she had been as lost in staring at him as any stary-eyed young miss.

Which she certainly was not, she reminded herself grimly. She was a scheming woman of no morals at all—

or so he believed her, as she was reminded in the next moment when Moreton came to announce dinner. With polished ease Roxham delegated Lady Mary and Olivia to Andrew to escort while he took Lady Beatrice and her for himself. Even over so short a distance as that from the rose salon to the family dining room, it seemed she was not to be trusted in Andrew's company.

Not that Jessica actually minded being led in by someone other than Andy. Given the boy's present mood, she was only sorry she must sit across from him at table. Happily his mother, seated at the foot of the table, was between them, and the conversation was general enough that she could avoid his eye.

The family had a great deal to ask Roxham of the news from town. Andrew was extremely eager to know the particulars of a curricle race he'd heard of, and his cousin was able to confirm that a mutual acquaintance had reached Bath in record time, driving a pair of blacks they'd both had the opportunity to admire.

The ladies of the group inquired after friends and acquaintances, and Jessica had to admit the earl answered all their numerous questions patiently. No, she did not do him justice with so pale a word. He was not merely patient, he was entertaining, she granted half-vexedly as he made some sally about a lady who was so fond of the ices at Gunther's that her husband complained she might never thaw.

Indeed, she herself laughed with the others, though not for long. When the earl flicked his gaze to her, she sobered abruptly. Though his expression was unreadable, Jessica felt accused of presuming. Who was she, he seemed to say, to be laughing when Ned must languish in Italy?

The conversation turned from London to Bleithewood when Lady Beatrice asked her nephew if he intended to survey the estate with his man, Millers, the next day. "I wish you to take a basket to Mrs. Kenting if you do. Her mother died of the ague this winter, did you know?"

"Yes to all your questions, my dear." The earl nodded, surprising Jessica, who knew from Lady Beatrice that the Kentings were only minor tenants on what was an enormous estate. "I intended to extend my condolences tomorrow, and I shall gladly carry out your commission. I thought you might like to go around with me, Andrew?"

It did not surprise Jessica when Andrew shook his head, saying he would prefer to work his hunter the next day.

"I would say it is past time for you to learn what is involved in managing an estate, Andrew," his cousin replied, an eyebrow arching. "You've only two years before you take over your own."

If Andrew had, indeed, imbibed heavily before dinner, he had not moderated his course during the meal, and now he shrugged unsteadily. "There's little enough to apply myself to." He waved his hand in the air. "I intend to retain the man you've sent over. He's good enough, and it's a certainty he knows more than I ever shall. Who knows? My decision may be the making of the Fitzgerald estates." Andrew smiled crookedly. "The squire's done well enough paying only passing attention to what his man does."

Jessica thought it possible that Andrew only raised their neighbor's name in an effort to discredit him and, by extension, a connection to his family through marriage. If so, judging from the earl's response, it seemed he needn't have bothered.

"The squire's tenants are the worst-treated in the county," Roxham informed his younger cousin grimly. "That man of his, Meeks, is poorly named. He charges exorbitant rents, which pleases the squire only because he is a fool. All his best tenants depart as soon as they are able, leaving him with a recalcitrant, shifty lot who must be whipped harder each year to come up to scratch."

"Looks to me as if their coffers are running over," Andrew muttered, emboldened by drink to argue a subject upon which he had already admitted he knew next to nothing. "At any rate, if one family leaves, there's ten more to take their place. Every enclosure means another farmer is without enough land to make his living. The squire's got men fairly knocking on his gates every day, pleading for work."

"Well, that doesn't mean he ought to treat the ones he's got as shabbily as he does," Lady Beatrice joined the fray with a determined glint in her eye. Having lived at the manor all her life, but for the few years she'd been married to her deceased husband, Lord George Carstairs, she had a strong interest in everything that went on in the neighborhood. "What think you, Jess? Is Andy right to say there's no harm in behaving as callously as you please as long as the rents come in?"

Startled to be included in the argument, Jessica glanced searchingly at Lady Beatrice, but seeing nothing that might explain the older woman's motive, she could only say what she thought. "I think every landowner has an obligation to those who work for him! There is the matter of having stable tenants which Lord Roxham has addressed, and there is the responsibility anyone who is born to wealth has to those less fortunate. . . ."

"Oh, I say," Andrew protested weakly before Jessica could add that she thought he would rise to meet his responsibilities when he came of age. "I feel the veriest ogre when you and Aunt Bea say such things, Jess. Ow!"

Jessica bit her lip as Andrew turned an injured glare upon Olivia, who sat beside him, and when the young viscount leaned down to rub at the shin Olivia had deliberately injured with the heel of her slipper, Jessica was forced to look away for fear she might add insult to injury by laughing aloud.

By purest chance, glancing away from Olivia, she encountered the earl's eye. Their gazes locked an instant, and then Roxham turned to engage Livy with some question. Still, though the contact was brief, it had the dismaying effect of setting Jessica's pulses leaping.

And why? she demanded as she attempted to bring herself under some control. When she looked into the earl's eyes, she had seen an amusement there to match her own.

It was an absurdly small thing to prompt such a reaction, she upbraided herself, and no matter what laughter might be lurking in Roxham's eyes, it did not mean he had changed his opinion of her.

That assessment was proven to be only too accurate when the gooseberry tarts were being served and Olivia reminded her elders that the annual spring fair in Altonborough, a town only a few miles distant, was to be held the next day, Saturday.

"Kate and her mother are going, and I should like to go too. Jess could go with me. She's never been, of course, and they've such nice gewgaws at the Altonborough fair. I remember last year. . . ."

It was the first Jessica had heard of the fair, and though she could not help but be pleased that Livy should care to include her, she did wish the girl had spoken to her first. Roxham was not likely to be pleased at the thought of his aunt's companion cavorting happily at the local fair.

He was not. "I should think Miss Winslow's duties with Aunt Bea would preclude her having time to join you on such an outing, Livy," he observed coolly.

"Oh, please," Olivia pleaded sweetly. "Jess ought to have some fun. What say you, Aunt Bea? She is your companion, after all."

"I think you are absolutely right this once, my dear." Lady Beatrice gave her niece an approving smile before she rounded upon Jessica as if she expected disagreement. "You've not had more than an hour to yourself since you've been here. No protest, now," she commanded when Jessica opened her mouth to say an afternoon at a local fair was more than an hour. "I wish you to go. All this evening I've thought you seemed a trifle peaked, and I'm convinced the outing will do you good."

Jessica, though she was the subject under discussion, was not given, even then, an opportunity to register her opinion. Andrew, taking her participation as a settled matter, spoke up to include himself. "And I shall go along as well. Two such lovely ladies will have need of an escort."

Had Andrew been beside her, Jessica might well have given his shin another blow, but as it was, all she could do was to turn calmly to his mother. "I think it would be most unfair for all of us to enjoy ourselves and leave Julia and Giles behind. May we take them as well, my lady?''

"Oh, no, Jess! The twins are a bother."

"Nonsense," Lady Mary summarily dismissed her daughter's protest. "I think Miss Winslow's sentiments are very nice indeed. They would enjoy the outing immensely, I am certain."

"Why don't we all go? Surely you haven't forgotten your taste for the Altonborough spring fair, Mary?"

It was cleverly done, Jessica admitted. Rather than play the tyrant and forbid the outing altogether, Roxham would simply come along to assure himself she did not lead his cousin astray while the boy's siblings looked on.

"Do you know, I do remember the queen cakes they were used to sell at the Altonborough fair," Mary said before agreeing that she, too, would enjoy the expedition.

7

The next day, when the Altonborough fair burst into view, the twins cried out in astonishment at the crowd assembled and Lady Mary lifted herself to peep over Julia's head. "La! You are not mistaken," she exclaimed rather less pleased. "I do believe the fair has grown since I last came I do not know how many years ago."

"But there are always a great many people on Saturday, Mother," Livy said. "This is the day the spring lambs are brought to be sold."

Julia clapped her hands at the prospect of seeing acres and acres of the sweet creatures. "Oh, Livy! Shall we see any?"

Lady Mary wrinkled her nose. "Ugh! I pray we shall not. They are such smelly creatures."

"Look!" Giles waved excitedly out the window as their carriage rolled to a stop. "There's Justin."

Noting the high color in the earl's cheeks and the way his eyes sparkled, Jessica revised her opinion that he'd only challenged Andy to a race across the fields to keep his cousin away from her. He looked like a man who had enjoyed his hell-for-leather ride purely for the excitement of it.

"Who won, Justin?" Julia called out.

"Mars by a length!" He laughed. "I hope your wagers are not lost."

Both children giggled. "Livy owes us each a piece of her gooseberry tart next time we have some," Giles confided, and Lady Mary turned to smile a question at her eldest daughter.

"You thought Andy's new hunter up to Mars, Livy?"

"Well, someone had to stand by the Fitzgeralds," Olivia declared stoutly, her sentiment earning her a shout of approval from her brother, who now joined them.

When the carriage steps had been let down, Lady Mary was handed down first. As she descended, she waved a plump hand toward a boy standing nearby. "Fancy! There's a child with a queen cake."

Roxham smiled as he gave her over to her son. "We shall make you and Andy the pathfinders, Mary. I doubt you'll be able to attend to any other pleasures until you've followed the boy's trail of sugar and currants to the source."

"Oh, you!" Lady Mary swatted at him with her ever-present piece of linen. "You are a tease, Justin, but you'll regret your fun when I do not order a cake for you."

Clutching his heart as if he'd received the direst threat imaginable, the earl sent the twins into whoops and then turned to hand Livy down, remarking, as he did, on her dress. "I believe it is worthy of Hyde Park, Livy, particularly with that charming parasol to match it."

"Do you really think so?" Livy twirled her parasol gaily. "I found the pattern, but Jess chose the material and thought to use what was left over for the parasol."

Roxham extended his hand to Jessica after the twins had clambered down unaided. "I commend your efforts on Livy's behalf, Miss Winslow."

His remark was followed by a swift inventory of her

appearance, and this time there was no mistaking the mockery gleaming in his eye. Unable to account for it, Jessica took refuge in defiantly lifting her chin. If his intent was to make her uncomfortable by comparing her appearance with Livy's, she would not give him the satisfaction of seeing her put out. She knew very well her sensible, long-sleeved dress of drab bombazine did not hold a candle to Livy's jaconet walking dress with its dashing spencer and its gaily ruffled hem.

"Thank you, my lord." She released Roxham's firm hand the moment she was on secure ground.

Livy linked arms with her at once and they set out after Andrew, who had taken on the role of escort to his mother without demur, to Jessica's vast relief. Just behind them came Roxham with the twins.

There were a great many sights at which to marvel and Livy made certain to point them all out to Jessica. The gypsy wagon, she said, was one of her favorite entertainments, for she dearly loved to have her fortune told. Julia came running up then to exclaim over a little monkey that was performing leaps and vaults for the odd coin or two, and Roxham's deep voice sounded to observe they were passing an area set aside for a puppet show. Both the twins ran forward forthwith to beg their mother to allow them to return in an hour's time to see it, and though Lady Mary only said, "We shall see," they cheered happily, for they knew they always won out when she was not adamant.

They passed a staggering number of booths selling a bewildering array of tools, trinkets, and foods, and when they reached the booth selling the queen cakes, everyone appreciated the excuse to stop.

"They've their name because they were originally made in honor of Queen Anne's ascent to the throne," Lady Mary explained as the three ladies found a bench upon which they might wait for the gentlemen and the twins to bring their refreshments. "The secret of it has been handed down from father to son in this family all these years, and I do hope they've not lost the magic of making them since I last had one."

Lady Mary need not have worried, for the cakes were

delicious and even the twins were content to enjoy them quietly. Andrew found a barrel for his seat while Roxham was content to sit upon the ground, propped against a tree with a twin ensconced on either side. To Jessica's surprise, he looked entirely at ease in the rustic pose.

"There are Kate and Lady Anne!" Olivia broke the air of companionable silence that had settled over the group as she gestured toward two ladies in the distance.

"Fetch them, Andy," Lady Mary implored. "I should like them to join us."

After Andy had departed upon his errand, Lady Mary glanced at her cousin with an unhappy sigh. "I vow Anne's dress is over a year old. They are only just making do at Roselawn, Justin, but Augustus has not the least care for the economies his wastrel ways force upon his poor wife. I declare, I cannot fathom the man. He seems intent upon landing them all in debtor's prison."

"At the rate he's burning his candle, Augustus will not have sufficient time to do that much damage," Roxham replied with what Jessica considered a deplorable amount of sangfroid. "Still," he continued, "I admit I should not care to be in young Philip's shoes when he inherits. He'll not find it easy work restoring the estate."

"Philip!" Lady Mary shook her head. "I wish the boy luck, of course, but I declare I cannot understand why Anne does not demand he go to town to seek an heiress to marry. A good match is the only possibility he has for bringing Roselawn around, yet she allows him to remain at school though he's a good two years older than Andy."

"That is not the least fair, Mother," Olivia rounded hotly on her mother in defense of the heir to Roselawn, an estate that bordered Bleithewood to the south. "Philip need not marry an heiress! Unlike Andy he believes a good mind is an asset, and he is learning all he can about the reforms in agriculture. He believes if he institutes them—as Justin has done at Bleithewood—he'll be able to restore Roselawn without resorting to a mercenary marriage!"

"Livy!" It was all the reproof Lady Mary was able to give. She would have to wait until later to point out that an advantageous match was to be prized, not scorned, for Andrew had just returned with the female half of the family in question.

As neither of the Verney women had seen the earl since his return, they greeted him first with obvious pleasure. Lady Anne, slightly older and a good deal slimmer than Lady Mary, then took the seat Jessica gave up and accepted a queen cake.

It was Kate who said with a great show of innocence that they'd just seen the Multaneys. "They are coming this way," she added, giving Andy a knowing grin. "I fancy we shall see them at any moment."

Andy's response was to wink gratefully. "And I saw Tom Cathcart," he exclaimed at once. "Told him I would seek him out when I could." He waved jauntily to his mother before she could gather her wits to say he must stay. "If I don't see you later today, I shall see you at home. Until later!"

He'd not left a moment too soon. Even as everyone looked after Andrew with various degrees of understanding in their expressions, the Multaneys arrived.

The squire, a broad, stout man whose fine clothes made him resemble a farmer attending a costume ball, hailed the earl with great gusto. "And you know the vicar, of course," he boomed, clapping a sandy-haired man of medium height on the back.

"Of course. Headley." Roxham nodded toward the vicar, who stumbled off balance.

"My lord, we are most honored see you." Mr. Headley's head bobbed up and down when he'd recovered his balance. "I trust your stay will be a long one."

"I shall stay for a time," the earl replied with what Jessica thought irritably was intentional vagueness. How long would she have to prove herself? She could not help but wonder.

Dismissing the vicar, Roxham turned back to the squire to discuss horseflesh, and Mr. Headley, who had little knowledge of the subject, excused himself to go around to where Jessica stood with the twins. He was their tutor in mathematics as well as their vicar, and so the children greeted him quite politely, if not enthusiastically.

Jessica sketched a smile as she bid him good afternoon. "Yes, it is a very good afternoon, indeed, I should say! I doubt I have ever seen the sky such a clear, deep cerulean blue. It is the blue of spring, the blue of re-birth . . ."

The twins fidgeted as Jessica's smile dimmed. It was ever thus with Mr. Headley, she thought with a sigh. He was agreeable enough. He was not homely, though he was not handsome certainly, and he had an adequate living. But despite the learning she could not help but ad-mire—Mr. Headley could read Latin, although not Greek, with some fluency—she almost invariably experienced a desperate desire to yawn when she found herself in his presence.

"Jess, the puppet show must start very soon." Julia, after a whispered consultation with Giles, pulled upon Jessica's arm.

Jessica could not blame the children for their impa-tience. Exchanging pleasantries was something they could do as easily in the rose salon at Bleithewood as at the Altonborough fair, and she was willing to present their case to their mother.

Lady Mary, distracted by the necessity of excusing An-drew's absence to the Multaneys, only nodded vaguely in reply, but when Jessica took the children's hands and made to leave, Roxham called out, "A moment, Miss Winslow! You and the children must have an escort. One can never be too careful in a crowd, I think. Ah . . ."

The earl scarcely needed to pause before Mr. Headley burst into speech, saying he could have no more pleasing mission than "to provide Miss Winslow and the dear lit-tle ones, too, company and protection."

When Roxham smiled faintly, Jessica felt a spurt of anger at that triumphant expression. He'd played the vicar like a plump trout, arranging matters to his liking with-out having to exert himself. The vicar, by Roxham's de-sign, would be along to act as Andy's protector, not hers, lest she should chance to meet the boy in the crowd.

None of her feelings showed, however, as she smiled graciously at Mr. Headley. "You are very kind, sir. The twins and I shall be delighted to have you with us," she said with all the sincerity she could summon. Above all things, she was determined Roxham would not guess how he had thwarted her, for in truth, on that bright, spring afternoon at the Altonborough fair, she would really rather have had almost anyone else's company than the good vicar's.

In the event, Mr. Headley's company was not so overpowering that she and the twins were kept from enjoying their puppet show, and if he persisted in referring to the simple entertainment as "a most entertaining example of the thespian's art," Jessica was able to concentrate more on the children's shrieks of delight than she did on the vicar's prosiness.

When they left the show and were walking slowly along in the direction of the place they had set to meet the others, Jessica was even forced to admit to some gratitude at having the vicar by her side.

His eyes gleaming suspiciously, Andrew appeared suddenly from a side lane to greet them. "I knew I should find you here," he cried, cheerfully ignoring the frown Jessica gave him. "And, Headley, you sly dog!" A mischievous gleam in his eye, he bowed a trifle unsteadily in the direction of the vicar. "I believe I can guess the origins of your interest in puppetry."

Mr. Headley colored and, not caring at all for the jest, gave the young viscount only the stiffest of greetings.

"I thought you were with your friend, Mr. Cathcart," Jessica spoke up then.

Andrew merely shrugged as he gave her a wide grin. "Tom saw a wench he fancied, and . . ." He snapped his fingers to indicate the speed of his friend's desertion. "But now, you see, I am pleased to declare that I am available to win everyone a prize at the ring-toss booth." Andrew was careful to include the twins in his statement, but it was upon Jessica that his sparkling eyes came to rest.

The twins were instantly in favor of their brother's notion. "I want a tin whistle." Giles began to hum the tune he intended to play.

Julia clapped her hands. "And I should like a cloth doll."

Jessica hesitated, but seeing the children's excitement

and reasoning that little harm could come of the expedition as long as the vicar was with her, she capitulated. Her reasoning, in the end, proved faulty, but Jessica could not blame herself. Nothing in her experience of the vicar could have warned her how adversely the combative atmosphere of the ring-toss booth would affect him.

When they stopped before the ring-toss booth with its four rows of shelves some ten paces back, each filled with green, long-necked bottles over which a small ring had to be looped to be counted a winner, Andrew slowly shook his head. "Actually I've never been terribly good at the ring toss," he confessed. "I always knock the blasted bottle down."

At the next booth, only a few feet away, he seemed more confident. Here the shelves were some twenty paces back and rather than bottles, they held wooden pins painted to resemble the men in Napoleon's defeated army. The object was to knock the pins down with a small wooden ball.

"How about you, Headley?" Andrew turned suddenly to the vicar. "Care to make a sport of this child's play by taking the ring toss while I tackle the ball throw? The first to win a prize shall have the honor of presenting it to Miss Winslow. I fancy giving her one of those painted birds, don't you?"

Jessica was not won over in the least by the size of Andrew's lopsided grin. "I do not care for a prize, my lord," she warned. "You said you intended to win prizes for Giles and Julia, and they would be severely disappointed if you did not try."

Andrew, who had imbibed quite as much ale as Jessica feared, was beyond reach of her protests, though he was not so far gone that he did not find it expedient to drop his gaze from her speaking look. He glanced down to pat his younger siblings upon the head. "I shall do my very best by you both," he promised. "But first, I think I ought to try for Jess. She should not be the only girl to leave the fair without a gewgaw. What do you think?"

The twins were very devoted to Jessica, as Andrew knew, and the reminder that she could not buy the profusion of scarves and ribbons and handkerchiefs in which their mother and sister would indulge themselves struck them forcibly. "Oh, yes," they cried in unison. "Win Jess a bird."

Jessica deliberated stamping her foot in frustration as Andrew, considering the matter settled, buffeted Mr. Headley upon the back and shouted exuberantly, "Timidity will gain you nought, sir."

What prompted Mr. Headley to take up Andrew's challenge, Jessica simply could not imagine. She thought it quite likely that he'd never so much as noticed the ring-toss game before, yet there he was plunking down a coin in the booth owner's broad, outstretched hand.

Certain they would have their own prizes eventually, the twins cheered lustily for both of the contestants. It was not, sadly, a sense of fair-mindedness that prompted their evenhandedness, but the surprising fact that the vicar quickly ringed two of the five bottles needed for one of the painted birds.

His aim affected by the time he'd spent at the ale wagon, Andrew was slower at achieving even partial success. But in the end, after expending several additional halfpennies, he was the first to earn the prize.

"Let us see," Giles begged, jumping up to catch a look. Mr. Headley glanced once in Andrew's direction, nodded, but though Jessica exerted all her mental powers to will him to come to her side, he did not leave off his own pursuit of a prize.

With a great flourish Andrew bowed before her. "Your bird, Miss Winslow." He held out the trinket in the palm of his hand, and Jessica, feeling a fool but seeing no way out without being churlish, accepted the gift.

"And now I claim a kiss!" Andrew's eyes sparkled as he swaggered roguishly. "It is my right as the winner."

He had gone too far. "Then you must keep your prize, my lord." Jessica held out the bird in her turn.

Andrew blinked uncertainly. He'd not planned for failure. Realizing dimly that Jessica was well and truly put out, he essayed a smile, and before she could see he meant to capture her hand, not merely the bird, he closed her hand around the little thing. "Nay, Jess, the bird is

67

yours." His smile became a grin, and swiftly, lest she escape, he lifted her wrist to his lips.

Jessica retrieved her hand with a jerk and opened her mouth to tell the foolish boy he went very much beyond where he ought, but the words died upon her lips.

Andrew was looking over her shoulder. "Oh, Lord," he swore, and Jessica, turning around, echoed his unhappy sentiments.

"So." Roxham did not burden himself with the formality of a greeting as he strode up; he looked coldly from Andrew to Jessica and then to her clenched hand.

"I merely won Miss Winslow a bird," Andrew found the strength to mutter.

He'd not the power, however, to hold the stony gaze that was his cousin's response. "Your mother wishes you to meet her by the gypsy wagon, where she is having her fortune read."

Andrew was nearly a grown man, but the steel in those terse words had the power to send him on his way after he flung Jessica a quick, contrite look. When he had gone, Jessica, feeling strangely calm, lifted her eyes to meet Roxham's scornful gaze.

The impact was of such force she felt she'd been dealt a slap. Her cheeks heated, but before he could give her a tongue-lashing, the twins came skipping back from Mr. Headley's side to greet him.

"We didn't see you come, Justin. Mr. Headley has won Jess another bird," Giles said happily.

Jessica swung around with a start. She'd nearly forgotten the vicar altogether, but here he came, a green, blue, and yellow bird in his hand.

"Here is your winsome little fellow, Miss Winslow." He presented the foolish thing to her with a beaming smile.

Keenly aware of Roxham's derisive amber gaze, Jessica did her utmost to keep it from affecting her. "Thank you very much, Mr. Headley," she responded with a quite natural smile. "I like it exceedingly."

The earl had affected her, of course, as she would never have given the vicar such fulsome thanks for so small a thing, but that she wished to defy Roxham.

The ceremony completed, Mr. Headley looked up to see there were other people in the world. That the one closest to him, but for Miss Winslow, was the Earl of Roxham caused him to flush. "Y-your lordship," he half-stammered, then made a weak gesture to the bird he'd given Jessica. "Couldn't have Miss Winslow the only lady at the fair without a trinket, what!"

In the extremity of the moment, he had repeated almost exactly what he'd overheard young Andrew say, but no one remarked the fact. Certainly Roxham, who had not been present, did not; he merely inclined his head a fraction and arched an eyebrow in a cool way.

He might as well have said the vicar was a fool and she no lady, Jessica thought angrily. Certainly he reduced poor Mr. Headley to tugging at his neckcloth in a most nervous way.

Fortunately the twins had no intention of allowing the uncomfortable moment to last very long. They had their own prizes to worry over.

"Has Andy gone off?" Julia asked in her piping voice. "He left before he could win our prizes."

Giles fixed Roxham with a pleading look when he realized his sister was right. Their brother had left. "Justin, would you try the ball throw?"

"Or the ring toss," Julia suggested brightly. "I do so want a doll, and Giles was promised a tin whistle."

It relieved Jessica that the earl did not take out his ill humor upon the children. For them he summoned a charming smile as he tousled their heads. "We shall need to make short work of the game," he said, striding off to the ball throw. "Your mother is waiting."

Jessica sent up a prayer that the mighty earl would prove inept at throwing. She did not beg that he actually lose. She wanted the children to have their prizes, but she also wanted Roxham to experience some difficulty, however small. But—and she admitted her petty request deserved to be overlooked—he proved to have a particularly accurate eye.

Six soldiers were required for a tin whistle and eight for Julia's doll. Moving right to left, Roxham dispatched all fourteen pins without a miss.

Jessica had thought the vicar, who stood watching with her, would be discomfited by the earl's prowess, but she was wrong. When the final soldier fell, he clapped as loudly as the twins.

"By Jove! Lord Roxham, has an excellent eye, does he not, Miss Winslow?" he enthused as Giles and Julia returned with their booty, their cousin just behind them.

"Indeed," Jessica allowed, looking up from an examination of Giles' whistle to flick a glance from Headley to Roxham. "It would seem leveling all manner of things comes easily to Lord Roxham."

Roxham merely bowed, as if to accept a compliment, but when the twins and Mr. Headley had moved a little ahead, he leaned down to remark softly in Jessica's ear, "I like to keep in practice, Miss Winslow."

Jessica acknowledged the threat implicit in his words with flashing eyes. If he intended to level her after his practice with the wooden soldiers, he'd find her a more difficult target. He could be sure of it.

8

"I think this calico the prettiest of the kittens, Giles." Jessica smiled as the young boy held up a black ball of fur, one white patch over its eye, and announced to her, his sister, and Nanny Budgett where they sat on a bench beside the kitchen door, that "the patched one" was his favorite.

"Mind, now," Nanny Budgett called. "There's one getting away. Run after him."

Shrieking excitedly, both the children chased a tiger-striped kitten around the side of the manor, and Nanny Budgett heaved herself up to follow. "Don't want 'em losin' the little creature," she said half to herself.

Jessica made no move to rise, for she had charge of four of the kittens, all of them in her lap.

"You've quite a skirt." Livy laughed when she came

out and saw what Jessica held. "It seems to be at least a dozen colors, and it moves. Oh, look! What a dear little thing!" She scooped up another calico that had particularly long and graceful whiskers, and plumped herself down in Nanny Budgett's seat.

Rubbing the head of a friendly white-and-gray kitten, Jessica greeted her with a smile. "I see Annie found you. The twins particularly wished that you not miss Mother Cat's newest litter."

"I am much obliged to them." Olivia rolled her eyes at Jessica as she nuzzled the calico. "And not merely because I adore kittens. I vow I need a peaceful respite." When Jessica lifted her eyebrows in question, Olivia nodded significantly. "Annie found me just after I had left Justin's study!"

When Olivia shivered, half in earnest and half in play, Jessica very nearly shivered as well. She'd spent much of the day awaiting her own summons to go before the earl, but as yet, it had not come.

She had seen him when he had accompanied Lady Mary, Livy, and herself to church, but he'd made no reference to the fair: indeed, he'd scarcely acknowledged her presence at all.

This was not so with Mr. Headley, Jessica recalled with an uncertain frown creasing her brow. The vicar's eyes had come to rest upon her so frequently as he gave his sermon on the "Divine Purpose for Womanhood's Noble Gentleness" that she'd felt her cheeks heat.

"You'll be vastly proud of me, Jess," Olivia reclaimed her friend's attention with a triumphant smile. "I told Justin the truth: that it was I who kissed Martin, and not he who approached me!"

Having no difficulty recalling just how very intimidating Olivia's cousin could be, Jessica meant it when she said she was, indeed, proud. "Was it very hard?"

"At first!" Olivia grimaced dramatically. "You've no idea how Justin can pierce one to the core with a mere look." Jessica had a very good notion how cutting the earl's glance could be, but she did not interrupt Olivia to say so. "You won't countenance it, Jess, but when Justin bade me tell him what happened that day, he said I should

71

think carefully upon my reply. If he found Martin had tried to take advantage of me, Justin told me he would be obliged to take a whip after him.''

It was a harsh threat to make, but Jessica could not fault the earl. From the scandalized look on Olivia's face, it seemed he had succeeded in making the young girl aware her actions could have dire consequences for others.

''Of course, I could not have Martin whipped,'' Olivia continued. ''And so I explained that Kate had teased me, because no one, not even Ph—ah, no one at all, that is, has ever tried to kiss me. And just afterward, when I returned home, there was Martin in the stables. I have known him ever so long, and so I just . . . well, I acted very foolishly. If only old Jenkins had not arrived in time to see!''

When Olivia threw up her hands in disgust, Jessica could not restrain her smile. ''And how did your cousin respond to your honesty?''

''He was very stern.'' Olivia lowered her brow in such a credible imitation of Justin at his most formidable that Jessica laughed. ''He lectured me about my responsibilities to those less fortunate than I and pointed out that it was Martin, not I, who had suffered the most. I felt very low by then, but I did tell him you had already read me the same scold and that I was very sorry—which is the truth,'' she finished mournfully.

''And Martin?''

Olivia gave Jessica a pained look. ''Justin says that I must apologize to him. I shall be ever so embarrassed.'' Biting her lip, she agonized in silence for a moment over the thought of the interview, before she recalled Jessica's question. ''But he'll not be turned off, though he will have to remain in the fields for a time longer. Justin said his punishment is to teach him to resist temptation.'' A mischievous sparkle that reminded Jessica of the girl's older brother crept into Olivia's eyes. ''I never thought of myself as a temptation,'' she allowed, her mouth curving. ''Do you think I am, Jess?''

Taking in her gleaming hair and large eyes, Jessica

72

smiled. "You are a very pretty young lady, Livy, and therefore most certainly a temptation."

Pleased, Olivia dimpled. "I wish I could present a temptation to. . . ." Her voice trailed off as she allowed her eyes to drop to the kitten in her lap.

Jessica smiled, though Olivia did not see. "Now let me see. Whom might you care to tempt?" She made a show of tilting her head to the side. "I should say it might well be Philip Verney."

Olivia started. "However did you guess?" she demanded.

"Be at ease, I cannot read your mind." Jessica laughed. "I guessed, because you defended him so strongly yesterday. Does he return your feelings, Livy?"

"I cannot be sure," the young girl admitted unhappily. "Of late, when he's come home from school, he has seemed to favor me, but I am his sister's best friend, after all. And he has said nothing, nothing at all." Olivia frowned balefully as she absently petted the little kitten she held. "Of course, he must know Mother would not favor a match between us, because his pockets are nearly to let. It is Ned, Justin's younger brother, she favors for me."

Jessica could not help but recall Edward Stafford with distaste. "Do you care for him?" she asked quietly.

Olivia shrugged in response. "I like Ned well enough, but he is like a brother to me. A very silly brother," she added, rolling her eyes. "He's always falling into dreadful scrapes with what Mother calls, 'that sort of woman.' Justin has had to save him twice from their clutches, you know."

Being careful to hide her surprise, Jessica managed to say in normal tones, "He sounds a foolish young man, indeed. Twice?"

She needn't have worried that Olivia might think her unduly interested. The girl was eager to relate her cousin's history. "The first woman actually persuaded Ned to elope with her," Livy confided in scandalized tones. "They were halfway to Gretna Green before Justin caught up with them and forced her to admit she was already married. I don't know what she intended to do with that

73

husband when she returned to town as Ned's wife, but it is Mother's opinion that she had it in mind to force Ned to pay her to keep the scandal quiet.''

Olivia shook her head rather sadly. ''After that Ned became dreadfully cynical. He was forever making slighting remarks about all women—so much so I didn't care to be around him and Aunt Bea forbade him to carry on in that vein when he was with her. Still it seems he did not learn his lesson, for he fell into the same sort of scrape again. I don't know the particulars. Neither he nor Justin mentioned it, but Mother heard from a friend in town that Justin was obliged to buy off a woman who claimed Ned had compromised her.''

''Miss Livy!'' Nanny Budgett appeared around the corner, a kitten trotting at her heels. ''James Footman says Miss Kate's come for you.''

Jessica's farewell to Livy was a vague one. She could scarcely think of anything but the implications of what she'd been told. If Olivia's story of Edward's first love were correct, then it was a deal easier to understand why he had acted so callously toward her and why his older brother had been so set against her. They'd both judged her by the standard set by the first woman.

The new information did not exonerate either man. Ned, in particular, ought to have made certain what sort of person she was before he brought her to such a disastrous end. But Roxham. . . . to be confronted at some revelry or other by Sally and to have her demand his brother marry an unknown quantity. Yes, she could see— if not forgive—his being so predisposed against her.

''Now, there! Aren't they the sweetest creatures?''

Jessica looked up with a start to find Bleithewood's amiable cook, Mrs. Appleby, bending down to tickle one of the kittens who'd wandered onto the bench, and Nanny Budgett behind her, watching with a broad smile.

''They are, indeed, Mrs. Appleby.'' The old nurse nodded stoutly. ''And there's a pile of 'em. The children have another three around the corner near the chicken coop.''

As if on cue, the happy shrieks of the twins seemed to rise in volume. All three women smiled, but when they heard Andrew Fitzgerald's deeper tones mingle with the children's, Jessica made a strangled sound.

"Now, don't take on so," Mrs. Appleby hastened to say. "Just come in through the kitchen, love. We'll not tell the lad where you've gone. He's not a bad boy, but he can be devilish worrisome, as more than one maid would say."

Jessica gave the good woman a smile. "Thank you, Mrs. Appleby. You are a dear, and you've helped me escape Lord Avensley often enough in the past. But today," she announced as she put the kittens in the box at her feet, "I've a mind to say a word to Lord Avensley."

As the two women watched Jessica depart, Nanny Budgett turned to the cook with a twinkle in her eye. "Has the light o' battle in her eye, does the lass?"

"She's fire aplenty, Nanny," Mrs. Appleby agreed, a wide smile spreading across her ruddy face. Clucking sympathetically, she went on, "I'm thinkin' his lordship may get an earful today, and time it is he does! It's nothing fair, simply because she's a beauty, that the girl must be forever runnin' through here to get away from him. Chases after her worse than he ever did any of the maids, and her a lady as anyone with sense can tell!" Mrs. Appleby winked broadly at Nanny Budgett. "I'm that glad she's had enough."

Mrs. Appleby's analysis was absolutely correct. In relation to Andrew Fitzgerald, Jessica had, indeed, had quite enough. The boy might think his pursuit of her a marvelous good game, but it was she who must wait for the earl's summons with white knuckles, not he.

Andrew was bending down beside Giles to ruffle a stray kitten's fur when she approached. "Lord Fitzgerald," she called in her low voice, and waited for him to straighten. "I should like a word with you."

Andrew took in her stern expression with a lopsided smile. "Lord, Jess! You look as if you intend to flay me."

She made no assurance that she intended nothing of the sort, and looked significantly at the two children still playing with their kittens before she turned to walk away from them. After a few paces, Andrew fell in beside her.

"I suppose this is in relation to yesterday." He glanced quickly at Jessica as he raked a hand through his hair. "Have you spoken with Justin?"

Jessica's tone of voice was glacial. "I've not had the honor as yet."

"I have!" Andrew's mouth curved in a rueful grin. "And I can tell you he read me a peal all about how anxious my mother is for me. The truth is he made me feel a pretty fool."

Jessica stopped short, causing Andrew to stumble slightly. "You behaved extremely foolishly yesterday, Andrew." She used his given name with emphasis. "I know how provoking the prospect of marriage to Marianne Multaney is, but nonetheless, I cannot allow myself to be the means you use to shock your mother into agreeing to your own plans for your future. I must work, if I am to eat and have a shelter, and although Lady Bea is extremely tolerant, the earl is not so forgiving. He will turn me off if he thinks you are serious."

"But I am! You could marry me!"

Jessica gave in to the impulse she'd had the day before, and stamped her foot. "You are no prospect for matrimony, Andrew Fitzgerald," she stormed in reply.

Treated, for the first time, to the sight of Jessica's eyes flashing in earnest, Andrew found the effect daunting. "Here now! I'm not so bad as all that," he protested, though his voice wavered as if he were not entirely certain.

Jessica fixed him with a stern stare that made the cajoling grin with which he'd thought to pacify her fade abruptly. "Two days together, after you've indulged in an excess of drink, you have behaved in such a way as to compromise my position here. I could scarcely wish to ally myself to a man who would behave so badly."

Andrew flushed. In truth he'd not given any thought to the harm he might do Jessica. "I did not truly believe you would be faulted," he admitted, once more raking his hair with his hand and disordering his valet's careful work beyond recognition. "I thought I'd receive a scold and then Mother would consent to buy my colors simply to get me out of the trouble she'd see in you." After an unhappy moment he gave Jessica a frank smile that had nothing mischievous in it. "And, too, I do think you very beautiful."

"Thank you," Jessica returned and, smiling a little, teased him lightly. "I am flattered, for I know you are a connoisseur. But truly, Andrew," she went on, her blue eyes imploring him, "you must believe that I will, indeed, suffer for your actions. Your cousin has said so."

"I say, I am sorry, Jess!" Andrew looked as unhappily contrite as Jessica could wish. "I cannot stand for you to look at me quite so beseechingly. It makes me feel a perfect scoundrel."

Jessica said nothing, but waited for some tangible promise for the future. It was not long in coming.

"I shall be a new man in future, I swear it. I shall not find it easy," the boy could not help adding with something of his usual spirit, "and I hope you appreciate the sacrifice, but I shall try very hard to behave circumspectly where you are concerned."

"I hope you will not forget." Jessica smiled then, her eyes lit with her relief. "And I shall, I assure you, appreciate your efforts."

Andrew looked as if he might like to linger to talk, but Jessica did not care to put his resolution to the test with an amiable, lengthy conversation. Satisfied the young man would give some heed to her situation in the future, she took herself off to Lady Beatrice's rooms, where that lady was having her regular Sunday-afternoon coze with her good friend, Helena Dalymede.

For his part, as he turned toward the stables, Andrew decided he would rather face Justin's scowl than Jessica's flashing eyes. At least Justin didn't make him feel a perfect beast as Jessica had done—with, he acknowledged shamefacedly, a great deal of justice.

If he were to keep his promise to her—and he did not care to face her, if he did not—he'd best find some new distraction in the neighborhood. At the thought he grinned. Tom Cathcart, if he recalled correctly, had made mention of a new maid at the Lion's Head Tavern in Rushton. She'd lush charms, so Tom said.

* * *

"Read me some Swift, will you, my dear?" Lady Beatrice, tucked into her bed, watched Jessica reach for the tome she requested and added, "As I missed Headley's sermon today, I've a need for some improving sentiments."

"I think you are better off with Swift." Jessica chuckled as she reported the subject of the vicar's discourse.

Lady Bea grimaced. "I don't doubt you were the inspiration," she said, watching with interest as a blush rose in Jessica's cheeks. She said no more on the matter, however, for she'd not the strength just then to investigate Mr. Headley's undoubted interest in Jessica with the care the subject deserved. "I doubt I shall be awake long," she said instead with an unfeigned yawn. "Helena and I gossiped overlong, I fear."

As the older lady closed her eyes and composed herself to listen, Jessica began to read in her low, pleasant voice from *Gulliver's Travels*. After only a chapter, when she glanced up, she found as she'd expected that Lady Beatrice had fallen into a doze. Smiling to herself, she marked her place.

"If it is your intention to begin where Aunt Bea's attention left, off, your marker is misplaced. She fell off some four pages back."

"Sir!" Only just biting back a cry, Jessica swiveled about in her chair to look accusingly at the Earl of Roxham.

He lounged in the doorway, one shoulder propped against the door frame and his arms crossed over his chest, in a lazy posture that suggested he had been listening to her read for some little time without betraying his presence.

After waiting on tenterhooks all day for his summons, Jessica was not pleased to have him take her unawares. Her eyes flashed. "You startled me."

"You read well, Miss Winslow." He uncoiled himself and stepped into the room. He looked very fine in a coat of blue Bath cloth and biscuit-colored breeches, but Jessica ignored the momentary spurt of pleasure she'd experienced at his praise, preferring to concentrate instead on the fact that he appeared to find her not worthy even of an apology for startling her.

He certainly said nothing when he stood beside her, frowning down at his aunt. "I did not realize Aunt Bea took her nap so late. Is it her second today?"

Reminded they might disturb the sleeping woman, Jessica rose and gestured to the door leading to Lady Beatrice's private sitting room. With a nod, Roxham followed her lead.

"It is Lady Bea's second rest," Jessica confirmed when the earl had closed the door behind him and she'd taken a seat on the edge of a chintz-covered chair. Her back was very stiff in anticipation of the attack she knew his sudden appearance in his aunt's rooms portended. "She slept while we attended church, for she spent a restless night last night. Mrs. Dalymede, though Lady Bea enjoys her, can be exhausting."

"I spoke to Dr. Mayes after church today," Roxham revealed, still frowning. "He says her condition is, over all, no worse, though she will have both bad and good spells. He also said you have been very good for her."

Jessica merely inclined her head and watched as the tall, virile man set out on a prowl of the feminine room. "I've another thing to commend you for as well," he went on in a tone Jessica could not read. He picked up a dainty china figurine and half-scowled at it. "I've spoken to Livy and know the truth of her tryst with the groom. You were within bounds to step in and save the boy from being turned off. He did not deserve so harsh a punishment in the circumstances. You are something of a heroine to the servants, you know."

Jessica lifted her shoulders slightly. "I only acted to prevent an injustice being done."

As he returned the little shepherd to its place, Jessica eyed him coolly. He owed her an apology for the ugly accusation he'd made in regards to Martin, but she did not think he would be so generous with her.

"I apologize for my hasty words at our first interview," he said as if he'd read her thoughts and wished to confound her. If so, he succeeded, for her brow shot up. "Livy says you scolded her roundly, though not so thoroughly as I."

Astonishment held Jessica silent, and Roxham flicked her a close look. "I see you shall have to consider whether or not to accept my apology." His golden-brown eyes not leaving her, he came to lean upon the arm of the chair next to hers. Perhaps by design his position put him above her. "I suggest you do so," he advised her in a dry tone that seemed to indicate he did not much care one way or the other. "I do not often humble myself."

Jessica had to arch her neck to look up at him, but she endured the uncomfortable position. "I accept your apology, sir," she said stiffly, in a tone she hoped conveyed she only just did.

He was very close to her. She could actually see the changeable gold lights at the center of his eyes, if she looked. But she forced her attention to the grim line of his mouth.

"You are fortunate," he said, breaking the silence that had fallen, "that I chose to speak to Livy before I spoke to you, Miss Winslow. Had I not, you might well have been on your way from Bleithewood by now. I thought we had an understanding that you would keep your distance from Andrew."

The moment had come, and now Roxham's amber eyes were as cold as Jessica had expected them to be. "Nothing at the fair in Altonborough occurred by my invitation," she said firmly.

"You maintain that you did not smile archly and beg Andrew outright to win you a trinket, though you liked them excessively, I believe you said."

He watched Jessica flush at the reminder of her exaggerated thanks to Headley. Too late she rued the rebellious impulse that had prompted her to speak so immoderately.

Her lesson learned, she held her tongue then. There was no point essaying to defend the indefensible, and at any rate, her remarks to Headley were not the issue that lay between them.

Roxham was not affected by her simmering silence. After only a brief pause, he paid her the compliment of saying, "I do not think you so unsubtle as to ask outright for the boy's company, Miss Winslow. You must know he would likely boast of his conquest. Your smiles are potent, however. You've enchanted the lad, and he merely wished to please you with what was, I know from him, entirely his proposal.

"But . . ." He paused and his gaze sharpened. "You did give him your hand to kiss, Miss Winslow. There is no denying that, for I saw. You did not keep your distance from Andrew then, my dear ma'am. The lad was near ready to swoon at your feet."

"Lord Avensley took my hand," Jessica informed him tartly, a dusting of pink tinting her cheeks. "I did not give it to him."

"Ah!" Roxham gave a short, sardonic laugh. "So, the whole is Andrew's fault just as the affair in London was Ned's."

Flicked on the raw by the scorn in Roxham's expression, Jessica battled a desire tell him he could find another to act as companion to Lady Beatrice and stamp from the room. She could not afford such a grand gesture, and she knew it.

"I should not have allowed Lord Avensley to persuade me to go with him yesterday," she admitted, her strained voice particularly low. "I was foolish to believe him when he said he wished to win prizes for the twins, but I thought that with Mr. Headley accompanying us—by your design," she could not resist adding, "nothing untoward could occur."

"Untoward?" Roxham queried, taking care not to allow himself to be affected by the hoarseness of her voice. A vixen with her experience would know too well how to play upon his sympathies. "From your point of view, I should imagine what occurred was anything but untoward. You had two men vying for your favors, as I recall. It is a common-enough wish among females of a certain sort to have men brawling for them. But I warn you," he continued remorselessly, though Jessica's face flamed at his words, "you waste your efforts upon Andrew. I shall never allow him to take you as his wife."

Jessica's eyes flashed hotly. "Your warning is entirely

unnecessary, neither Lord Avensley nor I have the least interest in marriage."

The earl disregarded Jessica's denial of her interest. He had expected as much. "You think Andrew has a less honorable goal in mind?" he inquired with lazy provocation.

"No!" Jessica flushed painfully at the implication of his words. "I meant that Andrew's flirtation is designed to relieve his boredom and to force his mother's hand, but not to end in wedlock to me."

"To force his mother's hand?" Justin echoed. "Speak on, Miss Winslow. You do intrigue me."

Jessica doubted his sincerity. The look on the earl's handsome face as he lounged with his long, muscular legs stretched before him, his arms crossed comfortably over his chest, indicated he was willing to hear her out, because, and only because, it amused him to listen to Banbury tales.

"Oh! What is the use?" she demanded angrily. "You'll not believe me, no matter what I say!"

"I insist," the earl returned, allowing just a hint of steel to enter his voice. "You've little risk to incur. I shan't bite you."

Roxham observed the fine line of Jessica's jaw sag, for in her opinion he'd done little, figuratively speaking, but bite at her since they'd first met. And then he looked to see her eyes widen so much that he could detect the clear white all around her very blue irises.

Deep in his eyes a light flickered. "I shan't bite now at any rate," he amended.

Jessica was forced to clear her throat. She'd not missed that sudden flash of humor in Roxham's eyes, and as it had before, his amusement unsettled her more than his anger.

"Ah, well," she began uncertainly before she gathered her wits. "I believe marriage holds little interest for Lord Avensley, because he has it in his mind he would very much like to buy his colors and make a career of the army. Lady Mary will not give him her permission, however. She believes the army too dangerous and," Jessica hesitated before she decided she was not betraying a confidence, "she has only limited funds. Even if she were able to buy his colors, Lady Mary does not believe there would be sufficient funds remaining in the estate to provide her son an income beyond the limited one the army would provide."

"Two compelling reservations," Roxham observed dryly. "And I might add my own: the boy's too unsettled to capably take on the duties and responsibilities of an officer."

Why she spoke up for Andrew, Jessica was not entirely certain. He had done little to deserve her support, but it was true she thought she could detect a spark in him that it would be a shame to waste.

"I think Lord Avensley not quite so lost to all hope as you believe, my lord." The earnestness of Jessica's tone was such that her words were robbed of all contentiousness, though Roxham did lift a tawny eyebrow fractionally. "He reminds me of one or two of the young men my father, who was an officer, brought home from time to time. They were too young yet for the settled life of marriage, but they desired a challenge. Lacking it, they'd have gotten into one scrape after another out of sheer boredom, or so my father said. Your cousin seems much like them. He only drinks to excess on occasion and acts wildly because his future seems so very grim." Jessica made an uncertain gesture with her hand. She did not care to try Roxham's patience by rattling on overlong.

He surprised her by saying, "An eloquent argument, Miss Winslow. I doubt Andy could be half so convincing. You've persuaded me that Andy's future deserves more consideration than I've given it heretofore." The earl was silent for a moment as he contemplated his young cousin, but he was not finished with Jessica, and when he recalled her, his eyes were cool once more.

"But you have failed to convince me that the boy is impervious to your charms. Nor could you, however eloquent you are. I have seen how he reacts to your presence." The earl's lids seemed to sink over his eyes as he continued to regard Jessica. "Content yourself with Headley, Miss Winslow. I should say you've fertile ground aplenty in the vicar. In church today he seemed sinfully tempted by your visage.''

His taunt drew blood. Jessica's cheeks heated, but Roxham knew he'd been unfair. Given the picture his aunt's companion had presented that morning, it was little wonder Headley had been unable to look away from her for long.

She'd worn a gray silk gown. It was her best dress, Roxham suspected, and though it was not cut on fashionable lines, it did fit smoothly over her young, slender figure. Its color, a somber hue on most, had the felicitous effect of heightening the pearly sheen of her fair skin while at the same time providing a subtle backdrop for the glory of her hair. In truth, in the gloom of the fourteenth-century church that served Bleithewood Village, she'd stood out like a beacon.

''Yes,'' Roxham continued, his voice harsher than it had been, ''I should say Headley would be delighted to make an honest woman of you.''

''Is that all, sir?'' Jessica's eyes snapped with indignation as she came to the edge of her chair. An honest woman, indeed!

''Stay still, Miss Winslow.'' The growl was a command, and if Jessica had been uncertain, she'd only to encounter the challenge in the earl's steely gaze. There was nothing she could do but submit, though her eyes conveyed the message that she did so only because she had no other course to follow. ''It is customary for me to dismiss those in my employ,'' he informed her curtly. ''I expect you will not forget it in future, as you will not forget to veil your charms when Andrew is nearby. Have I made myself clear?''

''Completely.''

''Then you may go.''

''My lord.'' Jessica curtsied just to the degree decorum demanded, and then treated the earl to the sight of her rigid back.

She would not have been the least pleased to know that it was to her hips the earl flicked his gaze. However militantly she marched from his presence, it seemed she could not keep her hips from swaying gently.

Roxham's mouth curved almost of its own accord. There was no question the girl was enticing, even angry.

Particularly angry. The fire in her eyes could blaze as brightly as her hair did in the sunlight. He shrugged as Jessica snapped the door closed behind her. There was no harm in admiring her beauty. Knowing what he did of her character, he was in no danger of falling under her spell.

9

Jessica saw little of the earl, or Andrew either, for much of the following week. Lady Beatrice's condition worsened as the weather turned rainy, and despite all Jessica's hot-water bottles, healing salves, and soothing possets, the older lady suffered too greatly to descend for tea or dinner with the others.

On the few occasions when Jessica did chance to see Andrew in the hallways, he kept the promise he had made to her by limiting his remarks to a cheerful greeting. Though grateful, Jessica responded with equal restraint.

Roxham she saw from a distance when he rode out on Mars, and at closer hand when he came to his aunt's rooms to look in on her. Jessica did not stay on those occasions, excusing herself on the grounds that Lady Bea should be allowed to have her nephew to herself, and when Lady Bea protested that Jessica need not play least in sight, Jessica, ignoring the knowing gleam in Roxham's eyes, departed anyway.

She too greatly needed a respite from the man. Even when he directed his attention entirely at his aunt, Jessica found she could not ignore his presence in the room as completely as she would have liked. More often than not she would find herself darting his back defiant glances, and then she admitted—unhappily—as had happened more than once, her eyes would linger to note the breadth of his shoulders or, dropping, to remark the narrowness of his waist.

There was one person Jessica could not avoid had she wanted to. Toward the end of the week, when Lady Mary came to visit her aunt, she begged Jessica to stay.

"I've a request to make of you, my dear." Her hand fluttered out to pat the seat beside her on the couch. "Come and sit, I pray you. I am hoping you will take pity upon me, Miss Winslow, as you know how easily overset my nerves can be."

Jessica took the seat offered, but regarded Lady Mary with some wariness. Any request couched in such terms would be difficult to deny, as Lady Mary had no doubt realized.

Some half-hour later Lady Mary tripped from the room, delighted to have had succeeded in securing Jessica's agreement to organize in her stead a festival held annually at Bleithewood on the feast of St. Barnabas in early June.

The day's festivities were an old tradition, it seemed, and though the neighboring landowners attended, the honored guests were the estate's own tenants and the local villagers. "Their tastes, you know, are not always what ours are," Lady Mary had revealed confidentially. "For several years we've been fortunate to have Mr. Headley lend his advice. He is perforce familiar with the sorts of games and music they prefer, and I am certain he will be vastly pleased to lend you a hand this year, Miss Winslow."

Doubtless Lady Mary did wish to save herself the trouble of planning a rustic entertainment for so large a group, but Jessica suspected she had been asked to take on the task particularly because it would throw her into company with the vicar.

Lady Beatrice agreed. "Matchmaking and no mistake!" She delivered her opinion in a voice only slightly subdued by pain when Lady Mary had left. "Mary believes if you marry Headley, she'll get you away from Andy and yet keep you close enough to look in on me." The old woman chuckled for the first time in several days. "I declare I never believed Mary half so clever."

Jessica still was not convinced on the subject, but she did not say whom she believed to be the author of the scheme to wed her to the vicar. She had no proof, only the knowledge that Roxham was cannier by far than his cousin and that he had remarked on Mr. Headley's apparent interest in her.

"And it is a scheme not without merit," Lady Beatrice continued with her own thoughts. "Headley's a bore, but you can't remain at my beck and call forever. I shan't last so long."

Jessica smiled at the sally, happy to see Lady Bea feeling well enough to jest. "And what makes you believe Mr. Headley will be so obliging as to fall in with Lady Mary's scheme?" she inquired lightly

"Oh, Headley!" Lady Beatrice lifted a dismissive brow. "He's a man with eyes, after all. His interest is not in question. It is the question of your willingness to take him that must give Mary restless nights."

At the thought of Lady Mary missing a moment's sleep, they both laughed. "Well and all," Lady Beatrice declared after a time, "you must decide for yourself, and that is why I encouraged you to take on Mary's duties. Work with the man a time and decide if you can abide him for life."

The damp, dreary day Mr. Headley was to come for their first meeting, Lady Beatrice's pain reached such a level she requested a dose of laudanum, though she loathed the medication that rendered her unclear and groggy.

Jessica, her heart heavy with frustration for how little she could do, was just fluffing Lady Beatrice's pillows when the twins appeared at their aunt's door, breathless with running, to inform Jessica in between gasps that they had found a hurt puppy in Squire Multaney's woods and that the animal was even then whimpering piteously in the stables.

"Go on, child," Lady Beatrice whispered in a weary voice. "I shall not need you when I am asleep. Only ask Annie to come and look in on me."

After she had left instructions with Annie as to where she would be, Jessica proceeded to the stables with the twins to investigate the puppy they'd left in a cozy bed of straw.

A mongrel, whose black-and-white coat, long silky ears, and long, thin legs, attested to a mixed ancestry, the puppy possessed a pair of great, dark, liquid eyes that he turned upon Jessica as she knelt beside him, heedless of the straw adhering to her skirt.

"I believe his leg is broken through," Jessica pronounced when she'd inspected the leg lying at an excessively awkward angle.

When Giles asked what was to be done, Jessica replied that he must ask Jenkins where stray sticks for splints might be found. She would ask Mrs. Appleby to supply old cloths to be used as bindings. Julia, it was decided, would remain with the little fellow to keep him company.

"He's done nothing but cry terribly," Julia said when Jessica and Giles returned with the materials they would need. "Is he hurting so awfully, Jess?"

As if to answer the question himself, the pup gave a long, low whimper.

Jessica nodded. "I am afraid he is, Julia. And frightened besides. Stroke his head, will you? That should help to reassure him."

As she talked, Jessica set to work to realign the bones in the pup's leg. It was to be Giles' task to hold it in place while she bound the splints in place, but after two failed efforts, they had to concede the boy was not strong enough to keep a firm grip when the little dog resisted their well-meant but painful ministrations.

"I cannot do it," the child cried miserably.

"Will I do?"

It was Roxham. He spoke from the doorway where he stood regarding their little group with a quizzical expression. Dressed in a pair of tight buckskins, a bottle-green riding coat, and a pair of gleaming black Hessians, he'd obviously intended to ride, despite the rain falling in a fine mist.

"Justin!" Giles ran to pull on his cousin's arm. "Come, help us! Jule and I found a puppy in the woods. A trap broke his leg and Jess says we must set it, but I cannot hold it straight."

The earl did not respond to the boy's disjointed explanation, but arched his brow sternly. "You were in the squire's woods if you saw a trap, my boy, and I know very well you've been told not to venture there. Your legs could be hurt as easily by a trap intended for a poacher as that little fellow's was."

"But we only went a little way. Really!" Giles' hazel eyes were very wide. "And we only went as far as we did because we heard him crying."

"It was a terrible sound, Justin," Julia spoke up, near tears. "We could not leave him there. And now we need your help. Please!"

Roxham came to kneel down on one knee and stroke the pup's silky head, an action that was rewarded with a great, wet lick. "I've not had much experience at this sort of thing," he allowed. Then, looking for the first time to Jessica where she knelt in the straw just across from him, he added, "But I suppose I could take direction from Miss Winslow."

Jessica's skepticism that he could so humble himself showed in her expression, and on the instant Roxham's eyes lit with an amused gleam. "I am always willing to bow to the expert," he protested.

The twins exclaimed happily while Jessica, aware that her heart was pumping at an absurdly quickened rate, spared a moment to wish that it had been anyone—Jenkins perhaps, or even Nanny Budgett—who'd come to their aid, but with the puppy before her, she did not think to spurn Roxham's offer.

"We need your help to hold his bones straight while I bind the splints into place," she explained in her low, quiet voice. Rather to her surprise, Roxham nodded obediently, though, as she could plainly see, a twinkle lingered in his amber eyes.

Jessica turned to Giles and Julia. "If you two will stay by his head, he will be less inclined to pull away from us."

When the children were in position, Jessica took a deep breath before once more struggling to slide the pup's bones into a proper line. As they snapped together, she looked to Roxham, and he bent down to take the pup's leg, his large hands holding the fractured bones in place with ease. The dog, perhaps sensing there was no use in struggle, lay still, and Jessica, concentrating so she had her tongue between her teeth, quickly fashioned a credible splint.

Finished at last, she rocked back on her heels, a pleased smile on her face, while the twins cheered wildly, "You did it! You did it!"

"We all did it," she corrected, and still smiling, she looked from the twins to their cousin. "Thank you, my lord. You were just what we needed."

For a moment only Roxham stared at her, finding it difficult to credit she had been so capable. Her long, slender fingers seemed too fragile to have carried off such a task.

"It was my pleasure."

"Look! He is investigating his new leg."

Jessica was grateful to Julia for her cry. The odd look Roxham had given her unsettled her so she was afraid her cheeks might betray her by heating.

The pup was, indeed, sniffing his strange bandages. Roxham rubbed his head calling him "a brave fellow" before lifting him so he might test his leg. "See, it works rather better now," he addressed the pup as it took an experimental step.

"He does not seem to mind the splint," Giles observed happily as the little animal turned in a circle before sinking rather tiredly back down into the soft straw.

Roxham patted him again. "He'll be as good as new with some rest. I don't doubt by tomorrow he will be recovered sufficiently to demonstrate his gratitude to you and Julia, and, of course"—he glanced back at Jessica with a faint smile—"to his brilliant doctor."

Jessica arched a brow, uncertain whether or not he mocked her. " 'Brilliant' is doing it up a bit brown, I think, my lord," she protested even as the twins cried that it was not. "Actually," she addressed the children, "I ought to confess I was not at all certain what I was doing."

"But you seemed to know exactly," Julia observed in wonder.

Jessica gave the little girl a wry smile as she stroked the pup's fur. "Well, I did once watch my father set a dog's leg, but in truth, I found watching and doing quite different matters."

The little puppy rolled over, the better to lick her hand in seeming gratitude, and to her surprise Roxham chuckled. "None of us would have guessed, most particularly not your grateful patient."

She cast him a quick smile, but was not sorry that Giles spoke up then to draw his cousin's attention from her. She was too doubtful of Roxham in this unusual mood to be comfortable when he addressed her.

"Justin?" Giles said. "Do you think . . . Well, that is, could you possibly speak to Mother for Jule and me? After all we've done, it would be a terrible shame if we could not watch the pup to be certain he recovers, but, well, as you must know, Mother has never much liked dogs."

Giles dived down to pet the puppy more closely before the earl could answer, and when his face was licked, the little boy squealed.

Jessica laughed sympathetically at once. "Did that lick bring the strangest tickle to the very back of your throat, Giles?"

"Yes!" He looked up astonished, and Jessica, laughing again, said she'd always experienced the same feeling when her dog licked her face.

Julia promptly put her face to the puppy's that she might test the theory, and she too was soon giggling. "Try it, Justin," she urged when she came up for air.

His smile was very amused. "I think I shall pass on that particular treat," he said, shaking his head, and Jessica could not help but chuckle.

It was an oddly perfect moment. The sound of the children's happy laughter warmed the air as the rain drummed steadily on the stable roof.

Across from her Roxham sat with his legs stretched before him and leaned his weight back upon his hands. When their eyes met, Jessica, her heart beating giddily, thought she had never seen such beautiful eyes as his, when laughter warmed them.

"Will you speak to Mother, Justin?" Giles asked again.

The earl's mouth curved as he glanced down at his young cousin. "Perhaps. What think you, Miss Winslow?"

Jessica, who had the absurd feeling that she had just been released from a spell, did not think it would be wise to look back at Roxham just then. His smile seemed to render her mindless.

Wisely she kept her eyes upon the puppy as she gave her opinion that he would make a very fine companion. "As long as you both agree to limit his excursions to the nursery and the out of doors," she added, looking at Julia and Giles with a question in her eyes.

"Oh, yes, we will!" It was Julia who spoke up, but Giles nodded in vigorous agreement. "Will you speak to Mother for us, Justin?"

The little girl had a very persuasive look against which Roxham proclaimed himself no proof at all. "Julie, my dear, with such a look I doubt I could say no even if I were so inclined." He held up his hand before the twins could shout for joy. "But please keep in mind I've no magic to work with Mary. I promise nothing."

The children knew better, however. Their mother would never deny Justin, and to show their appreciation, they assaulted him with their embraces so that he fell off-balance backward in the straw, laughing aloud as he took both children with him.

"Miss Jess?"

A smile lighting her face, Jessica glanced around. "Annie," she exclaimed, suddenly anxious. "Is it Lady Bea?"

"No, miss." Annie shook her head at once, seeing Jessica's concern. " 'Tis Mr. Headley. Lady Mary says you are to go to him in the library."

Jessica had quite forgotten Mr. Headley's intended visit. "Oh, yes, of course, Annie. Tell him I shall be right there."

The maid ducked her head, and after casting a quick, inquisitive glance at the the unusual sight of the master romping in a pile of straw with Lady Mary's children, she hurried away.

"But why must you go to Mr. Headley, Jess? He's not tutoring you now, is he?"

"No, Julia, I am not to work my sums with Mr. Headley, but to arrange the St. Barnabas Day festival with him." Jessica used the excuse of having to shake out straw from the folds of her dark dress to avoid glancing in the little girl's direction. Roxham was too close beside Julia, and were Jessica to look that way, she might meet his gaze.

She'd too much pride to chance that, for she was unhappily certain that he'd have discerned the turmoil into which Annie's announcement had plunged her. Like an idiot, she'd allowed the man's unusual warmth to lull her almost into thinking they could be friends.

To her the earl could never be the man with warm, laughing eyes. To her he was the man who wished to marry her off to Headley simply to relieve himself of her presence.

"Thank you," she said to Julia when the child came running with her shawl. "Promise me you will not take the pup to your rooms before your mother has given you her leave to do so," she added as she wrapped the shawl about her head to give her some protection from the rain.

In the sweet-smelling gloom of the stables, with her lovely face framed by the shawl, she looked like some biblical heroine. "Oh, Jess, you are so pretty."

Startled, Jessica looked down at Julia as a blush rose in her cheeks. "Why, thank you, my dear."

"And we shall not take our friend in," Giles rushed over to assure her.

"For what it is worth, I give you my assurance that they shall not," Roxham spoke up, his voice nearly bringing Jessica's gaze around to him.

She resisted the temptation to see if there was, still, approval in his eyes. Her head bowed, she curtsied. "Thank you, my lord."

"Miss Winslow."

At the direct call, Jessica turned and, unable to do otherwise, looked to the earl.

His eyes cooled abruptly. He had deliberately waited until she was near the door where her face would be illuminated by what light there was outside, and as a result, he could read all too easily the defiance sparkling in her blue eyes.

He interpreted it to mean she intended to encourage Headley and dared him to make any remark upon the fact. As Julia had said, she was lovely. She'd have little difficulty persuading Headley to provide her a roof of her own.

He ought not to condemn her. After all, the majority of marriages were based upon mercenary impulses.

"Give my regards to Mr. Headley," he said, idly brushing a piece of straw from his sleeve before he looked up to fix her with a sardonic look. "He must look forward to his work on the festival more this year than ever in the past. But remind him for me, will you, that he is to keep his mind upon his work. We all look forward to St. Barnabas Day very much, you see, and it wouldn't do if he is too distracted to carry out his duties properly."

How had she thought, even if only for a moment, that the man was not utterly insufferable, Jessica wondered, her hands balling into fists. He was the one sending her into Headley's arms, and yet he'd the effrontery to warn her in that mocking way against being a distraction.

"I think you worry overmuch, my lord," she replied, her chin proudly high. "I am certain Mr. Headley will manage as well as always."

Enormously pleased that she had had the last word, Jessica turned to go out into the weather without giving the earl a curtsy, a farewell, or even so much as a nod of her burnished head.

10

As she hastened through the rain, Jessica considered a number of other more trenchant, more scathing responses she might have made Roxham, altering them here and there to more effectively put the man in his place.

It was not until a footman hurried to open the library door that she bethought herself of the vicar waiting within. And that only showed how powerfully angry Roxham could make her, for Mr. Headley surely deserved more. Everyone, from Lady Beatrice to her nephew, seemed to consider him her best opportunity to escape a future spent companioning old and infirm women.

Jessica winced at the bleak prospect. If Mr. Headley asked her to marry him and she accepted, she would have a house of her own, a garden, and best of all, children.

As Mr. Headley leapt from his chair to greet her, Jessica flushed at the thought of the intimacy involved in starting a nursery.

Her eyes scanning him impartially, she noted the vicar was scarcely above her height, and though he'd a trim figure now, Jessica thought she could detect the signs of an incipient paunch.

But he was not sharp or accusing or infuriatingly superior, she defended Mr. Headley as he pumped her hand and then preceded her, talking all the while, to a seat.

Taking herself in hand, she concentrated upon the man's mind. As husband and wife, they would converse a great deal.

After an hour, however, she'd little choice but to wonder if their conversations would always be so one-sided. For most of the time the vicar had lectured her in detail on the history of the St. Barnabas Day Festival and then had enumerated at length each variation in timing or entertainment that had occurred over the years he had been participating in the planning of the affair.

"And now, with you to assist me, Miss Winslow"— he eyed her raptly—"I am certain this year's festival will shine for many years in the minds of all the participants as the very brightest festival they ever had the pleasure of attending."

Jessica inclined her head and said he was undoubtedly correct, though to herself she remarked the vicar's wording. She had understood from Lady Mary that she was the organizer of the affair and Mr. Headley the adviser. She did not truly care about their relative responsibilities, of course, but she found it impossible not to recall how the earl had willingly taken direction from her when they'd set the puppy's leg. Somehow she doubted Mr. Headley would concede her such authority, even on those occasions when he knew less on the subject at hand than she.

"I think this has been a most instructive meeting and I believe we shall be even more productive next time we meet," she said, deciding more eagerly than perhaps she ought to end their session. "I must go to Lady Bea now." She invoked the older woman's name to keep Mr. Headley from protesting they could accomplish more just then.

As she had expected, he was sent on his way forthwith, and she was free to return to Lady Bea's rooms to await that lady's awakening while she occupied her hands with embroidering a handkerchief for her mother and her mind with thoughts of Mr. Headley.

The good man did not, to be sure, send her howling from the room, but neither, as Jessica told Lady Beatrice later while the older woman partook of a light broth, did she feel a desperate desire to marry him.

Lady Beatrice grunted in reply, "I don't doubt if you do decide to take him, you'll have to settle for modest interest. Headley wouldn't inspire desperation in a spinster of forty years. And there's no hurry in all this, child," she went on as Jessica's brow knit in thought. "You'll decide in your own good time. But while you wait, you may as well fetch us some cards that I may amuse myself by trouncing you. I am feeling just well enough to pull the trick off.''

"I don't doubt you could trounce me in your sleep," Jessica laughed, for Lady Bea was an exceptional cardplayer.

The older lady was not so sharp that evening, but she did manage to win. Sadly her reward was a renewed assault of pain in her shoulder. Determined to bring some relief, Jessica went to the kitchens for a hot compress.

"You're a wizardess, Jess.'' Lady Bea smiled when Jessica had finished the treatment with the application of some warm oil.

Jessica's heart went out to the old woman, there was such relief in her smile. "I am glad I can help," she said simply before leaving to go to her own bed.

It was early yet, but she'd a feeling Lady Beatrice would not sleep through the night.

When she'd been asleep several hours, she was proven right by the tinkling of Lady Beatrice's bell. Stopping only long enough to slip on the cotton dressing gown she'd left on her chair, Jessica hurried to answer the summons and found Lady Beatrice plucking fretfully at her covers.

"Child! I am sorry to disturb you so often like this!''

"But that is why I am here," Jessica assured her, taking her hand to give it a squeeze. "Now, what can I get you? A posset from the kitchen perhaps?''

"No." Lady Beatrice shook her head wearily. "I'm tired of possets and that blasted laudanum as well. I should like something more substantial. Perhaps a sip of Justin's brandy will be the thing.''

Knowing the earl often retired to the library for a glass of brandy, Jessica hurried there and found a goodly portion yet remained in the decanter. Lady Beatrice, sipping slowly, emptied two full glasses while Jessica read another chapter from Swift. She'd just begun on a second when she was interrupted by a gentle snore.

A rueful smile curved Jessica's mouth as she looked up. She'd had none of the earl's libation and had never felt more awake. There being little point in tossing rest-

97

lessly in her bed, Jessica went to the trouble of returning the brandy to the library.

She'd replaced the decanter on its table and stood, a single candle in her hand, scanning the bookshelves for some massive, sleep-inducing tome when the door opened behind her.

"Oh!" She spun so quickly she extinguished her candle.

"A guilty conscience, Miss Winslow?"

Even had she not recognized the mocking tones, she'd have known who it was. Though the fire had been banked earlier by the servants, the embers were sufficiently bright to reflect off Roxham's tawny head.

"I did not realize anyone else was awake," she returned sharply, put out at being frightened.

Abruptly, without waiting for a reply, she turned toward the fire, intent on relighting her candle and absenting herself from her employer's library and presence.

Though she'd no notion of it, the light of the smoldering embers outlined her body through the thin cotton of her nightclothes, affording Roxham a shadowy view of her long, well-shaped legs, smoothly rounded hips, and small waist. His eyes narrowing, he fancied he could almost make out the hollow down the center of her straight, slender back.

When she turned around, lighted candle in hand, her soft breasts swayed freely beneath her costume. Roxham did not miss the gentle movement, for his eye had fallen to the single braid in which she'd bound her hair for the night. Almost as thick as his arm and glowing a dark copper in the firelight, it had settled in the valley between her breasts.

"I wonder if you would be so kind as to satisfy my curiosity as to what it is you are doing in the library in the early hours of the morning?"

A tremor of alarm coiled Jessica's stomach into a knot. It was not yet panic she experienced, but she was undoubtedly unsettled by the look in the earl's unusually heavy-lidded eyes. It reminded her that she stood before him without so much as a chemise beneath her nightclothes.

Granted those nightclothes were made of thick, unadorned cotton and could not be as revealing as those he had undoubtedly seen on other women, but the thought did not comfort. Jessica had never been so exposed before any man, even her father.

Too overset to placate, she went on the offensive. "I've not come for an assignation, if that is your concern," she snapped.

"Nor did you come for a book, it would seem."

Jessica's cheeks flamed. She had followed the drift of his gaze to her hands and had seen it linger first upon her breasts. She lifted her free arm to cover herself, and though one arm, alone, could make little difference, it did at least help to steady the arm holding the candle.

"I-I came to replace the brandy." She hated stammering, but she scarcely noted how she stumbled over her explanation of her presence. She was too disturbed by the look Roxham fixed upon her. Lazy but intense, it somehow informed her he knew very well she wore not a stitch of clothing beneath her nightdress.

The gleam in his eye was not precisely like the one with which Charles Godfrey had used to regard her, but it reminded her enough of her stepfather to make her breath come in shorter gasps.

Of their own accord her eyes dropped from his and fell to his chest. What she saw then dismayed her.

Roxham wore only a black satin robe. It lay open to the waist, revealing not nightclothes but a thick patch of light, curling hair.

"You needed brandy to sleep?"

Only later would it occur to her to wonder if Roxham actually slept in no clothes at all. Just then she seemed able to think of nothing but that they stood together in a darkened room very close to a state of complete undress.

"Lady Bea desired a glass of brandy for her pain," she said in a voice that sounded strange to her.

"Aunt Bea was in such pain?"

Jessica could hear the frown in Roxham's voice, and his concern for his aunt steadied her. She looked up swiftly, before she lost her courage to find his eyes reflected nothing more than worry.

She nodded in reply to his question. "Yes, she has had a difficult time much of this week and did not care for another dose of laudanum. It makes her restless and gives her odd dreams, you see."

Roxham's frown did not lift. "Why do you not keep brandy in her room, if she has need of it?"

"She very rarely asks for it," Jessica explained. "There's little point making room for it when Lady Bea desires it less than one night in a month."

"A convenient excuse, Miss Winslow. Or were you hoping to meet another, if not by assignation, then by chance?"

The soft menace in Roxham's voice reignited all Jessica's fears. Then, without warning, he began to advance toward her.

Though her heart drummed painfully in her chest, Jessica attempted to keep her alarm from her expression. Her father had told her it was best never to show fear to a enemy, but she found it a difficult precept to follow when Roxham came so close he could reach for her without extending his arm.

"I wonder what Headley would think if he found you so scantily clad in the public rooms of his house?"

As the earl's eyes raked her with studied insolence, Jessica experienced her first taste of real panic. It bubbled up from deep within her and constricted her throat so she could make no reply. She could not even think of one; she could only shake her head fiercely back and forth.

Roxham made little of her agitation. He thought she merely played the innocent to evade his questions. "Come, come, Miss Winslow," he chided softly. "You are not generally at a loss for words. Tell me, at least, what I should do with you now I've found you in my library in dishabille." As he spoke, he reached out to lift her thick braid and in the process he deliberately allowed his knuckles to graze her breast.

"Please!" Jessica jerked back, all pretense at bravery abandoned. In her fear, she'd forgotten the candle in her hand, and it swayed in its holder as their shadows whirled crazily about the walls.

"Put that down!" When his command seemed to have no impact, Roxham quickly wrenched the holder from Jessica's grasp. "You'll send yourself up in flames and the manor with you," he said impatiently, even as he noted that her breasts heaved with her deep breaths.

"You are afraid." The words escaped him before he had judged the truth of them, but Jessica reacted as if he had accused her of a crime.

"No," she denied so vehemently that his brow lifted. "I am insulted," she cried when she realized she'd only succeeded in intriguing him. "First you accuse me falsely and then you, you touch me." Her voice broke and she averted her head.

Staring, Justin could see she bit her lip hard enough to draw blood, but any actress could do as much. Her arms hugged her chest as if she would protect herself, but again the gesture might be feigned. Only the waxy paleness of her cheeks argued her distress was real. That he could not be certain even then annoyed him.

He stepped back slightly. "You are distressed, Miss Winslow, and well you might be," he told her in a deliberately cool, aloof tone. "You have been found in a public place dressed only in your nightclothes. Take this meeting as a lesson. You are to leave your room only when you are properly covered."

Thoroughly shamed, for Roxham had succeeded making her feel a fool by putting the matter so baldly, Jessica could not meet his condemning gaze and only nodded mutely in reply.

With her head hanging and her lip still caught firmly between her small, even teeth, Jessica, her chin wagging up and down, resembled nothing so much as a little girl admitting to some mischief.

Without thinking, Roxham reached to lift her chin with his hand, asking as he did so, "Do you understand?"

At his touch, Jessica cringed. Her action took Roxham so by surprise that he lost his hold on her chin and dropped his hand to her shoulder. He could feel her shaking through her nightclothes.

"Yes! Yes," she cried quickly as she tried unsuccessfully to elude his hand. It felt large and powerful on her

101

shoulder. She swallowed, though her throat was painfully dry, and looked wildly for the door only to find Roxham's tall figure blotted her one hope of escape from her sight. He was a much larger man than Mr. Godfrey.

Dizzy with fear, she rushed to say anything to placate him, scarcely aware what words she spoke. "Of course, my lord, of course I shall do as you ask. I had no notion anyone would be awake, but that is no excuse, I know. Of course it is not. I only thought, you see, to hurry down, return the brandy, pick a book—"

"Jessica! Look at me!"

At the sound of her name, Jessica's eyes went wide and flew to meet his.

Roxham thought he'd never seen eyes so wide or dark a blue. "I would never hurt you." The blood seemed to drain from her face, and Roxham had an impulse to shake her. "I make it a policy never to assault anyone in my employ, regardless of how provocatively they are dressed." He had the pleasure of seeing the color surge back into her cheeks, and he knew she would not faint.

Carefully he dropped his hand from her shoulder and stepped two paces back. With each step he took, Jessica's breathing seemed to slow, and when he crossed his arms over his chest, her shaking subsided, albeit slowly.

"You were afraid." Roxham regarded her gravely, his eyes betraying a hint of puzzlement.

Jessica was not yet sure enough of her voice to speak, and she'd not the strength to deny the obvious. Oddly, as her breathing came under her control again, she found she did not feel humiliated that Roxham had witnessed her loss of control. Just then she only felt very tender, as if he could rout her merely by grimacing.

He did nothing of the sort. He gave her a searching look she found it impossible to sustain. He looked too deeply and she had exposed enough of herself.

"It is normal for a young woman to be unsettled by a man's touch, but not to be undone, I think."

Jessica, her gaze upon the polished floor, only shook her head abruptly. He knew as well as she her reaction had not been normal, and she knew she had Charles Godfrey to thank for the panic that had overwhelmed coherent

102

thought. Had she been able to think clearly even for a moment, she'd have known Roxham would never force himself upon her.

She could not reveal the whole, however. Her stepfather's desire shamed her too greatly.

"I believe in the days of old the maiden-in-distress was allowed to tell her knight-in-shining-armor at least the whereabouts of her particular dragon."

Jessica lifted her head at that, and Roxham suffered a jolt at the sight of her wet, spiky lashes. There were no tears on her cheeks, but her eyes shone with them, and with question. It was obvious she did not know what to make of his remark, nor, Roxham admitted with a quirk of his eyebrow, did he. Certainly he was not making a bid to play the knight to her lady.

It was also obvious from the appeal in her eyes she did not care to have him delve further into the subject. He gave her an easy bow. "It is not gallant of me to press you."

When her graceful shoulders sagged with relief, Roxham was not unaware that he experienced a powerful urge to fold her in his arms. He thrust his hands into the pockets of his robe and distracted himself with speech.

"I did not mean to allow my curiosity to intrude upon you. I imagine I only behaved so boorishly from the novelty of having a woman shrink from me."

His amusement was directed more at himself than at her, and Jessica found she could smile. It was a shaky effort, but brave nonetheless, and Roxham nodded before he spoke again in a quiet but authoritative voice. "You need never be afraid in this house, Miss Winslow, you have my word on it. No matter what occurs between us, neither I nor anyone else shall lay a hand on you."

Fresh tears pricked at Jessica's eyes. She believed him, and believed as well that he had no obligation to be so understanding. "Thank you, my lord," she said, finding her voice at last.

The huskiness of it—as if she still suffered from unhappy memories—affected Roxham to such an extent he opened his mouth to demand, sternly, that she tell him who it was had originally frightened her so badly.

"May I go now?" Jessica asked before he could speak. She was grateful indeed for his quite unexpected understanding, but she was also at the end of her stamina and in desperate need of privacy.

The earl seemed to understand, for he stepped aside at once. "Good night," he bid her as she passed, and he detected the faint, woodsy scent of violets. She cast him a quick, almost startled look.

"The same to you, my lord," she said, and then continued on her way, shielding her candle from the draft with her hand.

When she'd gone, Roxham poured a glass with what remained of the brandy his aunt had left him. Sipping it unhurriedly, he contemplated the enigma of Miss Jessica Winslow, a young woman who had schemed to entrap his brother into marriage, though she was afraid of men, or rather, he amended, of a man's seduction.

Well and truly afraid. Her reaction had been no pretense. He recalled her uncontrollable shivering with a grimace.

No woman, he told himself, not even a jade, should have been treated in such a way that she should experience panic at a man's lightest touch.

His aunt's companion, in particular, ought to have reacted to his advances—if she truly did not care for them—by flying at him, her eyes flashing.

Roxham tossed down the remainder of his brandy. It was all a mystery, but then, he recalled as he stretched lazily, he'd always rather enjoyed solving the puzzles his tutors had set him.

11

"I am glad you are feeling so much more the thing today, Aunt Bea." Livy smiled gaily at her aunt, who sat in a comfortable chair by the window. "We've missed you frightfully at dinner. Conversation has been insipid in the extreme without your sharp retorts."

The young girl giggled as her aunt swatted at her with the newspaper she held in her lap. "Have you in your life ever beheld such disrespect?" Lady Beatrice addressed the question to Jessica, who smiled but did not answer, for Lady Bea had already turned back to scowl at the younger girl. "Enough of this useless flattery, baggage. What I want is news. I haven't had a good coze this entire week."

Olivia laughed again and proceeded, as she sipped her tea, to tell her aunt the news of the neighborhood. Jessica listened absently as she made her neat embroidery stitches.

". . . and somehow Justin has persuaded Andy to go 'round the estate with him. I've not the least idea how he pulled it off, perhaps he threatened to cut off all Andy's claret."

Jessica's ears pricked at Livy's mention of the earl. It was two days since she'd returned Lady Bea's bottle of brandy to the library, and she had yet to reach an understanding on the subject of Roxham.

In the one night she had been exposed to two sides of him. First there had been the familiar, accusing, mocking Roxham who held her in such low esteem that he thought her fair game for improper advances. She could yet feel his hand graze her. Jessica flushed and looked up from her embroidery, forcing her mind to the other Roxham, the man who had displayed the greatest understanding, even sensitivity. That man had assured her of his protection.

She'd always known he could be generous. Lady Mary had remarked it, and even now Livy was saying he had offered his assistance to Lady Anne at Roselawn; but that he should behave with any consideration at all toward her was, in short, astonishing.

The lowering suspicion that he had only behaved kindly out of pity caused Jessica to give up her ruminations— whatever he might do in an extremity, he still believed her an unprincipled jade—and to return to listening to Livy.

". . . tomorrow," the young girl was saying, "he and Andy will meet with the estate manager at Roselawn while I take tea with Kate and her mother."

"I don't doubt you shall have a grand time," Lady Bea observed dryly. "Think you the three ladies will discuss the absent Philip, perhaps, Jess?"

Glancing at Livy's pink face, Jessica smiled. "I imagine the young man's name will work its way into the conversation," she agreed, and Olivia giggled.

The ladies who gathered at Roselawn for tea the next afternoon, however, did not discuss Philip Verney. They had not the time. Disaster struck first.

Jessica first heard of it when Olivia burst into the nursery exclaiming shrilly, "Justin's been hurt!"

That the injury was serious was obvious from the girl's unnatural pallor, and Jessica was too concerned that Livy might faint, to wonder at the sudden constriction in her chest.

"What has happened, Livy?" she demanded with such authority Olivia was steadied.

Gulping back her tears, she sank into a nearby seat. "We'd just sat down to our tea, Kate and Lady Anne and I, when a groom came running to say the stables had caught fire. He did not know how, but I don't doubt some fool had left a lamp on the floor for one of the horses to kick over.

"The stables went up like dry leaves in the autumn. There was an awful roar and such confusion, with men darting about frantically! Justin and Andrew helped, of course, but saving the horses was slow going as they were half-maddened with fear.

"In all the chaos, Kate's mare was left until last and by then it didn't seem she could be saved. Kate had raised her herself, and when Justin saw how distraught she was, he wrapped a wet blanket 'round himself and ran back inside, though Lady Anne and Andrew protested that he should not.

"He did manage to bring Circe out unharmed, but he was not so fortunate himself. Just as he reached the door, a flaming timber fell on him, burning him badly on his side. If he'd not thought to take the blanket, I cannot say

106

what might have happened. As it was, he lay so still, I, oh, Jess, I feared he was dead.''

With the twins looking solemnly on, Olivia wept out her fear and anxiety upon Jessica's shoulder.

''And where is the earl now?'' Jessica asked when she thought Olivia could continue.

Olivia wiped away the last of her tears and sniffed. ''Lady Anne thought he should stay at Roselawn, but Justin demanded we bring him back to Bleithewood. Dr. Mayes arrived as we did, and is with him now.''

''Good,'' Jessica exclaimed, relieved that the earl would be seen to without delay, for burns could be very nasty wounds.

''I hope he has something for Justin's pain,'' Olivia worried. ''Poor dear, he was nearly gray with it by the time we reached the manor. I have never seen Andrew so undone, but he held Justin's head all the way.''

''Will Justin recover, Jess?''

It was Giles, his eyes enormous in his pale face, who asked the question in a hushed little voice. Reminded that the twins could remember their father's death, Jessica forced a confident smile to her lips. ''Your cousin is very strong, Giles,'' she assured him. ''With the care of Dr. Mayes I feel certain he will recover rapidly.''

Jessica's prediction proved accurate. But as the earl battled a raging fever that set in the night he was brought home, it seemed to everyone at Bleithewood a very long time before Dr. Mayes pronounced his patient out of danger.

Then, as the earl began his convalescence, the question became not whether Roxham would survive his injury—they had their answer to that—but whether the household would survive the master's forced inactivity.

Dr. Mayes did allow his patient to sit up in his bed, but he absolutely forbade him, though the earl growled fiercely, to leave it. ''I cannot promise the exact moment you'll be free of those sheets, my boy,'' the crusty old man, who had looked after Lady Beatrice for years and had learned a thing or two from her about handling even the most difficult patients, exclaimed. ''But I can promise that if you do not take heed, you'll open the wound and be flat on your back all the longer.''

On the fifth day after the accident in the early afternoon, Lady Mary came to sink weakly into a chair in her aunt's chambers. "I vow, my nerves have never been more overset," she wailed so faintly Jessica thought that for once she might truly be undone. "I adore Justin, you know it, Bea." Her hand fluttered to her throat. "But how does he repay me? Why, by throwing us all from his sickroom."

She looked quite scandalized, but when Lady Bea did not, Lady Mary cried, "You understand he must have someone with him at all times. He cannot move without considerable pain, and even if he could, there is the danger that he may reopen his wound. I only went to offer him my comfort, but he thanked me by snapping at me bearishly and saying I prattled so about the dangers he'd overcome that he suspected I wished to put him on display as a miracle worker.

"Why," she continued, throwing an indignant look at Lady Bea, who had had the poor grace to chortle, "he even railed at Livy, and she only cried out of pity for him. He looks quite dreadful, I assure you. And just moments ago he even gave Andrew his dismissal. Justin said Andy's expression was lugubrious enough to make him feel he'd rather have died."

Lady Bea gave her niece's indignant expression a wry look. "You are acting as if Justin deliberately intends to insult you, Mary," she chided. "But he was never a good patient, even as a boy. He's always been too energetic to take to his bed with any grace."

"Grace!" Lady Mary threw up her hands. "I am only asking for simple courtesy. And the way he is driving poor Hanks! The man is devoted to him, but I don't doubt he will go to his grave before the week is out," Lady Mary clucked righteously. "With all Justin's fretting and ill humor, the poor man's not gotten more than a few hours' rest since the accident. Nonetheless, Justin refuses to allow anyone else near him. I vow I do not know what I shall do."

Silence fell for a time, and Jessica, who had been listening closely as she busied herself with some sewing, looked up to find Lady Beatrice regarding her oddly.

Jessica's stomach tightened. "Jess . . ." She could not evade Lady Beatrice's keen look.

"My lady?"

"I can't imagine why I didn't think of it earlier." The older lady shook her head as Jessica turned to face her squarely. "It is so obvious. Who better than you to sit with Justin while Hanks takes his rest?"

Jessica's stomach executed an unsettling roll. "No," she objected firmly. "The earl would never—"

But Lady Mary interrupted before Jessica could finish. "I do believe Aunt Bea has arrived at the answer." She tilted her head consideringly. "You've experience in the sickroom, Miss Winslow, and you've just the healing touch Justin needs. There is propriety, of course . . ." Lady Mary frowned pensively before her brow cleared. "But, after all, Justin cannot move much at all without assistance. If we left the door open—"

"Don't be a goose, Mary," Lady Bea cut in. "Justin would say you'd put him on exhibition if you left the door to his rooms open that anyone passing by might look in. There's no need anyway. No one will think anything of Jessica reading to an injured man."

Lady Mary nodded convinced. "And you needn't attend to him, ah, bodily after all, Miss Winslow. You could call a footman if there was a need for that sort of thing."

Out of respect to Lady Beatrice, she did not go on to say that Jessica was also experienced at skillfully accommodating persons with difficult tempers, but she did think it.

"You may as well say the chit's got experience handling difficult tempers, Mary!" Lady Beatrice laughed heartily when her niece had the grace to look uncomfortable. "Bah! You needn't look so sheepish, my dear. We all know I can be a tartar. After me, you'll find Justin the veriest lamb, Jess," she added so innocently that it was only when Jessica saw the twinkle in her eye that she realized she was being roasted.

* * *

Roxham awoke by slow degrees from his sleep. Lying on his good side, facing the windows, he became aware first of the throbbing pain in his side.

Reminded he must not move abruptly lest the pain become a searing one, he scowled, then opened his eyes to search the room for Hanks.

His brow lowered ominously when he did not find the man in his usual chair. Blast him! Why could he not be about when he was needed? He hovered anxiously enough when he was not!

His detestable dependency upon others borne in upon him yet again, Roxham nearly swore aloud. He did not only because at that moment his restless gaze abruptly jerked back to the windows. For several moments he simply stared, well and truly diverted for the first time since sustaining his injury.

Jessica Winslow sat in a chair, her burnished head bent gracefully as she concentrated on the work in her lap. It was some sort of sewing, he realized when her needle flashed in the light.

He recalled their last interview. It seemed an eternity ago, and if he did not have such a strong recollection of it, he might have thought it some absurd dream. There was nothing the least panic-stricken about her today. Far from it, her expression was entirely serene as she plied her needle in a steady, unhurried rhythm.

Looking upon her, the observer had only one clue from which to deduce she was not always so cool and collected. Anyone with such glorious, coppery hair must have strong passions.

Roxham scowled visibly at the thought, recalling Ned and the girl's strange fear of a man's touch. Before the fire—when he'd had the leisure to think—he'd realized there was no great mystery as to why she'd been so set on marriage to Ned, though she feared a man's passions. While the marriage bed might not interest her, the marriage settlement did.

Still, there was the mystery of the origin of her fear to solve. He hadn't forgotten how she leapt back so abruptly after he merely touched her chin.

Jessica lifted her eyes from her work to glance absently

110

at Roxham. At the discovery that he was both awake and watching her in silence, her deep-blue eyes widened, indicating she was startled.

It pleased the earl to have confounded her, though he'd have been hard put to say exactly why. Perhaps it was that she seemed so vitally healthy while he lay before her weak and incapacitated.

"Good afternoon, my lord. Would you care for water?"

Unerringly she'd guessed what he wanted more than anything. "For what reason are you here, Miss Winslow?" he growled, though his throat was so dry it was difficult for him to speak. "You are paid to sit with Aunt Bea, and yet you seem to spend precious little time with her."

Jessica calmly put aside her embroidery frame and went to pour a glass from the pitcher on the nightstand. "I am here at your aunt's direction, my lord," she answered in her slightly husky voice when she stood beside him. The light from the window behind her turned her hair into a halo. A crimson halo—one not the least appropriate to heaven, Roxham thought with the ghost of a smile.

His amusement lasted until he realized she did not intend to hand him his glass of water and have done with it. Without a by-your-leave, she had placed her arm behind his shoulder and lifted him slightly so that he might drink more easily.

Once again, he caught the faint, woodsy scent of violets.

"What's this?" he snapped, and with an annoyed grunt made to lever himself away from her assisting arm. But he'd forgotten his burn, and hot pain shot through his side.

"Damn you, girl," he swore, flinching.

Jessica was not disturbed. She merely held him the more firmly. "I am here to help you. Be still and you will not hurt yourself," she told him reasonably.

Though he scowled thunderously, Roxham had little choice but to accept her assistance. He could not throw her off in his weakened condition. However, when he had slaked his thirst, he handed her his glass and informed

111

her tightly, "I am not a helpless invalid, Miss Winslow. Is this your idea of revenge?"

Jessica gave him a surprised look as she lowered him gently back to the pillow. "I would not see you hurt." Her solemn tone caused the earl to feel foolish, a feeling he did not relish. "Would you care to sit up now, or will you rest again?"

Roxham glared. "I am fully awake."

"So it would seem."

He did not miss the small smile that accompanied her remark, but he had no opportunity to say his ill humor was no more than she deserved as she'd come uninvited to his quarters.

Already she was gently lifting him again to place several pillows behind him for support. He could not see what she'd done, but the arrangement was more comfortable than anything Hanks had managed to contrive.

She then, again without consulting his wishes, moved the nightstand so that the pitcher and glass were within the easy reach of his good hand. To celebrate his independence, Roxham helped himself to more water and only realized after he was sipping it that Jessica had gone to the bell pull.

"Escaping the lion's den already?" He could not resist needling her, but before she could make an answer, he said, "And well you should! I cannot imagine what Bea was thinking. I've no need to be fussed over. And even if I did, I am not so past my prayers that it can be the thing for you to be here with me alone."

Jessica made no response to his various objections to her presence. Instead, she answered a scratching at the door, allowing Roxham to see she'd rung not for Hanks but one of the younger footmen. He had a tray he gave to her as well as, to Roxham's mind, a bemused smile before he peeked over her shoulder for a glimpse of the wounded master.

The master's expression sent him on his way so quickly that Jessica was left to balance the tray on one hand in order to close the door.

"I detest broth, Miss Winslow," the earl warned as she approached him.

"It is easily digested, my lord, and therefore will be more beneficial to you than something heavier." Roxham eyed Jessica mutinously as she'd settled the tray across his lap, and she smiled sweetly. "Are you able to feed yourself, or shall I help you?"

"No," he growled, and lifting the spoon, he ceded the battle of what he was to have for sustenance without testing her resolution. From the twinkle in her eye, he suspected she might enjoy pouring the broth down him.

"When I am finished with this invalid's fare, I shall require something more substantial," he barked as she returned to her chair to continue her needlework.

"As you will, my lord," she replied over her shoulder, and when he finished with the broth, which he had found tastier than he would ever concede, he knew why she had made him no argument. Very likely she'd known that after he wrestled with the difficulty of lifting a spoon full of broth to his mouth with his left hand, he'd be almost as tired as if he'd engaged a mountain lion in single-handed combat.

Of their own accord his eyelids drifted down, and he only opened them briefly when he felt her lift his tray away.

She saw that he'd awakened, but she hadn't the heart to ask whether he cared for steak or roast beef. He looked very weak, lying back on his pillows, with his eyes scarcely open. Normally his skin, a light bronze, had a ruddy, healthy sheen, but today it was tinged with gray, and his amber eyes, now that he was fatigued, were a dull brown. Even his hair was not unaffected by his bout with the fever, for it lay flat on his head and seemed more brown than gold. An unruly lock had fallen upon his brow, but Jessica restrained the impulse to smooth it back. He would declare that fussing and such be within his rights.

"Do you care for more water?"

Roxham smiled faintly. "Yes, but no ham, if you please."

His self-mockery surprised a chuckle from her. It was a rich, merry sound that had the effect of making Roxham's smile widen slightly.

"You'll be up to ham soon enough," she said, balancing his tray on her hip as she handed him his water. Leaving him to finish it, she went to put the tray outside his door and rang for someone to fetch it. When she saw, on turning around, that Roxham's eyes were closed, she returned to her sewing and the exceptional view of the gardens the earl's rooms commanded.

Quite some little time passed as Jessica concentrated upon making small, neat stitches before she looked up to find the earl's amber eyes upon her again.

"Aren't you supposed to entertain me?"

Jessica carefully completed her stitch before replying, "Lady Mary said you did not much relish entertainment."

Roxham grimaced at the mention of his cousin. "My foolishly earned wound gives me little patience with Mary's solicitous but effusive chatter—or Livy's tears or Andrew's drawn expression. They'd have me with one foot in the grave."

Jessica smiled, but was serious when she said quietly, "I do not think saving a helpless animal foolish."

Roxham cast her a dry look. "Your opinion is scarcely unbiased. Look at the effort you expended upon a worthless pup. By the by, Mayes says you did a better job of that splint than many a quack he's seen." He did not give Jessica the time to relish the old doctor's flattery. "Caesar!" His fine mouth lifted at the corner. "I wonder what Headley is about if his pupils believe that mongrel of no lineage worthy of such a name."

"It was the brave manner Caesar adopted toward our painful ministrations that put the twins in mind of the noble Roman," Jessica explained.

Though her tone was mild, the earl did not miss her point. "A manner this noble Englishman might do well to emulate, Miss Winslow?"

"I would not be so presumptuous," she answered, but the ghost of a smile she could not subdue betrayed her.

"Hmpf." She was given a long look, then the command, "You may read to me."

Jessica laid aside her work and went to an Adam table across the room. "At Lady Bea's suggestion, I've brought

114

Childe Harold's Pilgrimage, Voltaire's *Candide*, and the philosopher Hume. What is your pleasure, my lord?''

When her question was met with silence, Jessica glanced up from her perusal of the books to find the earl regarding her with one eyebrow arched in amusement. ''I doubt you would care to hear it, Miss Winslow.''

Jessica flushed hotly in response to Roxham's slow, lazy drawl. At once she turned on her heel, dropping the books in a heap on the graceful table before continuing on to the door. ''I see you are in the right,'' she said crisply as she went. ''I have no business being here, if that is the sort of remark you feel free to make, I shall send a footman to you.''

Her blue eyes sparkled with indignation but, Roxham noted, not a trace of fear. ''Send Hanks! I'll not have anyone else.''

''Hanks is fagged half to death, and is, hopefully, sleeping the sleep of the dead, my lord. I shall send in James, who is just outside. He can hand you the book you choose, and you can read to yourself.''

''Damnation,'' Justin roared, rising up as if he intended to throttle her for her disrespect.

It was he, however, who was throttled, for a searing pain lanced his side and he knew he'd reopened his blasted wound. Though he tried, he could not repress a strangled moan.

At the sound, Jessica whirled about and ran to him, hastily throwing aside the pillow she'd fluffed behind him so that he might lie flat. Without considering the liberty she took, she then jerked back the bedcovers to his waist and laid open the top of his nightshirt.

''Oh, dear! You've started it bleeding again.'' Gingerly she pressed on the bandage to stop the slight seepage coming at the edge of the long burn.

''Shall I die, do you think?''

It was a noble attempt at levity, considering how gray he'd gone, and Jessica gave him a faint smile. ''Not within the hour, at least.'' After a few moments she looked again at the long, ugly wound and sighed with relief. ''It looks as if the fresh bleeding has stopped. I shall just apply some basilicum powder and rebandage it.''

"You've a healing touch, Miss Winslow,'' Roxham remarked quietly as she worked.

"I've had ample opportunity to develop it.'' She glanced up and was glad to see a more normal color had returned to his face. Undistracted by anxiety, she was struck suddenly by the realization that she'd half-stripped a man of his clothes.

Too late, Jessica jerked her eyes from his bare torso to his wound. The triangle formed by the curly mat of hair she'd first caught a glimpse of in the library was burned in her mind. It was wide at the top across his chest, but tapered to a thin line before disappearing from sight beneath the sheets.

Flushing unhappily, she forced her thoughts to the bandage she must apply as painlessly as possible. The task accomplished, her hands wavered irresolutely over Roxham's chest and his unfastened nightshirt.

"I think I can do that.''

Jessica nodded, avoiding his eyes, for she was certain he would mock her for her relief. She had no business being here, he was right. On the thought, she said, "I shall just get James,'' and turned to go.

"Stay.'' Roxham's soft command interrupted her progress, but she did not obey him to the extent that she sat down. He eyed her position sardonically, poised on one foot in preparation for flight. "Will you force me to beg you? The footmen can read little above nursery rhymes, and I am too fatigued now to hold a book. Sit down and read to me.''

Jessica ought to have obeyed without question, but she could not. Her determined chin lifted. "Whence the change of heart, my lord?'' she asked warily. "I shall not stay to be insulted.''

It was impossible not to be affected by the picture she made, with the afternoon sun revealing the deep blue of her eyes and imparting a fiery radiance to her hair.

"I did not expect you would,'' he informed her with a half-smile. "I promise to school my tongue to politeness and not rouse you merely to relieve the devilish tedium

116

of seeing nothing but these four walls and this bed day after day.''

It was as close to an apology as she would get, Jessica decided, and it was close enough. Besides, her sympathies were aroused by the fatigue that showed clearly on his face. It was not easy to be a bear in pain, she thought, smiling to herself as she inclined her head and went again to fetch the three books she'd brought.

12

''You are late.''

Jessica breathed deeply. She had hurried and was out of breath. ''I did not know you expected me at a specific time, my lord,'' she replied. ''Would you—''

''Was it Aunt Bea who kept you?''

Jessica shook her head at the earl, who, with only two pillows behind him for support and a dark, silk robe around his shoulders, looked far different than he had when she'd first seen him five days before.

His hair, newly washed, gleamed a tawny gold, and his skin had lost entirely the dreadful gray pallor that had so alarmed Lady Mary, and looked, if not sun-bronzed at least healthy. Even his eyes had regained their luster. They sparkled now, though not, it seemed, with pleasure.

Jessica was not vastly surprised. The earl's temper had kept pace with his health by deteriorating in equal proportion to his body's recovery. Lady Mary had been heard to say—and the servants unanimously agreed—that the day Dr. Mayes would allow the earl to leave not merely his bed, but his room as well, simply could not come soon enough.

Jessica echoed Lady Mary's sentiments, though for another reason. The earl's temper could put her out of countenance, but what concerned her more was an experience she'd had the day before.

When she entered, she had found Roxham asleep. With his face relaxed and free of lines, he had appeared years younger and, somehow, touchingly vulnerable. His tousled hair had only added to his boyish look, and as she had stood quite still, unable to look away, she'd experienced a burst of startling, thoroughly disconcerting warmth.

Only just restraining her hand from reaching out to him, she'd conceded that the sooner she was taken from such close companionship with the earl, the better.

"Your aunt is very well," Jessica replied, avoiding Roxham's question as she went to place the stack of linens she carried on the washstand.

"What kept you, then?"'

Her jaw tightened as she reached for a chess board and a box of ivory pieces. "Would you care to play?" she asked, for they'd been accustomed to playing each afternoon.

"I have been waiting all day for a match," Roxham snapped. "Now, what kept you?"

Jessica crossed to his bed and, more intensely aware now of his dark gaze, briefly flicked her eyes to his as she set up the board. "As I said, I was not aware there was a precise time you expected me. Lady Bea only said originally that I should keep you company from sometime after luncheon to some time before tea; however, if you wish to know what it is I have been doing since luncheon, then I should tell you that I have been in a discussion with Mr. Headley on the subject of the St. Barnabas Day Festival."

"Aha."

In response to that knowing sound Jessica's mouth tightened mutinously. The subject of the vicar called up all that was unhappy between her and the earl.

"And how is Mr. Headley?"

"I cannot imagine you truly care, my lord," Jessica replied less than gently as with exaggerated care she placed the ivory pieces upon the board.

Roxham might have been put out with such a response, which lacked respect, but his mood was strongly affected at that moment by the picture Jessica made. She put him in mind of one of the new breed of schoolmistresses he'd read of. Clad in an undistinguished cotton twill dress of dark blue that sported a thin edging of white lace at the throat and wrists, she looked utterly prim and decorous until one noted the color of her hair or the spark in her eye, or her seat. She sat upon his own bed with her legs curled beneath her. His bed was too high from the floor for her to see the game unless she wished to stand.

"Come, come, Miss Winslow. You needn't stiffen," he chided, his brow lifted in an expression of extreme innocence. "I only asked because I must languish here in utter boredom. A little news must relieve the tedium, don't you agree?"

Jessica did not trust the gleam in his eye. She did not answer that question, but she did say, to have the matter over and done with, "Mr. Headley is very well," before studiously returning her attention to the board.

Roxham, whose turn it was to play first, looked at the top of her head. There was almost as much gold in her hair as there was deep red. The combination was what gave it its coppery look. "And Headley's suit? How does it progress?"

Jessica took a calming breath before she looked up. Idle tone or no, he was cutting close to what was none of his affair. "I understood you to say you wished to play a game of chess, my lord. It is your move, you know."

"I said, his suit—how goes it?" This was the Earl of Roxham, the man of the flat, commanding look.

Their eyes, one pair of blue and the other of amber, clashed. "His suit progresses nicely."

It was a lie. Mr. Headley had bored Jessica to tears, but the truth was not reflected in her proud look.

"How nice for him." Roxham held her gaze in silence a long moment. "You may inform your good swain I wish him to detain you at some time other than the hour you are to come here. I care not precisely when he comes, only that you are not late here."

"As you wish, my lord."

"You've no cause to look daggers at me, Miss Winslow," Roxham protested easily. "I am well within my rights. I do employ you, and I do not care to wait upon

Headley. An hour, when you are in a sickbed, is an eternity, you see."

Jessica could not let that pass. "It was half an hour only."

"Even a quarter of an hour is too much," he snapped, his brow lowering in earnest. Jessica nodded stiffly, and, silence reigning, Roxham moved a pawn before speaking again. "What was it you discussed?" he asked abruptly.

Jessica looked up, astonishment not unmixed with exasperation in her expression. Really! She knew he was truly bored, but this inquisition seemed absurd.

"We discussed the relative merits of the different sets of musicians who have played for the festival in the past."

"And you decided upon which ones?"

Jessica called upon all the patience she had to keep a civil tone. "I am to discuss the names with Lady Mary before a final decision is reached, my lord."

"I am not to be consulted?"

In response to Roxham's absurdly surprised tone, a spark lit in Jessica's eyes. "I beg pardon, my lord," she cried, smiling sweetly. "I had not realized you wished to be consulted, but as I mean you no slight, allow me to inform you of the various possibilities. There is a group in Altonborough that plays for the fair there each year, and—"

When Roxham laughed aloud, Jessica's heart leapt. His strong smile might have charmed a stone. "Enough," he commanded, his golden-brown eyes gleaming with lazy amusement. "I will not allow you to bore me to death with the same list Headley put you half to sleep with."

He knew! It was all Jessica could think as she quickly dropped her gaze from his. She was afraid he'd already seen the confirmation of his suspicion in her eyes, but if he had not, she would withhold it. The vicar might one day be her husband.

"I believe it is again your move," she said, her gaze focusing once more upon the board between them.

Roxham smiled but accepted the change of topic. In truth, there was little more to be said on the subject of Richard Headley.

"So it is," he remarked as he moved his knight. "And I must pay attention, for I've a loss to avenge."

"But you've avenged it the last two days," Jessica protested rather absently as she contemplated her own move.

"Good Lord! It will take several victories to atone for a loss to a woman," Roxham explained in mock amazement.

He was at his most dangerous then, with a smile playing around his mouth and his eyes warm with laughter.

Jessica experienced a giddy feeling in response to that look, but managed to cast him a look of reproach.

"You think women have the same reasoning abilities as men, then?" he provoked her.

Her answer was firm, though she knew he teased her. "I do. If women were tutored in the strategies of the game as men are, most would give a good account of themselves. They do not only because women are trained from birth to think of little more than gewgaws and dresses."

It was on the tip of Roxham's tongue to say, his eye dropping to her plain blue twill, that it was obvious she had not suffered such superficial training. But he restrained himself. Had anyone asked him why, he'd have said he wanted to get on with their game, but to himself he admitted he did not care just then to banish Miss Winslow's smile.

"Well, I admit your play has been a pleasant surprise," he allowed. "Who taught you, if I may ask?"

"Of course," she replied easily. "My father did." As was generally the case when she recalled her father, Jessica smiled, and her partner found himself as aware of the soft light in her eyes as he was of her answer. "Father instructed me in self-defense when he was sent home once with a leg wound and was bored to tears." She laughed at the similarity of the situations, but Roxham did not pursue it.

"Was your stepfather an army officer as well?" he asked curiously. Somehow it did not surprise him to see her luminous expression fade so quickly it was as if a candle had been doused.

"No," she said curtly, looking away from his interested eyes to the board. "My mother met Mr. Godfrey after my father's death. Your move is an unusual one, my lord. I find I must concentrate to defend myself."

And with that abrupt statement, Jessica cut off further conversation on the subject of her stepfather. Roxham did not force the issue. There was something about the set of her mouth that indicated she'd simply have rebuffed him again. She would be within her rights, he granted, for he'd no license to pry.

Still, so strong a reaction was food for thought, he decided, returning his attention to the chess board. It could very easily have been her stepfather who had given her her fear of a man's touch.

The next day, when Olivia came to pay him a visit before luncheon, Roxham was feeling in quite a good humor. Just an hour earlier Dr. Mayes had proclaimed him well enough to rise from his bed.

"Well, Livy, and to what do I owe this brave return to the bear's lair?"

Livy giggled. "I know from Jess you are feeling more the thing and will not cut up at me for coming," she replied, assured by the twinkle in her cousin's eye that she could be as saucy as she liked. When he proved her right by laughing, she twirled to show off the real reason she'd come: her newest evening gown, a white gauze affair over a white satin slip. At the hem, it was trimmed with lace entwined with pearls.

Roxham gave a low whistle. "What do you think, really, Justin?" she demanded with a coquettish grin. "Will it turn heads at my supper dance?"

"They'll positively swivel," he assured her, and she flew to give him a kiss on the cheek. "But what supper dance?" he asked when he'd disentangled her from around his neck. "This is the first I've heard of an entertainment, and I think it is poor-spirited of you to plan one when I cannot be present."

"Oh, but you will be there," Olivia exclaimed, throwing herself down beside him on the bed. "Mother has agreed to set the date a fortnight away, and I am certain you will be quite recovered by then."

"I am pleased you have such faith in my recuperative

122

powers, minx. Dr. Mayes might dispute with you, however."

"Dr. Mayes!" Olivia wrinkled her nose dismissively. "You won't be bound by him much longer, I'll wager. Mother says you are growing extremely restive. And I do so hope you will be able to come. All our guests will be quite disappointed if you are absent."

"They'll not be satisfied with a glimpse of the fair Olivia and an invitation to Bleithewood?" Justin queried.

Olivia, though she blushed happily at his flattery, shook her head. "Indeed not! They may have me and Bleithewood almost anytime. It is you who are in short supply and who will bring them flocking."

At the thought of the neighbors all flapping about him, Roxham chuckled and then asked what the supper dance was in honor of.

"Why, your recovery, of course," Olivia said a little too smoothly. When her cousin cocked an eyebrow at her, she shrugged elaborately. "Well, we've not had an entertainment in some time, and I thought we were all in need of one. So many people have returned home lately: you; Andrew; Sir Elkland's son, Percival; and Philip Verney. He's just come home from school, you know. But Justin," Olivia rushed on when her cousin began to look amused, "I've something to ask of you."

"Nothing dangerous, I hope," Roxham responded with a wry smile. "I'm off heroics for a bit."

"Oh, no! Nothing like that," Olivia assured him. "It's only that, as my supper dance is to be a small gathering, just friends from the neighborhood, I thought it would not be amiss to include Jessica as a guest."

"A guest?" the earl echoed, his expression impassive.

"Yes!" Olivia leaned forward eagerly. "It would be the greatest shame if Jess should have to attend as a companion. She'd be obliged to sit among the old biddies, holding Aunt Bea's shawl and watching the rest of us enjoy ourselves. I've a nice blue gown that would suit her admirably, and she does love to dance."

"Does she?" There was no mistaking the coolness in Roxham's voice, but Olivia, her thoughts elsewhere, did not heed it.

"Jess taught me the waltz, actually," she confided. "And I only hope her efforts are not in vain. Mother has not yet agreed it may be played, but I am still in hopes that I shall win her over by the time the dance comes."

"The waltz is danced in London daily, and so I can see no objection to it," Roxham said, causing Olivia to clap her hands with relief. She had not expected it would be so simple a matter to persuade him to take up her cause on the matter of the rather scandalous dance. "However," he continued in a tone of voice that caused Livy's delighted smile to falter, "nowhere does a companion attend an entertainment on the same footing as a member of the family. It would not be at all appropriate to present Miss Winslow as anything other than what she is."

"But, Justin," Livy cried, taken aback. "Do not tell me that, like Mother, you are afraid she will cast Marianne in the shade."

"This has nothing to do with Marianne Multaney," Roxham replied firmly. "You would put everyone in an awkward position with this whim. Think, Livy," he commanded curtly when the young girl opened her mouth to make another objection. "Desiring to please a friend is a commendable sentiment, but it is wise to carefully consider the ramifications of what you do. You would present Miss Winslow to our neighbors as a friend and guest, and to humor you, for that one night, they would follow your lead, treating her as you do. But they know her true status. They would not invite her to their dances, and after her taste of life as something other than a companion, she would again be nothing more."

"Well, I think it is positively gothic," Olivia declared unhappily. "Jess is as gently behaved as anyone. But I see your point," she allowed in the next breath, her mouth turning down. "I should not care to make her feel her place any more keenly than she must already."

The witch!

The words exploded into the silence when Olivia had left Roxham's room, and he did not refer to his cousin. It was Miss Winslow—and she alone—who had soured his mood.

She thought to turn Livy's friendship to advantage. While his cousin—and Bea, his aunt must not be forgotten—looked on approvingly, she would cavort among the local gentry on equal terms and essay to entice the heir to some neighboring landowner.

With a black scowl he reminded himself how little interest she had displayed in Headley. And why should she, if the vicar was only to be left dangling in the background in the unlikely event her grander scheme did not come off?

Very likely, Roxham admitted, his gentler treatment of her after their encounter in the library had led her to believe he'd not object if she used his family to establish her credit.

That he had come to anticipate her arrival in his sickroom with some interest, he did not think she had marked with any significance, if she had remarked it at all. It was too obvious he was bored to tears and any passable-looking female with the ability to keep quiet when he did not want her chattering would have brightened his day.

Damn, but he'd not forgotten Ned, nor the shuttered expression the boy had worn much of the year after his encounter with Miss Winslow. And she would soon learn to her sorrow that he had not.

When Jessica entered the earl's room that afternoon, her face lit at once with a smile. "But this is good to see," she exclaimed, crossing to where he lounged upon a chaise Lady Mary had loaned him. "How good it must be to escape the confines of your bed."

He looked very well, indeed, in a burgundy robe worn over a soft cambric shirt. The chaise was not small, but his slippered feet hung off the end and Jessica was reminded just how tall he was.

"I am very glad to be up, if not about," Roxham allowed.

Jessica's smile died and did not return when she looked more closely at his face. Distracted at finding him out of bed, she'd not glanced first at his eyes. Had she, she would have seen he was regarding her in the cold, impassive way she dreaded. That she had allowed herself to hope that particular expression might be a thing of the past, she only realized as her heart seemed to shrivel.

To Roxham, Jessica looked damningly beautiful.

The twins had taken luncheon with their Aunt Beatrice that day, and afterward Jessica had accompanied them and Caesar on a walk. A high wind had made a mess of her hair, and late as it was when she returned, Jessica had accepted Lady Bea's advice that she simply tie her hair back with a ribbon rather than take the time to pin it up, a laborious process with such long, heavy tresses.

His gaze only turned the more frigid as he noted how her color was up and her bright, red-gold hair rippled in a fall down her back. "Your hair is in a rather girlish style for one in your position, is it not?" Roxham demanded before he motioned her to a seat.

Jessica stiffened and, in a voice quite as cool as his, said, "The wind played havoc with it when I went out with the twins, and Lady Bea thought you'd rather I wore it down than be late, but if you prefer, I will go and pin it up."

Roxham ignored the thought that her hair was too lovely to be offensive. "I've not the inclination to wait on you," he said instead. "Sit down, I've something to say."

He waited until she faced him from the chair she'd sat in to do her sewing. She was not so seemingly comfortable now. She sat very straight, her hands held tightly in her lap, it pleased him grimly to see.

"I had a visit from Livy earlier," he began, his amber eyes not leaving her face. "She came to ask if you might attend a supper dance she intends to give—as a guest," he added after a significant pause.

Jessica's brow shot up in surprise, but Roxham recalled how she'd denied as well flaunting her charms before Ned. "I commend you, Miss Winslow. It was subtly done. Livy never knew she was being managed."

Even as her chin came up, Jessica fleetingly recalled how, once, Roxham had used her given name. She put the thought aside as quickly as it had come. She was first and foremost the scheming Miss Winslow to him, and she had best remember that.

"You'd only to say you love to waltz and later, offhandedly, make some mention how at a dance you would be obliged to sit by Bea with the other dowagers. A companion would not join the others of her age upon the floor, you might add then. Livy's affection for you would supply the request. You'd no need to make it outright. Forthwith she'd rush to me to decry the unfairness of the situation and to propose the remedy—an idea of hers, alone."

"It was her idea, alone," Jessica retorted. "I not only did not propose it, I did not suggest it. It is true I said I like, not love, to waltz, but that was when I first arrived at Bleithewood. As to where I would sit, I've not given a thought to the matter. But pray, my lord, if I may be so bold as to ask, why is it you imagine I should like to play Cinderella at the ball?"

Roxham held Jessica's flashing eyes with ease. "Because, of course, my dear, you hope to get a handsome prince," he quipped, his eyes mocking her. "There will be several, if not princes, then wealthy young gentlemen attending. And if you cannot wed Andrew, you may as well try for one of them."

He gave her a measured, considering look. "With your looks you might even inspire a desperate *tendre* in a single evening, though the odds are against the smitten lad's family countenancing such a connection." She colored fiercely as his barb hit home, but he did not pause. "It matters not, however, for I told you once I would not allow any other to be cozened in the place of Ned, and I repeat that warning. Content yourself with Headley, if you can stomach him."

Jessica clenched her hands so tightly, her fingertips were bloodless. It was the only way she could control herself. Otherwise she'd have lashed out, saying anything she could think of to humiliate him as he humiliated her.

To have to bear such treatment in silence was almost more than she could endure, and when he dismissed her, saying, "I have no more need of you now," she actually experienced a spurt of gratitude.

"Inform Aunt Bea that I shall come to her room for tea tomorrow to celebrate my newfound freedom," he told her as she curtsied.

Jessica acknowledged the demand with a single, abrupt nod of her head and left the room swiftly without saying a word. She could not speak, nor could she school her steps, though she detested giving him cause to suspect he had affected her.

But had she lingered or lifted her eyes to his or tried to speak, he'd not have needed to guess at his effect. Then he'd have had the satisfaction of seeing the loathsome, revealing tears burning her eyes.

13

Forewarned, Jessica made certain to be absent from Lady Bea's rooms next day when the earl, walking slowly but without assistance, came for tea. She had said she must have a walk, and Lady Beatrice, aware the child had performed a laborious task nursing her nephew, did not deny her.

As she was not present, Jessica did not hear Lady Beatrice sing her praises, nor Roxham respond by allowing she had a "nice touch."

"I think you ought to thank me for sending her to you, Justin," Lady Beatrice said then, not well-satisfied with such blandness. "After all, she's a great deal easier on the eyes than Hanks."

But her nephew was not to be drawn on the subject of Miss Winslow. "I do thank you. I know you sacrificed to do without her. And as to looks, as you say, Miss Winslow has the advantage over Hanks. But, Aunt Bea, tell me how the devil it is you and old Mayes manage to remain on friendly terms." Roxham smiled charmingly. "I'd never realized before what a tyrant the man is."

His ploy succeeded admirably. With his aunt off on one of her favorite subjects—her dear friend and treasured enemy, Dr. Mayes—the subject of Jessica Winslow was avoided, and the earl was spared the difficulty of parrying his aunt's shrewd gaze. He might not care for the treacherous chit personally, but she did have a soothing hand, and he was not yet prepared to acquaint his aunt with the truth about her. He did not believe she would keep the girl on, if he did.

Olivia and Lady Mary, upon returning home from an outing into Altonborough, were informed by Moreton of the momentous news that the earl had left his sickroom and was just then with Lady Beatrice.

Lady Mary, leaving her hat and pelisse with the old man, went at once up the stairs to congratulate her cousin, but Olivia, told upon asking that Miss Winslow was in the gardens, went out in search of her friend.

She found Jessica sitting beside an ornamental pool where several pairs of amazingly large goldfish resided. "I am glad to find you, Jess," she exclaimed, smiling. "I've been hoping to speak to you since yesterday, but a certain addition to our neighborhood has quite distracted me."

At the sight of Livy's sparkling eyes, Jessica's spirits lifted perceptibly. "And how is Philip Verney?"

"Very well, indeed," the younger girl exclaimed with a happy sigh. "He's changed so very much since Christmastime. That was only a few months ago, I know, but he seems a man now, not a boy. You'd be amazed how handsome he is, Jess. And even Kate has remarked that when he smiles at me, he does so with a particular warmth."

Jessica smiled fondly. "I don't doubt it."

"My only problem now is Mother," Livy went on, making a comical face at the fish staring impassively at her. "When she learned Philip brought me home yesterday, she flew up into the boughs. It is true we were unaccompanied, but I cannot see that Mother had cause to take on so. We were in an open curricle, after all."

Livy shrugged her shoulders in vexation. "Of course, her real objection has nought to do with propriety, anyway. She must always mention how low their funds are at Roselawn. But I know Philip will set matters right in the end. It will only take time."

She turned so abruptly the goldfish stared. "Jess, I have been wondering if you would speak to Justin for me?

129

He's the only one who can persuade Mother, and he would listen to you where he would not to me.''

Before Jessica could gather her wits enough to say Olivia had very much mistaken matters, the younger girl laughed. "I declare it amazed me the way you managed him. Dare I admit I thought you'd not last a day in his sickroom? It's true.'' She grinned at Jessica's look of surprise. "He was such a bear to all of us. I thought when he acted badly to you, you'd put him in his place and then he'd send you out the door on the instant. I suppose I should have known you'd find a way to bring him 'round, just as you did with Aunt Bea. Please, Jess,'' Olivia cried urgently, "I am certain he'll listen to you."

Recalling vividly her last scene with the earl, Jessica strove to keep a bland countenance. "Your cousin accepted my efforts to nurse him, Livy, but that does not mean he would respect my opinion in regard to your future. You must not hope for it."

But Olivia was not to be persuaded. "Only promise that if the moment should seem right, you will try,'' she beseeched so earnestly that Jessica could not deny her.

"If the moment is right,'' she conceded, but added conscientiously, "though I doubt it ever will be."

Something in her tone caused Olivia to glance sharply at her. "Justin's said nothing, ah, about anything to do with me in the last day or so, has he?''

Jessica was proud she could smile. She would rather not have had to discuss Olivia's supper dance, but she had no intention of enduring a repetition of the humiliating interview she'd had with the girl's cousin on the subject. Even now she could not recall it without coloring.

"Yes, Livy,'' she said in a tone she strove to keep light. "The earl did speak to me of your wish to invite me as a guest to your supper dance."

"Oh! I wish he had not,'' Livy moaned. "I did not mean for you to know unless he agreed to my plan."

"I suppose your cousin thought I must know so that I could then discourage you from making similar requests in future."

"Well, I think it positively ancien régime that my request has caused a to-do. It is not as if you are of disreputable birth, after all. Why, I daresay your family is as good or better than the squire's, and Mother wishes her son to make an alliance with his daughter.''

Jessica nearly said it was her character, not her birth, the earl suspected, but she bit back the bitter words. ''I thank you for your sympathies, Livy, I truly do. But I must agree with your cousin. I could never attend your dance as a your guest, my dear. I am not a guest at Bleithewood, I am your aunt's paid companion and it would embarrass me greatly to behave as something I am not. Can you understand, Livy?''

''I understand your pride's as devilish prickly as Aunt Bea says,'' the young girl retorted. ''And I still don't entirely see the harm, though I do see you are unhappy and I regret that I have done something to overset you. It was not my intent.''

Jessica squeezed Livy's hand affectionately. ''You are a dear girl. And be at ease, nothing you've done has overset me. Only promise not to surprise me with such kindness again, and I shall be restored to my usual good spirits.''

''A blackmailer!'' Livy laughed, rather relieved that Jessica did not look so intent now. ''But I shall do as you ask. After all, you have promised to speak to Justin on my behalf.''

Jessica was just on the point of reminding Olivia she might never have the opportunity to plead her case when they were interrupted by a call from the terrace. Turning, they saw Mr. Headley descending the steps to join them.

Olivia greeted him politely enough, but after Mr. Headley had compared their beauty at eloquent length to that of the flowers in a nearby bed, Livy suddenly recalled an urgent errand she must carry out for her mother and departed.

Mr. Headley, his eyes upon Jessica, seemed to care not at all that Lady Mary's daughter displayed only scant interest in his company. ''Dare I hope you are free to meet with me today, Miss Winslow?'' he inquired, beaming hopefully. ''Or are you engaged to sit with the earl again?''

131

"I am free for a time, Mr. Headley," Jessica responded. "The earl has left his sickbed."

"Oh, that is good news!" The vicar nodded happily. "I hope he takes care to go slowly. It is easy to overdo at first."

Thinking that was very likely what the earl might do, Jessica only agreed that overexertion could be a problem, for which she certainly offered no solution. Were she to speak to Roxham on the matter, he would either growl that her advice was unwelcome or go for a bruising ride just to prove her wrong.

"Shall we adjourn to the library, Mr. Headley?"

The vicar said that would suit him, and they turned toward the room in which they were accustomed to meeting. In addition to being comfortable, the library held a plentiful store of the pens and paper that were required for planning a festivity the size of the St. Barnabas Day Festival.

As they walked, Mr. Headley enumerated, with various chatty digressions, all the tasks he'd accomplished since they last met. But Jessica listened with only half a mind.

Her latest contretemps with Roxham had convinced her she could not remain for any great length of time at Bleithewood, beneath his roof and subject to his authority.

From the first she'd known it would be difficult to live with his suspicions of her, but she'd thought, foolish optimist that she was, that eventually he would come to see the truth about her.

She'd even begun to mark some progress in that direction. There had been his gentleness with her in the library after he had frightened her, and in his sickroom he had acted, on occasion, as if he actually enjoyed her company.

All absurd fancy! She'd not overcome the least of Roxham's suspicions. Perhaps it truly was the scandalous color of her hair, or perhaps it was something else—something she'd no notion of. But whatever it was, he remained so prejudiced against her, Jessica half-believed that even if Edward Stafford were to come home and swear to her innocence, Roxham would likely call the boy a fool.

That his continued lack of faith hurt, Jessica admitted reluctantly. She ought to have been above caring what such an obstinate, arrogant man thought, but she was too clearheaded to lie to herself. She did care and therefore she must leave Bleithewood. She would only come to despair if she remained.

Having come to that decision, she had decided as well there was every reason to give Mr. Headley greater consideration than she had done. It did not seem likely that life with the vicar could be worse than a life spent depending on the precarious goodwill of employers.

They did have disagreements between them. For one, the vicar believed young girls had little need to understand much beyond receipts and women's circulars. And though he had received the news that she played chess with relative equanimity, Jessica had not challenged him to a game. She did not think Mr. Headley would take being defeated by her in good part—unlike . . .

Jessica at once returned her thoughts to Mr. Headley. It was he, she considered, and no other. And he undoubtedly admired her. The extent to which he yearned for her good opinion was, indeed, to come clearer to her at their subsequent meeting several days later.

The interview began rather strangely. While Jessica, sketch in hand, made suggestions as to the placement of the food tables, Mr. Headley said little and several times shot her brief, unhappy glances. Often he seemed on the point of speaking, but when he did at last, he only launched into a long, rambling, almost incoherent monologue on the disaster to be invited by placing the ale table close to the section he'd set aside for the use of "the ladies of refinement."

When Jessica agreed and the matter was resolved, her companion fell into an abstracted silence. "Mr. Headley, is something amiss?" she asked, concerned.

"Amiss?" the vicar echoed, his voice oddly loud. "Amiss? No, no, nothing's amiss," he repeated as if to reassure himself. But almost at once looked up to say, "Miss Winslow . . ."

133

Jessica met his anxious glance with a reassuring smile. "Yes, Mr. Headley?"

"Miss Winslow, ah, I, ah . . . I received a missive in the post this morning." Mr. Headley tugged unhappily at his cravat before adding quickly, "From my mother. She, ah, she wishes to come to Bleithewood for a visit."

Mr. Headley fell silent, and Jessica, who still could not fathom what the problem was, said, "I shall look forward to meeting her."

"Ah, yes!" Mr. Headley exhaled and tugged more vigorously at his fast-wilting cravat.

Mystified by his reaction, Jessica waited a trifle impatiently for him to decide whether he would speak. His father was a clergyman, she knew, and Mr. Headley had once told her that it was his uncle who had funded his education. A merchant who had married a woman distantly connected to the Staffords, it was the uncle who had gained Mr. Headley his living in Bleithewood Village. Of his mother, however, he had said nothing.

"Mother is a good woman," he exclaimed at last, avoiding Jessica's eye as he spoke. "But she's not had, ah, well, you know, advantages. She's never come to visit me before, nor ever met, ah, anyone," he added, glancing quickly at Jessica and as quickly away.

That half-chagrined, half-embarrassed look revealed as much to Jessica as his words, and though she faulted Mr. Headley for feeling he must excuse his mother to her, a relative stranger, she also felt a certain sympathy for him.

"I shall be very happy to meet your mother, Mr. Headley," she assured him firmly. "It is she who reared you, after all, and the proof of her person is in the results of her efforts."

Had she conferred a knighthood upon him, Jessica was certain Mr. Headley could not have turned a more rapt look upon her. Grasping her hand between both of his, he pumped it up and down. "The beauty of your lineaments, Miss Winslow, is but a pallid reflection of the beauty of your soul. It is an honor, an honor, indeed, to have met you." And before Jessica could avoid the gesture, Mr. Headley raised her hand to his lips.

"I am interrupting, I see."

Mr. Headley let go Jessica's hand as if it were a hot brick. "My lord! Ah! No! No, of course you could not interrupt. You honor us with your presence. Miss Winslow and I were only discussing the St. Barnabas Day festivities. We've everything well in hand."

"As I could see," Roxham observed, flicking a look at Jessica.

He'd not entirely regained his color and he was a trifle thinner than he'd been before his accident, but on this afternoon, dressed informally in a loose cambric shirt that fit comfortably over his bandages and a pair of the finest buckskins, Jessica did not think one could say his looks were in any way diminished. He was still tall, possessed of a pair of quite unusual amber eyes, and effortlessly commanded attention.

"We have decided after a great deal of careful consideration to locate the festivities on the south lawn, where people will be less apt to trample Bleithewood's most magnificent gardens. I recall last year . . ." As Mr. Headley rambled on, Jessica returned the earl's sardonic gaze with what she hoped was one of cool indifference. After all, there was no reason Mr. Headley should not be kissing her hand, and she would not be made to feel guilty. She was not poison, however much the earl might think she was.

". . . and, of course, Miss Winslow has been marvelously helpful, my lord. She is so very capable."

The earl arched an eyebrow at the vicar. "Oh, I don't doubt that, Headley," he allowed before looking back to Jessica. "Miss Winslow is capable of a great many things, or so I have found."

"Yes . . ." Mr. Headley, his head bobbing, darted an anxious look from the earl to Jessica. Seeing her composed expression, however, his uncertainty over the earl's tone resolved itself into a smile. "Yes!" His head bobbed more vigorously. "Just so, my lord, Miss Winslow is most capable."

He cast a fond look at Jessica before recollecting he'd other appointments to keep. "I must go now, Miss Winslow, my lord." Mr. Headley bowed to each of them. "Mrs. Multaney is expecting me shortly. I shall return in two days, Miss Winslow, if that suits you?'' Jessica said it did, and after making Roxham another, deeper bow, the vicar departed.

The moment the door closed behind him, Jessica rounded angrily upon the earl, but he'd been watching her, not the vicar, and spoke before she could. "What strides you are making, Miss Winslow. I do believe the little vicar is in your grasp.''

"How easy it is for you to mock," Jessica cried, her eyes glowing bright blue. "You, who are safe and secure with your vast wealth and established position! I cannot imagine why it is you concern yourself with the unworthy likes of Mr. Headley and me. Why did you go out of your way to have him doubt me?''

Roxham lifted his brow innocently. "I merely said you were capable of many things, which is true.''

"I thought it was only the gentlemen of the neighborhood you considered beyond my touch," Jessica blazed back at him, ignoring his reply. "I did not realize you had placed even the vicar off-limits to me.''

A great many unredressed grievances rankling, Jessica did not, perhaps could not, stop. Balling her hands into fists, she leaned forward to challenge the earl. "What grounds have you, may I ask? It cannot be that his family is above mine. They are certainly not. And he knows very well I am a 'mere' companion, not a guest of the house. Nor is Mr. Headley's position in society above my capabilities. I think I could carry out the duties of a vicar's wife as well as any.''

Seeing Roxham's brow lift, Jessica made an angry frustrated sound. "Oh! I suppose you think I am too depraved. Well, it seems rather late for you to have second thoughts. What else did you intend by throwing me in company with him almost daily?''

"Forgive me, Miss Winslow, but I fear you much mistake the matter." He carefully straightened his unwrinkled sleeve before favoring her again with his ironic gaze. "I neither requested you to work with Mr. Headley, nor did I accept the request in your stead.''

Jessica did not believe he lacked all responsibility and said so. "You were not so direct perhaps. But I would

136

wager it was at your suggestion Lady Mary devised her matchmaking scheme. You would rid your house of me and the problems I pose while you would secure me close to Lady Bea."

"If I wished to rid my house of you, Miss Winslow," Roxham replied coldly, "I would have Moreton show you the door. I am not the author of any scheme to throw you into Headley's company in the vague hope he might take it into his head to relieve me of your presence."

Though she held Roxham's gaze, Jessica flushed. He'd succeeded in making her notion seem absurd. He would never be so indirect, she saw that; he might even look upon a marriage between her and the vicar without favor. As Mrs. Headley, she would remain in the neighborhood, where her pernicious influence might still pose a threat.

Jessica's shoulders sagged a fraction. She'd not anticipated that even the course of wedding the vicar would be denied her. "You mean to tell Mr. Headley your objections to me, then?" she asked, unable to keep the strain from her low voice.

Roxham swore beneath his breath. That she should be so dismayed at the thought of losing Headley caught him off-guard. "No." An image of Headley clasping Miss Winslow to him as his wife came and was quickly sent on its way. "What can it matter to me if you are not the saint Headley obviously imagines you to be?" Roxham shrugged negligently and watched as Jessica's eyes came alive with outrage. Angry, she did not seem the least vulnerable. "He's a grown man and must be responsible for himself. You may have at the good vicar without hindrance from me, Miss Winslow." He bowed with insulting largesse.

"How very kind of you, my lord." Her eyes dealt Roxham the slap she wished she could give him in earnest. "Good day." She curtsied gracefully and in a swirl of skirts left the Earl of Roxham to languish in his library undisturbed.

14

Hearing a lark break into song, Jessica caught her breath. Still as a statue, she listened rapt until it trilled its last clear note, and then she silently gave thanks to Lady Bea for giving her the afternoon to herself.

"I've told Appleby to prepare you a basket, Jess, so you needn't argue. The matter is decided," the older lady had said in her gruff way. "With Helena coming, I shall be maliciously occupied for the entire afternoon, and you need a respite from the lot of us here at Bleithewood. You are looking a trifle strained, if I may be so bold as to note it . . ."

Jessica had glanced away from Lady Bea's searching gaze to knot her thread. When she looked up, she had managed to sketch a smile and reply lightly that, if she did indeed look strained, it was only because she had the burden of attending to the twins' growing menagerie of infirm pets. First there had been the bird, then the puppy, and now they'd taken under their wing a kitten Mother Cat did not seem to want.

"Those infernal children!" Lady Bea shook her head and with a wave of her hand sent Jessica on her way. "What you need is more than an hour to yourself, I'll be bound."

Lady Beatrice had been quite right, as usual, Jessica decided as she followed a beam of sunlight that had found its way through the thick canopy of leaves. Landing upon a bed of wild woodland asters, it deepened their yellow to a tawny gold.

She walked on abruptly. She did not care for the color. It reminded her of Roxham, and Jessica had quite enough of him at dinner now that both he and Lady Bea were well enough to descend.

The courteous but utterly impersonal manner he

adopted toward her in company was almost as loathsome as the angrily suspicious attitude he displayed in private.

She might as well have been a statue, the way he looked through her. The thought chafed, but Jessica did not care to think on why it did. Instead, she continued with her catalogue of Roxham's sins.

Only once had the earl looked at her with any emotion, and that had been when Ned's name was mentioned in general conversation. In reply to Lady Mary's query as to where the younger Stafford was just then, Andy had spoken up to say he only hoped "old Ned" was feeling more the thing wherever he was. "The boy seemed a bit off his feed before he departed for the classical climes."

Jessica had stared quite determinedly at the succulent spring lamb upon her plate. She placed a bite upon her fork and lifted it to her lips.

"Ned will recover his spirits in time. He has a strong constitution, but the scars he carries, though they might not show to curious eyes, are deep nonetheless."

Jessica returned her fork to her plate, the bite upon it untouched. She did not turn her head, but still her cheeks heated. Roxham, after making his pronouncement, had fixed his gaze upon her. She could feel it, dark and brooding, upon her. Her head tilted defiantly, she reached for a sip of wine and allowed the footman to take her plate away entirely.

At that rate, she was likely to lose two stone and wither away entirely, she told herself grimly. She had not eaten more that night, and was conscious that her appetite had not fully recovered since.

She must leave Bleithewood, but though she accepted her future course, she'd not made any push to find a new position. She'd not written the agency in London where she had gone before, nor had she discreetly tried to pump Lady Bea and Mrs. Dalymede for the names of elderly ladies in need of a young companion.

She was relying, it seemed, on Mr. Headley; yet, truthfully, she'd not exerted herself to bring the good vicar to the point of asking for her hand either. She knew the ways a lady could sweeten a man's attitude toward her. She'd watched Sally Renwick at work, after all, but somehow she could not bring herself to bat her lashes at Mr. Headley and tell him he was just the sort of strong gentleman she'd always dreamed of.

Impatient suddenly with her heavy mood, Jessica kicked a rock that had found its way onto the gravel, and she had the satisfaction of seeing it sail a good way into the woods. She must treat Roxham in the same way, she decided, amusing herself with an image of Roxham arching through the air after receiving a well-placed kick from her sharp toe. If she could not do so in fact, she could at least dismiss him from her thoughts and enjoy her afternoon to herself as Lady Bea had ordered.

Her brave resolve made, Jessica took the first step toward realizing it: she lifted her head to look at the world around her and found to her surprise she'd entirely traversed the woods. Only a short distance away she could see the road to Bleithewood. A strange sound caused her to look more intently in its direction.

Not particularly wide, it separated Bleithewood from the squire's estate, and in the grass on the far side, Jessica made out the figure of a woman. She was kneeling over a form, moaning.

"What has happened, ma'am?" Jessica asked, her concerned gaze shifting from the woman to what she realized with horror was a small, extremely thin child who seemed to have collapsed, for her blue-veined eyelids were closed.

"Ma'am? May I be of assistance?" Jessica persisted, reaching out to touch the woman, who did not seem aware of her presence.

Startled, the woman jerked her head and cried hoarsely, "It be my Carley, ma'am."

"Has she taken ill?" Jessica knelt by the child and lifted her tiny wrist. The child's pulse was not strong, but it was steady. Her brow was very warm. "I am Jessica Winslow from Bleithewood, and I should like to help. Has Carley a fever?"

The woman, who was thin to the point of gauntness and clad only in a faded, often-mended cotton shift, moaned faintly. "Aye, the fever. There be little food . . ."

"Your child is ill from hunger?" Jessica demanded when the woman's low voice trailed away.

The woman nodded slowly and Jessica wondered if her dazed manner might be attributed to a lack of adequate food. "The vicar . . ." the woman sighed, shaking her head. "I 'oped to see 'im, 'oped if I showed 'im my Carley, 'e'd lend us a bit more from the relief roll."

"Well," Jessica said briskly, for she'd decided the woman was not capable of thinking what should be done, "I do not believe either of us can carry your child into Bleithewood Village. Do you live far from here? If not, I can manage to carry her there. I shall leave you the food I have in my basket, and I shall return as soon as possible with more."

Jessica rose and lifted the child, though the woman said nothing. "You can manage the basket, I think," she directed, and finally it seemed the woman understood, for her eyes widened. "Where do we go, Mrs. . . .?"

The woman straightened, gaping at Jessica. "Crenshawe," she whispered. He eyes fixed fearfully on Jessica, she reached slowly for the basket as if she thought there must be some trick.

Her timidity wrenched at Jessica's heart. "Yes, good," she encouraged Mrs. Crenshawe quietly as she adjusted her painfully light burden in her arms.

Mrs. Crenshawe, her hand tight on the basket's handle, then pointed down a path that led onto the squire's estate. "We live down 'ere."

As they walked, Jessica encouraged the woman to speak of her predicament. It was not easy. Mrs. Crenshawe was a woman of few words and seemed, at first, unable to countenance that her troubles could truly be of interest to a stranger.

Jessica persisted, however, and succeeded at last in learning that Mrs. Crenshawe and her five children were tenants of the squire. "With my Tom dead, it's 'ard to meet the rent," the woman confided in her slow way as they walked. "The squire's rents are 'igh, 'igher than t'other landlords 'ereabouts. I weren't left with much after the winter and all." The woman stared into the distance with large, fearful eyes. "No 'un wants to 'ire on my

141

boy, Jem. Say 'e's like his da, shiftylike an' all. We've na' a farthin', and the vicar says we 'ad all we can from 'is relief.''

They rounded a bend in the overgrown path and a small, rude cottage came into view. Even from a distance Jessica could see the bare spots in its thatched roof. It would offer some protection from the elements, but not a great deal.

The floor of the one-room cottage was made of dirt, but it was clean, she noted. Beside the wall facing the room's only window was a single pallet made of straw. When Jessica laid little Carley upon it, she awakened and began to whimper pitifully. While Mrs. Crenshawe made some ineffectual efforts to comfort the child, Jessica soaked a piece of Mrs. Appleby's bread in some cider the cook had included in the basket.

The child was persuaded to take a few bites, but she had not the strength to eat more. Once her eyes closed again, Jessica rose to go. "I shall go to Bleithewood and fetch more food," she told Mrs. Crenshawe.

The poor woman stared up at her, clearly at a loss as to how to respond to such unlooked-for generosity. "You're so good," she whispered at last.

Jessica flushed. "Nonsense," she returned stoutly. "It's the least I can do."

A noise at the door caused her to turn and she found three young children, all thin and dressed in dingy garments, gazing wide-eyed at her. She smiled, but they only stared solemnly.

They looked from Jessica to the basket upon the table, then to their mother. When she jerked her head in a nod, the three scrambled to it, grabbing at the contents until Mrs. Crenshawe went to dole out the bread, cheese, and cold meats evenly. "Jem'll need a bit as well," she said, setting a portion aside for her fifth child.

As if on cue, the door opened and a boy entered. Slight and thin, he looked in size to be about eight years of age. Only his eyes, looking out upon the world with an unsettling sharpness, indicated he might be older than that.

'' 'Tis a lady from the earl's,'' Mrs.Crenshawe said by

142

way of introduction. Jem doffed a battered cap, though his too-wise eyes asked a question. "Carley fell down sick in the road and she brought 'er home. Yon is 'er basket, too."

Jem nodded his head more respectfully and looked to where his brothers and sisters were eating.

"I am Jessica Winslow from Bleithewood, where I am companion to Lady Beatrice Carstairs," Jessica explained, addressing the boy with the dignity she'd have accorded the man of the family, for despite his years, it was obvious he was just that. "I must go now, but I shall return," she added rather grimly.

"I think your little girl will do well enough with some food, Mrs. Crenshawe," Jessica said when the woman accompanied her out of the low-roofed cottage. "But she will need food regularly to grow properly. What will you do if Jem cannot find work?"

Mrs. Crenshawe made a hopeless gesture with her shoulders. "I dunno. Per'aps Jem and me'll find work in Birmin'ham town. But I fear to go." She shook her head as tears appeared in her eyes. "I 'ad a sister there, and all her little 'uns died of bad lungs before they was full grown."

Very nearly in tears herself, Jessica patted the woman's rail-thin hand. "Don't despair yet, Mrs. Crenshawe," she advised gently. "I shall talk to the vicar and the earl, and we shall see what may be done."

"Jem be a good worker," Mrs. Crenshawe said, a spark lighting in her pale eyes for the first time.

When Jessica returned to the manor, she learned that she had only just missed Mr. Headley. He'd come by unexpectedly and had chanced to encounter Lady Mary, who had had the happy notion to invite the vicar for dinner the following evening. "I thought it is only fair to ask him to dine, he was so disappointed to miss you," she told Jessica with a pleased smile.

Any other time Jessica would have been undone to learn she must eat side by side with Mr. Headley while Roxham looked on, but just then all she could think was that Lady Mary's meddling had given her opportunity to see the vicar sooner than she'd expected. As a result, she smiled gratefully, to Lady Mary's particular satisfaction.

Unfortunately she was not able to see Roxham as soon as she'd hoped. He had chosen that afternoon for his first outing. Accompanied by Andrew, he had driven out in the carriage to inspect progress made on a drainage project.

Jessica instructed Moreton to tell his master that she wished to see him, then decided to apply to Lady Beatrice for permission to take broth and bread to the Crenshawes that afternoon.

"But, of course, child," the older lady exclaimed at once when Jessica recounted all she'd seen. "It's a frightful shame they should be in so sad a condition, and I lay the fault at the squire's door. He has too much greed to have a care for his tenants."

Mrs. Appleby, a warmhearted North Country woman, was not the least put out when she was asked to supply bread and soup for a family of six. "You've a kind heart, miss," she said, fixing Jessica with an approving look. "Not many's would care 'bout a parcel o' poor tenants."

"And not many cooks would take so kindly to supplying their supper, Mrs. Appleby," Jessica returned the compliment with a smile.

"Get along with you now." Mrs. Appleby shooed Jessica back to Lady Beatrice's rooms. "We've a boy goin' to the village. He can take the victuals hisself."

In Lady Bea's rooms, Jessica was too restless to read or play a hand of piquet. One ear tuned for the sound of Roxham's carriage, she tidied the already straightened room while Lady Beatrice played solitaire and watched her with a faint smile.

Two hours, nearly an eternity later, they heard Andrew calling something to the twins, and almost in the next instant a footman came to say the earl awaited her in his study.

Lady Bea chuckled as Jessica flew out the door. "I vow the lad has responded to her request for an audience with remarkable speed. Didn't even wait to wash the dust from his face. I do wonder if he is that concerned with my health?" With no one in the room to answer her question,

Lady Bea answered herself, laughing aloud. "No, and I'll be bound he only remembers me when she comes into sight."

15

In the earl's study were a pair of aged, richly colored Oriental rugs, but Jessica's eyes went at once to Roxham, who awaited her with his broad shoulders propped against the mantel, a glass of claret in his hand.

His outing had done him good. Along the line of his strong cheekbones there was healthy color, and his eyes gleamed with life. Jessica could not help but admire the figure he cut in his bottle-green coat and tight-fitting buckskins—and that, though he frowned.

"Nothing is amiss with Aunt Bea, I hope?" he demanded as she closed the door behind her.

Jessica shook her head. "No, my lord. I wished to see you about another matter altogether." She waited a moment for the earl to signify she might proceed, and when he lifted his brow as if in query, she began.

At first, she was aware of the conflict that lay between them; indeed she found it difficult to meet Roxham's eye when she recalled their last interview and how insulting he'd been to her on the subject of Mr. Headley. But, mindful of the importance of her endeavor, Jessica forced herself to face the earl and to do so without betraying even a trace of diffidence.

"I came upon a quite dreadful sight when I was out walking today, my lord," she said straightforwardly in her low voice. "A little girl of about five years of age lay collapsed upon the road to Bleithewood, faint and feverish with hunger."

As she spoke, describing the incident and then relating the full dimensions of the Crenshawes' plight, Jessica lost all her initial reserve. She had no time to think of her, by comparison, insignificant quarrel with Roxham when she told how Carley had lacked the strength to eat anything but a small piece of bread and how there were no funds to buy seed to grow the food the family needed just to live, never mind the crops they must give up to the squire for rent.

"Perhaps the worst shame is the old look in young Jem's eyes, however." Jessica shook her head as she recalled the boy's sharp gaze. "He's been given a man's responsibilities too early in life, though I believe he would make a fine worker. He has a dignity quite beyond his years."

All her sympathy for young Jem and his family was mirrored in her eyes, and Roxham, looking into them, was reminded of a tarn he had seen one summer in Scotland. He'd never thought to see such a rich shade of blue again.

"In all, they are in dire straits, my lord," Jessica finished her little speech by saying.

Roxham tossed down a swallow of his claret, then observed neutrally, "It's our good vicar who oversees the poor relief."

At once a faint line creased Jessica's brow. "Yes, I know," she replied. "It was to Mr. Headley Mrs. Crenshawe was going when I came upon her. It seems there is some problem there, and I intend to speak to him."

Jessica dismissed the problem of the vicar with a shrug. She would face Mr. Headley when she came to him; just now she knew she must concentrate entirely upon Roxham.

"But the poor relief is a temporary solution at any rate. I was hopeful that you might . . ." she hesitated, aware all at once she intended to ask a great deal. "Actually, I hoped you might take them on as tenants here at Bleithewood," she admitted in a rush, and before Roxham could reject her idea, she hurried to list all her good reasons. "Your rents are lower than the squire's, you know, and I think you would be more inclined to lend them a hand until their crops come in—"

Roxham cut her off, shaking his head. "I've all the tenants I need now."

"But the Crenshawes would work very hard. I know they would!"

"Undoubtedly they would try their best," Roxham allowed. "Though how a famished woman with only five equally famished children could satisfy even the most lenient landlord, I cannot imagine. But it makes no matter," he insisted steadily. "If I were to take them on, I should have to throw someone off to make room for them."

"But Mrs. Crenshawe is watching her children starve," Jessica cried, certain there must be room somewhere on the enormous estate for the little family.

The earl exhaled in an exasperated rush and pushed himself away from the fireplace to emphasize his point. "There is no room at Bleithewood, Miss Winslow. All the land here is spoken for. I cannot simply take a piece of land from men who have worked hard to earn their places here."

Jessica bit her lip in disappointment and the earl found himself adding in a dry tone not unlaced with sympathy, "I know it seems a vast estate with ample room to tuck away a family of six, but in truth the land is all spoken for and has been for quite some time. However," he added, and watched hope flare in her eyes, "you've my permission to apply to Mrs. Appleby for the food to supply their needs—within reason—until their situation is resolved in some fashion or other."

"Ah, thank you," Jessica replied gratefully as she debated whether to admit she'd already taken the liberty to do as much without his permission.

The issue was decided when Roxham noted the line of guilty color rising in her cheeks. "So, you anticipated my permission, I see."

Jessica colored more fiercely, though she could not decide if he was angry with her. "Their situation was such that I applied to Lady Beatrice—"

"And she is putty in your hands," Roxham finished for her, his brow arching. "Nor, I imagine, did Mrs. Appleby protest that she must have my express permission to deal freely with my food. I have it on good authority you could ask well nigh anything of that plump

147

lady and she would do her best to please you. You, I have been told, are the one responsible for the strawberries we are presently enjoying on virtually a daily basis.''

Jessica did not deny it. She had confessed to a penchant for the fresh, sweet berries, and they had, indeed, been served sometimes in pies, others times in custards or tarts, and on occasion in cream at least once a day ever since.

''I gave Mrs. Appleby an ointment for her grandchild when he was ill this winter, and she has treated me very kindly since,'' Jessica explained cautiously as she searched Roxham's expression. She did not want the cook to suffer for her rash actions, but she could not read his mood precisely. His gaze was impassive, as if the issue yet hung in the balance. ''I hope you will not be put out with Mrs. Appleby over this matter, my lord,'' she pleaded, taking a direct approach. ''I did not tell her I had not spoken to you, only that Lady Beatrice had given her approval.''

''You needn't look so anxious, Miss Winslow.'' Roxham's smile was only a faint one, but it had the power to relieve Jessica enormously until he added, lifting his glass in salute, ''Rest assured I know precisely where to lay the blame.''

Jessica looked a little daunted by that, but as he said nothing more, she allowed herself to hope he was not unreasonably angry and ventured to return to the subject of the Crenshawes. ''If you cannot take the Crenshawes as tenants, my lord, then could you hire Jem to do work on the estate? He is young yet, but I think determined and could surely do something in the gardens or the stables. It would mean so little to you, but so much to him.'' Jessica paused, but when the earl did not speak at once, she added, ''Please.''

Roxham knew that pleading did not come easily to her, and it was on the tip of his tongue to observe he'd never had a woman importune him so fervently on behalf of people completely unrelated to her. In his experience women only said ''please'' in that urgent way when they desired something for themselves, be it a new bracelet, a new gown, or a night in his bed.

148

He bit back the observation. It would be absurd to flatter the girl so. If she was altruistic now, she was, at other times, when her own interests were at stake, as hard and devious as the worst of her sex could be.

To the others at Bleithewood she'd only shown her good side. He'd even heard Mary sing the girl's praises for the time she spent with the twins. But he'd encountered her other side and seen its effects. And he was determined not to forget it.

"I shall have to see about the boy," he said, his voice made harsh by his thoughts. "And now, if you are finished saving the neighborhood, Miss Winslow, I've other matters needing my attention."

Jessica saw she'd lost Roxham's sympathy, but she could not understand how, though she thought it possible he had refused her simply because it was she who asked. The thought stung her deeply.

"I am sorry to have discommoded you with my trifles, my lord," she retorted before she could think better of angering him. "I see I shall have to rely upon Mr. Headley alone to play the Good Samaritan."

"I am surprised at you, Miss Winslow." Roxham looked down into her angrily sparkling eyes with a mocking smile. "First, you have lied. You are not the least sorry to have discommoded me. You only regret that you did not gain your ends." He was odiously right, and Jessica had no response to make but to tilt her head defiantly.

His brow lifted. "Second, you have been foolish enough to antagonize me when you ought to be doing everything in your power to turn me up sweet." The impossibility of that caused her eyes to flash, and Roxham actually laughed. "Last, Miss Winslow, I find myself amazed to learn you view your swain with such rosy optimism. Perhaps you are in love after all. But, as Mr. Headley is coming tomorrow for dinner, we shall have the opportunity to remark then the sort of Samaritan he is."

Jessica disregarded the earl's suggestion that Mr. Headley could not be brought around on the subject of the Crenshawes. He was merely trying to put her out of countenance.

Nonetheless she made a mental note to get the vicar off alone at some time. She did not care to have the earl looking on while she did her pleading. He would be too distractingly amused, she knew.

Even the thought of conversing generally with Mr. Headley while the earl stood by did not appeal, but she steeled herself to appear in the red salon with good grace by assuring herself, repeatedly, that Lady Mary would have the good sense not to matchmake with a heavy hand. Surely she would see neither Jessica nor Mr. Headley would care to feel forced into affection.

Jessica had reasoned correctly enough. Lady Mary was not, in normal circumstances, given to promoting anything with an excess of energy. Unfortunately the circumstances were extraordinary.

Only the day before, Andrew had refused more adamantly than ever to consider Marianne Multaney for a bride, declaring in a painfully loud voice that the girl was no better than a horse with two legs. Unless he were denied the opportunity of comparing poor Marianne with Miss Winslow on a daily basis, Lady Mary quite despaired of ever seeing him securely established.

Accordingly, the moment Jessica entered the salon, she made a great to-do over uniting her with the vicar. "Now, my dear Miss Winslow"—Lady Mary went forward to draw Jessica toward the couch where Mr. Headley was sitting—"You must sit here by the vicar. You two must be the greatest friends now. You have worked so very closely together these last weeks and we do want Mr. Headley to feel at home."

With a sinking feeling, Jessica thought to protest that she must stay close to Lady Beatrice, but already Lady Mary was leading her aunt toward a chair by Roxham where he lounged near the fire.

Short of being rude, Jessica had little choice but to take the seat beside Mr. Headley and greet him cordially. The vicar responded in like vein, and was only just saying how truly generous it was of Lady Mary to invite him to join the "sacred" circle of the family when his hostess rejoined them and proceeded to describe with a great many arch looks all the "quite wonderfully clever" things Jessica had accomplished since coming to Bleithewood.

Mr. Headley, far from resenting such an obvious ploy, rejoined by listing all the fine traits he had discerned in Miss Winslow, and Jessica was left to blush unhappily while he cast her rapt smiles.

Rapt and possessive, Jessica thought uneasily, and she found herself wishing Mr. Headley would not behave as if an alliance between them was a foregone conclusion.

Dinner was no better. Even Lady Bea spoke up to remark upon her "dearest" companion's soothing touch, and when Jessica shot her a sinking look, the older lady only chuckled delightedly.

Jessica could only be grateful that Andrew dined out with friends. He would likely have made matters worse by extolling her looks.

Nor was she to be given a respite after the dessert course was served. Flicking an idle glance her way, Roxham gave it as his opinion that the men should join the ladies in the drawing room without delay.

Mr. Headley rushed to agree. Though he admired the earl prodigiously, he had never felt entirely at ease with his powerful host. "To be sure, it is an excellent idea, my lord," he exclaimed grandly, his face rather flushed with all the wine he'd had to drink. "After all, the ladies are the light of our lives, and to be away even for a little is to be cast into darkness." He beamed happily and glanced at Jessica.

She, mindful of the request she had yet to make of him, managed a smile, though she was afraid it was a weak effort. If so, the vicar was not given much opportunity to note her reticence.

Lady Beatrice, in a loud voice, drew his attention to her. "Come, lend me your stout arm, Headley." She waved him toward her. "I shall rely on you, if I may. These others have to shoulder me about so often, they are quite hagged to death."

Leaving Jessica to her own devices, Mr. Headley hastened at once to Lady Bea's side. "I should be honored, my lady," he assured her.

When Livy fell into step with Lady Mary to request—futilely it seemed from her pouting expression—that she be allowed to visit Kate the next day, Jessica sent up a word of thanks that she was, for a moment, to be left alone to regroup.

"Miss Winslow . . . ." She'd forgotten Roxham. He appeared at her elbow, bringing her into step with him as he leaned close to whisper in her ear, "I never realized before what an utter paragon you are."

"Oh, leave off," she grumbled, entirely out of patience. "You know very well Lady Mary is only trying to be rid of me."

"Surely you are not ungrateful," he chided, assuming a look of great astonishment. "I thought Mary furthered your part with the vicar amazingly. Truly, by the time the strawberry tart was served, I was not at all certain whether he would not choose to eat you instead, he was regarding you with such enthusiasm."

The thought made Jessica slightly ill, but she declined to give Roxham the satisfaction of so much as a cool look. He eyed her lovely but unrevealing profile a moment, then asked idly, "By the by, you didn't have the opportunity to raise the subject of the Crenshawes, did you? In between the rounds of your praises."

Wondering glumly if she would ever have the opportunity to get the vicar to herself, Jessica merely shook her head and did not notice the satisfied gleam her answer brought to Roxham's eyes.

When they reached the drawing room, she set off at once to corner Mr. Headley, but everyone seemed intent upon foiling her efforts. First Lady Bea must end an argument with Mr. Headley as to whether or not young women should be taught Latin. He saw no use for it, and she thought it just the sort of training they required to think clearly.

Then Livy must come to ask Jessica if she would help put up her hair the night of her supper dance and to discuss possible styles.

Frustrated, Jessica was just intending to ask Mr. Headley if he cared to hear her play the piano, something she did not do with any great skill, but Roxham prevented her.

Strolling over with two glasses of port, he handed one to the vicar, who stammered his thanks at having the earl serve him. Then Roxham draped one arm indolently along the mantel and fixed Mr. Headley with a curious look. "Miss Winslow has encountered the Crenshawes, Headley. Has she had the opportunity to tell you of it?"

"My dear!" Mr. Headley cried, turning solicitously to Jessica. "I am so sorry you had to endure those rascals. They have been a blight on the parish for years."

Jessica suppressed an oath as she looked from the earl's suspiciously bland expression to Mr. Headley's anxious frown. She knew very well that Roxham had not raised the subject of the Crenshawes merely to make matters easier for her.

Her hesitation was unnoticed by anyone save the earl, for Lady Mary cried out in tones of disgust, "The Crenshawes! Why, the family is merely a pack of thieves and poachers."

"Nonsense, Mary!" Lady Beatrice entered the fray with customary relish. "They were poor but honorable enough until they lost their land. They couldn't manage to keep it when the squire enclosed the common lands they had depended upon for ages to help make ends meet. I didn't know they'd ended by being Multaney's tenants. What macabre irony that now they must pay rent to work the lands they once used for nothing."

When no one seemed prepared to argue with Lady Beatrice, Jessica broke into the ensuing silence to tell Mr. Headley of her meeting with Mrs. Crenshawe. "Without her husband to help her, she is experiencing great difficulty. I found it truly appalling to see how hungry the children were. Yet the poor woman says she would prefer to stay on as Multaney's tenant than to go into Birmingham to find work in the factories. She was most piteous when she talked of the horrors of taking the children into those places."

Jessica smiled hopefully at the vicar. "I know she has benefited from the generosity of the parish in the past, Mr. Headley, but I hoped to persuade you to extend her some additional assistance, as their situation is so wretched."

But Mr. Headley shook his head at once. "No, no, my dear! It is not possible. It would be a most unfortunate precedent to set, and the Crenshawes are, ah . . ." He cast an uneasy glance at Lady Beatrice, "Well, let us say they have received more than their share of the public relief. There are others who are more deserving and are in need also."

"But her youngest child is fainting from hunger," Jessica protested, her patience severely strained by the vicar's unyielding attitude.

Mr. Headley's response was to smile at her as if she were a pretty but untutored child. "Now, Miss Winslow, you mustn't upset yourself." He actually patted her hand. "I know you are generous by nature—did not Lady Mary say so?—but these people are not worthy of your sympathies. We cannot help everyone, and they are accustomed to having less than we. If Mrs. Crenshawe must move to Birmingham, then she must."

Jessica glanced to Roxham, but she saw she would receive no assistance from him. His expression was too innocent by half, and she suspected he was being well and truly entertained by her frustration with the vicar.

Well, she thought, if she must do it alone, then she must! She looked again at Mr. Headley, forcing a patient smile to her lips. "I think you have the wrong impression of Mrs. Crenshawe, sir. She is making a most courageous effort. I beg of you to visit her, at least."

"Visit the Crenshawes?" Lady Mary cried, so scandalized she did not think to fear Lady Bea's sharp tongue.

Mr. Headley shot his ally a quick, confident smile that set Jessica's teeth on edge. "Miss Winslow cannot know how rude their hovel is, Lady Mary." After apologizing for her, he turned back to Jessica with a smile that was fatherly in its patience. "It would be quite beneath my dignity, my dear, to visit such people," he explained. "Why! I do not imagine they even possess a chair. Some things are just not done. There are standards to maintain."

Jessica, her jaw set tightly, regarded Mr. Headley in

such a way that he reddened. "Believe me—" he began, but Jessica cut him off.

"I have been to the Crenshawes' hovel, Mr. Headley," she informed him coolly, and was unmoved by his gasp of astonishment. "Yes, it is rude, it is poor, and it is plain as well. They do not, as you fear, have a chair, only a single rough bench. They've mud floors . . ." Here Jessica paused, for she'd been about to say it had looked to her as if the mud had been mixed with ox's blood to bind it, but she thought better of being quite so forthcoming. It would do for her purposes to say only, "And they've a thatched roof that, I imagine, leaks even in light rains. But, for all that, the room is as neat as a pin. Perhaps it is not difficult to keep a room without any food in it free of crumbs, but with five children one might expect some untidiness. There is none.

"However," Jessica continued, taking a deep breath, "if you cannot be persuaded to show compassion for those less fortunate than you, then you cannot, and I see no purpose in continuing this conversation. It can only be tedious in the extreme to everyone else."

His complexion an alarming shade of red, Mr. Headley stared in shock, scarcely able to credit that the girl regarding him with contempt sparking her eyes was the beautiful, graceful girl he had come to know over the past months. The Miss Winslow he knew surely did not harbor such radical sentiments, nor would she ever lecture a man—her vicar, yet—in such a public, embarrassing manner.

But it was Miss Winslow who treated him to a view of her pure profile and made not the least effort to rescue the awkward situation she had created. The sudden silence seeming unbearably loud, Mr. Headley turned to his hostess, his throat working as he searched in vain for some remark.

Lady Mary was no help at all. Unlike the vicar, she'd long suspected Miss Winslow's strong temperament, but now, faced with a display of it, she could only utter a helpless, "Oh my" and reach for her glass of ratafia.

For a long tense moment, the only sound Jessica heard was a muffled choking emanating from Livy's area of the room. The girl had put her hand over her mouth as if she coughed, but the sparkle in her eyes gave her away, and Jessica quickly looked away. The worst thing she could do now would be to laugh aloud at poor Mr. Headley's astounded expression.

She regretted making a scene. She'd no wish to cause unpleasantness, but she could not regret her sentiments. Mr. Headley's attitude was unforgivably narrow, and she realized she could never ally herself to the man in marriage, no matter how greatly she might long for security.

As to Roxham, she did not consider glancing at him. He had suspected what the vicar's response would be, but Jessica felt too disheartened by her failure to improve the Crenshawes' condition in any significant way to give him his due.

Had she not been so cowardly, Jessica would have seen that Roxham's eyes quite lacked the triumph she expected to see gleaming in them. There was amusement shining in them, it was true, as he looked from her composed expression to Headley's undone one. But even a casual observer would have noted there was, as well, a spark of admiration.

But as it was to Lady Beatrice that Jessica looked, she saw only unqualified approval. "Bravo, child," the older lady applauded, clearly delighted. "I couldn't have put the thing better myself. You do me a world of good, as you must know."

The others—but for the earl, who remained preoccupied—stirred as the tension was broken. Mr. Headley reached for his glass and Lady Mary gathered herself together to make some remark on the weather, to which he replied at exaggerated length.

Eventually the tea tray was brought, and Jessica was visibly grateful when Lady Bea, her cup enjoyed, signaled the evening was at an end. "Come, lead me away to my bed, my dear," she said, then added mischievously, "It's time I retired if I'm to be fresh for this business of philanthropy."

Jessica just suppressed a smile and when she rose she managed to bid everyone, including Mr. Headley, a civil good night before she gave Lady Bea her arm.

The vicar did not linger, but rose to go only minutes later. When the door closed behind him, Roxham quickly held up his hand. "Nay, Mary!" He shook his head at his cousin, who had turned a most stricken look upon him. "There is no use your asking me what the prospects are now for your matchmaking hopes. I've no notion."

"Well, I am afraid I know very well," Lady Mary wailed, throwing up her hands. "They are dashed! Miss Winslow quite ruined herself with poor Mr. Headley, lecturing him in that forceful way."

"Poor Mr. Headley!" Livy sat up in her chair to glare indignantly at her mother. "The man's a fool and not worthy of Jess's little finger. I cannot imagine where you got the absurd notion that they would do together in marriage."

"But he is not unpresentable, and he has a comfortable-enough living," Lady Mary protested faintly.

Livy tossed her head in response. "Jess is a jewel worth a hundred Headleys, and I, for one, am glad she put him in his place."

Lady Mary accepted Olivia's stiff adieu and watched her flounce proudly from the room, but her thoughts were not on her daughter. After a sip of her ratafia she looked unhappily at Roxham. "The girl cannot afford such lofty notions." They both knew she did not refer to Olivia, but rather to Jessica Winslow. "She will live out her life a spinster, and she really is above such a dismal fate. She ought to be married."

"To solve your problem with Andy?"

Lady Mary nodded with a regretful sigh before adding, half to herself, "But that is not the only reason. The girl's too warm hearted not to have children of her own. I cannot think what she is about."

"I've no light to shed on the matter," Roxham said when Mary looked to him. He did not add that his inability to fathom Miss Winslow's game disturbed him, though it did. She'd as good as said she'd set her cap for the man, and he'd looked forward with grim interest to watching her retreat when Headley held firm against the Crenshawes. But in defense of a family of strangers, she'd

157

read the pompous man such a scold he was not likely ever to forgive her.

"You did keep an eye on Andy while I was bedridden?" he asked, kicking negligently at an ember that had fallen to the edge of the fire.

"He did not meet with Miss Winslow in secret, if that is your question. I cannot account for all of Andrew's days, but I can say the girl was too busy with Bea and you and the twins to carry on with him. That is not to say, I'm afraid, that the boy's not got an eye for her, however. He does not hide his admiration for her and his distaste for Marianne. Oh, Justin, I do not know what I will do with him."

Roxham smiled faintly at his cousin's pout. "He is near his majority, Mary. It may be time to allow the lad to decide for himself about his future." When Lady Mary's face fell, he said gently, "I cannot say that I should care to be shackled to Miss Multaney, but don't upset yourself with the thought. There is yet time for Andrew to come to terms with his future, whatever it may be, as long as he's not pushed into something rash."

It was not at all the speech Lady Mary wished to hear, but she was obliged to be content with it, for, after buzzing her cheek lightly, the earl took himself off to his study to enjoy his brandy and contemplate in solitude the surprise Miss Jessica Winslow had dealt him.

16

If Roxham had hoped to observe Jessica closely over the next days to determine precisely why she'd whistled the vicar down the wind, he was thwarted in his desire by both Livy and her mother. As the day of the supper dance approached, it seemed they had an unending list of tasks that could only be completed by Jessica.

There were flowers to arrange, place cards to be copied, the table setting to be decided upon, and so on. Lady

Bea gave it as her opinion that the wonder was not that Jessica had unerring taste, but that anything had ever been accomplished at Bleithewood before her arrival.

"After saying which"—Lady Bea chuckled, admiring herself in her pier glass—"I ought to be shamed to add I am pleased to my very marrow with how you've done my hair. But it is true no one else has done it so well."

Jessica only laughed at the older lady's play and went off to coil her own hair atop her head. In honor of the occasion she would wear her one "good" dress, her gray silk, and a string of pearls her father had brought her from Spain.

The simple strand could not hope to compare with the diamonds, sapphires, emeralds, and rubies sparkling at the throats of Livy's female guests Jessica saw when she and Lady Bea made their entrance after all the guests had arrived.

As they made their way across to Mrs. Dalymede where she sat among the other dowagers, Jessica took in the dazzling scene. Everyone seemed to be laughing, talking or dancing all at once. The music was a minuet, and there were at least twenty couples going through the motions of the elegant dance.

Quite suddenly she felt heavier of heart than she had in some time. Livy had been right: watching others at their play could not make for an enjoyable evening.

Roxham watched as Jessica entered, noting how heads turned in her direction, though she had only a string of undistinguished pearls to embellish the gray thing she wore on Sundays. She looked to the dance floor only once before taking her seat among the dowagers, all women who were, on the average, at least thirty years her senior. Her expression, he did not fail to see, was composed to the point of being aloof, even distant, as if what went on around her could not affect her.

"So, Justin, lad, are ye interested in her or no?"

Roxham turned a startled look upon the small, wiry man beside him and only recollected after a long moment that Angus MacFerson wished to sell him a filly. "To be sure, Angus." Summoning an image of Ned, he hardened his heart against Jessica Winslow and applied himself to what MacFerson was saying.

Jessica, too, had her thoughts turned just then, for Livy came to present Philip Verney.

He was a very fine-looking young man with an air of purpose that Jessica thought would nicely compliment Livy's lighter nature, as she said when he left them to fetch glasses of ratafia.

Livy's eyes sparkled with delight. "I vow he's almost as elegant tonight as Justin. And that is saying a great deal."

Feeling strangely reluctant, Jessica only turned to look in the direction Olivia indicated with an effort. She found the earl easily.

His lean, broad-shouldered body, elegantly displayed in the restrained black he favored, drew attention, though he stood entirely at ease, as if his finery were nothing exceptional at all. And, Jessica admitted, his dress could not compare to the man. Though he wore in his cravat a ruby of exceptional quality, it was the gleam of his sun-streaked hair and the lights in his amber eyes that she remarked.

"None of the ladies seems to mind in the least that he is not dancing in deference to his wound," Livy confided proudly. "That is Lavinia Marchant who has come now to hang on him, though he is discussing horses with Mr. MacFerson. But there." Livy's forceful gesture obliged Jessica to look again in time to observe Roxham flash a devilish smile at a pretty blond woman who batted her long lashes up at him and blushed like a schoolgirl. "It is little wonder he has her acting the ninny. He is not merely handsome and prepossessing but charming as the very devil."

"And Andrew?" Jessica asked, determined to have done with the earl. "How does he fare tonight?"

"Poor Andy," Livy cried, diverted. "Mother has come close to creating a scene because he refuses to dance with Marianne. He's danced with a dozen other girls, likely out of spite, but he is determined to avoid the Multaneys."

Philip returned then with their refreshments, and the

conversation turned to the progress made on rebuilding the stables at Roselawn. Jessica was glad to see that the young man not only spoke sensibly but that he regarded Livy with a warm twinkle in his eye. It would not do, really, if he were too serious.

Livy and Roxham had persuaded Lady Mary that the waltz could be played without causing undue scandal, and when the musicians struck up the first one of the evening, Livy tugged at Philip's hand. "Let us go, quickly, Philip! I do want to scandalize the neighborhood by being among the first to dance the waltz."

They would have to hurry if Livy were to cause scandal, Jessica thought rather wryly as she watched thirty or so other couples crowd upon the floor to be as daring.

When the music began in earnest, she found she could watch the dancers for a very little time only, and in the end she realized she could not, just then, remain in the ballroom at all. Leaning forward, she caught Lady Bea's attention. "If you can do without me, ma'am, perhaps this would be as good a time as any for me to take the twins the cakes I promised them."

Lady Bea subjected her to a shrewd look. "So you would rather escape watching others be gay than join them, miss? You could join them, you know. You are drawing attention, though you've dressed in imitation of a church mouse. I've half a mind to send you out on the dance floor in Andy's arms. What a sensation you would create."

"I believe you've the makings of a penny novel there," Jessica retorted dryly. *"The Poor Companion Defies Decorum* or some such."

Lady Bea laughed, delighted. "I think you are a silly goose," she cried. "I should be out there dancing and enjoying myself, but if you would rather go, so be it."

Grateful, for Lady Bea could have demanded she stay close by her the entire evening, Jessica gave the older woman a fond kiss upon the cheek before she went to heap a plate with custards, tarts, and Giles' favorite, seed cakes.

The children were beside themselves when she came to them, for they had not thought their aunt would give

161

her up. As they ate their treats, they told her they'd gone down to the minstrel's gallery to peek at Livy's ball. Julia reported that she had thought Justin as handsome as a royal prince, and Giles gravely gave it as his opinion that none of the ladies was as beautiful as Jessica. "Not even Livy, though she's got on a pretty dress and you haven't," he said with ruthless honest.

Jessica laughed and thanked him for the flattery.

"But it's not flattery, Jess," Julia protested. "Flattery is not quite the truth, and Nanny Budgett says you are the greatest beauty she has ever seen."

Unaccountably, the child's remark succeeded only in further lowering Jessica's already heavy spirits. Just then she had the bitter notion that her looks were nothing but a plague. Had she possessed mousy brown hair and pale eyes, she might have been dancing with the other young people her age.

Jessica excused herself soon afterward. Her thoughts were inexcusable. What she needed more than even the children's company was a breath of fresh air to blow away the self-pity into which she'd fallen.

Slipping out the library door onto the terrace, Jessica found the night cool enough to keep the guests indoors, but not so daunting that she could not enjoy it. Overhead the stars were bright and from the ballroom came the strains of a pavane.

The music enticed her, and before she realized it, her feet were executing the steps of the dance.

"I knew you would dance like an angel."

As Jessica took in the fact that she was no longer alone, Andrew caught her hand in his and, not missing a step of the dance, led her down the terrace steps.

"Don't protest," he begged before she could even open her mouth. "There can be no harm. No one will see— the air's too brisk for anyone to come outside."

Jessica laughed. "You are persuasive, sir." The temptation was too great. Just one dance, she decided recklessly, though she did retain sufficient judgment to determine first that Andrew's eyes were not sparkling in the feverish way they did when he was in his cups.

"What luck," Andrew cried in triumph. "I can

scarcely believe I should meet up with you just as I am fleeing the premises." He laughed richly. "Which is why we are making for the corner of the house. I want to be well away when Mother raises the alarm."

"And Marianne?" Jessica asked as they danced forward side by side.

"She has as little desire to marry me as I have to be wed to her," he declared shortly. "This marriage business is a silly notion concocted by our parents for reasons of their own. I only hope my desertion tonight will so offend the squire that he'll relinquish his hopes of a union with Bleithewood and urge Marianne on some man who'll actually care for her."

"Well, I think it is too bad you must resort to leaving altogether," Jessica told him with some feeling.

But Andrew laughed roguishly. "You are not to look the least sorry for me, my dear. The company at the Lion's Head in Rushton is quite congenial, I assure you. Besides, now I've had my dance with the only girl at the ball who interests me in the least, there is nothing left to look forward to."

They had reached the corner of the manor, and as if on cue, the music came to halt. Jessica stepped back to curtsy. "Thank you, my lord." She played her part formally, and Andrew responded in kind, bowing low over her hand, kissing it lightly, and then, with a laugh, making his escape in the direction of the stables.

As Jessica waved farewell, his form soon blended with the shadows and she turned to retrace her steps. Her thoughts on Andrew, she did not see the dark shape striding purposefully toward her until it reached out to take her arm.

She cried out in fear, though in the next moment she recognized Roxham's broad shoulders and tawny hair.

"You've every reason to sound fearful, Miss Winslow!" His voice was harsh in her ear. "You are well and truly caught out. Little wonder you would throw the vicar over when you cannot keep your clutching hands off Andy."

Roxham's tone was as fierce as his grip on her arm, and though Jessica shrank from both, she was powerless to prevent him half-carrying, half-dragging her up the terrace steps and through the French windows of the library. She blinked as her eyes adjusted to the light, then looked to Roxham's. His eyes, she saw with dismay, blazed almost as brightly with anger as the chandelier overhead did with its candles.

"Well?" he demanded contemptuously. "What the devil can you have to say for yourself now that you've been caught?"

His anger sparked Jessica's own, and she did not think it worth the effort to force herself to moderation. He would dismiss her now of a certainty.

"At what have you caught me, pray?" she challenged hotly. "At dancing a single dance? How very sinful, to be sure!"

Roxham's lip curled in a sneer. "I suppose you would see nothing in breaking your word. You've proven before what little sense of honor you possess. You do remember your vow to keep your distance from Andrew?"

Jessica reddened as if he'd struck her. "I did not break my word," she retorted. "I have kept my distance from Andrew. There is nothing between us. Our dance was as innocent as if he'd danced with Livy."

"Innocent! The word cannot apply to you, Miss Winslow, though you go to great pains to have the world believe it does. Even your drab clothes have been chosen for effect. The more pitifully you portray yourself, the better you play upon Aunt Bea's sympathies."

Jessica's eyes flashed as brightly now as her companion's. "That is absurd," she said flatly. "My clothes are in keeping with my station! And there is nothing wrong with them."

"They are old, plain, and without a hint of fashion." He dismissed her admittedly limited wardrobe with a slash of his hand. "And it is impossible you could be so free of vanity you would refuse Bea's offer to clothe you— yes, she did tell me you would have nothing of a new muslin—without some ulterior motive."

"No matter what I say or do, you think the worst." The words burst from Jessica as she returned the earl's furious glare. "If I were to dress in the muslins Lady

Bea has offered, you would accuse me of cozening her, but when I dress in the bombazine I believe better suited to my position, you accuse me of attempting to work some trick upon her. There is no point trying to reason with you. You'll not listen. You are too arrogant and . . . and pigheaded!''

Jessica whirled around, aware she had burned all her bridges and desiring only to see the last of the Earl of Roxham.

The earl, however, was not done with her. ''You are not dismissed, Miss Winslow.'' In one fluid motion he locked his hand on her arm and spun her about to face him. The gold lights in his eyes flamed angrily as he shook her for having the temerity to depart his presence before he'd given her leave. ''You will listen to me—''

''Have done with it!'' Something seemed to snap in Jessica. He had already consigned her to sit among the dowagers, a glorified servant old before her time, and now he intended to lecture her upon the evil she'd done capturing only one fleeting moment of innocent pleasure.

She was without a future. What more was there to say to her? ''Dismiss me,'' she lashed out, pushing furiously against him. ''Have done with the deed! After all, I am no better than a sack of grain to be hauled about at your pleasure. Send me on my way. It is what you have sought to do since you first learned I was in your home.''

Unable to free herself from Roxham's hold, Jessica hit his broad chest with her fists. ''I'll not listen to you revile me again! Send me on my way,'' she repeated wildly, unaware that, though her eyes blazed, they also glistened with unshed tears.

''I want to go. You have won the day, my lord. I shall be glad to see the last of you. Just as I was glad to see the last of your detestable brother. I never wanted to go to the park with him that day. And Sally . . . she left me in that wretched carriage with him. Fool that I was, I did not risk my life to leap out. I trusted him.

''Can you countenance it?'' Jessica demanded, laughing harshly. ''I trusted him! I'd no notion he was embittered against all women and would think it only my due when he forced that horrid, wet kiss upon me!''

At the memory Jessica shuddered. "I am glad I hit him," she declared fiercely. "I hope I bruised his jaw. He ruined me without a second thought. And you!" She pounded Roxham's chest. "You made certain there would be no amends. I did not want to marry the wretch, only to have the incident forgotten. But you! You thought a sack of gold all I was due. Ten pieces for my life."

When her voice broke on a sob, she wrenched free from Roxham's hold. "Now, look what you've done," she cried and bolted for the door.

But Roxham was there before her, blocking her exit. She could see his feet planted firmly in her path as she dashed at the hot tears streaming down her face, and she saw as well the linen handkerchief he held out to her.

"I believe you will need this before you rejoin the festivities."

Roxham's voice was damningly quiet, and Jessica stifled another sob. Now she had not even her dignity.

She took his handkerchief without thanking him. He, as much as she, was responsible for her tears.

Roxham watched in silence as she blotted her tears and edged away from him toward the windows. She was no longer the angry, spitting vixen who had berated him as no one else had ever dared to do.

Perhaps affected more than he realized by what he'd read in her expression earlier, when she would not look toward the gay dancers, he had seen beneath the sparks in her eyes a despair that had dismayed him.

And not merely because she was very young and too beautiful to have eyes that reflected such despondency. He'd stood quiet, in part, because he was the author of her despair.

Because he had decreed it be so, she could look forward to a life spent dressed in gray, following at some old woman's heels.

Then as he awakened to the scarcely comforting knowledge that he desired to take her into his arms and soothe her far more than he wished to toss her out of his home, he heard something she said and was brought, against his will, to question far too late if she even deserved the hand he had dealt her.

"What is your explanation, then, for not accepting Bea's offer of new dresses?"

The question was so unexpected that Jessica looked to see if it was truly Roxham who'd spoken.

Unperturbed by her astonishment, he shrugged as he propped his shoulders against the window opposite her. "I find I do not care to be accused of pigheadedness."

Jessica flushed. It was a childish thing to have said. Still, she shot him a searching look. She almost believed he merely wished to prove her wrong before dismissing her. But when he returned her a steady gaze, she was forced to allow even Roxham was not so cruel as to make her justify herself to no purpose.

"You've never thought what it is like to depend upon others for everything, my lord," she said at last, her husky voice very low as she looked away from him out the window. "The roof over my head, the food on my plate, the bed in which I sleep—even the books I enjoy—are all yours. Only my clothes are my own."

She looked very proud with her straight back and lifted shoulders, but the earl did not miss the sadness tingeing her voice as she addressed the window and the darkness outside. "Why do you not devote a part of your salary to refurbishing your wardrobe? I know you have enough."

"I send most of what I earn home to my mother. For pin money." Roxham did not think it the time to point out that she had a stepfather who ought to have stood responsible for her mother's out-of-pocket expenses. "You've made the precariousness of my position clear enough, but even had you not, I'd not have rushed to spend what's left. If I am dismissed, there is no one to feed me." She gave a futile little shrug. "The choice between a new muslin and food or shelter is no choice at all, really. And besides," she finished stubbornly, "my clothes are perfectly acceptable.

"Oh! This is absurd," she exclaimed with more spirit in the next instant. "What can you care? You intend to dismiss me. I must know how long you will give me to find another post."

Roxham noted the impatience flashing in her eyes, but

he did not answer her question. Instead, his eyes never leaving her, he asked, "Why did you say Ned was embittered?"

"Because he had a disillusioning experience with another woman before he met me," Jessica flared, irritated that with customary arrogance he had chosen to overlook her question in favor of his own. "Livy gave me to understand Edward seems to hold a bitterness against women, and I thought it some explanation for his callous behavior toward me. That, and my association with Sally."

At the recollection of the good name she'd lost by her own doing as well as Edward's, Jessica experienced another mortifying welling of tears. Swiftly, before Roxham could see them, she swung about to face the windows again. She would not have him think she tried to use womanly wiles upon him.

Though he could not see her face, Roxham could see her jaw quiver. He saw her lift a hand to her face in a posture that was intended to suggest she pondered something, while in reality she wiped her tears with her fingers.

When she missed one and it rolled from her cheek, he swore beneath his breath and twirled her about, not entirely gently. Without asking her leave or replying to the surprise on her face, he withdrew another piece of soft linen from his pocket and, taking hold of her chin, proceeded to mop her eyes himself.

"What are you about?" Jessica demanded, her voice hoarse with unshed tears.

"I am drying your eyes. Call it revenge for all the services you heaped upon me while I was helpless."

"But I am not helpless."

"You are too proud to help yourself," he returned rather curtly before stepping back to judge his handiwork. Had Jessica known it, her emotional outburst had left her cheeks flushed pink and her eyes sparkling with moisture. He stared into her blue eyes a long minute, and thought to himself she might not ever have looked more appealing.

"Not unacceptable," the earl pronounced, letting go of her. "But you are not good enough to return below."

"Lady Bea," Jessica gasped miserably even as she sought to subdue the spurt of vanity that made her wish to hide the puffy red mess she knew her face must be.

Roxham was surprisingly unmoved by her negligence toward his aunt. "I shall go to see about Bea in a moment, but I imagine she's requisitioned the assistance of that young footman who is forever hanging upon your coattails."

Jessica gave him a quick look. She could not think who the earl meant and feared he intended to start in on fresh accusations, but Roxham seemed unaware of her concern. Though he was frowning down at her, she had the odd impression he did not actually see her.

After a moment, his gaze sharpened as if he'd come to a decision. "I propose we cry truce for a time, Miss Winslow. I should like to write to Ned. I had not considered before that his encounter with Arabella Summers may have affected how he saw you."

When Jessica could only gape witlessly in reaction, Roxham gave her a rather cool look. "I am a fair man," he said curtly. "You have raised a legitimate question and I cannot in good conscience do less than ask Ned if it is possible he did not mistake matters."

Jessica had never asked for more than a fair hearing. But winning through to it after she'd behaved so outrageously left her without a coherent response.

The corner of Roxham's fine mouth lifted when she seemed only capable of nodding slowly in dumbfounded reply. "I do believe I've left you at a loss for words, Miss Winslow. As I imagine it is one of the few times in your life you've been rendered speechless, I think I shall take a certain pride in my accomplishment."

Quite suddenly, taking her by surprise, laughter warmed his golden-brown eyes. As her knees seemed to turn to butter, Jessica looked away nervously. "I should like very much to cry truce," she managed to get out in a soft voice.

"Good. We are agreed on it—and that you will maintain a distance from Andrew. No more dancing alone."

169

That brought Jessica's eyes back to his, but Roxham found that sparkle of indignation directed at him mild stuff compared to the fury he'd absorbed earlier. "Very good, my lord," she said with deliberate primness, and curtsied.

But once more when she made to leave, Roxham restrained her. On this occasion he placed his hand upon her shoulder, staying her but not turning her. "A strand of your hair's come loose," he informed her quietly.

Before she could draw away, he lifted the red-gold strand from her neck; long, thick, and silky. It was no easy task to tuck it into the braid encircling the top of her head. Taking his time, noting as he worked the faint scent of violets, the earl managed, "I doubt you would approve the effect, but it will do until you reach your rooms."

The look Jessica cast him over her shoulder lifted only as far as the ruby in his cravat. "Thank you, my lord," she mumbled stiffly before she hurried from the room, aware of little as she fled but that his fingers, where they had grazed her neck, had left a trail of such warmth she feared she might shiver in reaction.

17

"Is Jess here, Aunt Bea?" The twins ran into their aunt's room and did not pause to greet her before Giles inquired after Jessica.

"Or Caesar?" Julia chimed in. "We cannot find him anywhere."

"Whatever has happened?" Roxham demanded, striding through the door on their heels. "You two ran in here as if the house were on fire."

"We've lost Caesar!" Julia's alarm indicated she considered the loss of their pup to be a more frightful calamity than a mere fire.

"Jess was in the nursery doing maps with us," Giles

began his explanation, but he digressed at once. "Did you know there are birds in South America with red beaks, Justin?"

"Toucans, perhaps?"

"That's it!" Giles beamed at his older cousin with great pride. "Jess told us all about them." Then, seeing his sister give an impatient little hop, Giles recalled himself to the matter at hand. "We were very busy finishing our maps, for we wanted to surprise her when she came back to have tea with us, and we did not notice until only a little while ago that Caesar is missing. We cannot find him anywhere, not in the nursery or in the kitchens, and Moreton has not seen him in the front hall or ballroom where the maids are cleaning. Has he been here, Aunt Bea?" he asked, turning back to his great-aunt.

"No, he has not," Lady Beatrice said decisively. "But Jessica did not return here from the nursery either. She went straight to the Crenshawes' to look in on the little girl. Perhaps the pup followed her out of the house."

Roxham glanced out the window with a frown. "She walked there on a day like this? It looks as if it could storm at any time."

"She's a stubborn chit," Lady Beatrice observed wryly, "and rarely heeds my advice. Because she thought the child needed a salve Mayes left when he came to see me this morning, she went. I do hope she'll not come to harm," Lady Bea added, looking out at the sky herself. "I had not realized how dark the clouds have become."

"But surely something has happened already," Julia wailed, distraught. "Jess has been gone an age. We've worked on our maps almost all afternoon."

" 'Tis true," Lady Bea agreed gravely when her nephew looked to her.

The alarm he could discern in her eyes decided Roxham. "Mars has need of some exercise. I shall take him for a quick run on the path and see what has happened."

"Oh, do, Justin!" His aunt smiled gratefully. "Jess had no business going out today at all. Though you both conspired to keep it from me, I am certain she became ill last night. Of a certainty, I do not believe your absurd

171

contention that she retired before me merely because she was fatigued. Jessica is never fatigued.''

''Well, she was last evening,'' the earl replied firmly, though he looked away from his aunt as he made for the door. ''Livy and Mary left her hagged to death preparing for that affair,'' he finished, and waving farewell, departed.

He'd have been surprised to see the broad smile that immediately lit his aunt's face, and even more astonished to hear her say delightedly, ''Well! And I am so seldom grateful for bad weather!''

The twins, of course, did hear her, and they demanded to know what it was she meant. But their aunt only smiled shrewdly, ''Time will tell!''

Some half-hour later, when he had very nearly decided Jessica had lingered at the Crenshawes' Roxham found her, walking toward the path along a stream that had been swollen to the edge of its banks by the spring rains they'd had earlier in the season.

At the same moment that Jessica identified the horseman approaching her, Roxham realized that she carried Caesar in her arms, wrapped in her shawl, and that the skirt of her brown bombazine was wet to the knees.

A layer of mud stained the hem and sleeves of the dress, and she seemed to have lost her bonnet altogether, but dangling from the crook of her arm was an empty basket that had no doubt been laden with food for the Crenshawes at the outset of her journey.

When he saw that there were steaks of mud on her cheek and across her delicate nose, his eyes began to twinkle. ''It would seem, Miss Winslow, that you've been involved in a rescue mission at some cost to your apparel,'' he observed, his golden-brown eyes traveling lazily from Caesar, panting in her arms, to the dirt on her cheek, to, at last, her very dark-blue eyes.

''Well, you needn't look so pleased,'' Jessica retorted with spirit. Wet and muddy, she knew she must cut a sorry figure, and she could not but regret, as she took in the earl's gleaming Hessians and impeccable lightweight riding coat, that her appearance had only deteriorated from the last time he had seen her—and it had been bad enough then.

Roxham, far from being put out by her ill humor, laughed down at her. "I am afraid it is difficult to summon sorrow for that particular dress," he replied, a smile lingering in his eyes and prompting Jessica to admit to herself, if not to him that the brown bombazine was not her favorite either. "Did Caesar fall into the stream?"

Jessica nodded and, adjusting the pup in her arms, described how he'd dashed close to investigate something in the water only to have the bank give way.

She did not draw out her story, as she would later with the twins. The truth be told, she was disconcerted to encounter Roxham so soon after their last, tumultuous encounter. She had counted on meeting him at, perhaps, dinner, when there would be a number of other people present to provide sufficient distraction that she might gauge his mood before she must actually come face to face with him.

He'd have been within his rights, she acknowledged, to forget the truce he'd suggested and look upon her with amazement if not disgust.

After considering their interview for half the night, she'd been less and less inclined to forgive herself for her shocking loss of composure. True, she'd had provocation, but to upbraid him so wildly and then to take her fists to him! And that was to say nothing of how she'd cried openly before him! And not a few delicate crystal drops, she admitted, but hot, painful, eye-reddening tears.

Coloring at the memory of how absurdly she'd carried on, Jessica stepped around the earl and his sleek horse. "Excuse me," she muttered, avoiding his eyes.

"On the contrary, there's no need to excuse yourself," he said in the amiable tone that continued to have the effect of unsettling her. The one thing she had not expected from him, somehow, was amused friendliness. From the corner of her eye she saw him turn Mars about, but she continued walking. "Actually, Aunt Bea sent me out after you." He pulled up alongside her. "She feared you'd be caught in the rain."

Glancing up at the sky, Jessica saw with a sinking heart that it was not farfetched to believe they might be treated to a cloudburst at any moment. "I thank you for coming," she said, wanting only to be rid of his confusing presence until she felt more the thing. "You may tell Lady Beatrice when you return that I am not far from the manor now."

"You are at least half an hour away on foot, my dear," he corrected, and went on to displease her further by saying, "and as I am returning now, it is no trouble to take you up before me. Here, take my hand and put your foot in the stirrup."

Short of crying out the truth—that she'd no wish to ride in such close company with him—there was little to do but take his hand. It felt warm and strong when it closed over hers, and he lifted her up to sit sideways before him as if she were no weight at all. "Put Caesar in the basket and you'll free a hand to hold on to Mars."

Jessica nodded and did as she was bid, happy to be distracted from the realization that she'd never been as close to any man as she was now to the earl. To hold the reins he had perforce to encircle her waist with his arms, and unless she wished his hands to rest upon her hips, she must sit absurdly straight.

There was no possibility of keeping the full length of her arm from jostling his chest. Mars was a large animal, but not so large that she must not sit almost tucked against Roxham. Nonetheless, Jessica wriggled forward in an effort to put at least half an inch between them.

"It is not easy riding two on a horse, Miss Winslow, particularly when the horse is a spirited stallion, but it would help if you would sit still."

Jessica flushed a bright red and, quite unable to face Roxham, nodded as she fastened her gaze upon Caesar. The puppy looked up with adoration, but his liquid gaze could not keep her from thinking on how close Roxham's mouth was to her. When he'd spoken, his breath had ruffled her hair.

Nor could she fail to be aware of his well-muscled body. As the silence lengthened, she seemed unable to think on anything but the power she sensed emanating from it.

A flush was rising in her cheeks when she recalled, blessedly, a discovery she'd made at the Crenshawes'. "You hired Jem, my lord, and never said anything." She risked a quick glance at Roxham and as quickly let her glance slide away. His eyes, the color of warm honey, made her pulses leap distractingly.

"It seems the gardeners are all getting on in years and need a pair of strong young arms. I said nothing only because I waited to see if he would prove as dependable as you maintained."

"And what do you think?" she asked, her concern overcoming her self-consciousness. When Roxham said the boy was proving himself capable, she smiled, relieved. "I am glad, for Mrs. Crenshawe is quite beside herself at their good fortune. She views you as something of a savior."

Roxham shrugged and Jessica felt the muscles in his chest lift. "You're the one who pleaded the boy's case so effectively," he said, his voice as lazy as the horse's gentle pace. The sound of it seemed to shrink the already tiny space between them.

Roxham felt her stiffen as if she would avoid all contact between them, and glancing down, he saw her bite her lip as hectic color flooded her cheeks. With the smudge on her nose to complete the picture, she looked like a young and innocent girl cast in a situation she did not have the experience to handle with any composure.

If appearances did not deceive him, then she was not a vixen capable of seducing Ned. Surely a Circe such as he had imagined would not be so obviously agitated by her position within the circle of a man's arms.

A clap of thunder distracted them both. Roxham glanced back over his shoulder before kneeing his mount so it picked up its pace. "We can't make the house. We'll have to take shelter in the woods, but if we are to arrive even there intact, you are to sit stone-still." To enforce his command, he wrapped an arm around Jessica and took the reins in one hand.

She made no protest, though her stomach muscles

175

clenched tightly. She had little choice: without Roxham's hold, she'd have fallen.

When they were protected from the worst of the rain by a thick canopy of oak and hawthorn leaves, Roxham, his hands on her waist, lifted her from her perch.

She had not realized how much his body had warmed her until she stepped away from him. Feeling the loss, she shivered.

"Here. I think you have more need of this than I, as you are so wet."

Roxham held out the lightweight coat he'd donned in case of rain, but Jessica, embarrassed by all the trouble she'd caused him, shook her head. "No, thank you, really. I shall be quite fine. You need it more. You have not yet fully recovered from your wound."

"You wound me a great deal more with such sentiments," he chided her mildly. "And I am not the one shivering."

When he waved the thing rather impatiently, she gave in and, ensconced in its warmth, thanked him with a grateful smile. If she had looked like a girl before, she seemed almost a child now, with the streaks on her face and his coat swallowing her.

Roxham withdrew a handkerchief. "Luckily for you, I've set in a large store of these," he said, and watched with some amusement as she blushed at the reminder of her outburst the night before. "I would allow you to attend to your dirt yourself," he continued, "but I fear I didn't think to bring a pier glass."

Having explained his intent, the earl for the second time in not so very many hours cupped her chin with his lean fingers. He paused a moment when she stiffened and seemed poised to jerk away. Her eyes were very wide and blue, and the expression in them was oddly pleading, but before Roxham could react, she veiled her eyes with her lashes and stood quietly before him.

He worked efficiently and, he thought, impersonally, but when he had done, Jessica only flicked him a quick glance before going to kneel beside Caesar. Roxham watched her with a frown, for her uneasiness reminded him of her panic in the library. And he did not care to think she feared him.

Jessica, as she patted the little dog, felt nothing of the panic that had overwhelmed her that night, but Roxham's touch had unsettled her and she felt oddly shaky.

To her dismay, he did not allow her time to compose herself, but came almost at once to examine the pup himself. "He looks well enough," Roxham observed, reaching down to scratch the pup behind his ears. Inadvertently his hand touched Jessica's.

"Yes. I think he is only tired," she responded, withdrawing her hand carefully from the basket. She could not like the way her heart had begun to beat so quickly now he was beside her.

He tossed her a quick look then and, seeing she intended to rise to put some distance between them, remarked idly, "You'll not countenance it, but I admire this little fellow a great deal." He pointed at several old scars on the pup's head. "These nicks and cuts would seem to indicate that his first master did not treat him well, and yet, though he has reason to fear men, he is amazingly trusting of us. I think he's quite clever to distinguish between those who would treat him well and those who would not, don't you?"

The look he turned on Jessica was both direct and unwavering, and she could not return it. Sudden anxiety welling up in her, she rose and stepped away from him altogether. "I think we should return to the manor now," she announced, her voice low and breathless. "The rain has nearly ended."

Jessica knew he had mistaken her feelings. She was not afraid of him in the way he thought, only of the effect he had upon her. But in his error, he trespassed and pressed her for a history that agitated her greatly. Aware of his eyes upon her, she walked farther away, only stopping when she neared Mars.

Surrounding them both were the woods and the soft sound of falling rain. Roxham let the raindrops speak for themselves.

"Did your stepfather hurt you, Jessica?"

At the softly voiced question, a pained, unnatural moan

177

escaped her. A tremor shook her body and she flattened her hands to her side to keep them from trembling.

A wet twig broke beneath Roxham's foot as he rose and walked slowly to where she stood. She heard the sound as well as the shuffling of soggy leaves with a thrill of alarm. She could not face him.

He could tell she was poised to flee, and halted. Her decision hung in the balance a long moment, for he was within arm's reach, but when he made no further advance, she let out a long breath.

"Did he hurt you?" Roxham asked again.

When she shook her head, he let out a breath he had not realized he held.

"How did you know?" Her voice was a mere whispery thread, but he heard it.

"I guessed, merely. Your manner changes markedly when you are reminded of him. If he did not hurt you physically, Jessica, he has affected you."

The rough edge to Roxham's voice penetrated Jessica's senses. There was compassion in it—and regret, too—on her behalf. Like a balm, it seemed to reach some hidden, coiled place in her, and though she kept her back to him, she lifted her head.

Taking a faltering breath, she said, "Mr. Godfrey did not hurt me." She paused, another tremor shaking her as she recalled her stepfather's lascivious gaze. "But he made me afraid," she acknowledged, her voice a whisper. "I did not know what he might do. Everywhere I went, he followed me with such greed in his eyes. And I—I felt so shamed."

When her voice broke, it was simply not within Roxham's power to keep from pulling her to him. Blinded by tears, she seemed to lack the strength to resist him, which was just as well, for he brought her head to his chest with determination.

"You are safe now," he soothed her quietly as she shuddered with the force of her sobs. For her stepfather, he spared a murderous thought. It was as well the man was not within reach.

"You've nothing to fear now, Jess, and certainly nothing to be ashamed of," he assured, using her pet name

178

to some effect, though he did not know it. "It was none of your doing."

Jessica could make him no reply, though her sobs subsided. She could not seem to think at all, with her head lying upon his chest and his arms around her.

Her eyes closed, she listened to his voice and felt her fears and her shame dissipate before the power of it. Although Roxham now knew of the sordid interest she'd attracted, she realized slowly, she would be able to face him.

But not yet. Just now, in his strong embrace, she felt too safe to take herself away.

"You are beautiful, it is true." Roxham's tone, as he smoothed an unruly tendril from her forehead, was too detached to embarrass her. "But you must realize, you take a deal upon yourself to imagine you are responsible for how a man responds to your God-given lineaments. A painter might wish to paint you—"

A watery sniff interrupted his comforting. "I doubt anyone would care to paint me just now. I've mud everywhere and my eyes are red."

"Vanity!" He chuckled aloud. The sound rumbled in his chest in a most pleasant way. "And just when I was close to deciding you were not subject to that particular weakness. Here." He fished his handkerchief from out of a pocket. "I imagine you must need this."

"Again," she added mournfully. "Thank you." She accepted the ill-used piece of linen, and accepted as well that the time had come to be independent once more. Though it was not easy, she stepped out of Roxham's arms. "I seem to have become a veritable watering pot of late," she exclaimed as she attended to her face.

Her chagrin was so honest that he could but smile. "At least I've a goodly supply of linen, though I only thought to bring one handkerchief today."

She grimaced in response, but before she could speak, he took her by the shoulders, and she did not resist. When she looked up to face him bravely, though the subject he would discuss was appallingly difficult for her, Roxham had the most absurd desire to kiss her soft lips for the spirit she displayed. He did not, of course; rake he might

179

be, but bounder he was not. She trusted him—and the knowledge pleased him.

"Your stepfather is despicable, Jessica. How he came to be so, I do not know. I only know his nature has nought to do with you. If you are to live your life fully, then you must be brave and put him from your mind. I repeat: most men are not like him at all."

Immersed in Roxham's steady, confident gaze, Jessica was scarcely aware that he held her, or that she looked back at him with a surprising trust, considering the history of their relations. "But other men have looked at me in that way," she objected, and it was clear she found the attention her looks had attracted both distressing and unpleasant. "The dandies in London regarded me in the same manner. They'd certainly no interest in my thoughts or conversation, only . . ." She stopped, unable to put what had interested them into words.

Roxham put aside the thought that his brother was one of the dandies to whom she referred. "They were only young bucks with very little ability to think at all, and you were with Sally. They thought you fair game."

"And Mr. Ashcroft?" she demanded. "He'd a wife and daughters in the house. You've no idea how awful it is to be obliged to worry whether the master of the house is lurking around the next corner."

The darkening of her eyes said as much as her words, and Roxham experienced a wave of cold rage in relation to the unknown Mr. Ashcroft as well as her stepfather. His grip tightened on her shoulders. "You need never fear anything of the sort here. Andy . . ."

"Is not the same at all," she finished for him. "I do know it. I like him immensely for it!"

Though her blue eyes flashed at him, Roxham found himself half-smiling. "I do not fault you, Jessica. It is precisely what I have been laboring to hear you say: that not all men are the same, and that, in truth, most are entirely honorable."

There was a moment's intense silence between them. "As you have been," she summoned the courage to say, her gaze not wavering from his golden-brown eyes. "Thank you, my lord, for your . . . understanding."

He inclined his head and, realizing he still held her, let her go. "I am only glad you could bring yourself to speak of this Godfrey. It is wrong that you should feel shame when he's the one who ought to be horse-whipped." Aware he'd spoken with something approaching violence, Roxham shrugged the disagreeable subject of her stepfather off and gave Jessica a wry look as he changed the subject. "At any rate, I am also glad to know you realize I've looked upon you only with suspicion."

She smiled at that as he'd intended, and went him one better. "And mockery, my lord. I would say you've often looked at me mockingly."

Accepting her addition with a rueful quirk to his mouth, he brushed a tear she'd missed from her cheek. "We shall have to see about that in the future, Miss Winslow."

At the soft look in his eyes as much as at his touch, Jessica's heartbeat quickened, and she was very much relieved when Roxham stepped back away from her to look up at the sky.

"It would seem the rain has stopped and we may return." He flashed her a smile. "And in complete agreement, too."

She'd no thought of not returning his smile, her eyes very vivid and alive. "A moment to be marked, I should say, my lord." Then, not daring to look at him overlong for fear he might see precisely how happy the unusual accord between them had made her, she went to retrieve Caesar and his basket.

18

Some time later, as they came out of the trees arching over Bleithewood's drive, Roxham gave an exclamation of surprise. Jessica, looking forward, saw there was a strange equipage drawn up before the steps of the manor.

Red and gold, it was an impressive thing despite the

mud spattering its wheels. Its occupants, clustered upon the steps where Lady Mary greeted them, looked even at a distance to be as elegant as their conveyance. There were two ladies and two gentlemen, all strangers to Jessica.

When Mars, sensing other animals about, snorted, they turned to see who approached.

The woman standing closest to Lady Mary was the first to recognize Roxham. "Justin! Darling," she trilled in a high voice, and as the earl brought Mars alongside the steps, she tripped quickly down to meet him.

"Aurelia." The earl swung down from Mars and took the woman's outstretched hand to kiss it, bringing a winsome smile to her lips. "This is a surprise."

"A pleasant one, I hope?" the woman teased with a flurry of dark lashes.

He smiled lazily down at her. "It is always pleasant to behold beauty, my dear."

Roxham did not flatter her. The woman, whose name Livy had linked with the earl's, was indeed beautiful, with dark hair done in stylish curls, large brown eyes, pale skin, and a red, inviting mouth just to the side of which was a small mole that could with justice be termed a beauty mark. She was not young, being somewhere close to Justin's thirty years, and she was not tall. But neither her years nor her lack of stature detracted from her looks. Exquisitely turned out in a burgundy traveling dress cut to display her lush figure and a dashing hat with a black plume, she was the epitome of fashion.

"A moment, please. I must rescue Miss Winslow." Roxham laughed as the others came to make their greetings.

Jessica rather wished the earl had forgotten her. Led off to the stables with Mars, she would have escaped scrutiny. By any standards she was wretchedly bedraggled—without a bonnet, half her hair straggling down her back, and her muddy half-boots peeping out from beneath the hem of the earl's dwarfing coat—but beside the enchantingly turned-out Lady Aurelia, she looked worse than a scullery maid.

Perhaps something of her uncertainty showed in her

expression, perhaps not, but when Roxham lifted her down and deposited her between him and his guests, he allowed his hand to linger a moment upon the small of her back. Warm and supportive, it had the effect of lifting Jessica's chin to a lofty angle.

"Dashed if your coat has ever before shown to better advantage, Justin, you old dog," one of the gentlemen cried out loudly.

"I agree with you entirely, Alfred," his host replied easily. "Allow me to present Miss Jessica Winslow. She is acting as companion to Aunt Bea. Miss Winslow"—he gestured toward the man—"this reprobate is Lord Alfred Marling."

He was a short, fleshy man in his late forties, Jessica did not like on sight. He wore extremely fashionable clothing that did not show to any advantage on his paunchy figure, and his murky, bloodshot brown eyes reminded her at once of Charles Godfrey's. Just so had her stepfather's eyes looked after a long night of overindulgence. As Mr. Godfrey's eyes had often been, this man's were fastened upon her with hot interest.

Before she'd time to draw back, Lord Marling seized her hand and lifted the prize to his thick lips. "Charmed, charmed," he breathed huskily.

Jessica retrieved her hand as hastily as possible and only just kept from wiping the back of it on her skirt. Whatever Roxham might say about the nature of most men, Jessica knew instinctively this was a man she must distrust.

"Miss Winslow, you did get a soaking. And you've lost your bonnet. Oh, those Crenshawes! They are forever giving trouble."

Lady Mary, who had been detained giving Moreton directions as to the comfort of her guests, hurried up, her eyes reflecting true alarm as she took in Jessica's appearance. Reminded how frightful she must look, Jessica steeled herself against flushing. She might feel a quizz, but she did not care to have the others know it.

"The Crenshawes did not send me out in a cloudburst, my lady." Jessica managed a smile. "I was foolish enough to do that without assistance, I'm afraid, and it was Caesar here who detained me.''

"Oh, your shawl," Lady Mary cried when she, and everyone, looked down into the basket Jessica held, to see the muddy mess that had once been a serviceable cotton shawl. "But the twins will be so very relieved," she went on to say, casting Jessica a truly grateful look. "They have been quite beside themselves with worry over him.''

"Now we're assured the twins will not be going into a decline," Roxham said, "allow me to continue the introductions so that Miss Winslow and I may the sooner be on our way to our dressing rooms. Lady Aurelia Stanhope, Alfred's sister, is here." He gestured to the beauty who had come to stand close beside him.

She did not smile, only inclined her head to the degree civility demanded, and when the earl turned his attention to the couple standing across from him, Lady Aurelia's eyes hardened as she raked Jessica from her head to her toes with a decidedly unfriendly look.

"And over there we've Mr. and Mrs. MacDonald from the wilds of Scotland.''

Mr. MacDonald was dressed to a turn—his shirtpoints were so high that Jessica wondered whether he could see anything below the treetops—but when she encountered his good-natured smile, she forgave him his extravagance and smiled in return.

"The wilds of Scotland, indeed," he blustered, squeezing her hand. "Perhaps we are in need of civilization, though. Our companions are never so comely. You've a lucky aunt, Justin.''

Mrs. MacDonald was not so friendly. Her excessively thin eyebrows lifted faintly, as if she could scarcely countenance the novelty of being presented to a companion, and her sharp, bright eyes put Jessica in mind of a fox.

The presentations accomplished, Jessica made haste to excuse herself. She had little desire to be buffeted by Lady Aurelia's unfriendly gaze on the one side and Lord Marling's persistently smoldering one on the other.

"Actually we are the bearers of rather bad news," Mrs. MacDonald's voice carried to Jessica as she hurried up the steps. "Verney has just died, and it fell to us to bring Anne the news."

"And we've come to look in on you, Justin," Lady Aurelia added after he had asked after Lady Ann. "Mary wrote to say you'd been most frightfully injured. We half-expected you to be in your bed, but I should have known you are so strong that you'd make a marvelous recovery."

"With some assistance, to be sure."

Roxham's laconic reply floated up to Jessica, making her absurdly happy, though the emotion proved fleeting. As she disappeared through the door Moreton held for her, she heard Lady Aurelia exclaim, "Oh, my darling, your coat is quite wet. Surely you've not risked a return to your sickbed merely to save that healthy-looking child a wetting."

Her eyes flashing dangerously, Jessica sailed up the stairs. What a cat the woman was! Healthy-looking child, indeed!

"I suppose you know the worst has occurred while you were away." When Lady Beatrice looked mournfully to the ceiling, Jessica could not keep from chuckling. "You laugh!" Quick as lighting, Lady Beatrice's shrewd blue eyes impaled her. "I cannot inquire if you were drenched and will catch your death of cold, nor whether the Crenshawes still live, nor even if that mongrel pup has returned. I am too put out. The harpy is among us."

"You are very bad, ma'am," Jessica scolded, but her eyes, brimming with laughter, belied her spoken sentiments.

Reading her companion's expressive eyes, Lady Beatrice nodded complacently. "I am," she agreed. "But Mary is silly! Imagine! She wrote to tell Aurelia of Justin's injury. We are fortunate the mails are slow and the amusements in town diverting, or we'd have had the cat much sooner."

Lady Beatrice grunted unhappily. "That Verney should coincidentally stick his spoon in the wall at just this time is the sort of ill-judged action to be expected from one of his ilk. He provided Aurelia the perfect excuse to traipse up to Bleithewood.

"Not that she doubted her welcome, I imagine. She's been clever enough to cultivate Mary over the years. Whenever Mary ventures down to town, Aurelia goes to great pains over her. The two have exchanged letters for an age. Mary, the silly twit, is too overcome by such attention from one of society's leading lights to see she's only a means to an end."

"A willing means!" Lady Beatrice threw up her hands in disgust. "You will not countenance it, Jess, but she's actually invited all four of them to stay until St. Barnabas Day. 'It's the least I can do, after all Aurelia's done for me!' "

The older woman mimicked her niece's fluttery tones so accurately that Jessica could not keep from laughing. "Shall I brush out your hair, Lady Bea?" she asked, still smiling. "It is all the comfort I can offer."

As Lady Beatrice dearly loved to have Jessica gently brush out her long gray hair, she nodded at once. "That will do very nicely indeed, my dear. I shall close my eyes and plot my strategy."

In the ensuing silence, Jessica digested the news Lady Beatrice had given her. St. Barnabas Day was a fortnight away, which seemed a very long time to keep company with people she had not liked almost on sight. Mercifully, she tried to cheer herself, Bleithewood Manor was large.

"Aunt Bea! Jess!" Olivia, who never seemed to simply enter a room, flew into her aunt's, her hazel eyes sparkling with her excitement. "Have you seen them?" she cried, then, without waiting for a reply, went on to rhapsodize over the modish appearance of their unexpected visitors.

"Aurelia's hair is arranged in the curls you said were all the fashion, Jess. A trifle longer than mine, they were swept around to dangle over her ear.

"And her afternoon dress! I declare it was so fine she might have worn it for an evening gown. The neckline was certainly low enough. It was cut to here."

To her shame, Jessica looked to see where Aurelia Standhope's neckline came. It was very low, if Livy could be believed.

"Ha! Hussy," Lady Beatrice scoffed, eager to believe the worst.

"Oh! Is she really?" Livy breathed, clearly thrilled at the thought that they might be harboring a lady of low repute at the manor.

Her high hopes, however, were dashed in the next moment. "Of course she's no real hussy," Lady Beatrice admonished impatiently. "She's too highborn. I only meant she's got the instincts of one. I could tell it the first time I ever clapped eyes on her."

When it seemed that her aunt might not continue with her revelations, for Jessica was still brushing her hair with long, even strokes and she had closed her eyes to enjoy the attention undistracted, Olivia went to the extreme of grasping her hand. "Do tell, Aunt Bea!"

Lady Beatrice shot the girl a sharp look, as if she might reprimand her for the disturbance, but upon encountering the bright look in Livy's hazel eyes, she relented with a sigh. "Oh, very well! Aurelia was eighteen when she came out and took the town by storm, for she was beautiful. And even then she knew how to paint on anything nature had left off."

"No," Olivia gasped, fascinated.

Lady Beatrice nodded until she felt her hair pull against Jessica's brush. "That celebrated beauty spot is not genuine. I have it on good authority—her dresser left her to work for Liza Paxton. She can't keep servants, you know. She's a worse harridan than I. Still," Lady Beatrice conceded grudgingly after a pause, "she's natural beauty enough. And when she came out, all the young bucks hung on her. Even Justin paid her some court, though only in that offhand way of his that seems to drive women mad.

"And Aurelia desperately needed certainty. She did not have the leisure to pursue a mere possibility, however arresting his looks and wealth. The Marlings were one and all deep in dun territory at the time. Good family, don't you know, but with such a taste for extravagance and games of chance, they've always been only a step ahead of the creditors.

"When she clapped eyes on old Harry Stanhope, she

thought she could have it all. He was mad for her, rich as a nabob, and so old he'd turn a blind eye to any affair she wished to conduct. Of course, she told everyone her father forced the match on her, but I knew old Lord Marling. He was putty in any woman's hand, particularly his daughter's. The match was her doing.

"What Aurelia did not count on was Justin's sense of what was fit. Harry was an old friend of mine who had visited Bleithewood countless times. Of course, Justin wouldn't put horns on the old boy.

"Aurelia found other game, but she still wanted Justin. You could see it in her eyes every time she looked at him. Finally Harry obliged her by leaving his mortal coil, and even before her year of mourning was up, I'd word from town that she'd set her cap at Justin.''

"And the first step was her bed?''

Olivia did not blink when Lady Beatrice growled, "You shouldn't speak of such things, young lady. You are scarce out of the schoolroom.''

"But everyone says as much,'' Olivia pointed out reasonably.

"Well, that doesn't mean you ought to repeat Kate's prattling'' was Lady Beatrice's tart response. "Where that child gets all her tittle-tattle, I cannot imagine. Neither Anne nor the estimable Philip''—she tossed a knowing glance at Livy who blushed—"care for that sort of thing. But,'' she relented after casting a grudging glance at her niece, "as you know anyway. I suppose it won't hurt to say that it is widely believed Aurelia was pleased to show Justin a little of what he might look forward to after he wed her. In her defense,'' she added fairly, "knowing Justin, I don't think she had to work overhard.''

Lady Beatrice's observation did not surprise Jessica. Had she never witnessed the practiced ease with which he charmed women young and old, she'd have only had to recall the look that had flickered in his eyes when she had appeared before him clad only in her nightclothes to know that he did not lack for an interest in women.

Would he take his mistress to his bed while she was here at the manor? Fortunately Livy distracted Jessica from the unhappy realization that the Earl of Roxham's sleeping arrangements interested her a great deal more than they should have.

Just as she experienced a vaguely ill feeling at the thought of Lady Aurelia ensconced in the earl's room, she heard Olivia make mention of dinner. Jessica's ears pricked up at once, for she devoutly hoped Lady Bea would not care to join the family.

Lady Beatrice, however, felt differently. "Yes. Jess and I will be down," she replied firmly to her niece.

Jessica was quick to protest her inclusion in the affair. "But I should not join you when you have guests. I, I would be imposing," she improvised quickly.

It was a lame excuse. If Lady Beatrice invited her, then she was not imposing, and the older woman gave her reply the short shrift it deserved. "Nonsense," she admonished with a scowl. "Imposing, indeed! I wish you to be with me as always, and I shall be present. You don't think I intend to leave the field to that woman, do you?"

Had she not been so unsettled at the thought of joining Roxham's fashionable guests for dinner, Jessica might have laughed. Having none of her friend's distractions, Olivia did giggle at the idea of her ancient aunt competing with Aurelia Stanhope.

"Oh, Aunt Bea," she admonished indulgently before she turned eagerly to Jessica.

"Will you do my hair tonight, Jess? I should like to look the thing."

"Such praise for my simple talents." Jessica managed a light, teasing tone before inclining her head. "I would be pleased to do my best."

At least one of the Bleithewood ladies would look the height of fashion that night, she decided as she recalled Roxham telling her her own clothes were old, plain, and without the least fashion.

19

"Fustian! You were in the right, Jess. I shall need a heavier shawl. Will you fetch it?"

"Of course. James?" Jessica turned to smile at the young footman who hovered nearby. "Will you see Lady Beatrice down to the salon for me?"

Though he leapt forward eagerly in response to her request, the young man did not pull his rapt gaze from Jessica's retreating figure until he felt a cane sharply rap his ankle.

"Give over, lad," Lady Beatrice reprimanded, though not unkindly. "Moreton will have you polishing the silver all of next week if you don't practice a sight more discretion."

"Aunt Bea, is something amiss?"

Seeing Justin approach with Lady Aurelia and the MacDonalds, Lady Beatrice first acknowledged their guests and then addressed her nephew, a hint of wickedness gleaming in her eye. "Nothing's wrong, at all, dear boy. James is here to provide the stout arm I need. One of the pleasures of having Jess about is the surfeit of young footmen invariably to be found in the vicinity."

"Ah, yes," Roxham replied, an amused half-smile tugging at his mouth. "Andy calls it the Jessica Effect, you know."

Lady Bea chuckled delightedly at his answer, though she'd have admitted at once, if asked, that Aurelia Stanhope's annoyed frown afforded her an almost equal amount of pleasure.

When Jessica entered the salon alone, Lady Beatrice's shawl over her arm, she saw that the others had all arrived before her and were gathered at the far end of the room facing Roxham, who stood by the fireplace with Lady Aurelia at his side.

Dressed in an elaborately beaded gown of Nile-green silk with a profusion of diamonds sparkling at her throat and ears, Aurelia looked quite superb. In the dark curls arranged artfully upon her head plumes swayed, giving her height, and on her face there was a dusting of rice powder to turn her complexion the purest white.

There could be, Jessica knew very well, no comparison with her own toilette. She owned no paints or powders, had she wanted to wear them, and if her crepe was green, it was the only point of similarity between the two dresses. It struck her, as she noted the expanse of swelling bosom Aurelia Stanhope displayed, that the woman had likely not worn a dress with a high neck since she left the schoolroom.

But if Jessica believed her looks faded before Lady Aurelia's, there was at least one other present who did not agree as she was to learn when she caught the toe of her slipper in the fringe of the large Aubusson rug covering the floor and a heavy hand caught her elbow.

"Can't have our prettiest partridge stumbling." Alfred Marling's unpleasant voice rasped throatily in her ear.

Jessica contained a shiver. Marling's breath reeked unpleasantly of brandy. "Thank you, my lord," she said coolly, and having done the polite, she pulled away from the man's loathsome touch. He did not release her.

"Such a beautiful bird you are despite your drab feathers, my dear." With a knowing wink he whispered, "If it's Stafford's idea to rig you out like a wren in the hopes of throwing Rellie off the scent, it won't work, you know. She's up to every game. Bound to guess what a looker like you is doing here. Not a companion, I'll be bound—not to that old harridan, at any rate."

For an instant Jessica's eyes flamed with such a light that Lord Marling drew in his breath. "You mistake the matter completely, sir. Good evening."

Alfred Marling did not take his eyes from Jessica as she proceeded down the room. Her slender, graceful figure imparted to the plain clothes she wore an elegance they had never possessed hanging in her wardrobe, but it was the flash of spirit she'd displayed that caused him to lick his fleshy lips. It had inflamed his interest.

He gave no hint of that interest at dinner. He would not have done so even had he been able, for it would not do to ogle a lady at table, however uncertain her status, but he was given little choice. Between him and Jessica sat Lady Beatrice, and whenever he turned to catch a glimpse of Jessica's vivid red-gold hair, he only succeeded in encountering the older woman's sharp-eyed glance.

"That one's every inch the poisonous ne'er-do-well," Lady Beatrice commented later when Jessica helped prepare her for bed.

Jessica inclined her head, but gave no hint how strongly she agreed. She did not care to distress Lady Bea.

"And that MacDonald fellow," Lady Bea snorted derisively as Jessica tucked her into bed. "Forever chortling at every remark his wife and Aurelia made like some foolish courtier. Not that Aurelia's not witty," the old lady added in some disgust. "She's a clever way with an *on-dit*. Only, did you notice how everyone but Aurelia appears to disadvantage in her stories? And how tediously seldom an original thought is conveyed in all her bright patter?"

Before Jessica could be expected to answer, Lady Beatrice shook her head disgustedly. "Not that Justin seemed to notice how entirely self-centered and shallow she is. He regarded her in that amused way. It was a lazy-enough look, I grant, but Aurelia took it as flattery, particularly when it strayed, as it frequently did, to her décolletage!"

Jessica made some soothing, noncommittal noise as she unpinned Lady Bea's hair and brushed it out, but otherwise she made the lady no answer. She had, in fact, noticed everything Lady Beatrice had, and she had experienced some of the same dismay, which was absurd, she knew.

Lady Beatrice had every right to be concerned over her nephew's choice of bride, but certainly Jessica did not. What could it matter to her if Roxham's heavy-lidded gaze strayed openly to Lady Aurelia's bared bosom? And certainly she could not be affected if he chose for his wife a leader of fashion who would not know Ovid from

Homer and whose play at the piano in the drawing room after dinner was note-for-note faultless but as inspiring as a glass of hot lemonade.

Still, however absurd it was, Jessica could not deny that she'd lost her appetite as she had watched Aurelia hold forth. No harm was done. No one had noticed that she'd only pushed her peas about her plate or that she'd managed a single bite of the strawberry cake. True, once or twice she had glanced up to find Roxham's gaze had flicked to her, but he'd not watched her long enough to remark her eating habits. By some ploy or other, Lady Aurelia had invariably returned the earl's attention to her.

That night Jessica had difficulty sleeping. Confused images of Roxham, Lord Marling, Lady Aurelia, and worst of all, Mr. Godfrey haunted her. When she heard Lady Beatrice's bell, the sound came as a relief and she was quite glad to be sent to the library for some book that would, hopefully, deliver them both into a more restful slumber. Dressed fully—for, though she assumed all the manor's inhabitants were fast asleep, she had learned to be respectably attired whenever she left her room— she stood on the first step of a ladder just taking down a volume of Coleridge's poetry when a beefy hand clamped onto her waist.

"No," she screamed aloud before the man clamped another hand over her mouth and lifted her from the step.

Recognizing Lord Marling's foul breath, she kicked furiously at his shins, but he only laughed low in her ear.

"Don't be frightened, sweeting," he purred. "You are my reward for pushing away from the cards like a good boy. Told that nevy of Roxham's I couldn't lose again, and here I am."

A wave of panic overwhelming her, Jessica did not wait for him to say more. She bit down hard upon the hand covering her mouth.

"Blast," he swore, dropping it but tightening his hold cruelly on her waist with the other.

"Let me go!" Jessica pulled frantically at his hand. "Lady Beatrice has sent me for a book. She is expecting me at any moment."

Lord Alfred only spun her about in answer, and the

gleam in his small eyes made her mouth go dry. "Come! Come," he chided hoarsely, his eyes fastened on her lips. "You cannot be solely at that old harridan's beck and call. If you're not Roxham's doxy yet, you will be soon enough. He won't live long with the likes of you and keep his hands off, or he's not half the man I know him to be. Come, sweeting, give us a kiss with that luscious mouth."

Jessica twisted her head from side to side in desperation. "Let me go!"

"Marling! I say, Marling!"

The sound of his name penetrated Sir Alfred's senses only slowly. "Huh?" he grunted, turning partially about but not loosening his grip on his prey.

To Jessica, straining to see over Marling's thick shoulder, the sight of Andrew Fitzgerald could not have been more welcome.

"Let her go," the young man demanded as he advanced militantly into the room.

"You up to making me, lad?" Marling growled, facing toward the intruder.

Feeling her attacker's grip loosen as he responded to Andrew's challenge, Jessica put all her strength into one sudden, abrupt movement. Taking Marling by surprise, she broke free, and, eluding his effort to grab her, ran to link her arm with Andrew's. There was no time to hesitate if a very ugly scene were to be avoided. Before either man could quite fathom what had happened, Jessica had half-dragged Andrew to the door.

"Justin will want to know the sort of gentleman you are, sir," Andrew yelled over his shoulder as Jessica hurried him off. "Miss Winslow is under his protection."

His mind muddled by drink, Marling could not gather himself to respond before the two were safely away, and Jessica did not release Andrew until they standing at the head of the stairs.

"Thank you," she said, her voice trembling. "I owe you a great deal for that rescue, Andrew."

"The man's a beast," the young man cried in response. "Did he hurt you, Jess?"

194

"No, no." She shook her head. "I am quite all right, only a little shaken."

"You are so pale. And trembling like a leaf. I should go down and throttle him now."

"No! Please! You mustn't!" Jessica held tightly to Andrew's arm when he seemed prepared to return to the library. "I would not have you brawling with him. He is quite past rational thought."

Her breath coming under her control as her panic receded, Jessica attempted a smile. "Truly . . ."

"Truly you would die of shame," Andrew cut in abruptly. "Well, you needn't look so unhappy. I won't raise the household tonight, but I will certainly have Justin send him on his way tomorrow. He's a menace we shan't tolerate."

Jessica gasped. "No! You mustn't say anything to your cousin." The cry was a desperate plea from the heart, and seeing Andrew look at her in astonishment, she searched for some reason to sway him.

She could not admit the truth: that she was a craven coward.

Though Roxham had assured her only hours earlier that she need never fear the attentions of a man like Marling while she lived at Bleithewood, she feared to put his sympathies to the test: Aurelia Stanhope had come to Bleithewood in the intervening hours. However sympathetic the earl had been about her fears, he had held his doubts about her too long for Jessica to credit he would give her the benefit of the doubt when it was her word against that of his future brother-in-law.

It would only be the same as it had been with Edward Stafford. Roxham would fix her with a cold, disdainful gaze, and Jessica could not bear the thought of enduring it again.

Not now. Not after the way he'd looked at her in the woods. They had been friends, and she would not give that up.

As for Lord Marling . . . She was accustomed to taking care of herself. She'd no need to make the ugly scene public and to live with the questions she knew would linger in everyone's eyes. She would manage by avoiding the viscount in the future.

"Leave it, please, Andrew," she begged the young man. "As I said, Marling was in his cups and not responsible for his behavior. I shouldn't care to cause a problem for the earl's guests."

They both knew she referred to one guest in particular, and though he hesitated, Andrew eventually relented. "I cannot like it, but if you insist, I suppose I must honor your wish," he said, and Jessica gratefully squeezed his hand. "But you will take care he doesn't catch you alone again, won't you?" Andrew demanded, frowning.

Jessica nodded in earnest. "Of that you may be certain!"

"I would be obliged to call him out if he succeeded in mauling you, you know."

"Andrew," Jessica cried, surprised and not pleased.

But Andrew paid no attention to her dismay. "I would," he assured her solemnly. Then he kissed her hand and looked at her with something approaching a grin. "And to save my neck I should tell you Marling is quite a swordsman, despite his girth. Have a care, Miss Winslow, or you might lose me."

"I will exercise even greater caution now, I promise." Rather tremulously she returned his smile before going up on tiptoe to kiss him on the cheek. "Good night, sweet prince. Sleep well."

Andrew watched until she'd gained Lady Bea's door, the book she'd managed somehow to retain still in her hands; then he turned in the direction of his own room. As they went their separate ways, a door nearby closed.

Lady Aurelia had not slept easily either that night. She'd laid awake a long while, hoping Roxham would visit her bed, though he'd have been brazen indeed to do so with his elderly aunt sleeping only a few doors away. Hearing voices in the hall, she'd risen at once to investigate. Perhaps, she thought, Justin stayed up late playing at cards and was now coming to her.

The sight of Lady Beatrice's companion in earnest conversation with young Andrew Fitzgerald was not so pleasing as Roxham's powerful figure advancing toward her room would have been, but it was intriguing. Though she was clad only in her filmiest nightdress, Lady Aurelia cracked her door a little further.

She was frustrated in her efforts to hear what the two said, but she did note how often they touched each other, and that, at the end of their tryst, the chit was so bold as to kiss Mary's son.

It was a chaste kiss, she granted, but she recalled some remark Mary had made, hinting at a concern for young Andrew. Aurelia rarely paid Mary's chatter much attention, but she thought it all had something to do with the boy's lack of interest in an eligible *parti*.

And now here he was in the dead of night, when all honest souls were asleep, holding a rendezvous with Lady Beatrice's companion—most certainly an ineligible *parti*.

Lady Aurelia closed her door, her lips parting in a satisfied smile. She had not cared for the chit on sight. However drably she dressed, she was, still, too attractive for Aurelia's liking.

But how foolish the girl was to let the boy walk her up the stairs. Assignations ought to be conducted with a greater care for secrecy, as Aurelia knew. If they were not, people would see . . . and they would talk.

Aurelia nearly laughed aloud as she crossed to her bed. Yes, they would talk—to Justin, the head of the family, who would of a certainty want to know of the strange goings-on between his young cousin and his aunt's companion.

20

"Come in, boy. You needn't lounge by the door listening to Jess read in secret. Come see how cozy she's made me, dragging me to this window so the sunlight may warm my old bones."

"Surely, I did not drag you, my lady." Jessica smiled

as she marked her place in their book and looked around to see that Lady Beatrice addressed the earl. It seemed he had come straight from riding, for his tawny hair was windblown and he still wore a pair of tight riding breeches that displayed his long, lean legs very well indeed.

Lady Beatrice made a face at Jessica. "Coaxed, wheedled, whatever—you were determined I should come. And by gad, you were right," she ended by chortling. "It's perfectly delicious here."

Roxham bent to give her a kiss. "Even your cheeks are warm."

After receiving the salute with unmistakable pleasure, Lady Bea demanded tartly, "And what brings you to my boudoir? No doubt, like the twins, Livy, and everyone else, you've come for Jess, not me."

Not fooled at all by her gruff tone, Roxham smiled. "I've come for you both, in fact. First I should like a few words with Miss Winslow, and then I had it in mind to win back the small fortune I lost to you that last time we played piquet. That is, of course, if you can do with only me. The twins have begged me to request that Miss Winslow be allowed to take tea with them. They protest they've not seen her for all of a day."

"Well, what say you, Jess?" Lady Beatrice demanded. "Will you be pleased to take tea with two children and a dog. I don't doubt they put down a dish of milk for that ruffian."

"I fear you are all too right, ma'am," Jessica replied, and though the earl's demand for a private interview alarmed her, she managed a light shrug of her shoulders. "But in truth I do not mind. The ruffian has charmed me as well."

"Well, now that's all settled, take the girl off, Justin. But mind, don't be hard on her or you shall answer to me."

"Aunt Bea does not seem so drawn as she did last night," Roxham observed when he and Jessica were alone in his aunt's sitting room.

Jessica nodded as he went to lean his arm negligently across the mantelpiece, and she took the seat toward which he had gestured. "Lady Bea likely ought not to have gone down last evening at all, I suppose, but she forced herself, ah, on account of your guests."

Thinking precisely why Lady Beatrice had felt called upon to do her duty below last evening, Jessica swallowed a smile, but it seemed Roxham was not much fooled, for he gave her a quick, searching look. "She is not normally so punctilious," he remarked. "Nor did she seem to enjoy herself. She ate little, but then you had less than your customary appetite as well. Perhaps it was the food."

"Mrs. Appleby outdid herself, as always." Jessica leapt to the defense of the cook only to see Roxham's eyes light with amusement.

She flushed at how easily she'd taken his bait, but the earl, giving her no time to remark to herself how he had watched her more closely at table than she'd realized, was already asking, "How, then, did Aunt Bea sleep? She'd a quiet night I trust?"

At the mention of the night a certain wariness entered Jessica's eyes, but she said calmly enough, "No, actually, she did not. You aunt was restless in the night, but she did sleep late this morning to make up for it."

"A luxury in which you did not indulge, if I can judge by the smudges under your eyes."

Jessica dropped her eyes. She'd slept little at all the night before, but she did not wish to discuss the reason for her bout of insomnia.

"I'd have thought kissing Andrew would put a bloom in your cheeks, not make you unusually pale." Jessica's head jerked up, and she stared, stunned. A thin smile that did not reach Roxham's eyes curved his lips. "You did not know you were observed?" he inquired, mocking her.

"It was nothing." She had to force the words past very still lips.

His arched brow condemned her as surely as did his words. "An assignation in the dead of night? Whispered endearments? A kiss? Come, come, Miss Winslow. It was very much something."

Jessica sat still as a graven image, her blue eyes very

199

dark. There was nothing she could say. If she told the truth now, Roxham would only think she and Andrew lied to explain their tryst. Certainly Lord Marling would never admit to his brutish behavior.

Roxham's fist, when it hit the mantel, banged with the full force of his body and caused a pair of Queen Anne candlesticks to totter uncertainly. Jessica jumped at the sound and drew back in her chair when he stalked across the room toward her.

Not content with looming over her, he placed a hand on either side of her head and bent very close to demand thunderously, "What is your game, madam? Why do you refuse even now to tell the truth?" Before Jessica could gather her scattered wits and think how to reply to the anger heating his eyes, he snapped impatiently, "I know the story from Andy. He's not so blasted stubborn as are you.

"Why?" He shook her chair, then stood back and glared down at her as if he might do the same to her. "Why did you not wish me to know?"

Jessica kept her chin lifted. She would not let him browbeat her. If he knew the whole, there was no reason to have played a cat-and-mouse game with her.

"I thought it would be for the best if I merely took care to avoid Lord Marling in future, particularly when he has had an excess of drink. There need be no awkwardness for Lady Aurelia or you then."

"How noble of you!"

Jessica's eyes flashed at his dry tone. Sparing Roxham awkwardness had only been a part of the reason for her silence; still, she had considered him.

Roxham was not affected by her expression. "You needn't look daggers at me, miss," he growled harshly. "I am impervious to your black looks, potent though they are. If you think I intend to applaud the notion that a member of my household should leave herself open to attacks by a drunkard merely to save me the trouble of telling him and his sister I'll not tolerate such uncivilized behavior, then you are fair and far out in your reading of my character. I thought we had come to a greater degree of trust."

200

Jessica's cheeks flamed. He made her feel a perfect wretch. "Lord Marling is your friend . . ." She flinched as Roxham's brow drew down in a scowl, but she was not completely cowed. "I think I cannot be entirely faulted for fearing you might not believe my word over his."

She had a point, of course, but Roxham was not much mollified. "I see I need to be quite clear with you, Miss Winslow," he began, his gaze cool and unrelenting. "I am, yet, uncertain whether or not you would bid for the attentions of a young, attractive man of good family and some wealth. I am, however, quite certain that the attentions of a dissolute wastrel of middle-age would leave you as distraught as Andrew reported you were when he rescued you last evening. Nor, to continue, do I in any way believe you were responsible for Marling's inexcusable behavior. His lechery is well-known, and I consider that, if anyone aside from the man himself is to blame, then it is I. I ought to have warned him off you before he set foot in this house. Now I intend to deal with him by booting him from the premises this afternoon."

"No, please!" Jessica caught Roxham's arm as if she would physically restrain him. Beneath her fingers his muscles jumped and he looked down at her hand as if amazed by her impertinence. At once she drew back, flushing.

Mortified at having so overstepped the bounds, she stammered hastily, "Forgive me. I-I only meant to say I wish you would not require Lord Marling to depart."

Andy, when he'd been persuaded to speech earlier, had graphically described the brutal embrace to which Alfred Marling had submitted Jessica, and now, studying her unhappy face, with the feel of her slender hand still warming his arm, Roxham experienced a deadly desire to knock his guest into eternity. It was an absurdly extreme action to wish to take on behalf of a girl he was not certain he even trusted, but there it was. She was in his house, dependent upon him. He protected what was his.

"He does not deserve to remain."

Roxham's tone was so imperious, so much the lord-of-

201

the-manor that Jessica nearly smiled. She did not, however, for along with the flat look in his eyes, it gave her to fear she would not succeed in swaying him from his determined course. But the issue was important to her and she returned his set look with a level one of her own.

"If you send him away, my lord, there will gossip, and I shall be the focus of it, not he." She held herself courageously, but the shadows in her blue eyes revealed her fear of wagging tongues. "When I look for a new position, as I shall eventually be obliged to do, people will whisper that I bring trouble with men, and doors will close to me. It is possible someone will even recollect I was the girl who disappeared with Edward, and then there will be no hope at all."

The earl did not care for her reasoning. His aunt would live a long while yet. Jessica need not be affected by the inevitable gossip. And Marling must pay for his outrageous conduct.

"Please, my lord," Jessica begged in earnest when she realized he did not intend to relent. "You must see that it is I who will suffer from your punishment, not Lord Marling."

Arrested by the intensity of her concern, Roxham demanded roughly, "Is it your intention to leave within the year?" He saw her hesitate and he said quietly, "Bea would be distraught if you did, you know."

He'd succeeded at playing upon her sympathies, he saw when she flushed slightly. "I am very fond of your aunt as well, and I've no plans to go. It is only that my situation anywhere is tentative at best."

Roxham knew she was not telling the whole truth. She had considered leaving. The thought that she might, could, one day simply walk out the door left him oddly displeased.

But aloud he said only, "If you do not intend to leave, then the manor is for all intents and purposes your home. I will not have you afraid to walk the halls in your own home."

Jessica stared a moment before she could reply, "My lord, I am grateful for your concern. I truly am." There was no question at all she meant what she said. Her eyes shone with her gratitude. It had been a very long time indeed since there had been anyone to protect her.

But there was, as well, a shadowing of sadness in her eyes, as if she looked back to the time when she had stood alone and looked forward to when that time would come again. Had he been able to smooth that sorrow away by caressing her cheek, Roxham would have done so. Indeed, his hand came up, but Jessica, unaware of his intent, was addressing him once again.

". . . and I've no wish to worry what Lord Marling intends," he heard her say. "Now that you know what occurred, I should be grateful if you would speak to him. He would respect your wishes, I believe. As Andy would say, you've the devil of a look."

She smiled, hopeful that she had persuaded him not to make a great to do that would embarrass her. There was nothing coy in her expression. She looked at him quite steadily, even earnestly. And the faint sparkle he could detect was due entirely to her bit of humor about his supposed look.

"You make it difficult for me to do as I would like," Roxham said slowly. It was not easy to give up all thought of throttling Alfred, nor to concede to himself, if not to her, that her eyes had a power over him. But the truth was he did not care to see them dim. "If I do respect your wishes and do not toss Alfred out the door, then I expect you to come to me at once if he makes the least untoward move. Are we agreed, Jessica?"

The use of her name slipped out unnoted by him but not by her. To Jessica her name had a different sound when Roxham said it. It seemed they were friends again and her heart quickened even as she told herself she was being absurd. "That seems fair enough, my lord."

He was amused. She might have been a royal princess. "I am relieved you find it so."

It was impossible not to grin back at him. "But, my lord," she protested, "I always endeavor to give satisfaction."

"You endeavor," he corrected, "to give as good as you get, and you usually do."

The twins banged upon the door then and tumbled

through before they were invited. They had, they protested, been obliged to wait ages for their tea. "Are you not done with Jess yet, Justin?" Julia demanded of her cousin.

He did not seem put out by the children's uncivilized behavior. He only laughed at them and, after a last look at Jessica, took himself off to his aunt's room.

"Oh, I am glad Justin was not put out of countenance with us," Giles exclaimed, tugging Jessica out the door and toward the teapot in the nursery. "We thought he might be giving you a dressing-down, he kept you so long, but I can see he didn't," the little boy said, eyeing Jessica's rosy cheeks.

Jessica flushed brighter still. How did she look? Could Roxham know he had affected her? He had. Giddy fool or not, for a space of time whose length she could not judge, she had been aware of little else than that the earl looked down at her with teasing lights dancing in his golden-brown eyes. On account of them and his flashing smile, she had come close to forgetting even to breathe.

After his game of piquet with his aunt, Roxham sought out Alfred Marling and in concise terms he informed the man that if he ever again saw fit to assault Miss Winslow, he would first thrash him within an inch of his life and second call him out to finish the task with pistols or swords, whichever Marling preferred. Roxham's proficiency with blade or pistol being as celebrated as his ability in the ring, Alfred muttered an excuse that involved an excess of drink, and conceded the day without an argument.

Roxham's third interview on the subject of the previous evening's events brought him full circle, for the round had begun when Aurelia had hastened after luncheon to confide she'd seen Miss Winslow kissing Andrew in the hallway late in the night.

At her report, all Roxham's doubts of Jessica had rushed back. She was right, really to mistrust how he would judge any matter concerning her, he admitted. After he'd heard Aurelia's story, he had not taken the stairs two at a time to demand an explanation only because Jessica was still taking her lunch with his aunt.

He'd gone, as he had planned, to the stables, where by happy coincidence he had met Andy. Poor boy! Roxham smiled grimly to himself. His expression must have been threatening indeed, for the lad had paled visibly. It had been nothing to convince him to tell the full tale.

And as a result, he was now, once again, closeted with Aurelia. She was the only person he'd ever known to exert even a modicum of control over her brother, and he was determined that she would do so now on Miss Winslow's behalf.

Aurelia, however, was quite put out of countenance to have her plan to discredit Lady Beatrice's companion result in Roxham's championing of the chit. "But I cannot see what all the fuss is over," she cried pettishly when Roxham had told her what he wanted of her. "Alfie has spoken to me, Justin, and he is quite piqued, poor thing. He only meant to amuse himself, after all."

Not stupid, Aurelia saw at once she'd spoken out of turn. Justin had never looked at her so sharply. Truly alarmed, she spoke quickly. "Oh, believe me, Justin, I do understand! You think to protect a young, innocent girl living under your roof. It is an admirable sentiment, one I applaud. But, darling, you must see your error in this case. It defies reason to believe that a girl with her, ah"—Aurelia pursed her red lips as she chose the appropriate word—"provocative looks has not inflamed some man to passion ere this. Do not forget I saw her embrace young Andrew, and Alfie says she is a spirited chit."

The reminder that Alfred Marling coveted a taste of the spirit that undoubtedly filled every fiber of Jessica Winslow's being caused Roxham's eyes to flash with an unholy light.

"I will not say this again, Rellie, so listen well if you care to remain at Bleithewood with your brother. I will not tolerate a guest who forces his unwanted attentions upon any female living in my house—from the lowest scullery maid to my own cousin. If Alfred should forget himself so completely again, I would be obliged to boot him from the premises."

Aurelia yielded to Roxham's strength on the instant. "I understand, of course," she submitted breathlessly, her hand fluttering out in a supplicating gesture. "Only don't be angry with me, my dear, I pray. Alfred is my brother, and that is why I do plead his case to excess on occasion. And too"—she widened her eyes innocently—"I am the least bit envious. This girl has been quite successful at enlisting your sympathies on her behalf."

"But it was you who did the enlisting, Rellie." Roxham chuckled at the surprise Aurelia could not hide. "Had you not come to tell me your tale, I'd have known nothing. She had no intention of telling me, and I had to fairly pry the incident out of her."

It was only with great effort that Aurelia kept from gnashing her teeth in vexation, and when only a short time later she was alone with her brother, she felt no need for restraint.

Standing over Alfred, who lolled brandy glass in hand on a chaise in her boudoir, she pointed her finger. "Fool," she castigated him, "I have spent an entire interview with Justin discussing you and that wretched, little companion. I shan't forget that your stupidity has enlisted his sympathies on her behalf."

"Fiddle it, Rellie," her brother protested idly. "If you believe Justin's only just taking note of her, you're a bigger fool than I thought. Justin Stafford's not the sort to overlook a beauty like her. He's staked her out, and no mistake. Wouldn't have warned me off her so strongly otherwise. A man doesn't challenge a guest over a maid."

Aurelia slashed the air with her hand as she stalked from her brother's side. "That means nothing," she cried. "Justin couldn't be interested in such a nonentity. You only touched his sense of honor. As you have not got one, you would not understand, but Justin can be devilish touchy on some things."

Recalling his interview with the earl, Sir Alfred did not dispute her observation. "Devilish, indeed," he grunted. "He's a glare that could curdle milk. And perhaps," he continued after a moment, casting his sister a sly look, "it was affronted honor that nearly set him at my throat, my dear. But I take leave to doubt it. Tell me,

Rellie, what explanation has Justin given for staying away from town half the Season. You expected him to return within a sennight, did you not?''

Unable to deny it, Aurelia bit her lip. ''Mary says he's here to help her with the boy, Andrew. Something to do with his balking at marrying a squire's daughter.'' She shrugged as if Justin's absence from her side were explained satisfactorily.

''That boy couldn't hold out a day against Justin if he were set upon something,'' Alfred scoffed. ''There's more to it, and you'd best find out what it is. Your earl does not seem overly pleased to see you, my dear. As I told you in town, a man like Roxham doesn't care to be pursued.''

''Nonsense! He's enchanted to see me. And I am not pursuing him. I've every right, knowing of his injury, to look in on Justin. We are on those terms.''

''I only hope 'those terms' are not in your imagination for both our sakes,'' Alfred frowned at his sister over the rim of his glass. ''I've notes all over town, and Roxham's fortune means quite as much to me as it does to you. It was rumored,'' he continued, watching her closely, ''that the earl, the day he left, had a necklace—emeralds and diamonds, I believe—sent around to you. It is his custom, so the gossips say, to bid farewell with just such a costly bauble.''

Aurelia pinned her brother with a blazing stare. ''He has not given me my congé,'' she shrilled. That Justin had accompanied the stunning choker with a note thanking her for the ''memorable interlude'' they'd had, she dismissed. He'd meant the week they'd spent at a house party in Kent, she was certain of it. ''No man dismisses me. And certainly I shall not be passed over in favor of a companion.''

Aurelia's dark eyes glittered with anger, and Sir Alfred smiled admiringly. ''It's a pity you weren't born the son, Rellie.'' He saluted her, then settled his empty glass upon the table. ''But as you were born the woman of the family, my dear, see that you use your womanly wiles to catch Justin and his fortune in your toils. I should not like to see you passed over for this chit, if for no other

207

reason than I should miss my chance at her. I shall assist you as much as I am able," he continued, standing to go. "In the hopes that she will give us some means to turn Justin's interest into disgust, I shall watch her. Your only task in the meantime, my love"—Alfred turned at the door—"is to behave with grace and sweetness if you are able, for Justin will never abide the shrew you can be."

With an alacrity born of an extended acquaintance with his sibling, Alfred bowed himself out the door in time to use it to deflect Aurelia's shoe. Chuckling to himself, he continued toward his rooms, confident that Aurelia would do her best to turn Justin up sweet and that he would enjoy the task he'd set himself: keeping his eye on Jessica Winslow. Eventually, he assured himself, when Rellie had safely gotten Justin out of the way, he would have his chance at her.

21

"I know I ought not to say so, Jess." Olivia flounced away from her maid, Maggie, to address Jessica with a defiant pout. "But I am glad Philip's father is gone. I do not even resent having to wear this drab black that makes me look as plain as a church mouse. It means that that wastrel, who had not a care in the world for any but himself, is no longer about to plague Philip or Kate or their mother."

Jessica did not believe Sir Augustus would be greatly mourned by anyone at the memorial service that day, but as she had known the man herself, she asked after his family. "Have you had much opportunity to speak with Kate or her brother, Livy?"

Olivia nodded, tugging against a curler Maggie was unwinding so that she winced. "Kate is as incorrigible as I! She scarcely knew her father, he was so often away in London losing all their blunt."

When Jessica lifted her brows at Livy's use of the cant expression, the younger girl gave her a charming grin. "Well, I could scarcely say wealth," she protested. "They've not had wealth since Sir Augustus came into the title. Oh, Jess! Philip does not say as much as Kate, but he has a lighter step, I swear it. And his eyes when he looks at me . . ." Olivia broke off, smiling dreamily. "Oh, they seem so many things at once, you see. Glad and approving and pleased, Jess. I hope you will speak to Justin. I cannot marry Ned. Philip is a baronet now with land. Lots of it, really, and it will provide us a splendid living when he restores it.

"He is so wise," Livy rattled on. "He'll make it pay in no time. And he is so strong, and handsome. He's the most handsome man I know, excepting Justin—and he is rather old. What think you, Jess?"

The strength of her desire to object that Roxham was not at all old and was, by far, the handsomer of the two men surprised Jessica so she bit her lip. "Hmmm. Well, I think them both very fine-looking, and Andrew too," she added for good measure.

Olivia dismissed such evenhandedness with an airy wave of her hand. "You are too diplomatic. Andrew is too silly to be handsome. Now, if I asked Aurelia her thoughts, she would speak out so loudly for Justin that he would be certain to hear." Livy wrinkled her nose. "The way she throws herself at him is quite disgusting. Did you see her last night after dinner? She made a spectacle of herself, trying to get him off alone. Why, she even asked him to teach her chess. As if she could learn such a game. She only wanted the opportunity to lean over the board so he'd see her bosom in that dress."

Jessica continued to busy herself with instructing Maggie what to do with the ribbon they intended to thread through Livy's curls, but though she made no answer, Olivia was not deterred.

She gave a gurgling laugh. "But I vow Justin's up to every rig," she cried. "He turned aside her every effort with such smoothness. I thought I would laugh aloud when he told her she ought to ask you for lessons on chess, as you were the better player. He has such prodigious respect for you, Jess," Olivia added in awed tones.

Jessica inspected Olivia's curls and brushed one errant strand around her finger. "I'm not the better player by any means, as your cousin well knows," she said, dismissing the matter. "He was only trying to fob off the task of teaching a beginner on someone else."

"Aurelia thought it a good deal more than that. The look she gave you would have boiled you alive, had it been water."

Truly surprised, Jessica glanced at Livy in the glass. "But that is absurd! Lady Aurelia has no reason to feel anything at all toward me. I haven't spoken above five words with her since she came to Bleithewood."

With a merry laugh Olivia clasped Jessica's hand. "Sometimes, Jess, I think you are the younger of us. It is nothing you've said to her, dear. She's pea green because she cannot abide the thought that Justin holds you in high regard—as everyone but you seems to know."

It was true that Roxham had been warmer toward her since they'd agreed to cry truce. Even with his guests about, he found the time here and there to exchange a private word with her. Sometimes he asked after the Crenshawes or recommended a book he'd read. Jessica had particularly enjoyed the work of a new author, Jane Austen. And on occasion he had appeared unannounced in his aunt's rooms at the time when Jessica generally read to Lady Beatrice. When she stopped, he would wave her on, saying he'd come to listen to her.

Livy clapped her hands together, startling Jessica. "Just thinking of Aurelia clad all in black reconciles me to the idea of this service."

Jessica, grateful to have been rescued from thoughts of Roxham, smiled. "I thought you admired Lady Aurelia's sense of fashion prodigiously, Livy."

"Oh, I do find her clothes marvelously fashionable," Livy sniffed. "But she is so unbearably condescending in her manner that I cannot like her. Do you know she never fails to call me child?" Olivia's outrage became a sly smile as she looked as Jessica. "But I shall enjoy watching her face today when she sees you, Jess."

Mystified, Jessica frowned. "Whatever do you mean, Livy?"

"She'll not be so high and mighty, then," Olivia cried with reprehensible enthusiasm. "No matter how fashionable the cut of her dress is, she will be garbed in black, and for once she'll not have the advantage over you. I vow, when she sees how black becomes you, she'll be positively bilious."

Jessica thought Livy absurd and said so, and when she did meet Aurelia only a little time later, she had no opportunity to gauge the widow's reaction to her appearance.

Having taken longer than she'd expected arranging Olivia's curls, Jessica was hurrying to meet Lady Beatrice in the red salon, where they were all to congregate before leaving for Bleithewood's church. From the top of the stairs she saw Lady Aurelia below her, descending arm in arm with her friend, Mrs. MacDonald. A blur of movement caught Jessica's eyes, and from her vantage point she saw what the two ladies did not. The twins, Caesar prancing excitedly before them, were approaching down the hallway. Giles carefully carried something cupped in his hands and Julia pulled upon his arm, as if she were eager to see it.

Distracted, neither child watched Caesar, and when he detected a movement on the stairs, there was no one to prevent him bounding forward with a loud bark. From that moment on the scene became one of chaos. The ladies screamed in fright, causing Giles to inadvertently loosen his hold on the something in his hands, which was a frog.

In two amazing leaps, the frog attained the stairs and dived straight for the cover Lady Aurelia's skirt promised. Snatching at her skirts, she simultaneously rent the air with shrill screams and danced a maniacal jig to avoid stepping on the lively creature.

Caesar began barking wildly, excited by the commotion and then, adding disaster to disaster, jumped approvingly upon Lady Aurelia to show he enjoyed her dance. Seeing the dusty paw prints he left upon her dress,

211

she screamed all the more loudly and with the sharp toe of her half-boot gave the pup a savage kick.

Caesar sailed through the air, his bark now a pitiable yelp, and the twins added their piping voices to the mayhem. "You kicked him. You kicked him," Giles accused.

"He deserved worse," Lady Aurelia fumed, high spots of color on her cheeks.

"Oh!" Mrs. MacDonald screamed then, for the frog had hopped onto her foot. "Ahhhh," she went on, shaking first one foot and then another as she clutched at Lady Aurelia.

Rushing down the hallway from the salon, Lady Mary could scarcely be heard above the noise as she wailed faintly, "Oh, my! Oh, my! Whatever has happened?"

Lady Aurelia, displaying a side of her character Lady Mary had never seen, whirled furiously upon her hostess. "Those little hooligans have just loosed a monster upon us and allowed that . . . that mongrel to paw me."

Dismayed by the force of the lady's anger, Lady Mary put her hand to her mouth. "Giles, Julia?" She turned to her children.

"He was only being friendly," Julia protested, Caesar's continuing whimpers affecting her so she quite forgot her manners. "There was no need to hurt him!"

"Oh, my," her mother cried ineffectually as Mrs. MacDonald let out another hysterical scream when, in her efforts to evade the frog, she succeeded in landing squarely upon it.

"She kicked Caesar and hurt him." Giles' indignant voice added to the confusion. "She is—"

"Giles." In contrast to the others, Jessica's voice was low and, mercifully, had the effect of bringing everyone's attention around to her at once. "Lady Aurelia deserves an apology," she commanded quietly as she descended the stairs. "No well-trained dog musses a lady's skirts." She turned her attention to the little girl. "Julia, Caesar will recover. Please make your apology as well. You agreed to keep Caesar and any other pets in the nursery or outside, away from your mother's guests."

Having reached Mrs. MacDonald, Jessica stooped

down and with a swift motion recovered the frog. "James?" Jessica looked to the footman who had been following the scene from his place by the door. "Will you see this fellow's returned to his place—outside?"

Despite his best efforts to maintain a solemn expression, a smile curved the young man's mouth as the exchange was made and he proceeded out the door with the "monster," but no one aside from Jessica, who sympathized, noted his lapse. The twins had simultaneously begun making their apologies.

"We do apologize, Lady Aurelia," each one mumbled politely enough, though they avoided her eye.

"Now, take Caesar to the nursery," Jessica instructed. "I shall join you when I am able to see how he is getting along," she added in answer to their pleading looks.

As the children departed, their pup cradled in Julia's arms, Jessica turned to Lady Aurelia. "Is your dress in need of repair, ma'am?" she asked. "I shall be glad to see to it, if you wish."

Aurelia, her eyes cold, pulled herself to her greatest height, and though she did not reach Jessica's eyes, she did look imposing. "My maid," she said, her emphasis relegating Jessica to that lowly status, "is perfectly capable of attending to my needs."

"Unless you care to forgo this service for Verney, you'd best make do with brushing Caesar's dirt off yourself, Rellie. We are late as it is."

"Justin," Aurelia cried dramatically. The earl had come down the hall just as Giles and Julia had given their apologies, and his presence undetected, he had watched Jessica attempt to soothe Aurelia. "Oh, my dear, you will not countenance it, but I was attacked by that monstrous dog."

Her hand on her brow, Lady Aurelia swayed as if she might faint, but when Roxham made no move toward her, she made do with Mrs. MacDonald's arm. Half-reclining on her friend, she recounted in awful tones all that had taken place.

In return she received little sympathy. Her story done, Roxham nodded. "Well, all's quiet now," he observed with evident satisfaction. "You've powerful lungs, you

213

know, my dear. I could hear your screams on the terrace.'' He was smiling in such a way that Aurelia could not decide if he flattered or scoffed. She decided to sniff, but the pitiful little sound went for naught. Looking to Moreton, the earl instructed him to fetch the ladies' wraps. ''We must be off shortly. It wouldn't do to miss more than one eulogy.''

''We're all present,'' Lady Bea announced as she arrived on Mr. MacDonald's arm. ''Was there a battle royal taking place out here?'' she inquired loudly. ''I never heard such cacophony in all my days.''

As Lady Aurelia again recounted her bitter struggles with the twins and their menagerie, Moreton came. Jessica assisted Lady Beatrice with her shawl while Roxham did the honors for Lady Aurelia, which seemed to appease her, for she smiled tremulously at him.

Her sweet expression faded dramatically only a moment later when Roxham left her to take a simple cotton shawl from Moreton and wrap it around Miss Winslow's slender shoulders. Her eyes narrowing, she watched as, with the excuse of adjusting the girl's shawl, he leaned to whisper conspiratorially into her ear.

''I wonder where our wild animals are now, Miss Winslow?'' Roxham inquired. ''I shouldn't want them to be lurking on the steps outside. I fear our guests might never recover.''

Jessica could not help but smile. The scene had been so comically absurd she'd have laughed, had she not had to take charge. ''Caesar is recovering in the nursery and I gave the frog to James to return to the pond.''

''Hmm. I am certain James was prompt as always to do your bidding.'' At his dry tone, Jessica looked up quickly but found Roxham's eyes were twinkling as he queried her bravery. ''You were not afraid to touch so dangerous an animal?''

''No, my lord.''

''How commendable. You never cease to amaze me, Miss Winslow.''

Aurelia was powerless to prevent a line etching her brow as Justin's mouth curved in a half-smile and he bowed lazily to Lady Beatrice's companion. Nor could she be pleased to see that, when he turned back to her and the others, his smile faded.

On the drive to the church, Aurelia was seated across from Jessica. The close view she was afforded of the woman she had come to hold in intense dislike only added to her pique.

Really, it did not seem at all fair to her that anyone should look so, so—Aurelia could only bring herself to say—well in black. It was a dreadful color that quite turned her own complexion a dangerously sallow shade despite all her powders, while Miss Winslow's skin, Aurelia noted peevishly, seemed only to glow the more delicately.

Taking the opportunity afforded her as the girl joined in conversation with Olivia Fitzgerald, Aurelia darted her a close look, hoping to detect what coloring the chit used to make her eyes so deep a blue. She only just averted an ugly frown when she was forced to concede the chit used no artifice at all.

Not even on her hair—as Aurelia's maid had been ordered to discover from the other servants. Aurelia still found it difficult to believe no henna was used, but so her maid had sworn. Granted such a striking color was not the fashion. But Aurelia admitted such a nicety would matter little to a man. Contrasted with the black of the girl's dress, her hair seemed to burn like a flame.

Able to bear no more, Aurelia bit her lip and looked out the window. Andrew Fitzgerald was beside them, she saw, and leaning down to look in the window. Seeing his mother's attention was diverted, he looked directly at Miss Winslow and, grinning, bowed extravagantly.

It only infuriated Aurelia further that the young man did not so much as look in her direction. He was too callow to appreciate her, she supposed, but his preference for a mere companion rankled. Miss Winslow smiled and waved him on, rather as if he were her brother.

Was that dismissal done for the benefit of those in the carriage? Aurelia wondered. Likely so. The chit was clever. She'd managed to charm Justin into believing there was nothing between her and the boy.

Alfred was keeping his eye upon her, true, but Aurelia decided it would do no harm if they were both vigilant. She might see something her brother did not.

And if neither of them discovered anything? Aurelia smiled grimly. She'd find some way to discredit the girl. She must! Justin's interest in her was not to be borne.

22

"Mr. Headley is here to see you, Miss Jessica."

Jessica looked up from her needlework in surprise. "Thank you, Annie. Is he in the library?"

"Yes, miss." Annie curtsied and hurried from the room.

Jessica looked to Lady Beatrice. Her teacup sitting forgotten beside her, the older woman was concentrating on a game of piquet she played with Mrs. MacDonald. Free of pain for two days, she'd been determined to descend for tea.

"I must see what these self-invited guests are about," she had exclaimed, as if they might be making off with the silverware, and when Jessica laughed, Lady Bea had fixed her with a rebellious look. "Well, I haven't seen them for all of a week—since the day of old Verney's service when Aurelia screeched her head off over that pup. Egad, but she's a set of lungs."

As the men of the household had not yet returned from riding when the women gathered to have their tea, Lady Beatrice had taken advantage of the quiet to challenge Mrs. MacDonald, who had something of a reputation as a cardplayer, to a game of piquet, and though cardplaying at teatime was a trifle unusual, Mrs. MacDonald had readily indulged the older lady. Smiling to herself, Jessica thought that lady likely regretted her largesse, for it was obvious she'd had to struggle merely to hold her own against Lady Beatrice's shrewd play.

"Go along, my girl," Lady Beatrice called before Jessica could ask her permission to leave. "No need to keep Headley waiting. I'm well-occupied here for some little while."

When Jessica had left, Lady Aurelia looked to Mary, sitting on the couch beside her. "The girl has suitors coming to call?" she asked in a tone that indicated she was amazed by the latitude allowed a mere companion.

Lady Mary shook her head. "No, no, Mr. Headley is not a suitor. Leastways he is not now," she added unhappily. "He has come because they have charge of planning the St. Barnabas Day festivities."

Aurelia disregarded the last statement and returned to the more interesting topic of the vicar's lack of interest in Miss Winslow. "But Mr. Headley was the girl's suitor?"

"I believe he had some interest in her, yes," Lady Mary allowed.

"Some," Lady Beatrice crowed, for Mrs. MacDonald was not such a challenge she could not eavesdrop as well as play. "The man was forever underfoot."

"Whatever occurred to put him off?"

Lady Mary blinked uncertainly, unable to account for the relish in Aurelia's tone. "Ah, they had a disagreement over a local family. Miss Winslow thought the people deserved additional charity while Mr. Headley did not."

"Hello. I hope you've saved some tea for us." Mr. MacDonald came into the room, followed by Sir Alfred and Roxham. "My ride has whetted my appetite, and no mistake!"

"Justin," Lady Aurelia gleefully hailed the earl, who had stopped to speak with his aunt. Normally, she'd never have raised the subject of Miss Winslow, but she could not resist the opportunity to take the girl down a peg. "Come sit by me." She patted the couch beside her. "Mary is just telling me how Miss Winslow came to be rejected by Mr. Headley. It seems she was trying to teach the vicar charity."

Aurelia laughed at the absurdity of the idea, but Roxham only looked to Mary, his brow lifted slightly in question.

"It is only rumor," Lady Mary admitted, coloring faintly. "But there is talk in the neighborhood that Mr. Headley has asked Mrs. Wright, the widow, to be his bride."

"What famous news," Lady Beatrice exclaimed with obvious relish. "I cannot imagine that Jess and that prosy bore would ever have suited."

Sighing, Lady Mary nodded in agreement. "I think you are right, Aunt Bea," she conceded. "I had thought . . . Miss Winslow does need a husband and Mr. Headley a wife, but I saw the night they discussed the Crenshaws that Miss Winslow is far to, ah . . ."

Lady Mary's voice trailed away uncertainly and Roxham's mouth lifted. "Much for him?" he suggested helpfully.

"Well!" Mr. MacDonald weighed in with his opinion. "If Headley's the fellow who held the service for old Verney, I can't conceive of the two together. She has more spirit in her finger than he has in his entire body."

Aurelia's eyes flashed with annoyance. She had not raised the subject of Miss Winslow and the vicar to have the girl commended. Even now there was a faint smile playing at the edge of Justin's mouth as he looked his agreement at that witless fool MacDonald.

"Justin." Aurelia leaned forward to place her hand on his arm and return his attention where it belonged. "You know you have promised this age to show Cornelia and me the portrait gallery. Will you not make good on your promise this afternoon? I declare I have a longing to see that piratical ancestor of yours."

"He was a privateer, my dear, with a letter of marque from the crown," Roxham corrected her offhandedly. "And I should be happy to show him to you both after tea."

"I fear I shall have to go another time," Cornelia MacDonald spoke up quickly. "Mary has promised to show me the dress she will wear on St. Barnabas Day."

"Oh, well, if you prefer . . ." Mary began graciously to withdraw her invitation.

Cornelia, who'd received a rapier-sharp glance from Aurelia, firmly shook her head. "No, Mary. Truly, I should like above all things to see your dress. I cannot be certain otherwise what it is I should wear.''

Jessica did not rush to her meeting with Mr. Headley. On the contrary, her steps lagged conspicuously. The one meeting they had had since their confrontation over the Crenshawes had been very awkward. Mr. Headley had cleared his throat a good deal, cast Jessica reproachful looks, and they'd accomplished little.

He had not come again. Sir Augustus had died and the vicar had had duties at Roselawn, but Jessica suspected he'd been glad of the excuse to stay away. Now, with St. Barnabas Day fast approaching and a host of small matters to settle, he was forced to make an appearance.

Laughter coming from outside the window drew Jessica's glance. She did not soon look away. Roxham and Andrew were coming toward the house from the stables. Andrew was talking with more excitement than Jessica had ever seen him display, and his cousin was watching him with amusement.

They made a fine pair. Each was handsome in his own way. Both were fit and moved with athletic grace. But Jessica did not doubt upon which one most women's eyes would linger.

However appealing Andrew was, he remained, all in all, a boy. Roxham, though his expression was almost boyish as he made Andrew some laughing answer, was unmistakably a man.

There was no excess of fat upon his frame, but unlike Andrew, he had filled out as a man will. Even from a distance Jessica could see the muscles playing beneath his close-fitting coat. His chest was deep and his shoulders broad, and he held those shoulders with the easy confidence of a man accustomed to having his own way.

Jessica's head snapped back of a sudden. She ought to be proceeding to her meeting with the vicar, not staring moonstruck out the window like some . . .

She could not even finish the thought. Marching away from the window, her pace determined, she forced herself to think on the vicar of Bleithewood.

Resolutely she reminded herself that she'd decided the

vicar was to be pitied, not condemned for his lack of generosity. Mr. Headley, unlike another she would not think on, had had to grasp for advancement in life, and as a result, he was hardened to those who remained below him in society. They might have improved themselves had they but tried, he likely reasoned.

"Mr. Headley." She smiled brightly as she entered the room.

He did not smile at all and made her a stiff bow as he said, "Miss Winslow."

Jessica bit back an impulse to sigh. Though weeks had passed, he'd not forgiven her for lecturing him before the earl.

"Allow me to tell you how well our arrangements go here at the manor, Mr. Headley." She crossed to a table and withdrew the book in which she kept her notes. "With Lady Mary's permission, I wrote to the musicians you recommended, and they've agreed to come . . ."

Her tone decidedly pleasant, Jessica ignored Mr. Headley's baleful air and went on to describe all else she had done. When it was the vicar's time to speak, he did frown excessively, but in the end, because Jessica was determined on it, they came to agreement on most that remained to be done.

As Mr. Headley rose to go at last, Jessica breathed a sigh of relief that their session had concluded cordially enough, but when he halted irresolutely just as he reached the door, she wondered if she'd been precipitate in her happy estimation.

"Miss Winslow," he began, and looped his finger beneath his neckcloth, "I believe I should tell you of something momentous, that, ah, has, ah, occurred in my life."

"I should be delighted to hear of it, Mr. Headley," Jessica prompted when the vicar hesitated.

"Yes, er, ah . . ." He licked his lips. "I know I may have, ah, given you to believe . . . That is . . ." Mr. Headley started again, so clearly uncomfortable that Jessica waited with bated breath to learn what he intended to say. "I do not know how you will receive the news, but the truth is, Miss Winslow, I am overjoyed to say I have found my helpmeet at last."

The vicar looked at once so earnest and uncertain that Jessica smiled, though she was still unclear as to what he wished to tell her. Had he found a cook? she wondered and stifled an irreverent giggle. "I see, Mr. Headley. I am very happy for you."

She had said the right thing. Mr. Headley beamed. "I knew you would understand," he cried happily, seizing her hand between both of his. "You are so very good. It is only that I thought Isabella, Mrs. Wright, you know, more, ah, accustomed to village life. She has always lived in Bleithewood."

"And so you are betrothed to Mrs. Wright?" Jessica asked when understanding finally dawned. There was no mistaking her pleasure, for she returned Mr. Headley's pressure on her hands. "I think she will be a perfect wife for you, Mr. Headley. I truly do. You are a wise man to have chosen her."

Mr. Headley looked slightly confounded. He had not expected Miss Winslow to greet the news that he preferred another for his wife with such a radiant smile, but not a deep thinker, he soon found himself smiling happily back at her and reflecting that, if she was both foolishly generous and possessed of an unnaturally strong temperament, Miss Winslow did, nonetheless, want only the best for everyone.

Tea took a short while, but Aurelia waited patiently. She'd not managed to get Justin to herself for some time, and now she had, she was determined to make the most of her opportunity.

As he led her to the gallery, she locked her hand around his arm, marveling to herself at the strength of it. They walked slowly along the line of pictures, and though she found them generally dark and uninspiring portraits, Aurelia paused frequently to inspect one or another Stafford ancestor, being careful, as she leaned forward, to brush her breast across his arm with seeming casualness.

Justin made no response, but Aurelia was satisfied that he was pleased, for, she reasoned, he did not pull away. At the end of the gallery she saw a window seat and soon

221

made for it, intending to draw him down beside her in the narrow place.

"Oh, look how lovely," she cried, looking out to the gardens, though in truth she saw little. She was too entranced by how close Justin stood behind her.

"Indeed."

Something in his voice as well as a scarcely discernible change in his stance made Aurelia really look below her. The old lead panes obscured the view until she moved her head, but when she did, she saw, quite as plain as day, Miss Winslow, her burnished head bent to the task of cutting a selection of flowers, alone in the garden below, a basket and her discarded straw bonnet lying beside her on the ground.

Aurelia balled her hands into two fists and regretted deeply that the girl was not close enough to strike. She was just on the point of turning around and dragging Justin away when she caught a movement from the corner of her eye. Standing a little to the side, so that the glass did not waver, she saw Andrew creeping up on the unsuspecting girl.

Rooted to the spot now, she waited, well aware that Justin had stiffened. Oh, if only they would compromise themselves, she prayed.

"Jess," Andrew cried, and though the watchers in the portrait gallery could not hear him, they did see him jump out to lift Jessica to her feet, swing her about in a circle, and laughing, kiss her on the lips.

Aurelia caught her breath. It was too good! She dared not look at Justin, but she had little need. She could almost feel the intensity of his stare.

Miss Winslow was facing them, and when she smiled, Aurelia could not keep a similar if slier expression from her face. The chit did not even attempt to keep the boy away. No! She met him with a dazzling smile.

To Aurelia's disappointment, nothing of great significance occurred afterward. Miss Winslow stepped back from the boy, though she continued to smile and handed Andrew her basket while she linked her arm with his.

The young man was talking energetically, and when they turned to make their way to the manor, Aurelia could see from his smile he was exuberant. He gestured grandly, making the girl laugh. Aurelia regretted having to see her smile again, for Miss Winslow's face, when she laughed, was lit with a particularly vivid glow.

From the corner of her eye Aurelia risked a peek at Justin. Uncertainty swept her, for his face was utterly expressionless. Was he not angry? Surely he was. His eyes were too dark and his stare too hard.

The pair had stopped, Aurelia saw when she looked again. Andrew was speaking earnestly now, and though she could not see the girl's face, Aurelia could see it was tilted up toward her companion. When he stopped speaking, the young man bowed, lifted both her hands and kissed each one in turn.

After some response that brought a pleased look to Andrew's face, the girl dipped him a curtsy—a graceful one, Aurelia admitted grudgingly—and turned to make her way to the house alone, though Andrew remained watching her until she disappeared from sight.

"It would seem Miss Winslow has an admirer in your young cousin," Aurelia essayed cautiously when Justin continued looking out the window.

To her irritation, he started as if he'd forgotten she was there. "Andy admires her, yes," he allowed before continuing in a musing tone that gave no indication what he thought of the scene they had witnessed. "I fancy he was playing the part of the dashing soldier prematurely. I told him today that I would speak to his mother in support of his desire to make the army his career. He owes my change of heart to Miss Winslow, as he knows."

Aurelia's lower lip jutted forward in a vexed pout. Surely Justin was not as unaffected as he seemed! The chit was encouraging Andrew, it was plain to see! "I think the boy will do quite well in the army," she observed after a moment. "And once there, he will be well away from Miss Winslow, which can be only to the good, for the girl does not keep a distance from him as one in her position should."

Glancing up quickly, Aurelia caught a flash of emotion in Justin's eyes and knew with triumph he was angry.

True, his anger impressed her as excessive. She'd rather

have had him look bored or, at most, annoyed with the bother of having to reprimand the chit, but after all, anger was a great deal better than approval.

23

"Headley is a wiser man than I ever suspected," Lady Bea said later in her rooms after Jessica gave her the news about Mrs. Wright. "I have it from Helena the widow's a kindly, biddable creature—in short, a perfect mate for Headley."

And without bothering to ascertain what Jessica thought, for Lady Beatrice believed she knew the girl's thoughts on the subject of the vicar, she promptly nodded off to sleep. Her successful battle of wits with Mrs. Mac-Donald had tired her enormously and she needed her rest.

Her time her own for a bit, Jessica went to don her straw bonnet and, after requesting a flower basket of Moreton, made straight for a bed of irises the gardener had told her she might choose from. They were Lady Beatrice's favorites, and Jessica wished to have them for her when she awakened.

Andrew burst out at her when she had cut a dozen. Taking her by surprise, he lifted her bodily from the ground and then kissed her audaciously upon the mouth before she could do more than cry, "Oh!"

"I've always wanted to do that. And today I did."

Jessica gave him a rather bemused smile. Andrew was grinning so joyously, she could not be angry. "And now you are obliged to tell me what has you so elated."

"I am to go to the army," Andrew shouted, lifting his arms in victory.

Happy for him, Jessica laughed outright at his foolishness. "Your mother has agreed, then?"

"No." Andrew shook his head. "But Justin has agreed to speak to her. And therefore . . ."

". . . the thing is as good as done," Jessica finished. "I am glad for you, Andrew, very glad."

"I knew you would be, and that's why I've sought you out."

Jessica laughed again and handed him her basket before linking her arm with his and starting back to the manor. "When will your cousin speak with her, do you think?" she inquired curiously.

"Today, most likely," Andrew told her. "We went out together this morning to inspect some repairs being done on a tenant's cottage. Justin had put me in charge of them, after he was hurt, and when he saw how nicely I'd managed, he clapped me on the shoulder and called me Captain Fitzgerald. I didn't take his point for a moment," Andrew confided with an abashed grin. "Just stood looking at him as if he'd lost his mind, and then I saw the twinkle in his eye."

Jessica could, without even having to close her eyes, see that twinkle too. The golden lights in the earl's eyes would seem to dance and his mouth would curve up just a little on one side.

"Of course, you may imagine how I whooped," Andrew continued, oblivious to the fact that Jessica had blushed. "He said I had executed all the responsibilities I was given much better than he'd expected, and he realized you were right. I could make a fine soldier. That I would not make such a fine husband to Marianne he also thought was obvious," the young man added with a mischievous look.

They'd come to a dividing place in the path. One walk led to the stables and the other to the manor, and Andrew stopped, saying, "I'm off to tell Tom Cathcart my news." When Jessica wished him enjoyment of his task, he laughed. "Oh, I shall enjoy as much as anything seeing Tom's eyes when I tell him. He thought I should never bring Justin around because of Mother. But, then," Andrew bowed with a flourish, "Tom doesn't know you very well, Jess."

When Andrew looked at her again, his expression was more earnest. "I owe you a great deal, you know. I doubt he'd have listened to me. I had forfeited Justin's serious regard, as you must know, with my foolish starts." Lifting both of Jessica's hands, he placed a kiss on each. "I don't know what you plan to do in the end, Jess, but if you should find the idea of being a soldier's wife not insupportable, you've only to write. I should like very much saving you from the drudgery of being a companion. No! don't scold or protest or send me away. I am going anyway." He gave her a lopsided grin. "And I meant what I said, however much you may think I am only being grateful. Which I am. But I am also an admirer, and if you should ever need me. . . . ."

"I shall remember," Jessica did him the honor of saying. She would not call on him, of course. His cousin loomed too large in the background for her to ever go to Andrew, but she was touched that he'd offered. "You are very gallant, you know," she said with a smile, which pleased him so much Andy found it impossible not to watch her walk away and think on what might have been had he only been even a trifle more prepared to settle down.

Jessica had arranged the irises she had picked, had borne them all the way to Lady Bea's rooms, and had received that lady's thanks before she realized she had left her chip bonnet on the ground in the gardens.

When she had Lady Beatrice sitting comfortably in a chair, a glass of lemonade and the irises at her side, she excused herself to retrieve the errant headgear.

"There you are!" Jessica said softly when she spied the thing and was startled when it seemed to reply.

"Do tell!"

"Well . . . ," a higher voice began, and Jessica realized that behind a line of holly bushes bordering the iris bed and facing an ornamental pond, Lady Aurelia and her friend, Mrs. MacDonald, sat talking.

". . . Miss Winslow . . . ." Hearing Lady Aurelia say her name rooted Jessica's feet to the ground. ". . . was quite openly receiving young Fitzgerald's attentions!"

"Oh," Mrs. MacDonald breathed raptly.

"Yes," Lady Aurelia fairly crowed. "They exchanged a kiss on the lips. And in the garden." When Mrs. Mac-

Donald gasped, Lady Aurelia added, "And, by the veriest chance, Justin saw. I would not be in the least surprised if he did not . . ."

Jessica did not stay to hear what the earl might do. Sickened by the way Lady Aurelia had twisted her innocent, joyous encounter with Andrew, she fairly flew from the spot and only turned around to assure herself the London ladies with their ugly insinuations were not following behind her.

"Oof!" Jessica had the gasp knocked from her as her soft derriere came up against a hard pair of thighs.

Several things happened at once then.

Jessica jumped away, blushing with particular fierceness when she saw it was Roxham himself she had, however inadvertently, bumped so intimately.

Simultaneously, Lady Aurelia's voice rang out clear as a bell over the holly bushes. "But whatever Justin may choose to do, at least he must now recognize the chit for the forward creature she is."

Jessica's eyes did not waver from Roxham's as her heart sank. It was impossible to read his mood. He stood with his back to the sun, but she could see that he did not smile.

"A felicitous excursion to the portrait gallery, I should say, Rellie." Mrs. MacDonald's fashionable drawl came to them as they stood facing each other. "I'd begun to wonder . . . But never mind! Shall we walk to the pond? I see a black swan and I do admire them prodigiously, you know. They remind me of Prinny."

As Aureliea's tittering laugh faded into the distance Roxham made an impatient movement. "As you have chanced to hear, Aurelia and I were afforded the opportunity to watch Andrew give you the news that I've come around to supporting his bid for a career in the army. That is why he kissed you, is it not? Out of exuberance."

"Yes," Jessica nodded solemnly. "Andy was quite happy."

"And grateful. He seemed 'quite' grateful."

Jessica shot Roxham a wary look. This wry tone was not what she'd expected.

"Have a care how you respond to Andrew's happiness

and gratitude, Miss Winslow, or you shall cause him to forget his beloved military.''

''Oh, no!'' Jessica shook her head, for she was on firm ground at last. ''Andrew's head would never be turned so easily. He is truly enraptured with the thought of being Captain Fitzgerald.'' She'd added that last with the hope of making Roxham smile, but he did not seem to have heard her.

''You do not realize your effect upon the boy, I think.''

Though his tone had been musing, Jessica stiffened at once. ''I see, my lord,'' she returned in a cool voice, though the flash of displeasure in her eyes was warm. ''As usual, I am judged the temptress. You, like''— Jessica thought better of calling Lady Aurelia by name— ''others, without doing me the courtesy of asking for my version of events, have decided I am intent upon seducing Andrew because we exchanged smiles and one kiss. But then, I suppose it asking a great deal of one with your renowned sophistication to recognize so simple a thing as mere friendship. Nothing passed between Andrew and me but a shared pleasure that he should be so near achieving the life he desires. Nothing!''

Abruptly, Jessica made the earl a stiff curtsy. ''Good day, my lord. I shall take myself to your aunt's rooms, where, neither smiling nor laughing, I shall not offend the sensibilities of my betters.''

Proving even his laziest movements were efficient, Roxham possessed himself of Jessica's elbow and brought her around to face him before she had taken even one step away. ''No, no, my girl, you'll not leave me while your eyes shoot sparks,'' he chided.

Jessica's blue eyes were stormy indeed with indignation; she was just prepared to demand that he unhand her, but she saw he was smiling down at her. Perhaps it was the unexpectedness of his amused half-smile that so deflated her, or perhaps it was that that smile, expected or not, had the power to set her pulses leaping. Whatever the reason, the result was the same. Jessica caught her breath, her protest forgotten.

''Nor need you expect an apology from me for saying you are beautiful and tempt a man, Miss Winslow,'' he informed her softly. "For you are beautiful and you do tempt a man whether you set out to do so or not."

His voice, sounding deep and low, seemed to vibrate down Jessica's spine to her toes and in the process turn her knees to jelly. And though a part of her mind was obliged to occupy itself with keeping her figure upright, another, far larger part seemed capable only of entertaining the thought that Roxham was, of a certainty, a man. . . .

"I know," the earl continued, "that you did not see Andrew staring besottedly after you, because you had turned your back and were merrily continuing upon your way. But I did see him, and I tell you that with any encouragement from you, Andrew would hie off to his estates in Ireland and attempt to live his life as a farmer, bidding the army adieu once and for all."

"Andrew did ask me to marry him," Jessica heard herself say in a strangely breathless, throaty voice. "And I refused him, just as he expected me to do. Else he'd not have asked."

Lines Jessica had never particularly noted at the corner of Roxham's eyes crinkled upward as he smiled. "Though I advise you against testing my theory, I imagine that if you were to accept him you'd find Andy's banter was not all play."

Without premeditation, Jessica returned his smile. "You really do overestimate my powers, my lord," she remonstrated. "Only today Mr. Headley informed me he has asked Mrs. Wright, not me, to be his wife. Though," she added with a slight toss of her bright head, "I fancy you must take some of the credit for his change of heart."

She really was very beautiful with her indigo-blue eyes sparkling and her thick red-gold hair gleaming copper in the sunlight. And her mouth . . . though finely drawn, it looked very soft, and just now, moistened by her tongue, it tempted Justin Stafford.

His smile flashed. "I shall take no credit for sending Headley to another, Miss Winslow. I am not responsible for your temper. It was that, make no mistake, which sent the poor man flying."

Jessica laughed, acknowledging the hit. "Perhaps what

you say is true, sir, but you must admit you were responsible for the circumstances of its arousal."

The earl did not have the grace to look even slightly repentant, and when his eyes began to dance, Jessica's heart soared dangerously. "Guilty as charged. I shall not beg forgiveness. I'd not have missed the vicar's lesson on charity for the world."

"You are very bad, sir," she protested, but her tone lacked severity.

Roxham's response was immediate and dismissive. "And Headley's a pompous bore when you aren't setting him right." He paused, his smile fading as his gaze intensified. "It is my opinion he did not deserve you."

Roxham was very close—or so it seemed, for Jessica was aware only of him. She could feel her heart pounding painfully in her chest warning her to leave the man's dangerous presence, but she could not make her limbs respond. It felt to her as if they'd been turned to warm liquid by the look in his amber eyes.

"Justin! Jess! Justin! Look! Jess!"

It took two, perhaps three repetitions of their names before the sound made any impact upon either of them. Roxham started first, and looking over his shoulder, Jessica recognized Giles in the distance coming at a run, followed by Julia and Caesar. Farther behind them was Jem Crenshawe.

Julia waved, but Giles did not. He was holding something long with both hands. The children disappeared from sight then, for the walk bordered the pond before it came around the holly bushes to the iris bed. Just as Jessica remembered that Lady Aurelia and Mrs. MacDonald walked in that vicinity, a bloodcurdling scream sounded.

Swearing aloud, Roxham strode off at once, leaving Jessica to follow as the scream was repeated.

When they rounded the holly bushes, they found Lady Aurelia and Mrs. MacDonald cowering together upon a bench, both screaming, while the twins yelled and darted erratically about searching in the grass and flowers that grew to the water's edge. Jem Crenshawe, alone, stood back quietly, his hands thrust in his pockets, watching.

"Justin!" Lady Aurelia saw the earl first and cried out his name with what seemed to Jessica to be genuine fear. "They've lost a snake," she screamed, pointing frantically in the direction of the twins.

"We didn't lose it!" Giles stopped long enough to look up from the ground to defend himself. "He got loose when Lady Aurelia's scream startled me and I dropped him. Now I've lost him. He was beautiful, Justin. Long and black! Jem gave him to Livy and me after he found him in the woods. He knows ever so much about the woods."

"That I don't doubt," Roxham responded dryly, his reply and tone both mystifying Jessica, but with Lady Aurelia crying in earnest, there was not time to question him.

"If you will escort the ladies to the house, I shall help the children find their snake and remove it to some remote area."

Though Jessica detected a twinkle in his eyes, Roxham's nod was businesslike. "Capital idea, Miss Winslow. You won't be frightened to catch it?" he asked as an afterthought.

"I shall set Jem on the task and only supervise," she clarified.

His mouth quirked, but he made no further remark as he turned to Lady Aurelia, who still cried and craned her head wildly.

"Rellie! Stop that!" Roxham shook the lady's shoulders and she stared a moment before collapsing against him. "The snake is gone. It won't harm you. Come along to the house."

Murmuring soothingly all the while, he led the two ladies to the safety of the manor, and Jessica, having waved Jem down to help retrieve the escaped prize, watched him go.

Roxham held Lady Aurelia about the waist. And he'd called her Rellie! A sharp pain lanced through Jessica's midsection. Of course he would call her by her pet name. They were lovers.

Jessica dropped down hard upon a bench, unable to stand. Of a sudden she understood a great deal: why she

231

felt so odd when she was in the earl's company, why he could hold her transfixed with a mere look, why her eyes sought him out the moment she entered a room.

She'd fallen in love with him.

" 'E be gone, mum."

Jessica looked up, dazed, uncertain if Jem had spoken or to whom he referred.

"The snake," he reminded her patiently. " 'E wouldna 'ave stayed 'ere."

"No, no, of course, not." Jessica nodded, schooling her features and her emotions with an effort.

"But we cannot have lost him," Giles cried, bereft.

"I am certain Jem will find another in time," Jessica consoled, standing. "Thank you, Jem, and you needn't think anyone will hold this against you. It's Giles and Julia, both, who ought to have known better than to bring another animal close to the earl's guests."

"But . . ." Julia and Giles spluttered in unison.

Waving Jem off, Jessica took each child by the hand and, walking back toward the manor, reminded them that they knew their mother's guests were afraid of animals. "And you must respect their fears, as they are guests in your house," she added before extracting a solemn oath that they would not bring any other finds to the manor but would leave them at the stables where they could be shown off to the select few who accepted an invitation.

Though she spoke reasonably, Jessica scarcely knew what she was saying. In a dazed way she was still absorbing the awful implications of the discovery she'd made. Of a certainty now she would have to leave the manor, though she did not think she could make herself do so at once. She would stay at least until the St. Barnabas Day Festival, she decided. After it was done, she'd think what to do.

And until then she must hide her impossible feelings from everyone. It would not do, particularly, for Roxham to discover her secret. To know his aunt's companion entertained a deep emotion for him could only be the greatest embarrassment for him.

24

"Jess, do you believe Justin will accompany Lady Aurelia and the MacDonalds to Scotland when they go?"

Jessica's hands floated momentarily over the flowers she and Livy were arranging. "I've no idea. Why do you ask?"

Placing a white peony among the pink ones in her vase, Olivia stopped to survey the effect. "It occurred to me that, if he goes, we may take it as a sign he means to ask for her, but if he remains here or returns to town, then, it means he's come to his senses." She looked up with a mischievous grin.

Whatever answer she gave was adequate, for Olivia gave her no strange look, but Jessica did not know what it was she said. She'd thought it a foregone conclusion that Roxham would ask for Lady Aurelia. Though what, she asked herself sternly, did it matter if he did not? He'd simply ask another titled lady to be his countess.

Suddenly Olivia lifted a spray of greenery and spun around, bringing Jessica's head up and, blessedly, scattering her thoughts. "I know it's silly to be so excited, but I cannot help it," the younger girl cried with a laugh when she came to a stop. "After all, Philip will not dance out of respect for his father, though why he must respect that reprobate, I can't imagine. Kate and Lady Anne shan't come at all, but Philip told Andy that a Verney had not missed the St. Barnabas Day Festival at Bleithewood in two centuries, and he would not be the first. I imagine he'll only have a glass of ale to please the villagers, a glass of claret to please himself, and then go home."

Her eyes twinkling fondly, Jessica tipped her head to the side. "I imagine that before he goes, Sir Philip will allow his eyes to stray to the dancers, and thronged though the dance area will be, he will spy a certain young

233

lady with sparkling hazel eyes who will, by the merest chance, of course, be smiling dazzlingly back at him.''

Olivia dissolved in happy giggles. "Yes! I see it all too. She'll be dressed in her new sprigged muslin and look so ravishing Philip shan't be able to take his eyes from her.''

Jessica laughed as Livy twirled about again. "You may well have to watch the festivities from a chaise, if you go on like this,'' she teased.

Livy, gasping for breath, only grinned before returning to her flowers. "What shall you wear today, Jess?''

Her eyes were sparkling when she looked up, but Jessica assumed she was still thinking of Philip Verney. "I've a muslin I've been saving,'' Jessica answered absently.

"Oh! Is it new?''

"No.'' Jessica frowned a little, puzzled by the sharpness in Olivia's tone. "I've had it a year or two.''

"Or three!'' Olivia laughed, sounding strangely pleased. "There!'' She stepped back from her arrangement. "We've finished these flowers at last. You've a touch for it, Jess, but I fear mine are only passable. Ah, well!'' She shrugged philosophically. "I suppose no one will see them in here anyway. Are you going up to Aunt Bea's now?''

"Yes,'' Jessica allowed, looking around the drawing room a last time before, satisfied with what she saw, she led the way out.

Livy accompanied her up the stairs and to Jessica's surprise turned with her toward Lady Beatrice's rooms. "You are going to see your aunt?'' she asked. "I thought you intended to dress now.''

"Oh, I've something to ask Aunt Bea,'' Livy replied airily.

To Jessica's further consternation she found the twins cavorting in their aunt's room when she arrived, though they, like Livy, ought to have been dressing.

Julia rushed at once to Jessica, taking her hands as she laughed excitedly. "Giles and I have gifts for you,'' she announced, pointing to Lady Beatrice's bed, upon which there lay several brightly wrapped packages.

"Gifts?" Jessica looked from the packages to Lady Bea and Olivia. They were regarding her with smiles nearly as pleased as Julia's.

Giles, Caesar barking at his heels, jumped upon the bed. "It's like Christmas! Come and open them, Jess." The little boy grinned at her as she allowed Julia to pull her over. "Jule and I wanted to replace the dress you ruined saving Caesar that day. Well," he considered briefly, "Justin did suggest it and Aunt Bea and Livy picked the modiste, but Jule and I helped pick the style from a book of plates that Livy has. We thought it ever so pretty."

"Well!" Jessica was at a loss for words as she looked from Giles and Julia to the packages.

Lady Beatrice gave a great laugh at her predicament. "Go on, go on," she commanded, her gruff voice filled with affection. "After all, you cannot deny the children their pleasure."

"Why, I wonder"—Jessica's mouth tipped up as she glanced around again at Livy and Lady Bea—"do I feel as if I'm being cleverly maneuvered?"

"Because you are!" Livy erupted into giggles as she ran over to join her brother and sister upon the bed. "I do hope you like what we ordered," she cried, looking quite as delighted by the whole affair as the children.

In the first box was a silky Norwich shawl that Julia had picked herself. In the next was a pair of kid slippers and an assortment of lacy underthings, finer than any Jessica had ever owned. "I am responsible for those," Livy crowed. "I thought it only right you be new inside as well as out."

And last came the dress. As she drew it from its box, Jessica's eyes widened. It would be no replacement for the bombazine she'd lost. It was far too fine. Of jaconet muslin over a sarcenet slip of the creamiest yellow, it was flounced at the bottom with a triple row of delicate lace. The sleeves were long, for the festivities would be outside, and were edged at the wrists with another profusion of lace.

"Hold it up," Livy and the children cried, and when Jessica did, they clapped.

235

"Well, dashed if Justin wasn't right as rain," Lady Bea remarked when Jessica turned to give her a view. "He said that yellow would suit you admirably, but I was not so certain." Jessica could not keep her brow from lifting in surprise, nor, had she known it, a particular light from sparking in her eye. Lady Bea nodded in response to that look. "It was Justin who chose the color and consulted with the twins upon the style."

"But we did choose it," Giles spoke up proudly.

"And it is quite lovely," Jessica told him with such emotion he jumped down to embrace her.

"I'm glad you like it. Now your dress will be as pretty as you," the child said, looking up at her with a great smile.

Likely prettier, Jessica thought when she slipped on the dress later. As soft as silk, it fit her to perfection. Though her glass was not long enough to show her, she knew that its high-waisted style showed her long, slender legs to advantage. But she'd forgotten, she realized with a start when she looked into the glass, how little material there was in a fashionable bodice.

Her hand hovered uncertainly over the fichu she wore each evening as she eyed the soft and creamy swell of her breasts the au-courant neckline revealed. Even her nightdress covered more of her, she thought with a nervous giggle.

Livy's neckline would look much the same and Lady Aurelia's would no doubt be more daring, a little voice whispered. And the earl had approved the style, it added as Jessica recklessly dropped the fichu.

At least she had the satisfaction of knowing that the low neckline displayed the graceful curve of her neck and shoulders to advantage. Her hair was too long to wear down, had she needed to hide an imperfection. She'd already washed and brushed it so it gleamed a fiery red-gold. Now she braided it before pinning it atop her head in a coronet.

It was a regal style perfectly suited to her finely molded features, but Jessica stood suddenly uncertain before her small glass. The strikingly elegant young woman staring back at her seemed a stranger. The color of both her hair

236

and her eyes had been turned a deeper shade than usual by contrast with the creamy yellow of her dress.

Quickly, before she could lose her courage, Jessica darted into Lady Beatrice's room. If she were too finely dressed, the old lady would soon tell her.

But Lady Beatrice did no such thing. When Jessica came to stand irresolutely before her, she clapped, delighted. "Zounds, child! I wish I could claim you as mine."

"It's not too much, Lady Bea?" Jessica indicated the dress.

"Too much?" The older woman's echo was scoffing. "And how could such a modest garment be too much? It is quite perfect. Now, let's be off at once," she cried with astounding relish for one so old and so often in pain. "We shall call James to help us. I have shawls and reticules and my old bones to haul down. Besides," she added, a mischievous twinkle enlivening her eyes, "I've a mind to see if the boy's jaw will actually drop."

It did. When Jessica opened the door and the young footman took in who it was that stood looking so elegant and fetching all at once, he gaped. Lady Bea laughed aloud until she saw Jessica bite her lip. "Oh, get along with you, boy," she fussed then. "Take my things and stop gaping. Jess will not come down at all if you carry on so absurdly.

"And you, miss, may as well cease seeming so uncertain," she chided Jessica. "It doesn't become you. Nor is there time to change; half the village is already here. Been hearing them arrive this last half-hour. Come along, now."

Unable to hang back any longer, Jessica descended to her first St. Barnabas Day Festival. Celebrated for centuries, the festival had originally been nothing more than a day set aside for the lord of the manor to hear his people's petitions.

As petitioning was thirsty work, ale had gradually worked its way into the proceedings, followed closely by food. Where there is food and drink, there is often song, and after a time it became accepted custom for the lord and his people to take the time to enjoy themselves when the business of the day was concluded.

Gradually, as the courts of the land assumed the powers the lords had held, St. Barnabas Day became devoted exclusively to pleasure in the form of games, music, dance, and food. But though the original purpose had been lost, the earl, his lady, and family still attended. And the people of the county widely believed it was this tradition—where once a year the Earl of Roxham rubbed shoulders with his people—that accounted for how smoothly Bleithewood had run for so long.

As the estate had prospered and grown, so had the festival itself. Not only the Bleithewood tenants came now, but the villagers had included themselves in the affair, as had the older families in the neighborhood.

That particular eleventh of June in the year 1817—and Jessica sent up a word of thanks—was clear, with only a few puffy white clouds to emphasize how very blue the sky was. The late-afternoon air was neither too hot nor too cool, but felt warm and soft on the skin.

Everyone looked as pleased as she, for they one and all wore smiles, or so it seemed to Jessica when she and Lady Beatrice stepped onto the terrace. Even Lady Mary, whom they saw greeting the blacksmith and his wife, wore a bright smile.

"Mary seems particularly lighthearted today," Lady Bea observed, seeing where Jessica was looking. "I imagine it's the agreement she and Justin have come to. Not only will he buy Andy's colors, but he'll settle a substantial allowance on the lad. With peace here at last, she will not have to worry as much over Andy the officer as she would Andy the husband. And thank merciful heaven—Justin brought her to realize it."

Having heard the particulars of the agreement between Roxham and Lady Mary from both Andrew and Olivia, Jessica merely chuckled at Lady Beatrice's blunt way of stating her opinion. It was all she had time for, anyway, as they had reached their hostess.

"Ah, here you are, Aunt Bea, Miss Winslow." Lady Mary's eyes, when she turned, grew round. "Why, you are truly lovely!"

Jessica, as she curtsied gracefully, thought there must be madness in the air, for Lady Mary sounded not the least constrained. Perhaps she did, as Andrew had said, consider Jessica responsible for the earl's generosity toward her son. She was wrong, of course. Roxham would do only as he pleased, but Jessica would not dispute the result.

It seemed Andrew had inhaled a little of the same air his mother had, for when he appeared with his friend Tom Cathcart, he did not make the least effort to subdue his smile, though his mother stood beside him looking on.

"Jessica!" He grinned roguishly as he eyed her finery. "It is too bad of you to appear so exquisitely turned out. Now Tom will think I was lying through my teeth when I said you were merely beautiful and not a diamond of the first water."

Noting the tolerant smile Lady Mary wore, Jessica returned Andrew's grin affectionately. "I thank you, sir, though I must say such extravagant praise raises a question in my mind as to the amount of ale you've tasted."

"You mustn't think so of me," he protested. "I owe all my good spirits to this lady." To Lady Mary's astonished pleasure, Andrew turned to buzz her cheek. " 'Tis she, not ale, who's made the world a happier place for me today. Note, if you will, one and all, that the Multaneys, alone of all our neighbors, are not present."

"Oh, dear, so they aren't!" Lady Mary's plump face fell as she glanced around her.

"No need to fret, Mary." Lady Beatrice shook her head firmly. "Emily won't sever her connection to Bleithewood once she's got over the disappointment of not having her daughter live here. And if we're spared the greedy squire's presence altogether, I can't say I'll complain."

Laughing hugely, Andrew embraced his great-aunt and called her the greatest gun, after which he presented Tom Cathcart to Jessica. "And you're to watch out for him, Jess, he's a rum one," he teased.

Jessica greeted Mr. Cathcart amiably, saying he did not seem so very rum, which seemed to please the young man, for he grinned triumphantly at his friend. However, unwilling to press Lady Mary too far, Jessica ended the banter by saying she and Lady Bea must be excused. "Mrs. Dalymede is looking quite anxious all alone," she observed with a smile.

"Great heavens, so she is!" Lady Beatrice winked outrageously. "No doubt she has something vital to tell me," she whispered, to the general merriment of one and all, for everyone in the neighborhood knew of the two ladies' fondness for gossip.

Once she'd seated Lady Beatrice beside Mrs. Dalymede and had greeted that lady, Jessica saw that both Lady Aurelia and Mrs. MacDonald had already taken their seats in the area Mr. Headley had insisted upon setting apart from the crowd so that "people of refinement might have an area all their own."

Both women were regarding her with narrowed eyes, it pleased Jessica in the most objectionable way to see. Perhaps infected with the same madness as Andy and Lady Mary, she made certain to greet them warmly, though, for her pains, she received only a nod in reply from Mrs. MacDonald and a flash of something approaching anger from Lady Aurelia.

"Off, off, I say!" Jessica glanced around at Lady Bea with a particularly sparkling smile. The suspicion that Lady Aurelia's unhappiness had to do with Roxham's possible reaction to her appearance made her almost giddy. "Go and enjoy yourself, miss," Lady Bea commanded when she saw she had Jessica's full attention. "I won't have you sitting here among the dowagers."

The remark, said in a raised voice, was clearly meant for Aurelia. And it hit home, for that lady sniffed loudly and pointedly turned away.

Jessica shot Lady Bea an amused looked, but said only, "I shall fetch you and Mrs. Dalymede some punch, my lady, and then we shall see about the rest."

Little Annie was standing duty at the punch bowl, serving two tenants' wives and Olivia when Jessica approached. "Oh, miss," the girl breathed ecstatically, causing Olivia to spin around quickly.

"Jess," she cried loudly enough that everyone within

hearing must have turned, "you are a princess come to life!"

Jessica colored, though she managed a level voice. "Thank you, Olivia," she said graciously before adding with a little laugh, "though, truthfully, I wish I could say stow it! The fuss over a new dress gives me to believe I must look a fright normally, and besides, it keeps me from being presented to those with whom I'm not acquainted. I am Jessica Winslow," she continued, turning with an easy smile to the first of the two wives. "You are Mrs. Trubshawe, are you not? I recognize you from your likeness to your daughter, who has come to play with Julia."

Mrs. Trubshawe, who had followed the friendly exchange between Miss Olivia and Lady Beatrice's companion with sharp interest, the relations among the inhabitants of the manor being the substance of many of her conversations, smiled broadly, pleased that her daughter had been remembered. She introduced her friend, another tenant's wife, and after a few moments of conversation, the two departed to discuss Lady Beatrice's companion and to agree that the girl had not only looks but a sensible head upon her shoulders as well.

Before Olivia could remark again on her appearance, as Jessica judged from the girl's avid perusal of the muslin she intended to do, Jessica held up her hand. "No more! Truly, Livy, had I known the stir I'd cause, I believe I'd merely have added lace to my blue bombazine."

Olivia choked at the thought, but she had time only to say she thought Jessica a silly goose before she was hailed by several of her friends. Seeing she was about to be engulfed by a crowd of giggling girls, Jessica made haste to collect her glasses of punch from Annie and to bid Livy adieu.

As she made her way through the crowd, smiling a greeting at the people she knew, Jessica deliberately kept her gaze to a narrow path before her. She was more anxious about meeting Roxham than she cared to admit.

She'd seen little of him in the past week. She'd buried herself in preparations for the festival, and when they met at dinner, she'd been careful to keep her eyes averted.

But today she feared she'd never succeed at such circumspection. St. Barnabas Day seemed made for gaiety and laughter, not lowered eyes.

Besides, she wanted dearly to see his reaction to her changed appearance. There! She'd said it, she thought with a half-smile. And she wanted Roxham to look as wide-eyed as everyone else, she added for good measure as a Mrs. Goodbody, the village seamstress, called to her.

There was nothing surprising in the fact that she'd not already encountered the earl. Mr. Headley had long ago told her it was tradition that the lady of the house did the greeting while the lord spent his time mingling among the crowd and chatting at length with every guest.

"And you've not met my Mr. Goodbody, have you, dear?"

Jessica turned from the seamstress to smile at the ruddy-faced man who was her husband. They exchanged a word or two about the beauty of the day, and then, holding up the cups she held, Jessica turned away.

As if the moment had been staged, the crowd parted, clearing a length of space, and at the end of it stood Roxham.

He was dressed very finely in a coat of blue superfine, tight-fitting breeches of kerseymere, and a pair of gleaming Hessians complete with gold tassels. His frothy cravat was tied in a restrained but elegant knot, and Jessica thought the previous earls, looking down upon their day, would have nothing to complain about in their successor. Justin Stafford looked every inch the lord of the manor.

His tawny head gleaming in the sunlight, he spoke with an old man and looked up only absently to scan the crowd. Jessica held her breath as his gaze touched her, but unseeing, it passed her by. Absurdly let down, she made to go, only glancing his way one last time.

She was not looking to see where his gaze did stop, she told herself, but though it was a blatant lie, she was not punished. No sooner were her eyes upon him again than Roxham's gaze jumped back to her.

Unbelievably, his eyes did widen before a slow, potent smile spread across his face.

The old man with him looked to see what held his lord's attention, and catching sight of Jessica, he too, as he made some remark, smiled. Both men, young and old, then lifted the mugs they held and saluted her.

Jessica, her cheeks flushed, dipped them a pretty curtsy. And she smiled as well, a vivid smile that had not even a touch of restraint.

The earl's open admiration was too dizzying a thing to allow even a thought for caution. She would take this one day, she told herself as the crowd closed back around her, to do, for once, just as she pleased.

The smile that played around her lips was short-lived, however. Only a moment later it disappeared entirely, when Sir Alfred appeared suddenly from out of the crowd to stand directly before her. A glass of claret in his hand, he feasted his murky eyes upon her as if she were a newly roasted haunch of venison just set before him.

Swallowing past a suddenly dry throat, Jessica took a step back. Then, as quickly as he'd come, the dreadful man was gone.

Jessica arched her neck to look up at Roxham as her heart executed a somersault in her breast. "I've come to lend my assistance," he said, his smile obliterating all memory of Sir Alfred. Justin took the two glasses she held from her. "Ah, James, how happily predictable you are." His mouth quirking wryly, Roxham handed the glasses of punch to the young footman, who in truth only happened to be passing at that moment, and sent him off to Lady Bea.

"The lad's your devoted follower." He looked back at Jessica with an amused look that set her pulses leaping, but in the next moment, as he swept her with a measuring look from the tip of her coronet to the toes of her yellow satin slippers, he frowned.

Just as Jessica's heart began to sink in the face of his changed opinion of her looks, he looked up.

"I vow I have never found it so irksome to be an earl."

"I beg pardon?" she asked, for his words were so far from what she'd expected that they made no sense at all.

"It's true," he assured her, the slightest twinkle appearing in his eyes to give the lie to his so solemn expression. "I would vastly prefer to lead out the loveliest lady present for the first dance, but my duty calls me to the ranking tenant's wife, Mrs. Trubshawe."

"Fie on you, my lord," Jessica chided with a sparkling smile. "I daresay you say the same to all the ladies."

"You, however, Miss Winslow, are the only one has the honor of hearing the truth."

His teasing smile made her heart leap, but she knew she owed him thanks. "If I do look half so fine as you would have me believe, my lord, then I've no one but you to thank. It was a masterful stroke to have the twins present the dress to me. I found it impossible to refuse them."

Roxham grinned outright. "I did think it a clever ploy myself," he allowed with a lazy bow. Then, shaking his head with a laugh, he added, "I must say I had a hilarious time choosing a style with the two of them. Julia wished you to wear a silk evening gown until Giles persuaded her you'd be too cold. But," he paused to slowly survey her again, "we did well enough in the end, I think. Indeed, I'm nearly of a mind to order one of the maids to your rooms to burn your other dresses. I find, as I thought I would, that it is exceedingly pleasing to see you dressed as you should be."

Jessica dropped her eyes, afraid he'd see how happy he'd made her. The blush she could not control said enough.

Smiling at the sign that he'd affected her, Roxham very nearly, though they were surrounded by at least a score of people avidly watching the exchange between the earl and his aunt's companion, reached out to lift her chin and bring her blue eyes back to his.

He was saved the indiscretion that would have embarrassed Jessica deeply, for she did not have his ability to dismiss the curious eyes around them, by Mr. Headley. His intended bride on his arm, the vicar chose that moment to make his greeting to the earl.

"My lord, good day to you!" He bowed very low. "And to you, ah, Miss Winslow."

A frown darkened Roxham's expression, but the sight of Headley rendered speechless by Jessica in her finery amused him so he forgot his displeasure at being interrupted. "Headley . . ." He gave the distracted man a nod before turning to bow graciously to the woman beside him. "And Mrs. Wright. How very nice to see you."

Roxham swallowed a smile when Mr. Headley gave a guilty jerk and turned back to his forgotten betrothed, but it would not have mattered if he had given his amusement full expression. Mrs. Wright, a small, rounded woman with pleasant, even features and gray eyes that reflected her kindly if meek disposition, only dropped an awkward curtsy in his general direction and did not have the courage to look him in the eye.

When Mr. Headley was sufficiently himself to recall the necessity of introducing Mrs. Wright to Jessica, the widow attempted a smile of greeting, but under the strain of the moment her effort wavered painfully.

Jessica's sympathies aroused, she returned the woman her most reassuring smile. "I am pleased to meet you, Mrs. Wright. The twins tell me you have two delightful children." At the mention of her offspring, Mrs. Wright straightened visibly and Jessica's smile widened. "I look forward to meeting them when you move to the vicarage."

"Allow me to congratulate you, Mrs. Wright," Roxham said. "All of us at Bleithewood are pleased to know you'll be joining Mr. Headley at the vicarage."

Mrs. Wright's gaze veered in the earl's direction, but she could only murmur, "So kind, so kind," in a soft undertone.

"I should like to come to call upon you some afternoon," Jessica added, and the good lady nodded quickly.

"Yes, yes, please do," she replied with a real smile.

"Ah, I . . ." His betrothed having had her moment of attention from the earl, it was obvious Mr. Headley intended to reassert himself, but the earl had other plans.

"Look, there," he intervened smoothly, taking charge before the vicar could launch himself. "The musicians have arrived, which can only mean it is time for the dancing to begin. You'll excuse us, won't you, Mr. Headley, Mrs. Wright?" Extending his arm to Jessica, he asked, "Miss Winslow, may I offer to escort you to Aunt Bea?"

Jessica accepted his invitation with alacrity and grinned gratefully when they were a safe distance away. "Thank you, my lord. Mr. Headley looked ready to hold forth for hours."

"I see no reason why anyone on St. Barnabas Day should be subjected to an oration on connubial bliss or whatever subject Headley was preparing to expound upon." When Roxham winced comically, Jessica laughed at him. "You, particularly, did not deserve such a fate after you coaxed a smile from Mrs. Wright. I was afraid she might shatter before she got through the presentations."

"Well, it was an awkward situation," Jessica pointed out fairly. "She's bound to have heard my name linked with Mr. Headley's, and she was obliged to face meeting me with the high and mighty Earl of Roxham as a witness."

"High and mighty?" he sounded injured.

"Hmm." She nodded. "Amused high and mighty, I might add."

He laughed. "Headley came as close to regret as the pompous fool could, when he saw you. I would not have been amazed had he cast off poor Mrs. Wright on the spot." He chuckled richly, then startled Jessica by reaching over to brush her cheek with his finger. "But you, Miss Jess"—he gave her a look that was at once both teasing and tender—"never once thought to settle a score with him by flaunting your looks. Instead, you did your utmost to set his choice for a bride at her ease, thereby demonstrating, as I believe I once heard Headley say, you have as much graciousness of spirit as you have beauty of countenance."

There was no time for Jessica to respond, nor even to blush, for they'd reached Lady Beatrice and a chorus of voices called out for Roxham's attention. He left Jessica without another word to attend to this one and bend down beside that one. When he leaned down to speak with Lady Aurelia, Jessica could not but note their conversation lasted only for the shortest time, and then he strode to the platform where the musicians had gathered.

While Jessica watched him welcome his guests, her

ears rang with his last words. He thought her gracious! And beautiful! He's said the last before, but never with such undisguised approval. For the rest of the evening, as she danced, she smiled dazzlingly. And she danced nearly every dance.

It seemed there was not one gentleman present—excepting Lord Alfred Marling—who did not ask her to join him in one of the spirited country dances that were the order of the day at the St. Barnabas Day Festival.

Even Giles tore himself from the games the children played and came to beg her hand. "I should think it a great honor," he said with extravagant formality in his high child's voice, and Jessica accepted with a curtsy deep enough for royalty.

Roxham returned to her later. "I'll not deny myself a moment longer," he said then, not smiling at all. "I've had quite enough of watching every man here enjoy your smiles, Miss Winslow. It is my turn now."

25

Of the many eyes watching Jessica and Roxham as they danced, there was one pair whose expression differed vastly from all the rest. While the other guests observed the lord and his partner with pleasure, for they were an exceedingly handsome couple and would draw admiring attention even were he not the Earl of Roxham, Aurelia Stanhope looked upon them with something approaching hatred.

Justin had danced with her only once the whole evening, and then, when she'd thought he intended to come again to lead her out, he had not. He'd stopped beside that creature.

It was too bad of Justin, she screamed silently, not bothering to hide a vicious scowl. No one was looking at her, after all. They'd not been all evening.

She was not accustomed to being so markedly less-sought-after than another. But they were, one and all, boors, she consoled herself. It was only Justin who concerned her, and he made her sit here without anyone for company, Cornelia MacDonald having already gone up to her bed.

Alfred, when he came to whisper in her ear, did nothing to improve her mood. His breath fairly reeked of claret and she did not care for what he said.

"Justin's a deuced bright gleam in his eye when he looks upon his current partner, Rellie. It concerns me that he did not look upon you half so warmly."

"Damn you for a fool, Alfie," she hissed furiously. "You're too far gone in your cups to know aught. Justin is aware what he owes his position. He'll not take a servant for his countess."

In her anger, Aurelia did not guard her voice, and Lady Beatrice, who'd been observing her with relish, heard. Wishing—and succeeding far better than was wise—to rankle the woman she considered a spoiled, grasping harpy, Lady Beatrice spoke up.

"You speak as foolishly as ever, Aurelia, my dear," she chided, starting Aurelia so she gasped. "Jessica's no servant." Lady Beatrice snorted contemptuously at the thought. "She is my companion, a time-honored position for women of gentle birth who find themselves in straitened circumstances. And she is of gentle birth, mind. Her mother's family is an old, respected one in Hampshire, while her father's forebears are solid and honorable to a man. They're not of Prinny's circle, I grant, but they're the better for it, and the 'servant,' as you call her, has more nobility in her little finger than, ah, others have in their entire bodies. My guess," Lady Beatrice added with the greatest pleasure, "is that she'll be something more than my companion very soon."

When she looked significantly to the dancers, Aurelia followed her lead as if compelled. The music had just ended and Jessica was curtsying before Roxham, her face raised to his and lit with a smile so vivid it was difficult to look away from her.

Certainly the earl seemed in no hurry to turn his gaze away. His sensual mouth curved, he used the excuse of

248

lifting Jessica to her feet to hold her hands in his long moments after the other dancers had broken the line and gone for refreshments.

It was too much. The sight of Justin gazing with such open pleasure upon another sent Aurelia bounding from her chair. "I've the headache," she cried, and stalked away.

In the privacy of her room, she paced the floor, stopping only long enough to hurl any object that came to hand at the wall with all her might. "I must do something," she fumed aloud. She could not let Justin slip away. She could not! All the world knew she'd set her cap for him. She'd look a fool.

And no one else would do. No one could match him—not in lineage, or wealth, or looks!

She'd not let the chit have him.

And so it went until, exhausted, Aurelia sank into her chair and stared moodily at the window. Scarcely aware that the sounds of revelry had ceased long since, she continued to brood, though her eyes grew heavy and she sank into a restless doze.

"Rellie . . . Rellie." The quiet whisper seemed only a part of her unhappy dreams until she smelled her brother's breath.

"Alfie, wha—"

"Quiet," he hissed, grasping her arm so tightly that she winced. And came awake to realize the silence in the manor was absolute. "What are you doing here?" she demanded, shaking him off, though she heeded his advice to whisper.

"You've your chance, Rellie. Your chance! I swear, by damn, you can put the Winslow chit to rout tonight."

The excitement in Alfred's voice seized Aurelia. If he were part of a nightmare, then she welcomed it. "What do you mean? Tell me at once."

"I have seen her leave the house tonight," he cried, almost forgetting the need for quiet in his triumph. But Sir Alfred had participated in more than one unsavory affair and so recalled himself to his task. "I do not know where, nor why—though I know too that Andrew Fitzgerald is out. I swear there must be a kind of madness in the air, Rellie. Why should she jeopardize her chances with Roxham—and despite what you wish to hear, I'd say they are considerable—to keep a rendezvous with a mere pup? It makes no sense, but that's no matter to us. She's gone, as is he, and—"

"Oh, yes, my dearest brother, I do see. We've only to think of some means to alert Roxham . . ." Aurelia's eyes narrowed to slits as she considered the matter.

Content, Alfred sagged into a chair. Rellie would bring the matter to a happy conclusion, he did not fear. He'd only to find her an opening and he'd succeeded. What luck that he'd not been able to sleep!

Restless, visions of Jessica Winslow, so desirable but so out of reach, bedeviling him, he'd hied off to the library for a prolonged session with his host's brandy. Luckily, when the door had opened, his mind had been too fogged with the brandy to permit him to give himself away in surprise. From the shadows he'd watched in silence as a cloaked figure entered the room and made its way quietly to the French doors.

The lock was not easy, and he'd recognized Jessica's voice with a sense of elation when she let out a soft cry of triumph as it turned at last. Levering himself from his chair, he watched her walk swiftly across the lawn, passing the remnants of the festival the servants had left until the next day to clean, to disappear into the woods in the distance.

In his mind there was little question where she'd gone. He'd seen the lad, Andrew, slip unannounced from the house after the festival had ended.

For a moment, Alfred was tempted to follow Jessica and take her for himself. But rational thought prevailed. In the first place, he'd have been hard-put to catch up with her; and in the second, if he brought her into disgrace, as he hoped to do, she'd be far easier game, for she would be entirely without Roxham's protection. The thought made him lick his lips. Yes, he would have her.

And Roxham's money to boot, if the gleam in Rellie's eye was any indication. Alfred smiled to himself.

"I have it." Aurelia dropped down beside her brother. "Here's what we shall do, Alfie."

Some twenty minutes later Aurelia crept silently from her room and proceeded quickly down the long hall to the stairway. She stood quietly at the top, looking behind her first, then below to the vestibule. No light or movement disturbed the night and she crossed quickly to lift a valise from the shadows where Alfred had left it as instructed. Descending rapidly to the first landing, she heaved the thing with all her might so it rolled end over end to the marble floor below.

As it tumbled noisily, she ran beside it, crying out as if it were she falling to injury. In the vestibule, she hurriedly shoved the valise behind a column where it would be out of sight of anyone descending the stairs.

Still moaning pitifully, Aurelia then arranged herself in a graceful heap upon the cold floor and waited for rescue to arrive.

The first to come, pounding loudly along the hallway, was Alfred. "Rellie," he called out in frantic tones.

"What the deuce is going on?"

As they'd hoped, they had succeeded in rousing Roxham.

"Rellie's taken a fall," Alfred called back over his shoulder, and the two men descended the stairs with gratifying speed.

"I, I have been so foolish," she cried in a faint little voice when they reached her. "I've taken a fall and hurt my ankle."

"What the devil were you doing up at this time of night?"

Aurelia dismissed Roxham's querulous tone as natural for a man awakened from his slumber. "I simply could not sleep, my darling," she cried with an air of tragedy that she hoped would wound him, for, after all, it was indeed his fault she'd not slept well. "I was just coming down for a book—something to put me to sleep—but now I have hurt my ankle terribly. I don't think I can walk."

"Justin, whatever has happened?"

The anxious tones were unmistakably those of Lady Mary, and Aurelia smiled to herself. Miss Winslow was conspicuously absent.

"Aurelia's hurt her ankle in a fall," Justin said shortly. "I'll bring her to her room where we can have a look."

Aurelia waited until the earl had lifted her and she was firmly held against his broad chest. It had not escaped her notice that he wore only a dressing gown, and she savored the feel of his warm skin before she spoke again. "Justin," she began when they'd reached the top of the stairs and Mary reached out a sympathetic hand to her. "My ankle hurts most dreadfully. Would you rouse Miss Winslow, darling? Mary says she's the most marvelously healing touch."

She sounded so very weak and pitiful that, despite his first inclination, Justin did not refuse her. That Jessica would handle the situation more expeditiously than Mary was also a factor in his decision. He didn't relish being up the remainder of the night with Aurelia.

"Shall I awaken Miss Winslow, sir?" Miraculously Moreton had materialized—fully dressed, his master noted with appreciation.

Roxham nodded. "Yes, Moreton, do."

Justin had laid Aurelia upon her bed—and Mary, fussing extravagantly, had adjusted the pillows behind her so that she made a very pretty sight in the thin silk dressing gown she'd selected as her best and most revealing—when Moreton returned.

To keep Justin by her, Aurelia had grasped his hand, begging him not to leave her, and so she felt his hand tighten when he took in the expression on Moreton's face. "What is it, man?"

"Miss Jessica is not in her room, my lord," the old servant announced, clearly perplexed.

"Oh, my!"

The wail was Mary's, and Justin scowled briefly in her direction to silence her. "She's likely in the library fetching Aunt Bea a brandy," he said, and dropped Aurelia's hand without thought as he moved toward the door.

"She's not there."

Justin spun to face Alfred, a cold weight settling in his chest when he registered the thin smile Aurelia's brother made no effort to hide. "Oh?"

"No. I was in the library until only a little before Rel-

lie roused us. Miss Winslow was not there. However . . ."
Alfred deliberately lingered a moment just to savor the
look on Justin's face. He was not so all mighty now. "I,
ah," he continued so archly Roxham was tempted to
squeeze the words out of him, "I did see Andrew leaving
earlier. Just after you'd gone to bed, Justin. He . . . By
Jove, I don't relish telling this! However, he did have
someone with him. They set off across the lawns, but I
could not see clearly who it was who sat before him."

All the lamps in Aurelia's room having been lit, Alfred
could plainly see the flat, deadly look Roxham bent upon
him. "It's true," he insisted, eager to deflect that look.

Roxham departed the room abruptly. No one spoke as
they watched him turn toward Andrew's room, but Mary,
with a sobbing cry, fell to the floor in a swoon.

Moreton was torn. He was loath to leave at such a
moment, but he knew his duty. As Alfred moved ponderously to lift Lady Mary to a comfortable chaise,
Moreton announced he would fetch her dresser.

In the quiet that followed, Alfred quickly stored the
valise he'd brought, unnoticed, from the hallway. He
threw a quick, triumphant smile at Aurelia. She returned
it before composing her features as she heard Justin return.

His set face spoke volumes about what he'd not found
in Andrew's room, and Mary, who had revived to the
extent of opening her eyes, moaned pitifully. "No! He
cannot have done it."

Moreton, the sleepy-eyed dresser in his wake, arrived,
and Roxham waited until Lady Mary had been shep-
herded from the room before dismissing Moreton. "We'll
not need you now," he said, and stood watching grimly
until the old man closed the door. Then he turned to face
Alfred and Aurelia.

Both straightened almost imperceptibly, their earlier
mood of triumph evaporating like the mist before a tem-
pest.

"I do not know the particulars of how you learned
Andrew and . . . she had gone off together, Alfred, but
I am willing to wager, Rellie, that your ankle is as healthy
as mine own." He looked at Aurelia with such cold fi-

nality she gave a cry, but Roxham was not moved. "You'd have done better to come to my door and shout out the whole, not stage this absurd charade. As it is, I find the sight of you both all that is loathsome, and under the circumstances I wish you to be gone from Bleithewood by tomorrow at midday. I shall have my servants assist you in packing."

"Justin!" Aurelia's voice was infinitely more frantic than it had been when she'd supposedly fallen down an entire flight of stairs. She leapt from her bed, not caring that he would see his guess as to the health of her ankle was entirely correct. "Don't go! You cannot mean it," she cried, grasping his arm.

Roxham pried her fingers from his arm. "Oh, but I do, Rellie," he told her before dropping her hand like a stone. "I do. There was nothing more between us than the quick passion of an affair. You ought to have known it was over when I sent you that bauble. I believe I even said farewell in my note. I say it again."

With that he was gone, leaving Aurelia to stare after him, numbly shaking her head from side to side. Alfred quicker to see the game was well and truly up, sank into the chair Aurelia had occupied earlier, and laid his head upon the back of it to gaze fixedly at the ceiling as if he might find written there some suggestion as to how he would satisfy his most pressing creditors now that they'd lost Roxham's wealth.

The earl spared neither brother nor sister another thought as he made for his room, his blood pounding through his body as if he'd been at hard labor a full day or more. Unseeing, he selected the first pair of breeches he found, and stamped into a pair of boots. Flinging on a shirt, he made to fasten it but stopped his hands in midair.

He'd had some half-formed notion of chasing after Andrew and—he could scarcely bring himself to say her name—Jessica! Without thinking, he brought his tightly fisted hand crashing onto the table at his side.

There was no use in riding out. He would not find them in the dark. They might have selected some inn nearby, or settled for the woods . . . Jessica, her hair spread around her like a brilliant, fiery cloud, lying back upon the fragrant, mossy ground. . . . His fist crashed down again.

This time he sent the lighted candle upon the table flying. Darkness engulfed the room, and hot wax burned his hand, but he took no notice.

Jessica! Dear God, but in truth, he had not known he'd come to care so much. Pain, anger, and even now, desire streaked through him.

He stormed from his room, unable to bear its confines. His destination unclear, he made his way through the sleeping house and after a time he found himself before the decanter of brandy in the library. When he found it empty, he hurled it against the fireplace and derived a moment's satisfaction as it burst into a thousand bits.

The feeling evaporated too quickly and he charged across to pull at the bell rope like a madman. Moreton appeared before he'd had the time to pace the room twice.

Ever faithful, the old retainer had not returned to his bed. His master would have need of him, he guessed. From the corner of his eye he saw the shards of glass sparkling on the bricks before the fireplace, and he braced himself to face his master with some trepidation.

Still, he was not prepared. He'd never seen the earl's eyes blaze so hotly, nor known him so lost to all propriety that he appeared outside his rooms with his shirt undone.

"Brandy, Moreton. I'll have bottles of it," Roxham ordered in a harsh voice. "And then to bed with you, man."

The last was added in an angry tone, but Moreton was satisfied that the earl had not gone entirely mad. Wildly angry, yes, but he still remembered an old man's comfort.

26

Jessica, as she trudged across the park from the woods, remarked the light shining from Bleithewood's second floor. It was Lady Aurelia's room, she thought without much caring.

She was deathly tired. The St. Barnabas Day Festival had been enough to send her to bed for a week, she thought, and though she was exhausted, she smiled.

She would treasure her memory of that day for a long, long while. Since the day she'd learned of her father's death, she could not recall when she'd been so gay.

That she could attribute, at least in part, her enjoyment to Roxham's deliberate effort only made the day the sweeter. Why he had done it, she could not know, but it did seem he had set out to make her day memorable.

He'd been responsible for the new dress which had made her feel as attractive as he had told her she was. He'd danced with her twice, as much as propriety allowed. He'd taken, she learned from Andrew, the time to warn Lord Alfred Marling against so much as dancing with her. And last but certainly not least, almost as often as she'd looked up, it had seemed she'd found him regarding her with a pleased gleam in his eye.

Jessica's weary feet stumbled, and feeling a pain in her toe, she was reminded not all the evening had been so pleasant.

The twins had awakened her from a deep sleep only some hours after she'd sunk down upon her pillow. Struggling to open her eyes, she'd found a child on either side of her shaking her urgently.

"We went into the woods with Jem. He poaches, Jess!" Giles' voice seemed a shout in her ear, though he whispered.

"But he only poaches from Squire Multaney as he's so

256

steep with his rents," Julia rushed to say as Jessica struggled to sit up.

"It was Andy told us first that he likely did," Giles took up the story at its beginning when Jessica demanded with some asperity whatever in the world were they about awakening her in the dead of night. "Seems his father was suspected of poaching, but as he was never caught, no one could be certain. When we quizzed Jem, he denied it, but we thought he only feared to tell us."

As hanging was the punishment for poaching, Jessica did not doubt it. Squire Multaney did not seem the sort likely to press for leniency.

"For a lark, we thought to find out for ourselves," Giles whispered as Julia gripped Jessica's hand tightly. "We only pretended to go to bed when Nanny Budgett sent us up. The moment she left, we dressed and crept to the long gallery to keep watch on Jem until he left the festival. Luckily for us, he'd stayed to eat a deal more— he can eat more than Jule and me together—and we were in time. When he left, we hurried to follow him and kept very quiet until he'd entered the squire's woods. But when he took his first rabbit from a trap, we both"—Giles looked gravely at his sister—"made a noise. We were glad for him, you see. At any rate, he ran, thinking we were gamekeepers, and stumbled into a poacher's trap. Jess, we cannot get it off his leg."

"He's in the woods still," Julia cried, forgetting in her agitation to be quiet.

Giles hissed to her to have a care and then turned back to Jessica with such urgency, she was moved despite herself.

"Please, Jess! You are the only one we can ask. It's our fault he's been hurt. Please, will you go to him?"

The thought of the young boy huddling, cold and alone on the ground, a wicked trap biting into his leg as he waited for the squire's men and their dogs to find him, sent Jessica into the night—alone. She'd insisted upon that.

The children had described Jem's location carefully, and miraculously she only got lost twice finding it. Call-

257

ing out softly, she'd been led by a responding hoarse cry to the tree he lay beneath.

It was no easy matter to pull the trap apart. The metal jaws were made not to be broken, but she was determined, and best of all, she knew the principle of leverage. Using a heavy stick, she managed to pry the thing open just enough that Jem could drag himself free.

Her hands sweaty from her effort though the night was cool, she'd felt his leg and found, unbelievably, that the boy's leg was not broken, though it was horribly gashed. She thought it was the thickly padded pants he wore that had saved him. They were a trick his father had passed on, Mrs. Crenshawe revealed when they arrived at her cottage.

It had been a gruesome walk. Jessica was not strong enough to carry the boy, and he was in too much pain to walk. She'd had to half drag him along, though she knew every movement hurt. Once, they'd heard dogs howling and the hair on her neck had lifted, but in a raspy whisper, Jem had assured her they were not near. "May'ap another poacher off t'other side of squire's," he'd said.

At the cottage she'd attended his leg as best she could without the doctor the Crenshawes could neither afford nor chance calling in. What use to save Jem's leg if he were handed over to the magistrate?

To Mrs. Crenshawe's astonishment, Jessica had required boiled water. She'd no idea why her father had always insisted upon it. He'd not known himself, but he'd seen it keep the gangrene down he said, and so she used it to clean the boy's ugly wound before she sprinkled basilicum powder over it.

She'd also thought to bring laudanum and instructed Mrs. Crenshawe, whose face was white and strained, how to use it. But the poor woman had actually wept openly when Jessica handed her the last item she'd stowed in the pockets of her pelisse. It was the pouch Justin Stafford had thrown down before her so long ago. The ten gold pieces were still there. She'd never, out of pride, touched the money, though she had never thought to give it up before.

"I shan't need it," she told Mrs. Crenshawe when the

258

woman sought to push the gift away. "It was a reminder of a wrong done me, and now I find I'd rather not be reminded. Please"—she closed Mrs. Crenshawe's thin hand over it—"take it. You'll not have Jem's wages for a time, and perhaps now you'll not have to send the boy out into the woods at night."

Her head bowed, for she had not forbidden Jem the dangerous occupation his rash father had taught him, Mrs. Crenshawe nodded mutely.

Sighing as she quietly opened the library door she'd departed through earlier, Jessica hoped the boy mended steadily. She'd not be able to attend him often.

"Why the sigh, Jessica? Was your tryst too short?"

"What," Jessica cried out as she whirled to stare into the darkened room. "My lord?" she asked, seeing only a large shape uncoil itself from a chair.

A match hissed across flint and then a candle flickered to life. Jessica gaped at what she saw. Roxham was dressed, but only partially. He wore no coat at all and his fine lawn shirt hung open. Her eyes were drawn to the tawny, triangular mat of hair that covered his chest and, tapering to a thin line, disappeared into his breeches.

"Like what you see, my dear?"

The scathing mockery in Roxham's voice brought her head up with a snap, and Jessica stumbled back a step. He was livid with anger. His eyes blazed so hotly with it a surge of fear engulfed her, holding her silent.

"Come, come, Jess." His use of her pet name was an insult. "Tell me, how do I compare?"

Jessica retreated another step, then another. To no avail. Roxham's stride was longer. He advanced upon her with the slow, steady, ruthless intensity of a lion stalking its prey.

She gave ground again only to feel the French window behind her, imprisoning her. The latch! She searched frantically and found it. Too late. Roxham, his threatening eyes never leaving her, caught a length of her hair.

When she had hurried out to Jem, she'd not taken the time to put up her hair, only left it tied back with a ribbon that had come untied somewhere along the way. Now she could not know how wanton she looked with her fiery mane rippling loose to her waist.

Deliberately, Justin looped the strand around his hand again and again, reeling her in as he would a fish. The pain brought anger. "You are hurting me!"

"Am I?" he inquired with a grim smile that inspired as much fear as had his furious expression. "Then we are quits, for you sicken me, Miss Jessica Winslow. You, who play the innocent by day and then at night sneak off to be a harlot in the woods with Andrew."

"You are mad." She shrank as far back as she was able. The pungent smell of brandy was heavy on his breath, and though his speech was not blurred, she knew with faltering courage that he'd drunk to excess.

"Mad?" Roxham paused as if to consider the possibility. "Perhaps I am, but then I see this leaf." Without a care for her delicate scalp, he plucked a leaf from her hair. "And know you've been to the woods. Your skirts are damp." He roughly pulled her dress from her legs. "Your dress clings to your legs. And your back?" With one hand he untied her pelisse and flung it to the floor. Her eyes wide with fright, Jessica made to pull away, but he only smiled contemptuously as he took the liberty of examining every inch of her slender back with his hand. "No. Not wet. Did you lie upon his cloak?"

"I did no such thing," Jessica protested, shaking now. The man before her was a stranger. She had seen Roxham angry, but nothing like this. Nothing. He seemed to have no relation to the man of the St. Barnabas Day Festival.

Though his eyes were the same shape, they burned now with disgust. And the mouth that had smiled with such warmth was by candlelight a grim, taut line. Even his nose was changed, for his nostrils were flared, so intense was his emotion.

"Where were you, then?"

She could not tell him. She might have divulged Jem's secret to the Roxham of the St. Barnabas Day Festival. She had even considered awakening him before she left, and only had not, because she thought he'd be put in an exceedingly awkward position if he were found assisting a poacher on a neighbor's land.

260

But this Roxham she could never trust! How had she forgotten the earl who was accustomed to accuse and to condemn her without benefit of hearing?

A fierce hurting spread through her, for she had thought . . . She'd been the worst sort of fool.

"I will not say," she blazed back, her pain vanquishing her fear and emboldening her with sudden anger.

"You will not! You need not!"

A new light flamed in Roxham's amber eyes as they raked her. It frightened Jessica so her heart thudded in her throat. "My lord," she tried to recall him to his senses.

He ignored her. "You're a winsome lass, as you well know. Desirable, too." His voice was a low growl in his throat. "I'd have a taste like all the rest I do believe."

"You mistake the matter, my lord."

But the time for protests of her innocence was past— quite past. Roxham tightened his hold on Jessica's hair, forcing her head back and exposing her neck. He kissed it, first at the hollow of her throat where her pulse beat a frantic rhythm. Then higher and higher, his lips stroking her creamy skin.

"No!" She pushed frantically against him, ignoring the pain to her head.

But he was much stronger than she. He used his hands to still her body, pulling it tight against him, and he employed his mouth to cut off further speech.

There was only anger in his assault upon her mouth. He would punish her with his kiss, if he could.

Justin's single-minded pursuit of vengeance, however, did not last beyond his first taste of her. When he found her lips hard and taut against him, giving nothing, a throbbing desire to have more swept him.

When the change occurred, Jessica could not have said. One minute Roxham was deliberately, cruelly hurting her, but the next he was not. Not at all. His lips caressed her, coaxed her against her will. He still assaulted her, true, but so differently.

His lips were soft and warm now, and strangely sweet. A spark of some emotion utterly new to her exploded into life deep within her. It set fire to her blood and raced through her veins, leaving her trembling.

Later she would recall in shame that she arched her body into his and encircled his neck with her arms. When that was not enough, she opened her mouth to him and sighed with pleasure when his tongue flickered over hers.

Groaning, Roxham pulled her roughly up against his taller, harder body and, raking his tongue against her teeth, sent Jessica spiraling into some exhilarating abyss she'd never dreamed existed.

But when she moaned aloud, the abandoned sound penetrated Roxham's senses. Infuriated with himself as much as with her, he wrenched his mouth from Jessica's and flung her from him with a curse.

Reeling off-balance back toward the hearth, Jessica stretched out her hand to catch herself as she fell. It landed squarely upon a shard of the shattered brandy bottle.

The sharp pain in her hand was nothing compared to the searing pain in her breast, but Jessica cried out.

"What have you done?" Roxham demanded, his voice as harsh as his countenance. When he strode to her, Jessica shrank back. "I'll not strike you, though you deserve it," he growled. "What's amiss?"

"I've cut my hand," she told him on a ragged breath. Staring at him, she found she was in some perverse way pleased to see how heavily he breathed. If she'd been moved when she knew better, then so had he. The discovery gave her some courage, and when he imperiously reached out his hand, she tilted her chin belligerently. "I've no need of your assistance," she flared and, struggling to her feet, ignored his fierce gaze. While he watched, she refused to examine her wound. If she dripped blood on his fine rugs, it was no more than he— or she—deserved.

"Whether you care for it or not, you will accept my assistance later today," Roxham informed her in a biting voice when she was standing. "An hour from now, at first light, you will leave Bleithewood in my carriage to go as far as the coachman can take you."

27

"Lo, Aunt Bea! What's got Moreton in such a taking? I swear he growled when he told me to come along to your room. Can the old boy have had a surfeit of ale last evening?"

Grinning at his own play, Andrew leaned down to buzz his aunt's cheek, but was shooed off with a sharp rap from the fan she'd been plying in frustration all day.

"Get on with you, you vexatious boy. Where in the name of all that's holy have you been this night and day, when you've been needed here?"

"Needed?" Andrew asked in surprise. "Mother's not taken ill has she? Too much syllabub, I don't doubt."

"Will you be serious this once? Where have you been?"

"Now, Aunt, that's a devilish sticky question to be asking a young man."

"Out with it! At once," Lady Beatrice roared, unhappy to be reminded at that particular moment how like his Irish father Andrew could be.

The boy laughed. "Have it your way, then. I happily spent a goodly portion of the night at the Lion's Head tavern in Rushton. Need I be more explicit?"

"I thought as much." Lady Beatrice nodded gloomily. "That fool, Justin, was always a hothead about matters dear to him."

"Fool? Hothead?" Andrew echoed, clearly intrigued, and at once dropped into a chair across from his aunt. "Surely you are not speaking of Justin Stafford."

Lady Beatrice grimaced. "Would that I were speaking of someone else!"

"Oh, come now, Aunt," Andrew chided. "Give over, do! You've entirely succeeded in piquing my curiosity and now you must satisfy it. Whatever do you mean?"

"Do you see Jessica Winslow here in my rooms attending to me as she ought to be?"

Thinking to humor his ancient relative, Andrew made a show of looking about. "No, I do not see her. Shall I fetch her for you? Is she with the twins?"

"And did you perchance pass Aurelia, her brother, or the MacDonalds when you came up the stairs, lad?"

"Well, no, I didn't."

"Last but certainly not least," Lady Beatrice continued dryly, "did Moreton inform you where you might find your estimable, elder cousin, the head of our family?"

"No he did not, Aunt Bea, as I suspect you know very well."

It was Lady Beatrice's turn to give a chuckle. "That little glare was very good, boy. You'll learn, yet. And you are in the right. I do know Moreton made no mention of the earl's whereabouts, because I know full well he hasn't the faintest notion where Justin is. Or Jessica. Or those wretched others, blast their souls."

"None of them are here?" Andrew asked, bewildered.

"Not a one, not a one," Lady Beatrice shook her head mournfully. "While you were out enjoying yourself with some serving girl—you needn't look so sheepish, boy, you'd not be the first young man to visit a tavern for that purpose—mayhem and nothing less was let loose here. Perhaps it was some madness in the air," she observed half to herself.

"Aunt Bea!"

"Yes, yes, I'm coming to it! You needn't be so impatient. I'm old and deserve respect not chiding."

A choking sound from Andy received a glare, but at length Lady Beatrice told him what she'd learned of all that occurred the night before. "Of course, I may be wrong on some particulars. Your mother has lain in a near swoon all the day and been most unhelpful, but Moreton is not so vaporish. Luckily he was on hand during a great deal of it and after some prodding overcame his reluctance to discuss 'his lordship's' affairs."

Andrew cast her a dry look, thinking if any one could open the dignified old man's tightly sealed lips, it would be his Aunt Bea; but as he considered all he'd been told, his amusement gave way to amazement.

"I can scarce believe it," he confessed, shaking his head.

"I must allow when I began to learn the bits and pieces, first from Annie, then your mother, and finally Moreton, I suffered from the same lack of imagination. However, as I thought on it, the whole began to make some macabre sense.

"I am afraid I am not without my portion of the blame," Lady Beatrice admitted gruffly. "I could not resist goading Aurelia last evening by insinuating—in not very subtle terms, I am ashamed to say—that I believed Justin had formed such an attachment for Jessica he would ask her to be his wife."

Andrew gaped. "What?"

Lady Beatrice dipped her chin emphatically. "He's head over heels, though I don't think he realizes it as yet. More objectively I watched for signs. I'd hoped for it, you see. Who better for his countess?"

"But what of Aurelia?" Andrew demanded.

"A passing fancy." Lady Beatrice dismissed Aurelia Stanhope with a curt wave of her hand. "Her coming was, or so I first believed, a godsend. Any comparison between her and Jessica could do nothing but drive Justin into my pet's arms all the faster. And I was right in that respect. By last evening Justin was staring at Jessica with besottedness written all over his expression."

Andrew gave a great shout of laughter. "By Jove, I do believe you're in the right of it. Tom said something about Justin's eye lingering sweetly on Jessica, but I gave the matter little thought. In truth, I'd celebrated with enough ale to be incapable of much deep thought, and at any rate I believed Justin was simply watching to be certain Marling didn't force himself upon her again. I did watch that toad, and I can tell you he seldom lost sight of Jess. Whew! I can't say I'm sorry he's departed."

"No, nor his wretched sister, either," Lady Beatrice agreed. "If only I'd not shaken her confidence so! But, be that as it may, I did, and then, somehow she got wind of the fact that you and Jess were absent from the house.

It was a simple matter from there for her to have some accident and desperately need Jessica to attend her. When you were both found departed, Alfred had only to say he'd seen you leave together.''

"But surely Justin could see they were lying.''

"Ah, but there you are! He is in love, and love distorts the eye. He was too jealous to think clearly.''

"Jealous! Of me?'' A smile of considerable relish spread slowly across Andrew's face.

"According to Mary, there had been talk you were interested in Jess for yourself.''

"As I don't doubt you were well aware,'' Andrew returned. Then, with an openness Lady Beatrice could not help but like, he admitted, "But she never gave me the least encouragement, you know. Far from it, she dampened all my hopes. Repeatedly.''

Lady Beatrice nodded sagely. "Well, as I said, love is blind or, in this instance, blinding. And, too, Justin was faced with the fact that Jessica could not be found. Moreton assures me she was not inside anywhere. He even went to the nursery to see if she'd gone there.''

Andrew frowned. "Have you learned where she was?''

"No.'' Lady Beatrice shook her head. "That is the only mystery. No one seems to know. She left a note for me, but it only says farewell and that she will write. Poor thing!''

"When did she leave?''

"At dawn! Can you countenance Justin sending her off at that hour?'' Lady Beatrice glared balefully at her footstool, and Andrew suspected that if it had turned, by some miracle, into Justin, his aunt would have kicked it. "The rascal knew I'd never let her go, and so he did his evil work before I was up to put a stop to it. Bah! The stable lads told Moreton he watched her go from the drive, standing there with his legs spread wide and his arms crossed over his chest, like some Oriental tyrant.

"Now he's hied off. Took his leave soon after she did, hoping to escape his devils, I don't doubt. But he won't succeed. No, boy, you don't tear out your heart and then carry on with your life as if nothing happened!''

"Aunt Bea, may I come in? Andy!'' Olivia, who had

not waited for her aunt's permission to enter, stopped to glare at her brother. "I should say it is more than time that you came home, Andrew Fitzgerald. Though what good you'll do now the harm's done, I can't imagine. Gracious, it seems as if the world's gone quite mad."

"Good afternoon, sister mine." Andrew grinned, unruffled; then, looking beyond her to the door, he called out loudly, "And greetings to you, children, hanging back by the door looking guilty of murder."

"Oh! Though you are forever making fun, you are seldom amusing, Andrew." Livy turned from him to the twins, her expression in no way softening. "Come in here at once, you, two. You will tell Aunt Bea what you have told me. And don't delay. No one is going to be hanged."

"Hanged?" Andrew cried, starting, but Livy silenced him with a scowl Lady Beatrice would think to commend later, when she'd the leisure.

At the time, she was looking interestedly at Giles and Julia. "Do you know where Jessica was last night when we were all asleep?" she inquired, confirming her older niece and nephew in their estimation that age had not dimmed her mind one whit.

Reluctantly, in small voices, the twins said they did know, and then even more slowly, with a great deal of threatening from Olivia and coaxing from Andrew, they told where Jessica had gone and why.

"Devil take it," Lady Beatrice cried pungently when they had done.

Andrew whistled softly, and Olivia said, "Those Crenshawes!" with a wealth of feeling.

Livy was the first to recover. "I do hope we are able to straighten this mess out now." She pouted unhappily. "Jess never had the time to bring Justin around to supporting my intention to marry Philip and not Ned."

"Selfless as ever, Livy." Andrew laughed and received a grimace in response.

"Hush, you, I must think!"

Lady Beatrice's words had only just escaped her mouth when there was a knock on the door. "Yes," she called fretfully. "What is it now?"

"Mr. Edward, my lady," Moreton intoned as he swung open the door to allow an exquisitely dressed young man whose features brought the earl to mind, but whose slighter build and irresolute expression made his good looks less striking than his brother's.

"Greetings, Aunt Bea. And everyone," Ned Stafford added when he took in the Fitzgeralds.

"You're something of a surprise to see, boyo," Andrew expressed the general sentiment of those greeted. "We thought you'd not return for a year or so yet. Tire of the antiquities, did you?"

"Ah, well, no, not exactly." Ned looked uncomfortable. "I came to see Justin about . . . At any rate, Moreton says he left Bleithewood this morning. Too bad." Ned's brow knit in a frown. "I had hoped to make it home for St. Barnabas Day, but I'm traveling with some others, the Creightons of Broadmoor in Yorkshire, and the axle on their carriage broke, slowing us."

"Are your companions here with you?" Lady Beatrice asked with the concern of a hostess.

Ned nodded. "Yes. Moreton is seeing to them. But I do regret like the devil missing Justin. I had wanted him to meet them, particularly, ah, well . . . Dash it!" The young man grinned, reddening. "I have it in mind to offer for Miss Creighton. Met them in Rome, you know, and I wanted my older brother to approve her."

Olivia, to Ned's astonishment, went into great whoops and clapped loudly in response to his announcement.

"Never mind her, Ned," Andrew advised with a wink. "She's daft and suffers spells on occasion."

Livy stuck out her tongue at her brother, and naturally, he was obliged to grimace exaggeratedly back at her. Following that display of sibling communication, the two fell into a bout of laughter. "It's nothing you've said, believe me, Ned," Livy protested when she had, at last, sobered. "It's only just a, ah, family joke."

Ned did not look as if he much believed her, but as she said nothing more and Andrew was making a point of looking elsewhere, he let the matter go. He'd other things on his mind than some silliness of Livy's at any rate. "Aunt Bea," he began in an odd tone that at once caused everyone—including the twins, who sat chastened and silent upon the floor by their aunt—to look curiously at him. "I wonder, ah, is your companion here? Miss Winslow?"

"You know Jess?" The surprised query was Livy's, but she was only the first to voice the astonished thought.

"He does!" Lady Beatrice said with such triumph that Ned was clearly startled. "Ned," his aunt pounced, rapping her cane on the floor for emphasis, "was Justin by any chance acquainted with the girl before she came to Bleithewood?"

Livy looked at the older woman as if she'd gone mad, but Andrew tipped his head thoughtfully, and when Ned blurted out, "But didn't he tell you?" Andrew did not cry out in surprise as his sister did.

"That explains it," Lady Bea exclaimed triumphantly. "I always thought the two of them behaved deuced oddly when they met. It was as if Justin knew something discreditable about Jess, but when he said nothing at all, I thought I'd imagined things.

"Sit, boy!" Lady Beatrice jabbed at an empty chair with her cane. "And tell us the whole. We must know it if we're to know what to do. And you needn't cast another anxious glance at the door. Jessica won't come in to bite you. She left Bleithewood this morning. Now . . ."

Ned looked most uncomfortable and even pulled upon his exceedingly high shirt points in a manner that reminded everyone of Mr. Headley. But no one laughed, and in the end Ned made a clean breast of his entire acquaintance with Jessica Winslow, not omitting anything: not how he'd abducted her, not how he'd forced a kiss upon her, nor, finally, that he'd lied most shamefully to Justin about her.

"I couldn't write and admit the whole to him you see," he said miserably after he'd told them of the letter he'd received from Justin. "I thought I must face him. And her. To beg her forgiveness."

There was a great silence then, for all those facing Ned had come to love Jessica very much, and they all found it difficult to dredge up a feeling of forgiveness.

"I think you are very bad, Ned."

Ned swung around, and seeing the speaker, Julia, sitting cross legged on the floor before him gazing at him with great, accusing eyes, he flushed. Uttering a strangled groan, he buried his head in his hands. "I know," he cried in a muffled voice.

"Dear heaven! We shall all be in tears soon." It was, of course, Lady Beatrice who rescued the extremely awkward moment. "You are very bad, Ned. Julia is right. However, it is not for us to judge. At least not too harshly," she amended, for, in fact, the judging of others was something she frequently did. "It is Justin and most particularly Jessica with whom you shall have to right matters. And if we go about this correctly, I have a shrewd idea your youthful sins won't mean a great deal to either of them."

When Olivia exclaimed in surprise to hear her aunt say such a thing, Lady Beatrice proceeded to apprise her, and Ned and the twins as well, of her belief that Justin and Jessica were very much in love.

"Explains the whole, you see. Justin is jealous and Jess is too hurt by his doubts to tell him he's no reason to have them in the first place." Scowling, she shook her head and Andrew could almost hear her mutter, "Lovers!" in exasperation.

"What we shall do is this," she continued after a moment. "Andy, you shall go to Jessica's home in Kent, learn her whereabouts, and fetch her back. Likely you'll have to tell her I've fallen dreadfully ill to persuade her."

"But isn't that lying, Aunt Bea?" Giles objected.

A cool look cowed him. "There's no harm, if it's done in a good cause."

Andrew, who was enjoying himself immensely, roared with laughter, but Livy, who was in complete agreement with her aunt, only inquired earnestly what they should do about Justin. "We don't know where he's gone."

"No matter," Lady Bea advised. "He'll come home eventually, or we'll get word of him and drag him here somehow." She darted a sharp glance at Andrew, who only laughed again. "In the meantime, we'll have returned Jessica where she belongs, and she'll be safe from harm, waiting.''

The reminder that Jessica, away from Bleithewood, was open to harm made Andrew rise. "If I'm to start out first thing in the morning, I've packing to do. Adieu till dinner, then. And never fear!" He turned back at the door to flash them all an irrepressible grin. "I'll not fail to return with our beauty in distress!"

"See that you don't, boy!" His aunt's sharp command rang out as he stepped into the hallway, and Andrew smiled to himself. Here was a twist upon the old stories! Now it was the dragon saving the princess. He laughed aloud and made sure he would tell Bea his thought when he returned. She'd relish it.

28

"Good afternoon, Miss Winslow. And how did you fare today, then?"

Jessica sketched a wan smile for her landlady, Mrs. Twig, a widow who had from necessity turned her home into a boardinghouse for respectable young women. "Not very well, Mrs. Twig. The employment agency still had nothing, but perhaps they will tomorrow."

"That's the spirit, child!" Mrs. Twig clucked sympathetically. "You've only been here five days, after all. No need to be discouraged yet. I've known girls who had to be patient a month or more. Will you take some tea?"

Jessica shook her head. "No, thank you. I've some letters to write."

It was true that Jessica did intend to write her mother, but as she had the whole evening to devote to the task, she'd the time to linger over tea. Breakfast, however, was the only meal included in the month's rent she'd given Mrs. Twig, and Jessica had decided she must do without any other meal until she knew what her future held. Her funds were too meager to squander.

"Miss Winslow!" Mrs. Twig hurried back down the hall to halt Jessica's progress up the stairs. "I very nearly forgot to tell you. A gentleman called earlier asking for you. He said he would return later this evening."

Mrs. Twig thought Jessica too pale normally, but now, seeing the girl go paler still, she rushed to reassure her. "He didn't leave his card, but his clothes were ever so fine, and his carriage—"

"Please, Mrs. Twig!" Jessica rapidly descended the stairs to take the landlady's hand in an urgent grasp. "This is very important to me. I do not care to meet this gentleman. Please tell him I am not at home if he comes again."

"But . . ." the good woman began to protest. The gentleman had been exceedingly handsome, though she did not think it proper to say as much.

"Please, Mrs. Twig!"

The alarm in Jessica's voice persuaded her reluctant landlady. "I shall do as you ask, child, of course."

Shaking her head over the oddness of some people, Mrs. Twig left Jessica to mount the stairs, her shoulders sagging slightly. There could be no question now of remaining at the friendly haven she'd remembered from her first stay in town.

She'd no doubt at all who her caller had been, though she had not expected Alfred Marling to trace her so quickly. Only the day before she'd seen him and he her.

She'd been crossing the street. After a dray had moved ponderously by her, she'd begun to pick her way across when she realized a roan stood in her path. Looking up, she'd found herself staring into Marling's bloodshot, triumphant eyes.

She'd fled at once. The crowds were thick and she thought she had lost him when she darted down a side street, but it seemed she'd been mistaken.

Opening the door to her small, single room, Jessica bit her lip, determined she would not give way to tears again. There were other boardinghouses in London, she told herself. Eventually she would find employment, and if she were lucky, it would be out of the city altogether.

She shot the bolt on her door and lifted her hands to

untie the ribbons of her new, rutched bonnet when Mrs. Twig's voice, high and indignant, reached her ears. Jessica tilted her head to listen, forgetting her task. She'd never heard the landlady cry out in such scandalized tones.

A low-pitched man's voice answered the landlady, and hearing it, Jessica experienced a thrill of elation, only to cry out "Fool!" in silent anguish in the next moment. Of course it was not Roxham below. She must cease this constant thinking of him. He even plagued her dreams.

But in the next moment, just as she again lifted a shaky hand to her bonnet, she froze. The footsteps on the stairs were a man's. Heavy and quick, they were quite unlike the light clicks of Mrs. Twig's female boarders. Whatever could the man be about? Men were not allowed upstairs.

Holding her breath, she listened as his footsteps proceeded down the hall. On they came, and on farther. They halted at her room.

"Jessica!" It was Justin Stafford. He tried her door and, finding it locked against him, rapped upon it so it seemed a mere splinter between them. "Your landlady says you are not at home, but I know you are there. Open this door."

At the peremptory command, Jessica's eyes flashed dangerously. And why should I? she demanded of the door. Because you would have another opportunity to revile me, my lord?

"Jess! I shall break the thing down, if I must!"

"Oh, my lord!"

The pitiful cry was Mrs. Twig's. She was likely wringing her hands. The door would take time to repair, even if the earl made good the damages, and there were the other boarders to consider. Even now they'd be peeping around their cracked doors to see who it was that so rudely disrupted their quiet.

"Jess!" The door rattled wildly. "I warn you!"

"Oh, dear me! Please, my lord!"

Jessica shot the bolt and threw the door back with a violent crack.

"How dare you?" she cried furiously.

Mrs. Twig stepped back in alarm and raised a plump

273

hand to her cheek. Gone entirely was the pale, subdued girl of her acquaintance. The sparks fairly flew from Miss Winslow's deep-blue eyes now and her cheeks were stained with color.

"I am at the edge of my limits." The earl—Mrs. Twig had seen the crest emblazoned on the man's carriage and was fully aware of his rank—flared in his turn. "You, Jessica Winslow, are a witch and have afflicted me so there is only one remedy."

Having gained her door, Roxham easily stepped through, seized Jessica before she guessed his intent, and scooped her into his arms.

Jessica reacted violently. "You can't do this. You would ruin me on top of all else. Mrs. Twig!"

The earl entirely disregarded her outburst. Tossing her a grimly triumphant smile, he strode from her room, carrying her as easily as if she were a feather, while poor Mrs. Twig trotted along behind him clasping and unclasping her hands in dismay.

At the top of the stairs the landlady halted, her hand over her mouth. She was joined at once by those of her boarders home just then. One and all, they'd raced from their rooms to observe the very scandalous goings-on.

Their mouths all formed in O's of surprise, they watched the earl make short work of the stairs and, holding firmly to his wriggling burden, fling open the front door. When he did not race out but swept around to face them, they drew back as if he might attack them.

He did nothing of the sort. Though Jessica pummeled his chest and kicked her legs, he managed an elegant leg.

"I shan't harm her, Mrs. Twig, never fear!" He flashed the landlady a gleaming, roguish smile that set her heart, as well as the hearts of the seven women with her, racing excitedly. "Have Miss Winslow's clothes packed, will you, my good lady? I'll send for them shortly."

The effect of the earl's smile was such that Mrs. Twig found herself nodding, though she addressed a back and broad shoulders that were quickly disappearing from sight. Really! She began to smile. He was a handsome devil. Surely he did not mean the girl harm. And what

274

was she to do, besides? He was a nobleman. There was no setting the watch upon him.

Jessica, who had not been treated to Roxham's persuasive smile, was not so quickly won over as the landlady. "Put me down this instant," she cried out loudly.

As if she'd never spoken, Justin bounded down the front stairs of the boardinghouse to his carriage. "A guinea if you are there before dark, Samuel," he shouted to the coachman before disappearing inside the conveyance with Jessica still held firmly to his chest.

Before he was fully seated, the stairs were thrown up, the door closed, and the carriage jerked forward.

"Where are you taking me?" Jessica demanded, pushing hard at his arms, but he kept his grip upon her and sat her down, not gently, upon his lap.

Nor did Roxham give Jessica the benefit of an answer, at least not at once. To her vast annoyance he merely sat back regarding her with a pleased grin that, had she known it, very much resembled the one he'd thrown Mrs. Twig and all her boarders.

It was then Jessica noted that her abductor had a day's growth of beard stubbling his chin and that his eyes were rimmed with a touch of red, as if he'd not slept much the night before.

"You are foxed," she accused furiously.

He laughed. "I am never foxed. Though," he allowed rather cryptically, "I may be intoxicated." He ran practiced hands around her waist, and when his thumbs met, he frowned. "You are thinner."

"Whatever are you doing?" Jessica yelped in protest. Perched on his lap and with his warm hands upon her, she suddenly found it difficult to breathe. Curiously, she felt no fear at all.

Roxham blithely ignored her cry. "And wherever did you come by this affair?" He flicked the brim of her bonnet with his finger. "Hoped to hide your hair no doubt," he guessed with absolute accuracy. "Amazing," he continued, casually untying its ribbons though Jessica batted at his hands, "how I've missed it. There now . . ." He finished by tossing the bonnet onto the other seat, and then, catching both Jessica's hands in one of his, he proceeded to pull the pins from her hair.

When he was done, her hair hung in a waving coppery fall to her waist. "Lord, it's like silk," he said, his voice sounding a trifle hoarse as he ran his hand through it.

That very dangerous warmth she knew to be wary of from her last encounter with Roxham swept Jessica. Only with the greatest effort did she resist a powerful impulse to toss her head and allow her hair to glide teasingly across his chest.

"What are you about?" She managed instead to renew her efforts to squirm out of his grasp.

"I advise you to stop that at once." Roxham placed his hands upon on her hips to hold her still, and grinned lopsidedly. "You're only making matters much worse from your point of view."

Taking his meaning only dimly but nonetheless adequately, Jessica blushed to the roots of her hair, and he gave a laugh. "Such an odd little wanton you are to blush so."

When he brushed her hot cheek with his finger, Jessica shivered. Utterly confused, for his tender tone seemed to imply he did not think her a wanton at all, she tried to fix him with a firm stare. "What are your intentions, my lord?"

"Justin." The golden lights in his amber eyes sparkled and Jessica was very much aware that one of his hands remained warm and strong upon her hip while the other was again occupied with stroking her hair. "It is my firm intention not to reveal the least of my thoughts to you until you call me by my name. I have, as it turns out, long wished to hear it on your lips."

When his gaze settled upon them, Jessica only just kept from biting those lips. He would guess how nervous she was, if she did, and above all, she did not want him to know how he undid her, particularly when he smiled at her in just that way.

The corners of his firm mouth curved beguilingly and his teeth gleamed white and strong. She could distinctly recall how almost painfully sweet his mouth had felt on that last night.

Jessica jerked her gaze away from Roxham's mouth and fastened it upon his cravat. "I do not understand any of this. I thought you detested me."

He coaxed her chin upward with his knuckles so she must look at him with her blue eyes. "I do not understand any of this, what?" he prompted, his voice strangely unsteady.

Her heart was beating very hard. "Justin." She surrendered in a whisper, then, more firmly, "What do you intend to do with me, Justin?"

"Abduct you."

There was a twinkle in his golden-brown eyes, but only the flat certainty of his tone registered with Jessica. She drew back alarmed, and Roxham did not calm her fears when he added, "As my brother did."

Had he learned the truth from Ned? Jessica nearly spoke the question aloud, but another thought intervened: Roxham was taking her to the same inn where Ned had taken her. It was, she thought, just of a distance to be reached by dark.

"No," she cried, her voice near breaking. "I cannot be your mistress."

Roxham's fingers brushed aside her hair and settled upon the nape of her neck to trace slow, intoxicating circles at that sensitive spot. "No?" he challenged, his low voice caressingly soft.

How Jessica might have protested, or indeed, if she could have found the will to do so, was not to be known, for at that moment, the carriage bounced over a rut, and though it was superbly sprung, Jessica lost her balance and was thrown against Roxham's chest.

Her head landed without hurt upon his broad shoulder, and when Jessica looked up, she found his handsome face only inches from hers. His breath was warm on her cheek. He smiled, and though she noted the curve of his mouth, it was the lights in his golden-brown eyes that captivated her.

"You are my mistress, love," he told her gently in a voice that worked on her senses in anything but a subtle fashion. "The mistress of my heart," he added before slowly lowering his head to brush her soft lips with his.

It was not easy to stop there and so he tasted more deeply, caressing first, then teasing, until, feeling a rushing excitement build, he pulled back.

Jessica, her eyes wide and darkened to midnight blue, stared back at him, and her breath came in little gasps between her parted lips.

A low growl erupted from deep in Roxham's throat, and he captured Jessica's lips a second time in a far different manner. Fierce and possessive, his second kiss assaulted her.

She'd little chance against it. Her senses ignited, she moaned, unknowing and uncaring what that helpless sound revealed.

When Roxham released her some moments later, it was with an effort. He was breathing heavily and his eyes had turned the color of liquid gold.

"You cannot deny me, Jess."

She made no attempt to do so. "I cannot deny wanting you," she admitted, one corner of her mouth lifting. Hesitantly she traced the line of his firm jaw with her finger. "But, Justin," she emphasized his name by looking directly at him, though her eyes were still heavy with the passions he'd stirred, "I could never bear to have you leave me each evening to Aurelia."

His brow arched abruptly. "Why, pray, should I go to Aurelia each evening when I cannot bear the sight of her?"

Jessica, her head still comfortably ensconced upon his shoulder, shrugged his objection aside as unimportant. "Whoever she may be, I could not bear to share you with your wife," she told him quietly.

"Ah! But, you see, I am certain you'll not have any difficulty," he assured her flatly, and Jessica frowned in annoyance though he'd begun nuzzling the smooth hollow of her throat.

"Justin! Stop! You'll not persuade me!"

"You make much of nothing, love," he insisted, his voice muffled by her hair. "You'll have only yourself with whom to share me, after all."

"What!" Jessica gave the lie to her weak strength by violently shoving Roxham away from her.

He grinned and flicked the tip of her nose with his finger. "Did I neglect to say I wish you—and no other—for my wife?"

"You know very well you did!"

Roxham laughed, amused by the flash of her blue eyes. "My negligence is just punishment, I think, for the pain you've cost me these five days. You ought to have told me at once where you were that night, Jess. It was only your pride that put me through hell."

"So!" Jessica straightened as much as she was able with his strong arms cradling her once more. She succeeded in bringing her face only inches from his. It was difficult to keep her eyes from his lips, but she made the effort. "Now you've talked to Andrew and the twins, and you've decided to forgive me."

"No." He smiled, and she glanced fleetingly at his mouth, unable to keep from it. When she returned her gaze to his eyes, she nearly sighed. It mattered little where she looked, his mouth or his eyes. All his features seemed capable of captivating her. "I have not spoken to Andy. I left Bleithewood only a few hours after you, before he'd returned. I'd just enough sanity left to know I might do something I would regret if I saw the Viscount Avensley just then. As to the twins"—he shrugged negligently—"I never thought to question them. Were you with them that night?"

He truly did not know, Jessica realized. "Do you mean you've asked me to marry you, though you still do not know for certain I was not with Andrew or some other that night?" she demanded, ignoring his question for her own.

Roxham nodded and then lifted Jessica so she sat upon his lap once more. His gaze at once both tender and direct, he took her hands in his. "I've little memory where I was for the four days after I left the manor. I assuaged all my pain with enough good English ale to make a yeoman of me. But when I awoke this morning at Roxham House in town, I saw everything more clearly. *Post vino veritas,* I suppose," he said with a wry smile.

"I recalled how you had looked at me throughout the St. Barnabas Day frolics, your eyes sparkling so it seemed

279

you had found a means to capture starlight. A woman contemplating a tryst with her lover does not look so besottedly . . . Now! Now! I am only telling the truth," he protested, laughing as Jessica hit, albeit gently, at him. "No woman," he picked up where he'd left off, "could look so lovingly upon a man, if, all the while, she cherished his younger cousin. And, too, there was your response to my kiss. It was not"—Roxham's smile flashed—"and I've some knowledge of the subject, the response of a woman sated by another man's attentions.

"Jess?" The laughter in his eyes was replaced by an expression of deadly earnestness. "Can you forgive me? I was lost in a rage of jealousy. I should never have believed Alfred Marling, of all people, when he said he saw you ride off with Andy, but when your room was empty and the lad's as well . . ."

"You'll never countenance such foolishness again?" Jessica placed her hands on the earl's shoulders and shook him. "I do not believe I could endure this ordeal again."

Roxham cupped her lovely face in his hands. "I'm done with doubting you, my love. I believe in you completely, even to the extent that I now accept Ned lied to me about you. He must have, for I know you are not capable of ensnaring anyone into a marriage he would not choose.

"Forgive me for hurting you, for putting those circles beneath your beautiful eyes, and for costing you more than one dinner." Wincing, Roxham traced Jessica's cheekbones with his thumbs. "You are so dear to me, I shudder to think what life would be if I lost you, Jess. I've had women aplenty over the years, but I have never loved before. I did not recognize what it was I felt until that night, when you could not be found. I went quite as wretchedly mad as you accused me of being."

Swiftly, taking Roxham by surprise, Jessica bent to kiss him, her heart so full she felt it might burst. "I was a little mad myself," she admitted breathlessly when she drew back. "I was so mad with hurt, I could not bring myself to tell you where I'd been, though my destination was entirely innocent."

"And you'll marry me?" Roxham demanded huskily,

his hand entwined in her hair as he pulled her slowly back down to him.

Jessica jerked upright, abruptly resisting him. "What of your friends, Justin? And your family? What will they think? I could not bear to cause you embarrassment."

The earl allowed his hands to settle firmly upon her shoulders. "All my friends will be delighted by you. Like my enemies, they will envy me my good fortune. And my family?" He laughed indulgently. "Silly gudgeon. Andy himself wished to marry you. Livy and the twins treat you as their sister and mother respectively. Mary has already, happily, conceded you the running of Bleithewood. And Aunt Bea, the old harridan, has schemed from the first for a union between us."

"Lady Bea?" Jessica looked her surprise and tipped her head to the side. "You're gammoning me."

"I did not realize it myself at first," Roxham admitted. "When she sang your praises day and night, I only thought she sensed the rift between us in her shrewd way and thought to make me see how dear you were to her." He shook his head. "It was only when I saw her half-drag herself down to sit at the table with Aurelia, whom she's never liked above half, that I guessed what she was truly about. She wished me to make a comparison between you. It was, I might add, a quite successful stratagem. You are gold to Aurelia's brass, and there was no mistaking the difference. Poor Aurelia!" He chuckled suddenly. "Her arrival, far from persuading me I must ask for her, prompted me to realize I must have you for my wife.

"You do intend to say yes, do you not?" he demanded, and it was his turn to give Jessica a shake.

Jessica's smile illuminated her face. "It would be my greatest pleasure to marry you, Justin Stafford," she accepted his proposal, her voice huskier than normal, and to prove her words, she dipped her head for a kiss.

Both of them were flushed and not a little breathless, when, a few moments later, Roxham lifted her from his lap to place her beside him and tuck her into the curve of his arm. "Lord! You put my self-control to the test, my love." He grinned and quickly kissed her nose. "Divert me," he commanded, stretching his legs out to rest them on the opposite seat. "Tell me where you were that mad night. Did you take the twins fishing?"

Snuggling comfortably against him, Jessica recounted the story of her rescue of Jem Crenshawe. When she was done, Roxham called her a brave, reckless witch and forbade her to do anything so foolish again. "I admit to being glad, though," he said after a time, "that you left that pouch with Mrs. Crenshawe. I'd not have it as a reminder of the unhappy things between us."

Jessica reached up to kiss him then, though he had told her she should not. She thought to prove there was only happiness between them now, and she did. Indeed, the two of them were so lost to the rest of the world, they did not mark the progress Samuel coachman made until their carriage slowed upon entering a town.

"But it is Donbridge," Jessica cried, recognizing her home when she looked out the window.

Roxham's golden-brown eyes sparkled amusedly. "Where did you think I was taking you but to your mother for her approval of our plans?" Jessica did not answer, for at the mention of her mother, she stiffened. "Do not worry yourself, Jess," he said quietly, guessing the cause of her unhappiness. "I was here earlier today and I made certain Godfrey would not be present."

There was not time to ask how he had managed so high-handed a thing as to force a man from his own home, for their carriage was rolling to a stop before a modest brick town house, but Jessica did express her gratitude with a look and one last, necessarily brief kiss.

When they were shown into Jane Godfrey's sitting room, they did encounter a sight they'd not expected, for not only was Jessica's mother there and her two brothers, but Andrew Fitzgerald as well.

"It is something of a surprise to see you here, Andy," Roxham remarked after the happy greetings between Jessica and her family had subsided.

"It is entirely Aunt Bea's doing, I assure you," the young man replied with a grin. "Knowing in her prescient way that the two of you were head over heels, she sent me down here to find Jessica that we might keep her safely at Bleithewood until you returned to your senses, dear cousin. When Mrs. Godfrey told me you'd come pounding on her door early this morning to ask, first, permission to pay your addresses to her daughter, and second, her daughter's direction, I thought it wiser to await you here than to chance missing you on the road to London.''

When Roxham commended his cleverness, Andrew bowed. "Though I must say," he added, giving his cousin a searching look, "I was not so clever as to guess you'd return before dark. I'd almost believe you abducted the lass, Justin, you made such short work of persuading her to forgive you your abominable temper.''

When Jessica giggled, Roxham had the grace to grin. "Not a bad strategy when it comes to it, actually," he allowed lazily.

Andrew looked a trifle uncertain, but when he turned to Jessica, he saw the emotion reflected in her radiant smile, and lifted her hand for a kiss. "I wish you happy, Lady Jess. You deserve it even more than I knew when I last saw you. I've not had the opportunity to say so before, but Ned's returned and told us all of the wrong he did to you. He wishes to beg your forgiveness.''

"And I shall give it," Jessica said at once. "I'd likely never have met Justin, had Ned not played his trick. And, too, he was very young.''

"Your age now," Roxham reminded her with a frown.

But Jessica only laughed. "Ah, but I am blessed by the gods.''

The soft light in her eyes was too much to resist, and though Andrew, Mrs. Godfrey, and the two boys looked on, Roxham kissed her lips, albeit with restraint. "Nay, sweet Jess, it's I the gods have favored," he whispered gruffly.

Andrew, for his part, thought them both equally blessed by fate, and a remarkably indulgent grin upon his face, he sent up a prayer to the weird sisters in hopes that he might be so lucky in his time.

SIGNET REGENCY ROMANCE
COMING IN OCTOBER 1989

---·---

Anita Mills
Newmarket Match

Leigh Haskell
The Paragon Bride

Sandra Heath
The Pilfered Plume

---·---

SIGNET REGENCY ROMANCE

Watch for

"A REGENCY CHRISTMAS"

Five holiday tales of
love and romance.

by
Mary Balogh
Gayle Buck
Edith Layton
Anita Mills
Patricia Rice

COMING IN NOVEMBER

There's an epidemic with 27 million victims. And no visible symptoms.

It's an epidemic of people who can't read.

Believe it or not, 27 million Americans are functionally illiterate, about one adult in five.

The solution to this problem is you... when you join the fight against illiteracy. So call the Coalition for Literacy at toll-free **1-800-228-8813** and volunteer.

Volunteer Against Illiteracy. The only degree you need is a degree of caring.